ADAM THORPE

Nineteen
Twenty-One

VINTAGE BOOKS
London

Published by Vintage 2014

2 4 6 8 10 9 7 5 3 1

First Published in Great Britain in 2001 by
Jonathan Cape

First published by
Vintage in 2002

Vintage
Random House, 20 Vauxhall Bridge Road,
London SW1V 2SA

www.vintage-books.co.uk

Addresses for companies within The Random House Group Limited
can be found at: www.randomhouse.co.uk/offices.htm

The Random House Group Limited Reg. No. 954009

A CIP catalogue record for this book
is available from the British Library

ISBN 9780099597568

The Random House Group Limited supports the Forest Stewardship
Council® (FSC®), the leading international forest-certification
organisation. Our books carrying the FSC label are printed on FSC®-
certified paper. FSC is the only forest-certification scheme supported
by the leading environmental organisations, including Greenpeace.
Our paper procurement policy can be found at:
www.randomhouse.co.uk/environment

Printed and bound by Clays Ltd, St Ives Plc

'Rarely has such heat been associated with so strong a wind . . . Hour after hour passed and not a drop fell . . . on the parched and cracking ground.'

The Times, July 25th, 1921

FOR GEE-GEE
(RAGTIME GRACE)

I

Dragon's Breath

'I FEEL DWARFISH,' Joseph said to his friend Baz, once, on one of their Sunday rambles around London. They were crossing the heath just north of the pleasant village of Stanwell, having visited its fine church and green. The weather was bright and cold. 'Really dwarfish, really practically nothing,' he persisted.

'I can't help being tall,' his friend replied.

'I mean spiritually, in the head. Against the chaps that saw action, felt the heat.'

'Felt the heat? Jo-Jo, you sound like Horatio Bottomley on a bad day.'

'I'm living a half-life.'

'Oh, you'll be all right. Chances are you wouldn't be living a life at all, if you'd felt the real heat.'

'I'm a slat of young pine among seasoned timbers. I'm a hunchback valet—'

'Do shut it. Just get on with building the new world and — shut up. Appreciate the fact that you still breathe and are able to see all *this*.'

Baz swept an arm to indicate the wide heathland of south Middlesex: only the snorting of the Bath Road disturbed the calm. Firs whispering, the February sunlight clear, specks of distant cattle, white clouds swept up to the zenith: it was a landscape by van Ruisdael. They were thirsty, and after another mile or so reached the little village of Heathrow and stopped for a pint in its rather wintry pub. Suddenly, quite suddenly, there among the old boys snapping their dominoes, Joseph felt certain that the world would

1

not be drowned after all: that its very newness was their youth's advantage. He would not even have to be Noah.

This was before he had moved to the cottage in the woods – where sometimes he did feel like Noah. The lone survivor of some cataclysm, at any rate.

For the rest of that walk they discussed their fathers in a rather slow, gloomy manner. Baz's was long gone to India. Joseph's was dead – dead and buried some two years now, yet the mind obstinately refused to admit it. Were you not supposed to grow inwardly tall with the death of the father? But his mind would not admit it: it had not yet stopped sounding strange to his inward ear, this death of his father. He would not grow any taller until he did admit it, he reckoned. You could sport a black armband till kingdom come, for all the truth it told.

Of course, Pa Monrow *had* been short, physically-speaking, and even plump with it – though this reassured people, somehow; he would stand outside the shop and people felt that this short plump fellow had always been there, selling rugs and carpets. In fact, he had only got into carpets after groceries and then hardware, but the carpets were his thing, as shoes had been for his grandfather in old St Petersburg. Right by the synagogue, where tacky boots rang out business on merciless cobbles. Joseph's father had a soft rolling sort of voice which went with the softness of the carpets. He was always very good at arranging them in the window, suspending them on wires like wings. It gave vent to his artistic side. They were not solid heavy things any longer, those carpets: a puff of wind might take them up into the sky.

Joseph's first memory was of brown paper, a huge crackling sheet of it – and the terrific tearing noise when it was ripped away. The carpets disappeared inside it. Things kept rolling up and disappearing. His elder sister, for instance, who perished of enteric fever when he was five.

The shop was in black-browed Matlock. It was illuminated by Indian copper lamps which cast little soft spots of light everywhere and made it mysterious. There was even a bristle of Indian incense sticks, like a temple, and a papier-mâché model of a multi-armed *joss* squatting in the corner by the giant scissors. People would come in off the hard street with its gloomy black-stoned houses into this paradise of softness and the magic East, a chip off the Empire without the cholera. And they purchased. The terrific tearing sound went on all day: he could hear it through the floorboards of his bedroom, along with the murmur of the customers, his father's high laugh that sounded almost insane from up there.

In 1908, when he was ten, Joseph's family moved to a big cold house at the top of the hill on the edge of Youlster. Soft limestone country, this was, but scarce a mile away you hit the gritstone, lumbering in piles out of the moor. The house got all the winds, of course. Joseph's room had a grand view of the moorland and he started to write poems up there, secretly, with the winds whining around and the clouds chasing up from off the barren peaks. Not surprisingly, the poems had a lot of stuff about temples and Hindoos and flying carpets. His model was *Songs of Travel* by Robert Louis Stevenson, borrowed by chance from the school library. No one could explain why the Monrow boy won the writing prizes and had poems in the *Derbyshire Times* now and again: there was no pedigree there, not for authorship.

His best friend was Basil Beardow, whose parents ran a hydropathic establishment outside the village. The two boys sat next to each other on their first day at school, blocking their ears simultaneously when the slate pencils started shrieking. Their names, when they wrote them out, finished up in the same way: OW, they wrote, laughing. And they both did very well academically, they rather chivvied each other along. Baz had the drier mind, always chopping and cutting – he could slice anything into its component parts to understand it – whereas Joseph was prone to handle things whole, feel the weave under his thumbs: he could even do maths that way. He was a dreamer and that stood against him at first – even the chanting of tables would have him drift – but it helped later. Baz never dreamed, or if he dreamed he hugged the coast, he never went deep. His mouth was very fine and firm while Joseph's was queerly lopsided and mobile. Joseph tried to copy the set of his friend's mouth: as well put a quart into a pint pot.

One fierce winter, when Baz was fifteen or so, his mother slipped on the iced-over frigidarium and died a week later without waking up. The hydropathic establishment was closed (the baths leaked and were slippery with algae, it had been nothing but trouble) and his father went off to India where he had family. Baz and

3

his elder brother Hanley won scholarships to a boarding school, or maybe someone in the family paid – at least paid for Hanley, because Hanley was pretty stupid. The school was near London, a long way away, and Joseph did not see his friend for three years. They wrote to each other at intervals and Baz was always being urged to come back and stay in the holidays. He never came north again, however; he was staying with aunts and that was his duty. He would shuttlecock between the aunts and was spoiled silly, but he was too serious to go rotten. His brother Hanley did, but that had always been on the cards.

And you could have foreseen what Joseph got, too: an exhibition to Oxford in 1915. Brasenose College, it was, which his mother said sounded like a snooty sniff. She gave plenty of those in the next few weeks, telling folk about it – and his father beamed at everyone from the shop doorway: on cloud nine they were. They almost gave the carpets away, they were so happy. His father unlocked the safe and produced his bottle of vintage brandy. He and Joseph drank a toast, and then another until they were dancing around the *joss* with incense sticks in their hands, Ma looking on with folded arms, shaking her head. She couldn't imagine what the *joss* thought of it, she declared. That made them laugh even more.

Because of the war, everyone else was miserable, and the dissonance made Joseph queasy. He was glad when he was on the train, going down to 'go up'. He took the Stevenson poems with him – a new copy, very smart, a present from the school with the school eagle pasted in. Not every day the establishment had an Oxford scholarship boy to boast of.

Joseph was surprised to find Oxford as coaly and dark-stoned as Matlock: in his literary mind it had been golden. He had never seen so many bicycles in his life. Faces whirled past him in rooms and lanes, jolly and shouting. His head only settled when, sitting on the river bank by Iffley Mill at the end of the first week, he watched the huge poplars aglitter in the breeze and felt himself being sewn back into his own life with a new, ineffable thread.

Bumping into Baz on Broad Street a few weeks later was a shock; he had grown very tall, shot up when Joseph was not around. Where Baz's nose had been was the knot on his necktie. It took a bit of adjustment, his features had stretched a bit too, but the old kinship burned through. They were glad of each other; Oxford was an eerie place at that time. There were a lot of empty rooms with names still screwed on the doors, names of those who should have been browning their muffins at the fire instead of splashing about in toast-coloured kit, killing and getting killed on the far side of the Channel. Enlistment came in, along with steel shrapnel helmets. Joseph was about to be eighteen, too. Baz and he had done a lot of talking, however, and they decided they were pacifists.

Their tutor was very thick with the Bloomsbury lot and his flat, sardonic face lit up when they told him. Baz had a good solid reason: Hanley had been killed at Ypres in the autumn push, blown to vapour. They debated whether to help the war effort as noncombatants, in the Red Cross or wherever. Joseph's ma was very keen on the Quakers, though not quite a Quaker herself, and he would go along to talks, good fiery talks against the war. There were a lot of young men like him, and a lot of others who simply did not want to get damaged, or worse.

They attended the medical examination, however. You could get in a great deal of trouble for missing that; it was considered high cheek to skip it, whatever your views. An open winter had snapped into a bitter March, and the room was hardly warm enough with a jacket on, let alone a birthday suit. The doctor was easy-going and pleasant but the whole thing was horrible – penis pulled about, backside publicly squinted up. The next day Joseph wrote a decent poem about it, 'The Bully', but no one would print it, not even the chap who knew him on the *Derbyshire Times*. The last verse alone would have done for it:

> And there like shiny pestles in a row
> The rubber stamps do lie; 'tis here the flesh
> Is judged, and the ink upon each name, still fresh,
> Ground into powder for war's breath to blow
> As Antarctic wind doth, howling over snow.

In fact, they were turned down. Just like that. 'C3', suitable only for light sedentary work. Eyesight. Neither of them had been able to get beyond a certain line on the chart and at that point the top brass would not suffer a four-eyes in a front-line trench. The two friends were disappointed, if anything, though relieved at not having to face the music – the tribunal would not have been at all sympathetic.

They fired each other up and took to hand-printing pamphlets. Joseph got introduced to some of the Bloomsbury lot and his work fell off. Literae Humaniores, it was; a queer time to be studying that. His wheels slipped onto a certain rail and away he went, further and further into conscientious objection, a deep landscape tinged with melancholy and mysticism on the one hand and a hard bright socialism on the other. He had certainly set his face against the majority. It dislocated him, somehow. It did not allow him to be his own man.

His parents had arguments about it, back in Youlster. His father, in a fit of anger among his anxious carpets (there was not the money about now for such luxuries), called him a 'shirker'. His mother defended him and there was a row. Then nothing more was said, not at home. In the street, though, it was different: complete strangers would approach Joseph and hiss at him like snakes – *slacker*, they would hiss. *Slacker!* Generally women. He would make faces back. One of them, rather posh, called him a *Jewish slacker*, which was the first time he had been called a Jewish anything.

Baz and Joseph were in neighbouring colleges, though not on the same degree. It was as if they were sharing destinies for a while, though Joseph saw pretty soon that Baz's height came with a bit of toffee nose on it; his Derbyshire twang had gone, for a start. As boys, both had been clouted for using 'thee' and 'thou' at home; it was almost mucky. But the twang had been theirs as much as their muscle and blood. The quads at Oxford rang to the vowels of the nobs, generally; Joseph learned to adjust, though the minute he was home he would lose the affected tone. The snobbery was awful – much talk of being a 'commercial', and so forth. And the Jew thing, now and again. The chap with the rooms next to his was a lord who regularly broke china against the wall; it was a ritual of some kind. Then he went off to the war and was immediately smashed up, like one of his plates.

D-D was the one don for whom Joseph felt some warmth, a twinkly-eyed Socratic type, the sort who cannot ever get out of the mould but shifts amusingly enough within it. D-D would hold court in his cluttered sitting room in Beaumont Street. His real name was Desmond Brown. He would dangle a sugar lump to 'sweeten conversation', make dastardly puns out of your name in Augustan verse, dance the flamenco with his teddy bear in his slippers, that kind of thing. He claimed to be a close friend of John Drinkwater's, too, which held him in good stead later on. Otherwise, Joseph found the dons impossibly narrow, tight little men in dull brown rooms.

One evening during the Michaelmas Term, Baz and Joseph took shelter from a sudden downpour in a university cricket pavilion. It was empty, abandoned-looking, smelt of linseed oil and mildew and coconut cake. Neither of them were cricketers, not even Baz – it had always felt a bit foreign, somehow. They started to talk about Youlster and the moors, steadily and slowly, like a long, steady innings in the darkness while the rain dripped off the mildewed eaves. They were very nostalgic, like old men. It was an aberration, almost, all that sudden northernness in their heads. Dropping stones down Jewitt lead mine that folk said was Roman; the secret camps in the upper woods; the days spent haymaking in the fields below the church; the doings that went on in Wakes week – horse muck stuck down the village band's tuba, that sort of thing. They held each other back, in one way, with this sort of shared churning-up. But never again were they so drugged with it as in that dripping pavilion. Gorged, they were, as if they had lifted the flap of the sweet counter and raided the stores behind.

And they were even comic, seen together: the tall and the short (though not really so short, only in comparison), wandering over the lawns in similar spectacles – the gold-rimmed oval type – earnest and quick at the same time. A sort of music-hall act. They were dubbed Pip and Squeak for a while.

It was only by a squeak that they missed the trenches.

Things were going rather poorly for the Allies in the winter of 1918, and when the spring came the bright boys at the top had a brainwave: throw more men at the Hun. So they did. They dragged the sick and wounded out of bed and the lads in their middle teens out of their sweethearts' arms, or their mothers'. And the near-blind would do; they reckoned that if you could see to stumble your way to death it was, oh, *quite* good enough. Baz and Joseph found themselves in the A category, called up for service in the lines. The swiftest promotion either would ever know: nothing was said about their pacifism, someone knew them better than they knew themselves. There was a terrible pride in seeing that 'A' on the card, like a mark at school. From dunce to scholar. The thing is, both were in good health and soft-spoken; it was the consumptives they were afraid of, and the firebrand political agitators. They were called up and somehow neither of them spoke out or tried to swing it. Baz did mention desertion at one point, going underground like one of their friends in a barn or a forest cottage. Their pacifism was threadbare: you could see the floorboards through it.

The first time they put on khaki, it was like wearing a solid rash. Baz's cap was too small for him and Joseph's too big. Baz grew a moustache, Joseph did not.

After a brief bout in Tidworth, they both ended up at the training camp near Etaples, though they were not in the same company. Just two weeks there and then it would be straight along to the filth and glory somewhere along the line, an overnight train ride. They were really hurrying them along now. It was May. Flowers in the hedgerows, peaceful sunlit fields, green corn splashed with poppies. They learnt to walk with a Blighty pack, heavy as a gas stove, miles and miles over flat country that felt, to a fellow under a pack, like the Himalayas. Even the smooth chalk roads seemed cobbled.

They had learnt to shoot – and Joseph enjoyed shooting, though he was no good and his shoulder was black and blue from the recoil. It was the age-old barracks routine; they had swapped college dinners for iron rations, books for ammo and gas masks, brain talk for slang and swearing. The clouds rolled over them, indifferent. (The camp was not close enough to hear the guns as more than a fluttery rumble.)

It was a weird thing, but Baz and Joseph were not displeased. They got on with it fairly well, the whole physical side, chivvying themselves along with private jokes, nursing their blisters and greasing their boots in equal measure, with care in it. Khaki never let you forget it was on you: like starched moss, it was. Yet the flutter in their stomachs was like love, love for the way this process turned them away from matters of the mind, from dead Greeks and bony scholarship. It had been a considerable effort, putting themselves up against the mass. Now they were swooning in recompense, like a man stood to attention too long,

8

limbs held too tense. A gun, uniform, a helmet once they were up at the line. Ludicrous, really. They were even awed by their first sight of men in full war gear, passing them one morning on the road, dusty as hell. And so they scrambled in and out of ditches, trotted through woods, chased each other with wooden munitions: it was good, boyish fun. Healthy, even – they were certainly fitter after only a few days of this. The unpleasant part was the base-wallah of a sergeant-instructor, his delight in screaming at your face so that you felt the spittle on it. That was the only really unpleasant part, until the gas chambers.

These were little deep dugouts four miles from the camp. The old type of gas mask was dished out – no more than a muslin bag with eyepieces – and the men were marched off. This was on the Tuesday of the second week. Baz and Joseph were among those who had the first bash. They climbed down into darkness and put the bags over their heads, looking like a cabal of the Ku Klux Klan. For the first time since he had joined up, Joseph was frightened, properly frightened. Claustrophobia, it was. A serious phobia, maybe to do with a shop cupboard locking on him by mistake when he was five. Or maybe not. Maybe it was just a rooted part of him, ordered by the stork. The sergeant-instructor was at it again – all the horrible things that would happen to them if they so much as breathed one mouthful of the atmosphere. Sweat misted Joseph's eyepieces and he had already taken his glasses off. The whole idea of it was unbearable to him. It was stifling down there. He was short of breath. He looked about him and the familiar faces of fellows he knew were now blurred and monstrous, terrifically primitive, something out of nightmare with black round eyes. Then the iron door shut on the sergeant's grin. Clang.

Pitch dark.

Joseph felt he had gone blind, he went a bit giddy, he always had to have some sort of handhold of light, just a spot or a streak would do. He heard shuffles and then a kind of hiss – he thought it was one of the fellows hissing between his teeth, but it went on and on.

Of course, it was the gas.

This did for him. It went against instinct, to be stifled with a bag over your head and not to whip it off. It was stinging him, stinging through the muslin – chlorine, it was – but they were told

9

to expect that, to expect the urge to remove the mask when it was only that bag of muslin between you and suffocation, you had to think contrariwise! He did not think at all, there was not the time to, the urge made sure of that. The urge was too deep for thought, it was animal, before thought was even born.

So he lifted up the cloth and sucked in a mouthful.

No air – the air had been pummelled to death by a sweetish reek which rammed its fist down his windpipe and stayed put, knuckles and all. He could not cough it up. He pulled his mask right off and was aware of himself flailing about. This caused consternation – the dugout was barely big enough to hold them stock-still, let alone with one of them flailing his arms like a windmill. A part of him, very dim, needed to find the door but there was no door, it was all sandbags and timbers and bodies of men themselves flailing now because in their surprise they had loosened the masks, they were pretty hopeless masks anyway, those old PH helmets. It was a basket of writhing snakes, that place, and no one opened the lid. Maybe no one heard them from outside. They all loved life and they were drowning. Raw wet mouths against hands. Hard teeth. Down a lime-pit, they were, in a place made to extinguish life, that little vulnerable flame. They were dancing corpses, really.

By the time the lid swung open, one of them (Joseph) had all but gasped his life out and the others were pretty seedy. The base-wallah of a sergeant laughed, but behind the laugh there was terror.

Joseph woke up in a clean if blurred white room feeling nasty in a very precise way, with what felt like a giant spiny bloater filling his mouth. Starchy sheets and nurses. Quills under his eyelids, moving inside his throat and nose and chest. Nausea. He still reeked of chlorine – even his breath, like a dragon's might. Baz and Joseph were out of action for four months, 'somewhere down in the F category', as a doctor joked. Acute gas poisoning, Baz keeping Joseph company with some further complication in the lungs. Their eyes were all right, after initial worries. It had happened before, they were told, it weeded out the weak and hopeless.

Joseph had the mark of Cain upon him, psychologically-speaking; and a burning desire to prove himself.

Not once did he hear a word of blame or accusation fall from Baz's lips. Or any of the others. He was not even sure they knew who had started it; at any rate, he never admitted to anyone that it was sheer funk. Faulty masks were not uncommon. One hated the sergeant-instructor enough to blame him, which is falling only a little short of the truth.

Joseph read the whole of Dickens in the sanatorium, Baz his law books. It was not so bad. It was even quite jolly, once they had fooled themselves they were veterans. There were disabled races, young men in Bath chairs – men without feet or legs or invisibly crippled by gas – rushing for the tape, tumbling, laughing, eggs on spoons held between the teeth, rolling over on the soft lawn, chaps cheering, the eggs bursting. But the lie played on Joseph's nerves. Baz, however, was equable, counted his blessings. The nurses hovered about in their blue uniforms, with handkerchiefs on their heads like Russian peasants – though some of them were ever so posh, young ladies fit for a ball, knew exactly how to pick up a handkerchief. Of course the men kept falling in and out of love like a rainy day. Joseph kept a diary, but he no longer had the urge to write verse, though he tinkered about. He wanted to be Dickens, that's what he wanted! The thought made him laugh.

Then Baz was given a job at GHQ, because they needed brains. Joseph bust a gut to get out to the Front, despite his wheeziness. They did not mind the wheeziness at all. This was early October 1918; they had used up too many men in the autumn push, they just needed to wind it up and so they were desperate. They would have sent up the men in Bath chairs if they could, everybody in fact but the women and smaller children. Joseph had nurtured his pacifist views in the sanatorium with its maimed young fellows – the whole war rotten, through and through rotten – but of course he had to go out and fight; it was the only way to scrub off the Cain patch, to give himself a touch of dignity. He felt so ashamed and hopeless that he was ready to die, though he was still young enough to believe that he would not die, not outright.

On the outside he was above suspicion, keeping his seasoned look. He had been gassed 'in France' – that was good enough for Ma and Pa and the neighbours. He was almost on the same level as the doctor's disfigured lad, with his nose that came away on a spring. Anyway, they kept off the subject. They had other worries: no one seemed to want carpets, these days. There was not the spread of money.

He crossed to Etaples again. The sergeant-instructor had been sent up to the heat; no one knew Private Monrow from Adam. There was a murmur going round in the barracks about Peace. And then it was the off. They wrote some 'last lines' to their 'people' and marched down to the station, tin hats wobbling about on their skulls like saucepan lids. Like an away game, someone remarked. The cattle truck was late, they waited on the platform with their waterproof sheets and ammo and packs feeling the thrill of it, despite the nasty yarns of the line they kept hearing from the transport men. There was a drizzle, it was cold, but somehow Joseph was warm inside, as if his blood was up.

Then there was a ripple among the fellows further down, a strange kind of ripple that reached him as a breeze passes along a line of osiers. He swayed. It was like the shock of hearing of an unexpected death — someone close. He felt as if he had been orphaned.

Peace!

The war's done with, finished, it's bloody over!

The Hun are smashed, they're cutting home!

Joseph sat on the platform among the match-ends and cried like a child, but then a lot of the men were crying. Nobody knew what they were crying for, there were so many reasons and all of them different. The war had been taken away from him, whipped away — from right under his feet. That was why *he* was crying. Big history, taking no account. It might have waited a couple of days. The men wandered about, like lost souls. Some of them were very happy, thinking they might be sent home smack off, on the next train that came puffing in. Drink appeared, strong stuff, as if from nowhere. The cattle truck never came. More and more men just wandered about or sat drinking. Songs, and jokes. Cheering. No one had to pull any more triggers in the history of the world.

His company was recalled. He spent several tedious weeks in England billeted with his own frustration and shame. His father caught the 'flu at a Thanksgiving service (like half of Youlster) and died painfully in December, telling everybody he was 'all right' to the end. Joseph found an unopened bottle of brandy in the shop and worked his way through it late at night, weeping among the rugs and carpets. He fancied the *joss* spoke to him in his father's voice. Each night, when he was small, his father would read to him from the Book of Common Prayer. Now the *joss* was doing it.

'. . . as by thy special grace, preventing us, thou dost put into our mindes good desires . . .'

His father would close the fat little book and kiss him goodnight. A sweet smell of pipe tobacco, chalk from the signboards, smothery bolts of cloth, incense from the sticks. And something else: a sort of bubble that rose up from underneath and burst its fragrance after his father had closed the door softly on the darkness. A smell that gleamed with everything he did not yet know about the adult world. Locked drawers, dark bottles, doors he could not open. As a boy, when he thought about God, he saw Him closing the accounts book and having His nip, just like his father did. Angels everywhere, golden spots of light and the dust dancing in the storeroom. Now here he was, full of brandy, and God was nowhere to be seen.

He woke up feeling dreadful, rolled up tight in a rug, a delivery man banging on the door.

His mother shut up shop and sold the cold house and bought herself a gas-heated flat in Buxton with room for the piano. She was happy, in her way. You could *smell* the happiness off her: coconut cakes and sherry. There were plenty of widows to keep her company, and she played a lot of bridge. She never became a Quaker, though. No need for it now, she said. Wars are finished. They're last year's model, Joseph.

Who caught 'flu, too, probably at the funeral; it did not do him much good except that he was invalided out of the army. He still wheezed a bit and his lungs recovered to about three-quarters capacity. It meant he was winded rather easily, nothing more, and if cold air got down him it was like swallowing icicles. He was in no way tubercular; he was quite fit and strong. But the flu caught him when he was still weak from the gas and he never quite got back, not completely. And he smoked a lot, too.

2

A Sunday Ramble

T HERE WAS THE hullaballoo of the Peace in the streets, folk not knowing whether to weep or laugh: Joseph simply got drunk and found himself arm in arm with a lamppost in Fenchurch Street. A constable with a scrubbing-brush moustache was somewhere in it. Joseph had no shoes on and his spats were lost. He was roaring out the hymn beginning 'Forty days and forty nights' in a light foggy drizzle. It was very early in the morning, quite black and cold, and his buttons were all too tight. That was how the new world began.

Baz shot back to Oxford like elastic the minute his uniform was off. He was just pipped to a First and came up to London to study law. This was in 1920. Joseph was studying the blank page in a boarding house in Clarges Street, off Piccadilly. The blank page was a mirror. He had forgone his degree, miscalculating the benefits of his small inheritance (half the proceeds of the shop). Really, though, it was the Oxford weather; nasty for the lungs, the damp was – and it somehow affected his whole self, creeping up from the chest. But he never admitted it. His first professional appearance in print was an article about the war for the *Daily Herald*, highly critical of the murderous dummies at GHQ. No one seemed to want his poems. They hung about. He felt quite sorry for them. Maybe there were too many poets around, they had not all got killed – at least not the bad ones. But this failure did not worry him overmuch as he was already embarked on the great work: secret, that was.

Baz was vexed because his old school had left off his brother's name on the bronze memorial plaque in the cloisters. The school, an insignificant runt of a place buried in woods near the unpronounceable Billericay, modelled itself quite laughably on Eton College, and, since Eton was having bronze in the cloisters, so would Lutteridge. Hanley had been expelled after a year or two for some unnameable misdemeanour. As far as Joseph could make out, Hanley had spent his later adolescence smoking cigars and bullying his mother. He was a lout, frankly. Baz was very keen on justice, worshipped his brother, and loathed his school. It was a fair fight.

The school authorities stood their ground: well, the bronze has already been cast, we cannot go doing another! Even the latest deaths had been mopped up, the ones who had taken their time about it. To have Hanley Beardow scratched in as an afterthought would draw attention to the fellow and look odd. There was some talk of a wooden plaque, the family to pay some ridiculous amount for it, but only if it was tucked behind a pillar. Baz was thus furiously engaged when he and Joseph started seeing each other again.

Baz enlisted his friend's aid, of course. Baz was full of passion – no talent for writing, though (it all sounded like legal footnotes), so his angry letters to newspapers were mostly phrased by Joseph. Some of these were published. The article for the *Daily Herald* was commissioned by another old boy from the school, an editor on the paper whose loathing for Lutteridge equalled Baz's. Joseph made it into a general attack on the insane devils that ran the war and on the society that bred it, and slipped in the business about Hanley towards the end. It caused some consternation and the friends received enthusiastic notes from the likes of Bertrand Russell and even Clifford Allen. Hanley had his name carved on a bench in the main courtyard: it was a bench Baz remembered fondly from sunny days in his last term, so everyone was happy.

It was about this time that they took to walking together around London on Sundays, seeking out solemn woods or mysterious green lanes in areas soon to be smothered in brick. And they talked a lot about girls.

Joseph had fallen head over heels for a beautiful dark-haired creature called Louise, the cousin of an Oxford friend. They saw each other at least once a week, always in the company of this friend, and she seemed not the slightest bit interested in Joseph. She would look at a fellow for just long enough to sting. Her parents had a large house in the country – near Stow-on-the-Wold, he thought, though she was always very vague about it. He was certainly never invited to weekend parties. He did not lure her with silly jokes but talked too much about politics and literature, emphasising his gas-induced wheeze as others did their limps. A lover likes nothing better than to be entertained, in the end, but Joseph did not know this; he behaved like a serious-minded hero in a romantic novel. This does not come off with spectacles, though he was quite good-looking behind them, in his long-faced, sensual way, with his queerly lopsided mouth. He was quite olive-skinned, too, which a lot of girls prefer to the pallid variety. And his eyes were dark as pitch, with lush lashes he was faintly shy of. But the smell of the closed study hung about him (or rather, of his land-lady's dogs and boarding-house stew). He had nothing really to boast of.

About a month after the article appeared, he and Baz were Sunday rambling. Their walk had taken them up one of those ancient sunken paths that attract gnats in the summer – near Hayes, it was; they were enticed into it by a broken stile. Mud a foot thick sucked at their boots and if they had been true veterans, well, their nerves would have been stretched a bit. Instead, they were rather enjoying themselves, daubed from head to foot in Middlesex clay and discussing whether Hylas was not to be envied, dragged down by the lovely wet naiads. They sat on a tuft for a breather.

'Moth-eaten lungs,' said Baz. 'How are yours?'

'Middling to fair today. Depends on what London's coughing up.'

There was not a whiff of coke out here, however. Only the sweet nip of cow and horse muck and the smooth November meadows, dazzling-wet.

'I wear my 'flu mask,' said Baz. 'It helps.'

'I can't,' said Joseph. 'It makes me twitchy.'

Although it was only a pad of cloth stuck to the cheeks with adhesive tape, it reminded him of the PH helmet.

'That germicide stuff they spray in the buses and tubes, it gets down my throat,' Baz added. 'So I have to wear the damn mask!'

'An anti-anti-'flu mask,' Joseph quipped.

Though the epidemic terrified them, underneath. It was mopping up what the war had missed, was the influenza. You could not help feeling nastily vulnerable.

Baz reached into his rucksack and passed Joseph a few letters, brushing crumbs off.

'Replies to the *Daily Herald* article,' he said. 'Some amusing, some sinister. The amusing ones spittle away about sacrifice and Empire and all that rubbish. The sinister ones remind me of the Count in *Dracula*.'

'The book or the film?'

Baz ignored the question. (He had never read the book, that was why.)

'They think we're, I quote, "*womanly*".' He snorted.

Joseph read them rather idly, skimming the blither. Then he was caught up short. A letter several pages long, in a neat hand, explaining why the slaughter on the Somme was justified – as one might justify, with careful scientific and social arguments, the existence of abattoirs to a vegetarian. Joseph could see that it was wrong, deadly wrong, with an icy conviction to its wrongness which chilled the gut – yet it gave him a terrible few moments. He had to struggle with it, really struggle with it. Joseph read it through again and shook his head.

'This one takes the biscuit,' he said. 'It's like the devil himself whispering in your ear.'

Baz was surprised – he had not read it properly. The signature, like the writing, was small.

'Frank Pitts will turn out to be a crusty old bloodthirsty fool with a limp from the Crimean campaign,' he declared, having run through it again too fast. 'Like all the others.'

'His handwriting isn't right for that,' said Joseph. 'It's rather feminine and young. And anyway, as you know, the shrillest lot are often the ones who were there, in the thick of it.'

'Justifies their suffering,' Baz said rather too casually, scratching his head.

Joseph nodded. 'You can put up with suffering until it feels futile. The basis of all religion, that.'

'Perhaps it's a hoax.'

'I don't reckon so. You can always tell a hoax. It's never quite flat enough. This is very flat. Ugh. Did General Ludendorff really write that, do you suppose?'

Baz read what the General had apparently written after the long Battle of the Somme – how the German army had been fought to a standstill and was 'utterly worn out'.

'My pacifism,' Baz stated, with an irritating *hauteur*, 'is not conditional on what a German general might spout in his memoirs.'

'The address is a wretched post-office box in London,' said Joseph.

'The postmark's Chertsey, though. We could go to Chertsey and bump Mr Pitts on the head with a wet fish.'

The path stretched out either side, trampled into glue by hooves and boots. It was so like a front-line trench that Joseph wondered whether Baz had brought him here deliberately. His seat was dry on the tuffet of grass and his boots were in the cold mud – he felt like a fly on a long strip of flypaper. He glanced at the letter again and began to feel incensed.

'I'm going to reply to Pitts point by point. I'm going to sit in a library and consult the appropriate books and papers, and deliver him a bone-dry, devastating counterattack.'

Properly incensed, he was.

'On his own terms, you mean?'

'Yes. Better than a wet fish.'

'Oh, what's the use, Jo-Jo?'

Joseph grimaced. He was not quite sure of that himself. He had his great work to think about: the novel had hatched to a fledgling of ten pages, not yet enough to be dispirited by. In order to earn a crust he was spending a large part of his week copy-editing thick tomes issuing forth from a legal publishers – it was owned by the head of Baz's chambers. The current tome, updating the law on a certain type of insurance, was six hundred pages long, its print minuscule and the myriad footnotes all but invisible. It did not pay that well, but it meant he remained unchained to office hours. He loathed literary hackwork; if he had been offered any he would have said no to it. He also detested literary *soirées* or the scrimmages in front rooms that went by the name of 'parties'. He had uncoupled from the Bloomsbury lot: they were all money, class and condescension, though he quite liked Mrs Woolf's latest novel. There were young Americans about, too, who unlike himself had no complexes about not having fought and got on with the business of taking over London while the natives squabbled or jigged about to jazz. Or so it seemed to him. Oh, the whole scene was quite nauseating. And when he saw the crippled hawkers and beggars in service uniform, holding out their tin boxes to indifferent passers-by, he wanted to scream, really scream.

'The only worthy thing to do,' he had said to Louise once, in the hothouse of Kew Gardens, 'is to write a giant novel of our times.'

'You mean one full of Bolsheviks and perms?'

'I mean one so caustic, Louise, it'll burn a hole in the fabric of hypocrisy and stupidity that the war did absolutely nothing to tear. On the contrary – it merely thickened it.'

Louise had nodded and turned without comment to her cousin, who was pointing out a huge tropical bloom sticking out its plump tongue.

Anyway, Joseph spent three days under the great booming cupola of the British Museum's Reading Room, swatting up on Generals Haig and Ludendorff (yes, there was the deadly comment), the Somme offensive and Passchendaele and all the rest of the shambles, and wrote a careful but stinging rebuke to Mr Frank Pitts under Baz's name. They received no reply. Not surprisingly, since the letter began with the immortal phrase: 'I found your letter not only morally repugnant, but ridiculous.' Joseph was proud of that.

The Sunday walks became a regular diversion: for a few more months, even through the depths of winter, they explored the numerous green lanes around London, hopping over smothered stiles and eating their lunch under hedgerows and talking – really talking. In dim and solemn woods they discussed Ruskin and William Morris. Once, caught in a storm on the south Middlesex heath, they sheltered in a cowman's lean-to, misquoting from *King Lear*. Now and again they reverted to boyhood and made bows and arrows out of sticks or threw clumps of moss at each other – whooping tinily under great, noble trees whose last hour was already come, along with the fields and all the busy creatures there.

3

The Rose Petal

IN THE EARLY April of 1921, a wealthy dilettante friend from Oxford days offered Joseph an ancient gamekeeper's cottage in the Chiltern hills at peppercorn rent, which he jumped at. He did not throw a party for his friends but slipped away, just like that. Louise had got engaged to the *cousin*! – Joseph felt tricked, somehow. The law book was off his back, and he was determined to eke out what remained of his inheritance with homegrown cabbages, poultry and such like. He had given himself until the end of the year: if the novel was a dud, he would seek employment in the Far East and never write again. It was now or never.

He walked from the little station down a steep and muddy lane overarched by budding branches. The wealthy friend had sent him a hastily-drawn map on brown bag-paper, and he was not at all sure this was the right lane. A toothless old woman in shabby black appeared, pushing a pram filled with rusty tins. He asked her the way. She pointed down the lane and then told him her life story, a long litany of grief and pain.

'Don't bide round here,' she said. 'It's finished muh.'

'I'm sure it hasn't.'

'Well, I tell you it has, boy.'

'You're not finished yet, I can see that.'

'Listen – at the end of the road there's a hole. And that's the truth. *That be all there is to't*,' she added, with a fierce spittly emphasis.

Like a secret, she told it to him. And barely greeted him in the subsequent months – as if she regretted giving it away, her secret.

The cottage, a little further on, was set down in a rather mouldy wood, about fifty yards beyond two rusty iron gates creaking on a pair of stone pillars each topped by something crumblingly heraldic. The lodge was a burnt-out ruin smothered under brambles. At the other end of the rutted drive lay the property, belonging until recently to the wealthy friend's dotty grandfather: a mansion, really. It was now as mouldy as the wood that enclosed it, the grandfather having perished of the 'flu around the same time as Joseph's father. The pile was mostly Hanoverian and quite handsome, but in so much need of renovation that no one in the family knew quite where to begin. Through gaps in the long shutters, out of a fetid darkness, Joseph could just distinguish gilded cornices and towering fireplaces in rooms the size of cinemas. Bats fluttered about in their curious, hesitant manner. He dismissed the idea of breaking in to explore.

It was a few days before the cottage warmed up and lost its urinous stink. The noise in the mossy thatch was rats, not mice: he could tell from the bulkiness of the thumps. There was scant furniture (scarcely the basics) and the midden was up against the kitchen wall. The parlour next to the kitchen was a mess of broken plaster and warped deal planks; he left it that way. The place had not been occupied for a year: mould on the walls, windows bleary with spiders'-webs, all that. Horsehair, from fourteenth-century horses, sprang out in tufts from the crumbling walls. But he was quite happy.

He would get up early, walk in the bare woods before breakfast, then write. He used the tiny spare room upstairs as his study. His ink-pot rested on a broken saucer alongside interesting stones from his walks; the crude little table that served as his desk had but one drawback: he could not cross his legs under it. Its wood was dark with old varnish and split in the middle, a real working-man's table. And it had a sort of queer, magnetic pull to its solidity.

If folk in the village asked him, he said he was writing a memorial volume. They never asked what a memorial volume was, exactly; they just pursed their lips sagely and nodded. It shut them up, at any rate.

Covering sheets of thin-lined foolscap, his novel talked to itself for page after page. He was glorying in it, here. He particularly enjoyed the reflective passages. He would in time set these off with the scenes of physical action – for the moment, for ill-defined reasons, he was setting them aside. The work was quite out of keeping with the slim satires then in vogue with his own set; it was weighty and raw, knitted through by symbolic references culled from the likes of Frazer, Levy-Bruhl, Jessie Weston. He really wanted it to have the force of ritual, of a nature myth; so it raged and devoured today's rottenness like a great ritual fire but always, always poetically. It thrilled to its own music, and he read his favourite poets continually. He felt them at his shoulder. In the rustling quiet of the countryside, they had gathered like refugees at his shoulder – Shelley and Keats in the forefront. He was quite blind to what he was doing, of course. He had no inkling just how floridly empty the writing was, not at this stage. No judgement, no standing apart.

No poems, though. That Muse had really fled at the first sniff of his prose. He was happy at that. It made life easier.

He would eat nothing but biscuits or porridge until evening. Then he would walk down to the village and sup in The Saddler's Arms. This was a rambling thatched building with a curious arrangement of windows – squint-eyed, it looked. It was generally packed, Cholesford being a thirsty village, and he would slip through the smoke room into the stuffy parlour where he ate his supper. He avoided the tap room completely: all boots and waistcoats and a porridge of dialect, that was.

Cholesford itself was a straggle, its scruffy old houses scarcely visible between the beech woods and the church (the latter's only point of interest was a mammoth's yellowed rib hung up near the chancel). It boasted a garage, a grocery store, a Post Office and a minuscule branch-line station. The garage doubled as a hairdresser's and the curious, gypsy-like folk, slightly of the ferret type, offered a variety of services. There was even a beehive maker who lived in a tent on the common – a proper gypsy, he was, with a big tumbling family. The village had an excremental stink about it that after two days Joseph did not notice. Cholesford suited him well.

He had this arrangement with the inn's landlady, Mrs Hamilton: for a derisory amount she would cook him something that steamed with gravy, and he would read to her in front of the fire for an hour or so. She had very poor eyesight, and her daughter and son-in-law did most of the work. She had a passion for Sir Walter Scott, unfortunately, but the advantage of this was that Joseph could drift off while in the act of reading. *Waverley*, it was. They fair shot through it. The queer aspect was the absolute concentration it inspired in Mrs Hamilton, knitting quietly in the private snug with its crooked beams and creaky floor. She only once interrupted, to ask which side Sir Everard was on; all she needed to keep in mind, he told her, was Sir Everard's support for the Old Pretender. He was, in truth, as bemused as her among the Whigs, Tories and Jacobites. The war was simplicity itself, in comparison. He made no comment on her black armband: it was still as common as crows, in the village. Anywhere, for that matter.

Baz came to visit after a few weeks, with what struck Joseph as a very loud voice to go with a loud battered old BSA motorcycle. It was queer, having someone erupt into his life, like a revolution in a peaceable country. Baz was doing very well, was fully articled or whatever it was and had just won his first case. Over supper in The Saddler's Arms (Mrs Hamilton insisted, as they had just started into *Ivanhoe*), Baz pulled out a letter from his pocket. The writing looked familiar to Joseph. He read it with horror.

Mr Frank Pitts! – not, after all, squashed for good. It was some five pages long, with a full page devoted to the Treaty of Brest Litovsk. Joseph had never heard of it.

'The Bolsheviks signed this treaty with Germany in 1917,' he read out loud. 'Russia would have lost 89 per cent of her coal output, 73 per cent of her iron output and 300,000 square miles. It had to pay an indemnity of 6 billion marks. Thankfully, the treaty was never ratified because we won the war.'

Brilliant and deranged.

'This man doesn't care a fig for human life,' he commented. 'It is quite horrible. And this business about looking at the war "objectively" – it makes me feel sick. Life isn't all iron output and square miles, is it?'

Baz smiled. 'At least we've a fencing partner. Keeps you on your toes, Jo-Jo. You'll sink into mental softness here, if you don't look out.'

Mrs Hamilton came in just then, waving her copy of *Ivanhoe*. They passed through into the snug, Baz lit his pipe and snuggled down into a dog-scored leather chair, and Joseph read *Ivanhoe* rather breathlessly, as if the knights were galloping about in a cinema film. Afterwards she offered the friends a tankard each

23

of murky home-made cider on the house. They talked about the strikes and Ireland and some grisly murder in the paper. Joseph was not reading the papers, out here.

'I refuse to sully my head,' he said, 'with second-hand reports of terrible matters.'

'I would miss that very much,' said Baz, puffing happily. 'Always makes me feel fortunate.'

Mrs Hamilton said she did not have the time, anyway, which seemed rather odd, in the circumstances.

The son-in-law appeared in the doorway. He glanced at the two men like nails, as if they had no right to be there – not both of them, at least. He was of average height but stooped like a much taller man, a man like Baz. It was the stoop of a man ducking the pub's beams when he had no need to. A miner's stoop, maybe, or a mild trench stoop.

'Nobbut knows where it is,' he said, mysteriously.

'Try the larder, Walter,' said Mrs Hamilton.

'The larder? Why the larder?'

Mrs Hamilton settled her knitting on her broad lap and smiled.

'You put things down to take things up,' was all she said. It had the air of a profundity. Baz blinked through his pipe smoke, nodding.

Walter had very large, spaniel eyes, but now he narrowed them.

'No, I don't. I don't do that.'

'I don't mean you *personally*, Walter. We *all* do is what I mean.'

'What's lost?' Joseph asked. 'I might have seen it.'

Walter swung his whole body towards him rather awkwardly, as if it had an Antarctic sledge attached to it. Walter was not lame, but he had rheumatism, though Mrs Hamilton had said once that he was 'hardly thirty-five'. With his greying hair and long bedraggled moustache, he might have been fifty.

'You won't know what it is if I tell you,' he said.

This was more cajoling than threatening. He would speak in a sort of loud mutter, with a northern twang – from Lancashire, he claimed. It was his wife who did the talking – that high-breasted merry type, she was; her only defect was an ugly laugh, a whoop that hit just the wrong note. They could hear this laugh now and again through the thick oak door that separated the snug from the bar proper. The snug was really Mrs Hamilton's domain: Joseph had never known any other customer venture in. This explained Walter's irritation, perhaps. At any rate, Joseph merely shrugged in a sort of diffident fashion and occupied himself with his cigarette.

Mrs Hamilton told him that it was a key that was missing, a key to some cupboard or other. Then she blew her nose.

'You feeling poorly, the missus?' That was Walter's pet name for her, 'the missus'.

'I'm quite fine, Walter, thank you.'

She started knitting again. Her eyes were very red, it was true.

'I won't bother with it,' Walter muttered.

'What's in there apart from the cloths?'

'The pickle jars.'

'Then give them mustard. Ham and tongue goes well with mustard.'

'None left.'

Mrs Hamilton stood up and tutted and swept herself out, leaving Walter looking rather bashful. He picked up the Scott.

'Boo-ooks,' he said, with a wealth of derision in the strung-out northern vowel.

'Another Walter,' said Joseph, lighting his pipe. 'The great Scott.'

'Who's that fellow up there?' asked Baz, pointing at a photograph on the mantelpiece.

Walter looked. 'That's the late Mr Hamilton,' he said. 'Fell in th' war.'

'Where, exactly?' Baz asked, as if it might matter to him.

Walter blinked uncertainly. 'Difficult to say,' he said. He put the book down.

'Missing, then?'

'No, not missing.'

There was a silence, the fellow in the dim photograph looking down on them like Judgement. Joseph caught Walter's eye when he did not mean to, both stealing a surreptitious glance, like a pair of burglars frightening each other in the dark. Then Walter turned and stole out, silently. The latch fell a little too hard, nervous rather than angry. Mrs Hamilton came in a few moments later, still tutting.

'The mustard were there as clear as day. Oh, Walter en't the same man, you know,' she said, sitting with a sigh. 'Slow, very slow, since he came back. He was a ray of sunlight, before.'

Hard to imagine this: a sunny Walter. You almost had to turn his moustache the other way up, to imagine it.

'Of course, he was with my Ted when he were took off.' She glanced at the mantelpiece, tears shining in her eyes.

'Yes,' said Joseph, 'we talked about that.'

'Did you? Did you now?' She seemed genuinely startled.

'In so many words.'

She settled back, closing her eyes for a moment. 'It was very clean, Ted's going. Didn't feel a thing. Just going over the top, they were. Then he fell back into Walter's arms with a rose petal on his brow. Just here.'

She pointed to the middle of her forehead. 'Very peaceful,' she added, with her eyes still closed.

'A *rose* petal?' Joseph could not see this at all: it was almost vulgar.

'His wound,' she murmured.

'Ah, of course,' Joseph acknowledged, contritely. A red petal with a glint of dew.

'That's how Walter put it,' she went on. 'A petal fallen onto his brow. Walter tried to brush it away. He even tried to brush it away, with his fingers. You could put that in your memorial volume, if you so wish, dear. If it fits in.'

'Thank you. I might.'

After a respectful little pause, during which Mrs Hamilton gazed upon Mr Hamilton's visage and snuffled a bit, the subject was changed to sundry village matters. The church bell struck ten o'clock, followed by the sound of tipsy men swelling onto the road, all beery bonhomie shot through with something dangerous, even cruel. The two friends sat in the warm little snug like two young boys sheltering in their maternal folds. They felt free of the world, they did; to the tick-ticking of the woman's needles.

4

The Living Image

J OSEPH WOKE UP in bed in the middle of the same night with
a startled jerk. Bang upright, he was. The bed squeaked as if ill
at ease. Rats rustled about in the thatch. The queerest hunch had
yanked him out of his dream.

Walter had been *responsible* for it!

In fact, it was a moment before he could remember what 'it'
was, beyond the notion that it was deadly. He could not even
remember very much of the dream, but it had featured a deep
conversation with the dead blacksmith on the mantelpiece. The
photograph had turned into Walter's stark-white face. This face
now seemed to hover in the dark little bedroom like the globe
of a gas lamp. It was ghastly, sheer terror. There was some sort
of distant, blood-curdling shriek. Then Joseph woke up properly
and sat up in bed to ease his breathing, upon which the nightmare
had an almost asthmatic effect. So he had not really been shot bolt
upright at all.

Baz was snoring next door. It was good to have someone else
within earshot.

Joseph went down to the kitchen and ate an apple, standing at
the back door. The night air was delicious, apart from a faint acrid
whiff from the midden. There was a real-life distant screech and
then the woods seemed to beat, as if they had a heart: a regular,
thudding type of beat. A friend had described how it was the
deep woods behind his position that had smashed his nerves up
in France, making the din of a barrage reverberate – 'ten times
worse, it was'. Joseph remembered that from childhood, playing

27

in the woods behind Youlster. Woods acted like a gramophone's horn or a speaking trumpet. The beating heart was some big owl flying past, he supposed, steadily flapping its wings. At any rate, it faded soon enough and he went back inside. The squeaky stairs disturbed Baz. At least, he stopped snoring.

Joseph lit his bedside candle and scribbled down his hunch about Walter. 'Hunch' was right: there was something crookbacked about it, slipping about like Hyde in the dirty shadows. But it gave him an arc, a kind of arcing stroke over the whole stretch of the novel: a man goes to war, does something that spears him on a shaft of guilt. Breaks him *inwardly*. He wrote the words INWARD WOUND very large across the middle of a sheet of paper, and underlined the first word three times. Then, quite a way underneath, in small letters – almost timid it looked, crouched down there – he wrote:

England

Angrily inspired, he scribbled off a rather vicious reply to Pitts. The ink-pot rattled on its broken saucer. 'A Freudian disturbance in childhood,' he wrote, 'must have been responsible for your chillingly pragmatic attitude to the most horrible of wars. Killing is never "objective" – you cannot look at the killing of a single human being "objectively". If you can, you are sinister: I would not like to meet you on the train.' Oh, he was very pleased at that. He could not tackle him point by point, after all. It was like playing cricket with someone who thinks they are playing tennis. But the rejoinder satisfied him. Now and again one simply had to bite the jugular.

He said nothing about any of this to Baz the next morning. The motorbike would not start and Cox from the garage took it apart. The two friends rambled through the beech woods around Tring, taking the main old trackway to Aylesbury, and hitched a lift back on a waggon, perching on its rather soiled boards – the cottage smelt sweetly of dung all the next day, to Joseph's delight. A most satisfactory excursion, with his ideas for the novel running softly underneath, like a secret passion.

Baz's motorbike, a truly battered affair, was deemed unmendable. Something really vital had bust in it.

'Well,' he said, rather cheerily, 'it's back to trains and horses. I'll bet you approve, Jo-Jo.'

And Joseph did.

He was much more conscious, once Baz had left, of his solitude. Solitude paling into loneliness, rather sickly. He would look out from his worktable onto the rustling greenery (responsible for the permanent gloaming in the room, like a woodland pool) and envy the birds their chatter. His book was full of comradeship. He fancied at one point that the characters were looking out from the page and laughing at him with their arms around each other's shoulders. Unhealthy, at any rate, to be cooped up like that. He sought relief in endless cups of tea, arrowroot biscuits, and brisk hikes round about. He would take a stroll up and down the sloped lane after lunch, scarcely meeting anyone except the odd woodsman, melancholically chopping. The woods were full of bluebells, violets, anemones and wild strawberry: gradually he explored them, though never going very deep.

Well, it was a queer lost nook, that part. There was enough beech about for a hundred bodgers — but they were a thing of the past, the other side of the war. The ones he had known as a boy were robust, jolly fellows who chewed on their pipes and spun tales of elves and goblins and imps. He fancied they actually believed in such things. It must be a very influencing thing, he reckoned, living as the aboriginal peoples of England did, in a little clearing in a wood. Their eyebrows and big beards were always white from sawdust, making them look older and wiser. The chairs in the cottage were bodgers' work, of course. Five bob a piece, thoroughly out of fashion.

Each evening he would repair down to the inn and come back later and later — pretty tipsy, sometimes, especially if he indulged in a barley wine or two in the smoke room. He never entered the tap room and saw very little of Walter, who usually served the rougher types there. He reckoned the fellow was avoiding him. Mrs Hamilton informed him one day that Walter was 'fey'. Well, Joseph had met quite a few countrymen with such reported gifts, it must go with a closeness to animals and trees; but he had never reckoned it up. Some of them, on the other hand, were more downright than anyone from a town.

'Can't help wondering,' she whispered, leaning forward, 'as

whether our Walter didn't have a bump on the head from summat, out there.'

Or an inward wound, thought Joseph. Ted Hamilton stared down at him from the mantelpiece; hard-headed, he looked. Wanting his life back.

The days passed. He began to feel stale, a little shoddy. The last buds had burst abruptly into vivid, sticky leaves that the sun entangled itself in, as if unable to get out; he could not match this budding within himself. His small parcels of words came out badly wrapped. The bluebells in the woods almost infuriated him with their blazing, dark-blue beauty. The primroses and late celandines, too. He could not even describe them. He felt like Adam: that all he could do was name.

He had seen an advertisement in the newspaper for a sketching week in Cornwall and on a sudden impulse took a week off and joined it.

It was not exactly a polar expedition. Still, the change of scenery and the sudden plunging into people was almost as dramatic in its effect. Even the sulphurous train down was a shock. He was not very skilled or gifted at drawing; what he used it for was attention, to firm up his visual sense, his memory. Otherwise he would get bleared by words and let the eye slip over things. Over half of the round dozen of them were elderly widows – it did not matter to Joseph: the sun came in and out most of the week and the rain frisked about in a Cornish way, it was always warm, they stood on the edge of cliffs and marvelled. Nothing better than the sparkle of sun on water, spume-dashed rocks, the scent of moorland blooms. The chatter of the venerable widows was blown away by the wind and Joseph spent many hours at one with the carbon pencil and the view, his thoughts streaming out into gusts of pure air and the perplexed mews of gulls.

Mr Douse was their tutor, serious and thoughtful, a little obsessive – the only concession to bohemianism was a floppy canvas hat; otherwise he stalked about the group in a smart tweed suit and tie, consulting his fob-watch every so often. Joseph learnt many useful things: tree branches always taper; the motion of the subject dictates the speed at which you draw; if there is wind in a sail there will be no reflection in the water; beauty is not a thing to see but an emotion to feel (this reminded him painfully of Louise). He went to bed early, full of sea air, and slept like a log. He thought the rest of the group regarded him as aloof, which was correct, but they forgave him because of his extreme keenness. On the last day he managed to capture sparkle on a breezy sea with quick, short lines of ink. He did not really know how, though. It was a kind of trick, like wax under a wash of watercolour. The salt air fogged his glasses a bit, but Mr Douse told him that Constable was short-sighted, too. It got rid of the fussy detail.

It was on that last day that he met himself, as it were.

The group had reported en masse to a smokery in a fishing village near Newlyn to celebrate the successful completion of the week. The smokery was a long, whitewashed affair looking out on a pebbled beach, with a tall fat chimney belching smoke and delicious smells over a row of flaking little boats. It was evidently very old. No sooner had they walked in than one of the number – a rather portly woman from the Midlands – grabbed Joseph's arm and cried out, 'Goodness gracious, it's your twin!'

He looked. A fellow was serving at a table, his back was turned at that instant but Joseph still felt an odd sensation, a sort of fluttering of coloured rags in his head. Then the fellow straightened up and Joseph saw the face.

Thin, rather hollowed-out. A lopsided mouth and a narrow, rather large nose. Thin neck, too – somehow onion-like, like the neck of an onion. Scrawny. The same oval spectacles – gold-rimmed, the standard type – if dirtier. Joseph was momentarily horrified that he might look like this to others, but only momentarily. Really, he did not believe them. The resemblance was superficial.

The fellow had rather fluttery gestures – these mimicked Joseph's own, he was told. The only difference was in the eyes; when the man looked up, Joseph saw they were not only a striking blue (Joseph's were dark), but bleary – a seafarer's eyes. That was a *great* disappointment to all concerned. Then the young man smoothed down his eyebrows with the ball of his thumb and the group gave a collective gasp. *That is my tic, too*, Joseph thought. He wanted to disappear outside, feeling quite shy all of a sudden, uncomfortable. The notion that this sharp-faced waiter with his fluttery, feminine gestures was in any way like him struck him as absurd, even offensive. The three or four men in the group were no help; they

31

joined in the chorus of subdued shrieks and sniggers with their own jolly remarks, serving only to get the women going again.

'We've seen right through you now,' said one of this number, 'there's a family secret here, admit it!'

She was a retired headmistress with a florid face. They were all sat down by now and her hand met the table with the kind of smack reserved for class assemblies. The whole cramped establishment fell quiet. The twin in question had disappeared into the kitchen. Joseph had got to know these faces surrounding the long table rather well, in the way you can familiarise yourself with people who a week ago meant nothing to you. And as quickly forget them.

'Why not ask *him*?' he said.

He was a little annoyed, but determined not to show it. Something about the whole business struck him as sinister, as if it had been planned. As if their tutor, Mr Douse, looking on as thoughtfully as usual through his glittery round glasses, had set him up on purpose for some elusive exercise in portraiture.

On cue, the fellow emerged from the kitchen and came over to take their orders. He was dressed in a clean white apron, his checked shirt rolled up at the sleeves. Joseph noticed with reluctant envy that, despite his fluttery gestures, his likeness had more muscle, he was a little firmer in the arms and legs. He was not really thin, or at least his thinness was of the wiry type. He was of the strong and wiry type while Joseph was merely wiry. The fellow had no idea what was going on; like Joseph, he could not immediately recognise his living image. But the group had become a united surge of amazement now he was hovering not two feet from his double, and even Mr Douse was nodding in appreciation. Joseph began to feel bewildered. It was like being on stage and having no clue of the lines. The ex-headmistress asked the poor man whether he was of any filial relation to Joseph. The man turned and looked. Joseph smiled nervously and studied the tablecloth. He was oddly sensitive about attention, about being the centre of it, most of the time.

'Never seen the gentleman in my life before,' the fellow muttered.

'What's your name?' said one of the group, puffing on his pipe.

The poor chap blinked uncertainly. He would have liked to have shooed them all out, probably.

'Hubert Rail,' he said. 'Now, how many smoked herrings was it?'

It was not the name that had the group almost rising up as one from their chairs; it was his voice. It sounded rather high and nasal, rather pukkah (they had expected a Cornish burr, at least), and was generally declared to be the 'wax recording' of Joseph's, complete with a slight mouthing northernness in the vowels. Through all this shenanigans, Hubert Rail kept a calm demeanour, more intent on getting the order than anything else. As if he had these sort of mad folk every day, and tolerated them as one tolerates a foreigner with appalling English. A thin little dark woman, a bit rodent-like, said it reminded her of a Kipling story, one of the *Plain Tales*, the one where that poor fellow falls for his love's likeness. She had all the same mannerisms and didn't she sing the same song in the same way? What was the song? Nobody could quite remember, or they would have started singing it there and then. It was a nightmare.

'I hope Mr Monrow won't fall in love with *himself*,' someone jovially remarked. This made Joseph blush. He was relieved to note that his likeness did not.

One of the men had a Kodak, and insisted they all stand outside the smokery together, Joseph and Mr Hubert Rail in front, to have their picture taken. He then took another of just the two of them, standing rather shamefacedly shoulder to shoulder, like Siamese twins. They had to comb their hair to get the same cut, but Hubert Rail's was too thick and unruly on the top. Since Joseph's tatty straw hat was irreproducible, the two men succumbed to the indignity of a couple of identical boaters borrowed from the group. Joseph's was too big for him, Hubert's too small. They swapped. Now Joseph's was too small for him, and Hubert's too big. They kept it like that.

'All neat and spick!' cried the chap with the camera. 'All neat and spick!'

Through all of this, oh, how embarrassed Joseph was! He covered it up with heartiness; his duplicate (whose chin's small mole rather ruined the idea, Joseph was glad to see) seemed completely unabashed. More than that, he seemed positively somewhere else, as if it was all but shadow-play. Joseph was rather envious of this cool. His supposed double made him shrink slightly inside himself. He absolutely refused to sing 'Poor Wandering One!' – which someone had discovered was the song in the Kipling story – or make ridiculous faces.

Mr Douse was delighted. He was very keen on balance and harmony, of course, and whittered on about honeycombs. Joseph did not understand what he was driving at. It had something to do with binary arithmetic. The morning had been spent in drawing reflections of posts and boats in glossy sand and then the same sort of thing on a wide stretch of water, the breeze making fantastic shapes of their subjects – quite distorted they were, they approached the wilder experiments of the kind of artists Douse disapproved of. Joseph had got tar on his trousers, and was not at all pleased with his efforts; he could not seem to find the vertical beneath the boats, and his reflections had seemed more solid and niggly than the real object. In the end, he turned his paper the other way up and signed it thus. Mr Douse did not see the joke.

Anyway, at his suggestion, Hubert Rail and Joseph were made to make mirror images of each other for the last two photographic poses, sticking their arms and legs out. By now the other customers were watching from the door, and the kitchen staff had emerged from the smoky side. A pale balding man was struggling to remember a quote from *The Comedy of Errors*. All were agreed that the whole business had made their day, and was remarkable, and the cook even suggested ringing the local newspaper. Joseph desisted at that, and said he was famished, and could he and his *doppelgänger* return to their respective roles, please?

Joseph shook hands with Hubert Rail and thought, honestly thought, that that was the back of the business, as far as he was concerned. They went inside.

'I subscribe,' announced Mr Douse, 'to the theory that in all the millions of our fellow-creatures, playing infinitely upon a limited range of features, there are one or more – perhaps many more – who resemble us down to the last whisker. It is simply that we never cross their paths, not in the usual run of affairs.'

'I hold,' boomed the ex-headmistress, 'to the much more interesting possibility of a dark family story.'

'A shipwreck, even,' said the pale balding man. 'In their infancy.'

'Oh, much darker than that!' She turned a beady eye upon Joseph. He bluffed it out by agreeing. He would ask his mother. He blew a large smoke ring over the dreadful woman's head. 'My problem is,' he added, looking anxious, 'well, I am due to inherit an enormous – positively *enormous* – family fortune. It would not do to have it halved, would it?'

This absolute lie provoked a hush, then a laugh from one of the men, who thought he saw through it. Hubert coughed and went out. Mention of fortunes makes people uncomfortable, the desire for it rises in the throat, so the doubles subject staggered on for a bit and then faded. Joseph had killed it. Even when Rail entered with a tray piled with smoked eels, it hardly revived. Oh, he did have such a pale, unappealing visage, slightly skewwhiff. As a boy Joseph had wasted much time in front of his mother's dressing-room mirror, a triptych affair which threw back the reflection of your reflection and enabled you to see yourself as others saw you, uninverted and at certain angles continuing on into infinity. Just such a skewwhiff impression had it given him, as if he had never quite known himself. As he cut into the fat charred flesh of the eel, he wondered if he had, yes, met his double. He felt so queasy at this that he could scarce swallow, and left half his meal on the plate. The ex-headmistress finished it for him with relish. Someone asked Hubert, busy clearing away the dishes, if *he* was a painter, too – she had noticed traces of paint around his fingernails.

'I do regard myself,' he said, in a slightly simpering tone, 'as the Cornish Constable.'

This engulfed the table in laughter, though it was hard to say whether Hubert was mocking them, or himself. At least, Joseph thought, he is not embarked on the great war novel. When asked if he had any of his paintings to hand, Hubert shook his head. He flatly refused to talk about it any further. He looked vaguely upset as he went off into the kitchen.

The room grew stifling. Joseph slipped out as the others waited for their batter pudding, all yearning for it (he could see this in their eyes, really burning for cold custard they were). He lit a cigarette and wandered down the pebble beach to the slop of surf, standing on the very edge of England where the land made sucking noises in its teeth. The day had turned grey and rather dismal and the movement of the little waves seemed to him rather cretinous.

The big slow swell stopped at the mouth of the little bay and ended up as this cretinous motion at his feet. He contemplated climbing on the rocks either side but they were slippery-looking. He heard a squirming of pebbles behind him and turned. It was Hubert Rail.

'Got a cigarette, have you?'

'My last one, actually.'

Hubert took it without a murmur, nodding his thanks. His hands, Joseph noticed, were slightly trembling.

'I need to sit,' said Hubert. 'Five minutes.'

He moved up the beach a little to a bleached log and sat on it. Joseph joined him. There was a vague peal of laughter from the smokery's open windows behind them.

'Now then,' said Hubert, 'let's have it fair and square. Are we related?'

'Not that I know of,' said Joseph. 'What a hullabaloo,' he added, lightly. 'All in the eye of the beholder, to my mind.' He felt superior, sitting with this fellow of his own age, to the older lot in the smokery.

Hubert looked across with a faint smile. The listless sea made clopping noises in the hollows and now and again a flash of spume shot up from the rocks, like somebody going white with surprise. Hubert, Joseph noticed, was very white, with traces of sunburn on his neck.

'Can you stand that crowd at all?' Hubert asked.

'Oh, now and again. One will do anything for art, you know.'

'Where are you from?'

'Youlster. Know it? Derbyshire—'

'I'm from Chesterfield,' Hubert cut in. 'My father died when I was six. We were very poor. My mother was an unhappy woman. I've always painted. I don't know where it comes from. I think I'm very good. But I need — one should do anything without needing money, but one can't. I can't afford decent paints, you know. And there's the time. The job sucks it all out of you — time, soul, what have you. Your genius. I need to meet people, folks like you. Other slaves to art. *Proper* slaves, I mean.'

He bent his head down and scooped up a few pebbles, rolling them in his hand. They made tiny shrieking noises as he rolled them together. Joseph nodded, feeling queerly wise and old.

'Do you paint the sea?' he said.

Hubert snorted. 'It's a long time since I've done that,' he said. He looked out at the sea as if it was a dreary lot of folk in bowler hats. 'Oh, a very long time.'

'Sweeping lines and confused hollows, the waves are,' said Joseph, scoffingly. He made a gesture with an imaginary pencil. 'That's what I've learnt this week.'

'As far as that, you've got? Well.'

Joseph felt an uncomfortable responsibility to the part of him that strove to be detached from the old order.

'It has to be drawn from the imagination,' he remarked. 'Whatever one paints or writes, it has to be drawn from there.' It sounded bossy, even to his own ears.

'Bourgeois,' said Hubert. Joseph was unsure whether this was an insult or a declaration, the word was flopped out that listlessly. He drew hard on his cigarette, already denying Hubert a certain reality, boxing him as a Marxian bore.

'We must first of all decide that life has no meaning,' Hubert went on. 'It is gratuitous. Therefore any act of artistic making is vanity.' He blew out smoke in an aggressive cloud and gave a light chuckle. 'Unless you give yourself up to life.'

'What do you mean?'

Hubert turned to look at him with ominous, red-rimmed eyes behind the spectacles. It occurred to Joseph then that the fellow might well be taking some sort of drug – cocaine, probably.

'Paint without meaning. Don't think about what you're doing. The sea doesn't, does it? So why paint the sea? We must do everything as nature does it. Killing, even.'

'Killing? There's been too much of that—'

'Ah, but it wasn't senseless, was it? That's why there was so much of it. It was calculated. Nature never calculates. Every act must be primal, and without sense.'

'What do your paintings look like?' Joseph asked, genuinely interested. At the same time, he thought Hubert somehow second-rate. The extreme views were what his father would term 'gassing', to hide the second-rate mind.

Hubert smiled, looking at his companion closely.

'Never mind that,' he said. 'Do you have lodgings in London?' This struck Joseph as an odd question.

'Why do you ask?'

There was a shout from the smokery. Hubert leaned forward, cursing softly. 'I need to be in London,' he said. 'I'm really dying here. Dying slowly but surely. It's a very slow death, but it's death all the same.'

'Oh, London won't help,' said Joseph. *It's full of your sort*, he wanted to say. 'I left in April and am much the better for it. I live in a wood—'

'Nevertheless,' the other broke in, holding Joseph's arm, 'I must get up there. I *have* to get up to London.'

'Then go.'

'I'm skint. You don't know how I live. In an old broken boat, on the beach.' He waved towards the beached boats, that did look old and broken, like clapboard huts with crooked chimneys. 'The only reason I don't starve is they give me scraps here.'

'What do you spend your wages on?' Joseph asked, slightly accusingly. There was something ungrown about Hubert that prickled.

Hubert drew deeply on his cigarette and looked away.

'My treatments,' he said. 'I'm not well.'

Definitely cocaine, Joseph thought.

'I have headaches,' the other added. 'Since the war. Someone keeps opening my head with a paper knife, as if it's an envelope. If I could find a girl . . . Isn't it a wonder, how cool girls' flesh is? You expect it to be hot but you touch their arms and the skin is cool. The books have got it all wrong. I'm like the sea without a moon, I have the passion and desire moving in me like a tide but there's no moon. That's the mystery. Their skin is very cool, isn't it?'

He got up and brushed his trousers with an oddly affecting gesture. Joseph stood, too. He knew what Hubert meant about cool girls and inner tides without moons. He wanted to agree with him out loud, yet something – a superior feeling – stopped him. He merely said: 'I've enjoyed talking to you, you know.'

On the way up the beach Hubert said, rather casually: 'You're lucky, not having to think about the readies. I could do so much if I was in your shoes.'

'I don't have the readies,' Joseph replied, firmly. 'I only just get by, you know.'

'What about the fortune?'

'What fortune?'

Hubert grinned under a sharp frown, his thumb poking Joseph's forearm. 'Don't pull my funny bone,' he said. 'You've got that fortune, you told everybody—'

'Oh, that!' Joseph laughed. He wished to tell Hubert how it came to pass, that fib. He nearly did. Then he caught the fellow's eyes and their stark blue was all aflame with yearning, it was quite startling. Hubert was staring at him, yearning from his two, pale-blue eyes in the whited face.

Joseph waved a hand about. 'It's all bound up,' he said vaguely. 'I'll probably never see it.'

He could not admit to the lie. It would have shamed him. Hubert blinked and nodded slowly, clearly disbelieving.

'You have to say that. If not then it's *hubris*, isn't it?'

He gave a short, coiling laugh, rather cynical. Then a man in a greasy-looking cook's outfit shouted at him from the kitchen door and he disappeared inside without a further word, leaving Joseph with a feeling that he had been cast out in some way, standing alone on the grim pebbles. He felt ashamed of the muddle about the fortune; there was something inelegant about it, something bony and coy.

That afternoon, which was very warm, Joseph bathed in a secluded cove, stripped to his fish-white birth suit. He felt a need to do this, though he loathed cold water. He hesitated for a moment, once undressed, feeling the delicious sensation of sun and breeze, the light Nereid fingers touching him all over, very cool and lascivious. It was positively carnal, but cosmically so. The *chaos* of the water – it was all seen by him now in terms of curves and angles, sharp and sweeping pencil lines, the foam a shifting mosaic at his feet. The moment he splashed in, yelling at the top of his voice, all this was smashed. He was once more purely physical, battling with the ocean (not really battling: it was calm, the breakers were far out) and glad to be so precisely delineated as himself – unique, that was the thing, once and for all time. Not twice! Half, perhaps – children were half. But not really, they were their own thing. He wasn't half his father. Life isn't arithmetic.

He swam out and then trod water, thinking hard. The events of lunchtime had affected him; Hubert Rail was an odd fish, a hook that went deep, he decided. He then realised, drying himself vigorously, that the main result of the week was to have him drawing like Mr Douse.

So, for that evening's exercise, he sketched a sunset from a cliff in what could only be called a Vorticist manner, violently scoring the paper in revolt. His body glowed from the swim. Poor Mr Douse, over supper, said only that he thought the drawing was 'lacking in restraint', and that Joseph should have used a BBB pencil. Joseph snorted, rather contemptuously, and lost the good feeling of the group for the last few hours of their time together. This is why he hated groups, he realised; their affections move about like a big clump of dangerous floating weed. He felt gloriously young, even wild with it.

'I wonder, what is your fortune in, young feller?' asked one of the men, a tidy little chap with a monocle who had drunk too much. They were sitting about in the hotel lounge, smoking. He was wearing a smoking suit a size too large for him; leaning towards Joseph conspiratorially, the collar almost touched his mouth.

'The horses,' Joseph replied, sick of this business.

'Good God. Well I never. Horses! Of course, of course! Horses!'

The man shook his head, wonderingly, his monocle popped out onto his lap. He had found the secret of great wealth. Joseph might have said 'Mexican whores', with the same result. He sketched the man as a toad, like something out of *Punch*. It was his best effort of the week, but he kept it to himself.

5

Cracks and Heartbeats

O N HIS RETURN, he immediately set to on the novel. The cottage was chronically damp and the hot summer seemed merely to make it fuggish, down the throat like a steam-bath's vapours. The weeks passed, he worked. Worked and rambled and ate and slept. He would remember little of that period: he must have been content. He ripped up a lot, of course. But he did progress. The mythical elements, all that sympathetic magic enthusiasm, all the Jessie Weston and Frazer and Levy-Bruhl – that had started to be dropped, like a husk. He had had the greatest difficulty in getting a character into and out of a room without stuff about rain charms or vegetation gods or wounded corn. Now, if one of his people went white, they just went white. That was an advance, he realised.

By early July the heat was, according to the newspapers that Joseph mostly avoided, 'unusual'. The mud outside the cottage door was now as cracked and dry as an elephant's skin, while the leaves on the trees were shrivelled – some even appeared to be turning colour, months early. Muck heaps and compost spontaneously burst into flame, having smouldered of their own accord.

He attended the unveiling of the village war memorial and almost fainted in the churchyard. Several people did actually faint from a mixture of grief and temperature, since they were all dressed heavily and in black. Someone informed him that it was the hottest July day since 1881. Sweat ran down the backs of his knees. The ungainly black crowd under their hats quivered in the blasts apparently surging from the browned grass; when the cloth was tugged off by two Boy Scouts, everybody had to shield their eyes against the stark-white lump.

The names were as small as newsprint, small and furtive. That was how Joseph saw it, at any rate. *Lance-Corporal Edward Hamilton*: that did look odd. One imagined a young fellow wet behind the ears, not the hard-headed fellow on the mantelpiece. There was a woeful piece of bilge read out by the local bigwig and the vicar sauced it with some religious rot. Mrs Hamilton and her daughter wept like the others. Walter, however, was nowhere to be seen. A boy cadet rasped a reveille on a gleaming trumpet – he would have made a prettier effect with tissue paper and a comb – and then a father read his dead son's poem, flowery light verse but the occasion gilded it and brought tears to Joseph's eyes. Afterwards, for a few good moments (perhaps more than a minute, it was not in any way planned), there was a silence so total that he felt the whole world might have slipped down into it, into a void of infinite soundlessness and futility.

He avoided the gathering for tea and biscuits afterwards, outside the village hall, preferring a good walk in shorts and his patterned silk shirt, the one bursting with bright red carnations. A protest, that was, though he encountered no one on the path. The bell tolled for seeming hours, like a pebble plopping into a deep pool – he could hear it from a long way away, at least three miles, with a wooded valley between.

There had been a blankness about the whole business that irked. A real dullness, apart from that silence. The silence was anything but dull – and it was apparently accidental. It was like the silence that can fall in a church before the coffin arrives: those wings of extinction passing overhead. A real nothingness, on this plane. A proper absence.

Perhaps he was growing dull to himself, in his own company; he had been a month without seeing any friends, since he had refused all suggestions of visits. He knew how easily distracted he was, and visitors rippled the calm no end. His fingers ached from the pen. Baz, anyway, was on a long and tedious case and had already started courting a girl called Agnes, which took up all his spare time. She was a surgeon's daughter and lived in Chelsea; that was all Joseph knew.

It was not all dull. There was the odd half-welcome invitation to luncheon from the local set: from the village doctor and his bristly, tennis-mad wife; the scholarly retired rector with a plump maid who breathed through her mouth as she served the vegetables; a prim young solicitor who 'wrote' – unpublished erotic stories, it turned out; a couple of dear old upper-class ladies on their rather derelict farm down a long track. And Joseph would come awake at the table, it seemed to him, turn mannerly and amusing. Then he would sink back into his creative torpor, in the cottage, and feel lonely.

With great suppleness, he fell for Mrs Hamilton's niece, who came to visit for a week at the end of June. He kept to mild gallantry over Scott – they were still ploughing through *Ivanhoe*. Quick glances, that was enough, coming over all in a heat as their eyes met. Saxon romance, it was. So dramatic an emphasis would he put on the 'love' passages that even Mrs Hamilton would stop her knitting. She actually broke in once.

'Are you all right, my dear?' she asked. 'You're quite flushed.'

Joseph looked at her as if from a great height, blushing tremendously. Clariss Hamilton, all of a rosy eighteen with striking chestnut hair left long and a quick, supple figure, made strange stifled noises behind her hands.

'Quite all right, thank you, Mrs H.,' Joseph replied. 'Do I not seem it?'

'I shouldn't wonder if it's not the long words as makes you giddy,' she said. 'They do carry on so, don't they?'

Then Clariss flushed as deeply as himself, biting her lip as if appalled. Though they were not 'carrying on', not at all. The week was over before he could even think about making an advance. The unveiling ceremony was like the nail in the coffin: no wonder he felt so inert.

The hunch about Walter had not flattened; it was growing into the chief plot-line in his novel. Forty-odd pages, and it was thickening into gristle. He saw little of Walter until the middle of that month, however; Mrs Hamilton's brother had a farm about twenty miles away and Walter was 'giving a hand' with the haysel. The uncle had put his back out some time before and his head labourer had a metal arm. This was why, to Joseph's regret, Walter had been absent from the unveiling ceremony.

Mrs Hamilton did let out, one evening, that her husband had died in a 'night attack'.

'I'm surprised Walter saw the wound as a red petal, in that case,' Joseph remarked, without reflection.

'Well, maybe there were lights. I dunno. Maybe there were them lights.'

She lay back in the chair and closed her eyes.

'Do you think Walter might be fibbing, then?' she said, quietly.

It was a rhetorical question, of course, yet with a hint of fear in it, or perhaps irritation. Joseph denied doubting Walter's integrity and changed the subject. It was now too delicate an issue to discuss with the widow herself.

He acquired an old bicycle and pedalled about in the cool of early morning. It sent him into a light trance, the pedalling, in which the unravelling countryside merged with his thoughts. It was almost clairvoyant, the way ideas came to him as if from some finished book leafed through in the darkness of the future. He sped down hills, singing.

A dissatisfaction remained, however; the prose was too weighty, he could not cut the fat.

'Stealth,' he would mutter to himself, speeding down a lane, 'stealth!' Meanwhile, his story was clod-hopping about like a milkcart's horse.

The fact is, he could not get away from the fact that he had missed the show. By a whisker. On this he would brood when he should have been getting the advantage off it; namely, that he was not smeared over with the waxy dullness of shock, the pale satisfaction of having 'done his bit' for the country, like the fellows who were veterans, yet to stir themselves into convulsions, wounded anger, those damaged men spitting with anger yet unable to shape it into words. This would take time, this stirring out of shock and lethargy, it would take positively years – ten or more of them. Meanwhile he just did not get the *advantage*, though he knew where it lay. Sweating like a pig in that little gamekeeper's cottage, he just could not find it behind him, that wind in his sails, the prow beating fast over the ocean. No, he was far from that, alas. He laboured on like a peasant tilling a useless field, with the two dreadful letters from Mr Frank Pitts propped on the windowsill among the geraniums like a threat of flood or famine. Like something ominous, anyway.

'Objectively', my foot!

But the story did creak on: the death of the Ted Hamilton figure loomed, Walter – no, the Walter-type *character* – to be responsible for it in some way not yet fathomed. This is why he needed to know whether his hunch had flesh on it. He had to be careful with his enquiries, even out of earshot of the family: he backed off at crucial moments. Cities are full of mouths, but villages are full of eyes. Watchful. This is why he avoided the tap room, he told himself. When really it was because he was timid, shy of the boots and the muck smell and the thick dialect.

The death itself was gruesomely hard to get right. It started with a bullet, then a shell, then – oh, this was nasty, this brought back a real nausea – a dose of gas. The son-in-law was still in some way responsible. He spent an hour noting down the possibilities, none of which satisfied, most of which seemed plain daft. He failed even to find a name for this Walter character; nothing seemed to fit but 'Walter', and he was not going to use that in a hurry. 'Walter' fitted it like a tombstone.

Then he wrote a version that lay a red petal on the fellow's brow like something out of Tennyson; it had a haughty tone, rather distant. He liked it. That surprised him. It was genuinely gallant and moving. But it made the war into something noble, in a long tradition of gallantry. This was the opposite of what he intended, yet he did not tear the pages up. He had to be patient. Later, later in the novel, he would rip up this gallantry, show it up as the oldest lie.

Then in the dank middle of one sweaty night he woke up with a most horrible notion.

The cottage was *moving*.

He stared at the wall opposite and heard it make sounds, sharp rapping sounds. It was exactly as if somebody was banging on it in the darkness with a hammer. Silence. Then tap, tap, tap – but disordered, quite crazy. His nightmare had been vague, filled with faces and limbs, all with designs on him. The isolated position of the cottage, the thought of the deep wood and the large empty house looming at the end of the overgrown drive, filled him with the kind of dread that overtook him long ago when his mother read *Grimm's Tales* each night. He did not want her to read *Grimm's Tales* at all. His mother reasoned that if she did not read to him

45

each night he would do no better than his father, stuck to a shop. She despised the shop, in some proud part of her. The flickering light of his bedroom, the whistle of the wind off the moors – no wonder he was scared. She read with relish, too, and a strange calm came over her at the end. She had dreamed in her teens of becoming an actress; she would go to all the touring theatre shows and sang in a local mixed choir. All her frustration went into those tales. It filled them up like green blood.

He lit his candle with trembling hands and raised it so that its light fell upon most of the wall. The rapping sounds continued, irregularly. No one – or no *thing* – there, of course. It was stiflingly close, the open window simply ushered in more heat. He breathed slowly in and out and went downstairs for a glass of milk. It was sour, the heat had already turned it, curdled it right through – and he had hailed the milk cart only that morning.

There is something fearful in such extremes, he felt helpless and almost frightened, if in a sullen sort of way. The large well in the grounds was so low that the pump spat rather than gushed, but he was stocked up with several bottles of lemonade, some Bass, and a small barrel of cider. He had, for the last few days, drawn water from the inexhaustible pump in front of The Saddler's Arms: still cold, it was. Joseph stood at the kitchen door with a glass of lemonade and looked out upon the small garden, the massed darkness of shrubbery and trees beyond, the fleet moon above. Just so had he stood after the other dream, the one about Walter, Walter's face as white as a gas lamp. He remembered this, this standing there the first time, almost with nostalgia. It was less than three months before. Like a maroon, he had lost any sense of time.

The heat had gathered itself all day in the wood and was now exhaling sweetly, but there was no coolness, not a breath of it. He heard a twig crack. Ah, there was a great drama in the village; he had been told all about it in the snug and he thought of it now. The schoolmaster was missing, he had complained of memory loss and then vanished at the weekend. Completely vanished! The police had peppered the villagers with questions, searched the school and apparently found two clues scrawled on the blackboard, as in a ninepenny novel: a large fish divided in four and *1666, London burned like rotten sticks*. Oh-ho! they cried, scratching their noses. But of course it was only schoolwork.

This had greatly amused Joseph, this clues business.

So maybe he was out there now, this schoolmaster, stumbling blindly through the woods with chalk in his pocket, wondering who he was and what on earth might a bead frame or a ruler be used for. Or a stick of chalk, for that matter. On the other hand, he might be on the Continent with a woman, or stone dead.

And the countryside *was* as dry as sticks: there had been fires in some of the ripe corn, spontaneously combusted, and a nearby barn, very old and big, had burned to the ground. He had seen the charred crucks, impossibly stout for their length, in a shambles on the ground. The lead in the church roof was said to be creeping, whatever that meant. Baz had written to say that he had endured with Agnes something called *The Peep-Show* at the Hippodrome, chosen because this last was said to be the 'coolest theatre in London'. It was not cool, not by any stretch, and quite a few in the audience had fainted. Stood there in that lusty night air, yes, oh yes, how glad Joseph felt that he was not jigging about in the city among the frauds and flappers! *That* sapped your strength, if anything did. It was a hot burning blast of soul denial, that's what it was! And most of them were toffs, anyway, with heads like horses. When you got down to it.

Some creature mewed, there were little busy sighs in the woods' deeps. The heat did not stop the animals.

Ah, it was good to be far from London. In Mrs Hamilton's *Daily Mirror* he had read about the outdoor frolics. It had made him feel monkish, reading that. There were full-page photographs, page after page, under the title 'The heart of London beating warm'. Tables were 'edging out tentatively onto the pavement', naked boys were 'plunging wildly' into the Serpentine, the capital was 'turning brown and brilliantly Mediterranean'. They quoted Keats under a couple of laughing girls splashing about in a fountain in one-piece bathing suits – 'Dance, and Provençal song, and sunburnt mirth!' A vague flush of envy, then – he had never felt in the running of it, all this 'having fun' lark, the dark perfumed underworld right under his feet but concealed as if from a child. He struggled to remember how it really was at those dances he had gone to – toothy girls with the musical jitters, their sexless bodies encased in tubes and their plethora of white necklaces bouncing about around the region of their belly button, harsh light and fearsome shadows, neurotic music, the sultry sweetness of hashish and alcohol and cocaine, jabbering talk about nothing . . . he would dream then of being South all right, among olive groves and orange orchards and long white roads in sunlight!

At the last party, at the Café Royal, among the fellows in their smart evening dress, all louche demeanour and glossy hair, he had recognised several of his closest literary acquaintances playing the fool. Juvenile delinquents, that is what they had become: no need to look farther, no need to wander the slums. They were too busy *working*, in the slums, to play the fool. He had felt that hard bright socialism rise in his mind like mercury, just watching his fellows muck about.

Joseph *should* have been knocked out by it all; instead he recoiled. He was brought up on the moors, that was the trouble. Moors and carpets and Chapel consciousness, and the Book of Common Prayer.

Then there was the heartbeat again – that thudding, thumping sound passing slowly beyond the nearest shadows of trees. Nothing like the rapping he had heard in the bedroom. Must be an owl, it must be. A big white barn owl. Or a phantom rider. Yes, it *might* be the padding of hooves over leaf mould. Ghosts galore around these parts, on the corners of dark lanes. Like the ruin on the way out of Youlster, at Orme Rocks: the kids would never play there, on account of some long-ago murder. The Saddler's Arms had its fair share, too. And even here, in Keeper's Cottage: a baby had died fifty years back, sucking lucifer matches, and now and again a sort of dim infant sob could be heard. Well, this was the story. He shivered, and went straight back inside. The invisible was thick with his imaginings, the products of his dream-soul. Yet a part of him kicked against it.

In the bedroom, by the uncertain candlelight, he noticed a crack running from ceiling to floor. It was fresh, he was quite sure of that. He could put his finger into it, comfortably. He took his blanket and slept out under the plum tree, waking up slightly chilled at dawn to a waterfall of birdsong, wondering for a moment where on earth he was in the world.

6

Sticky Feet

WALTER CAME TO see about the crack – he was a man of many skills and much called upon by helpless types. He was turkeyed up from his haymaking, red as a beetroot, with his usual shapeless green hat on. He declared the crack to be the result of subsidence. The drought had ravaged several of the flimsier cottages in the village, while the pond was an evil-smelling puddle palpitating with frogs.

Walter set to the next day on filling up the crack, working methodically. A telegram to the owner brought back the suggestion that the room be replastered anyway, and a *bon courage* for the novel. The dilettante was off to Antibes for the rest of the year, which somehow reassured his peppercorn tenant. The latter had to sleep in his 'study' until the completion of the job. He had mixed feelings about this invasion.

Walter had an irritating, tuneless whistle which the old latched doors could not shut off, and Joseph took to writing under the plum tree in the garden. He found it hard to write, out of doors; his thoughts would float off like smoke, there was no ceiling to stop them. The novel had ploughed into the sand, drops of sweat plopped down and blurred the ink. From time to time the thought struck him that he had chosen ill, that he should have studied law or medicine or gone into business or even entered a monastery. These were moments of despair, real flickerings of despair.

All he needed was a foothold. Then he could climb.

Walter emerged from the house one breathless day covered in white plaster, wiping his hands on his apron. He sat on the doorstep and lit up. He might have been holding a moth, the way he cupped the cigarette. Hanley, on leave, had lit up in exactly the same way, even indoors. A life-saving habit, Baz had explained – a night sniper could pick off a chap by the glow of his ciggie, let alone the flare of a match. Well, they had never been taught that, you picked it up at the Front proper. Common sense, really, in a crazy place.

Walter even smoked in the same way as Hanley, just the same way, sucking on the ciggie from within the palm, under cover of the arched fingers, so it looked as if he was just picking his lip until the smoke blew out. The man's whiteface was streaked with sweat, like a clown seen too close. Joseph felt sorry for him, suddenly. He sensed in him a hint of his own failure.

He stood up and invited him to have a cup of tea, there in the garden.

Walter was startled, deep in his own reverie, and mumbled a thank-you. Joseph stepped past him to settle the kettle on the hob.

He would probe the fellow. Not to extract a confession, exactly – no, that would burn fingers for certain . . . more a subtle interception, as you might intercept a stranger on a path and ask him the time. That's all, just the time. But by so doing you know – oh, so much more about him: gesture, voice, eyes.

'All I need,' Joseph murmured to himself, 'is a foothold – a little steady bit of the truth.' Then he would carry out the impossible climb, right to the icy peak.

When he came out into the garden with the tray of tea and biscuits, Walter had gone.

He was disappointed, even hurt. Perhaps the man was relieving himself. He called Walter's name and the shout flopped in the heat. He sat at the table and shook the pot gently, feeling faintly hateful about himself. Ah, the cottage looked quite charming through the low-hanging branches of the plum: he scarcely deserved it! He wondered who had lived here, keeping the woods, watching the carriages bump past in the days of the manor's glory. A queer sensation of decline and ruin fluttered through him, and he feared the trees as invading, living things intent on blind destruction. Woods are wilderness, in the end – even where lovingly tended by man they are just waiting to throttle him.

Then, after about five minutes, Walter nipped back around the corner, sprightly almost, clean and flushed. He was armed with a sponge cake whose top half had risen too high and was uncertainly balanced on the jam like a silk hat. He must have pedalled like mad and plunged his head under the pump, Joseph realised. Quite touching, it was.

'All me own toil,' Walter joked.

He did have this lugubriously joky side, Joseph could see that.

The wet hair dripped milky drops onto Walter's bare arms as the two men sat and chatted. The influence of strong tea, afternoon sunlight, the vegetable heat of a country summer in a secluded garden – most beneficial to the nerves, these are, and they began to relax. Out of the pub, Walter was altogether better, more companionable. He was clearly a bit cowed by women, despite the sponge cake. Though men's star is setting, some of them twinkle in the strangest ways.

The subject of the missing schoolmaster came up. Folk were worried. Joseph said that he did not know him by sight. Somehow, a missing schoolmaster was queerer than a missing doctor, he thought. The fellow's name was Jonson-Lois. Walter lifted his hand and said that the tips of Mr Jonson-Lois's thumb and forefinger were missing.

'How is that?' Joseph asked.

'How do you think?'

'Shellfire?'

Walter nodded.

'The beastly old war,' Joseph said.

'Stopped now,' said Walter, half to himself. 'We can laugh and sing now.'

Joseph shook his head. 'Oh, do you think it's stopped? The guns have stopped and we have jolly train excursions to the Front, but really it goes on and on—'

Walter broke in with a grunt. 'Was you against it, then, Mr Monrow?'

'Oh yes. But I was – I was in khaki, too. I was against it, yes. But I didn't run away from it, either.'

Joseph felt troubled, outmanoeuvred. The big face opposite gave nothing away but a slight irritation as it came a bit closer.

'Them train excursions are not *jolly* excursions, Mr Monrow. They're for them as lost their loved ones, visiting the graves.'

They sat in silence for a few moments. The younger man felt as if he had been peevish. What most enthralled the population was this dreadful grief. The most savage bloodbath in the history of civilisation was being coated over in layer upon layer of pathos, the pity of it all, the amber varnish of tears, until nothing of the original foulness and stupidity could be seen. He wanted to take a hammer and smash it.

Then Walter murmured something. Joseph asked him to repeat it.

'Sticky feet,' he said, and gave a little cheerful grunt, remembering. 'The flies had sticky feet, oh ay.'

An inexplicable thrill went up Joseph's spine.

'Sticky feet,' Walter repeated. 'Very sticky feet.'

The ridiculous sponge cake seemed to totter between them. It had been difficult to slice without the jam spurting out, but they had managed. A fly was crawling over the red jam. Joseph waved it away with his hand. Walter remained immobile.

'Sticky feet from the jam?' Joseph ventured.

Walter frowned slightly. Joseph knew what the fellow meant, what he was going to say – and wanted him to say it, just as he had wanted his mother to finish each horrible tale once it had begun, and then sit in her strange calm.

'Nay, from their flesh,' Walter said, as if he was dealing kindly with a dunce.

'Whose?'

Joseph was leaning forward, now. If he put a foot wrong, he would lose him.

'Oh, the dead 'uns,' Walter replied. 'Good place to lay their eggs.'

He put a finger into the strawberry jam leaking from the sponge and kept it there. Then he thrust the finger in further, right into the jam part of the cake. This is very bad manners, Joseph thought. It is what men with shattered nerves do. They are impulsive and strange. But he knew exactly what Walter meant, what he was showing him, and felt sick. Walter said nothing more. Joseph nodded slowly, but he was not being looked at. Walter pulled his finger out of the cake and licked it.

'Ay,' he said, 'ever so sticky feet. You could feel it when they crawled over you, them sticky little feet.'

And put his hands square on his big knees, as if he had just remarked on the weather.

Joseph was burning inside with excitement, though he felt stark white on the outside. He looked reflective for a moment or two. Then he said, 'Did you not think of burying them?'

Walter snorted in a quite ordinary way. Snorted, then dunked a last morsel of cake and swallowed it.

'Ay,' he said, 'them flies were wonderfully picky. Only the best for them.'

It was all quite matter-of-fact, that was the queerest part of it.

He stood up, thanked Joseph for the tea, dusted his hands free of crumbs and strolled back into the house.

Wasps had arrived, with their determined dismal drone. Joseph left his slice of cake to them. How abstract the concept of futility is, he thought, watching the wasps' enthusiasm. It never occurs to Nature to think of its great effortful work as futile, not for a single instant.

He started out on a brisk walk through the wood, which soon turned slow and sluggish, and he was drenched in perspiration by the time he reached the big house. Passing behind into the untrod field that was once a garden of lawns and fountains and stone statuary, he frightened away a host of red squirrels on the stone terrace. He made a wake in the long grass behind him: it was the very weight of life that he trailed about, heavy as a cadaver. Cadavers are heavier than the living man, that's the queer thing.

He had reached what had once been a gazebo made of iron arches twirled into spirals and wavy lines, as if it had grown there. The iron was bent and rusted and shrouded in ramblers sporting small roses that had left their petals inches deep on the stone bench. It was rather a comfortable place to sit. He wondered who had sat there before. Bored Hanoverian ladies in a rustle of silk, plotting love; the tight serge of the men, their plump and well-fed bottoms – the English are proud of their plump bottoms, it is what rolls England back to the vertical like a child's wobbly toy, no matter how hard you strike it – ah, it will roll and wobble back to the decent and upright, grinning like a fool! His own rather bony bottom released the heady scent of the rose petals – a scent for tubercular poets, that.

Joseph rested his head in his hands and planned. He must not be complacent. He must work Walter to the quick.

He stood and walked towards the great house, thinking. There was a dull, heavy silence about the house, as if it was immured in its own time. He peered in at one of the long windows; to his surprise, it opened at a push, rattling the old bubbled glass. In the dim light there was something, a *thing* squatting on a sideboard, some huge shape that he knew was alive. Quick as a flash it was hurling itself across the room, huge it was, noiselessly flinging itself and expanding out – and before Joseph could duck it had hit the half-open window with a great bang. Oh, it was shocking, that!

Joseph crouched by the window, his fingers on the stone still, trembling all over. The creature had returned to its perch on the sideboard and regarded him from the two great triumphant-seeming hollows that were its eyes. Joseph looked back at the great owl with fear and respect. Tawny owl, he thought. There was something humble in its triumph, though; and again, as if impelled to it out of this humility, the creature took to the air in the same way, circling the room and heading once more for the window – and this time Joseph ran, really darted away as though from gunfire, away from the window along the stone terrace with its smashed balusters and flagstones, right to the other end where the steps curved brokenly down.

He had fled not so much out of fear as out of respect. It was the respect side that was pulling him away; to leave well alone, to leave things as they were: the tawny owl and her nest, the house taken over by the animals. Ah, that was what we deserved – to be taken over by the animals. To be returned to the earth by flies.

He sat for a bit on the top of the curving stone stairs, panting with the shock, half-grinning to himself.

There was a second trampled track in the grass – he had not noticed that before. It crossed his own and weaved – no, *wriggled* – away and down towards the huge copper beeches that marked the lower limit of the grounds. Beyond their sunlit bulk lay the wood: like a black cliff it was, black as pitch against the light. This second track troubled him. Walter might have finished his work and come up here to do a spot of poaching. The thought of Walter not knowing he was also here, or choosing not to be seen if he did know, struck Joseph as sinister, and he hastened back.

Terribly uneasy, he felt. All the way down the dusty avenue, its length a kind of gulch in the thick hot wood, he felt the owl was watching him from one of those myriad blind windows. He glanced back over his shoulder now and again; queer, how the perspective of the avenue made the house loom, seem even grander than it was. The porch built for a giant, the windows huge. It diminished as you approached it. Now it seemed to expand, as he hastened away.

The cottage was empty. He was almost sorry about that. He took a page and wrote at the top, *Walter: notes from conversations.* And he scribbled under it the stuff about flies and their sticky feet. The Ted Hamilton business would be drawn soon enough. Sidled up to, snatched out painlessly. He could almost see it on the page, towards the bottom, like a drill of seeds. And the whole novel flowering out of it, full and heavy-scented.

The next morning Walter arrived with a large envelope addressed to Joseph in a hand he did not recognise. Dan the postman was giving his post to Walter this week, to save the nuisance of the steep and dusty lane. Inside the envelope was a brief note and three little brown photographs, one of them badly watermarked in the developing. The note was from the member of the painting group with the Kodak, who had taken the pictures of Joseph and his 'twin' in front of the smokery.

For a moment Joseph was caught out: he could not tell which one *he* was. The trouble was, they had changed sides twice, on the photographer's orders. And the brown print was poor.

But then he spotted Hubert's blue eyes; not that they had come out blue, no – but they were very pale. And the angle of the boater was rakish. Then it all fell into place and Hubert Rail was Hubert Rail, with his stony, sullen look. Embittered, that is what he was. Even behind the smile, you could see that plain as day.

They looked like something in a student rag. It was absurd.

The note assured him that if ever he wished to write an article about his experience, Dr Stephen Smith would gladly give his permission for the use of the 'snapshots', and that he had sent copies to Mr Hubert Rail, c/o the Old Smokery, near Lamorna. He very much hoped that they might both consider submitting themselves to a blood test and general examination from one of his august colleagues (a pioneer in the study of twins) in the near future.

What rot!

And oh, how Joseph laughed at it! People have to have a reason for every queer thing – scientific, of course. Quirks of chance do not come into it, they are twisted boles in a plantation of straight thin trunks. That's the modern world, he thought, with its grim plantations of science. Yet there was nothing to do with quirks of chance – they gave science the lie. No, you couldn't deny them: as good shelter in a shell hole on the basis that shells never strike the same spot twice. Oh, but they do, they do. Many the poor chap caught out that way, oh yes.

The fact is, if the sketching party had gone to another smokery, well, there would have been no 'remarkable phenomenon' to crow about. Put it another way: until somebody or other noticed the similarity, *that similarity did not exist.* Maybe, Joseph considered, God wanted a somebody or other to notice His Creation, His clevernesses. Thus Man. A play is not performed until the first night. A book is not read until it is opened. Hubert Rail and Joseph Monrow did not exactly resemble one another until Mr Douse and his gaggle stepped into the smokery near Lamorna. And that's a fact! Harrumph!

He tore the note up and threw it into the kitchen stove.

The floorboards creaked above him. He went upstairs. Walter was sweeping his plaster in smooth strokes over the wall, slapping and sweeping with the big plasterer's board to the usual tuneless whistle.

Joseph disliked the smell of plaster, particularly lime plaster. The sludge of it rested in a tin tray at his feet and pervaded the air in a damp invisible cloud. He realised that he would have to sleep in a newly-plastered room that would not dry out for several weeks. This depressed him. Walter nodded a greeting. The ugly dankness was already invading Joseph's damaged lungs. Didn't Schubert die in just such a newly-plastered room? He decided then and there to stay out of it until it was bone dry.

He sat down in the rush-bottomed chair in the corner and 'worked' Walter, as he had planned. He had already decided to give himself a few weeks in the trenches: a white lie, at best. If the war had not stopped dead when it did – well, the lie would have been the truth.

He did feel a tremendous haste inside himself to get results. So he veered very quickly into war talk.

'Cleaning your kit in camp – that was a joke, wasn't it?'

'Ay,' said Walter, with a gruff chuckle. 'That were a bit.'

'Were you conscripted?'

'Ay.'

'Along with Ted Hamilton? Same time, was it? What age would Ted have been? He was near the upper limit, wasn't he?'

Joseph's heart was thudding – best, though, to get it out in a rush.

'Forty-three,' said Walter. 'He were just forty-three. Only he didn't let on.'

'Ah, duty.' The word sounded derisory – he had not meant it to be.

'In his turn,' said Walter.

For several moments there was no sound in the room, beyond the thudding in his head, but the gritty shush and slap of the plastering, like a sullen sea falling on a beach of harsh sand. Then Walter, without turning, mentioned flies again. It was all flies, his talk.

'Remember them flies?' he said. 'You must remember the size of them flies. Champions for weight, they were.' He might have been talking about fish.

And he added, in his usual matter-of-fact tone: 'Them fly-papers'd drop 'em into your tea – that were the worst, weren't it? Right into the meat.' There were several dead flies on the windowsill and a few live ones were struggling on the wet plaster. His board came over them, swept their mangled bits for good into the wall. The flies business was a sort of mental fixation. Joseph mentally saw them as crawling all over Walter's talk. He would have to get Walter off these wretched flies or give up.

'That gas saw the flies off,' Joseph essayed, as if he had really experienced a cloud of it in the trenches. His heart seemed to be thudding in his right eye now.

Walter slapped on more plaster and grunted.

'Gas, or flies. Folk were never satisfied. Near potted out once,' he added.

'Potted out?'

It sounded as though he was referring to plants. There was a brief pause.

'Hit,' he said, a touch impatiently. 'Sniped at.'

Joseph saw how playing slow-witted was the way forward. He wiped sweat from his upper lip.

'You mean snipers, Walter?'

'Snipers snipe, don't they?'

The arm swept across the wall, the board making spiral shapes as it smoothed. Joseph had not read a newspaper for days. Walter was standing on the old ones kept for firelighters: now that was impossible to imagine in this heat – a fire in the hearth! The man's boots crackled over the newspaper – just like rapid firing, it was. Joseph felt rather foolish, a child asking questions of an adult. But that was all right. That was the way forward. He would get to Ted Hamilton soon enough, with the fatal skill of a surgeon.

'What happened?'

'When?'

'When you were nearly popped out.'

'Potted out. I were near potted out, that's all. You weren't, I suppose.'

'No. Just gassed. Night or day?'

'Night. That's nasty, to be gassed.'

'Were you lighting a ciggie?'

Walter stopped plastering but kept his back turned.

'Taylor, dangling his watch. That damn Taylor. The glass caught the moonlight, twirling about in his hand. Ping!'

'The watch?'

'Shattered. To tiny bits.'

Joseph expressed amazement. The scene was so vivid in his mind that he could hardly credit it as real. The man turned round to scoop some plaster and caught Joseph's eye. The fact that he was taking advantage of Walter was written all over his face, he was sure. Then Walter stared at the large slop of plaster, bent over it with his trowel. He smiled, and settled down on his heels. Joseph wanted to know why he was smiling, what he was seeing in the wet mound lightly steaming before him. The heat really was insufferable.

'He thought he knew the hell of a lot,' he said, very softly. 'That damn Taylor. Well, he kept trying to swing it, with his sciatica. *God damn my bloody sciatica!'*

Walter's voice had risen a quarter-tone, in imitation of someone effeminate. He was smiling.

'Kept trying to swing it. Know what I mean? Thought he knew the hell of a lot, that Taylor. But the flies got him.'

Joseph decided that the fellow was actually ever so slightly deranged, behind his matter-of-fact tone. Maybe, he thought, I should not have started him off outside the confines of a sanatorium.

'The flies got him. They don't hang about.'

Walter straightened up stiffly, plunged his trowel into the wodge of plaster and slapped the scooped stuff onto the wall. Within the minute it was indistinguishable from the rest. He paused. There was something rather wonderful, even admirable, in the way he could convert a scooped mess into the unadulterated face of a wall. Joseph knew that if he were to try it, he would make an ass of himself. But the fact of the pauses was disconcerting. It broke the rhythm demanded by this sort of task. New flies alighted on the wall, arrived from nowhere. Walter was watching them. So was Joseph.

'God damn my bloody sciatica!' came out again, in a kind of wail. Then again: 'The flies got him, smack off.' He grunted a satisfied little grunt. 'Could see right into it through the hole. Moving with what they flies had laid. Millions of eggs, they lay. Very impatient to lay 'em. They don't hang about. They get on with it.'

Joseph realised with a jolt that he was being looked at. He nodded. Walter's gaze shifted to his trowel.

'Moving with 'em, it was. Like it was thinking. Like he was thinking them clever cunning thoughts. How to swing it. It might have been, now I come to think of it; well, he was a bit wobbly on his pins, but you couldn't say as he wasn't thinking. Groaning a little groan here and there, he was, tottering about a bit. Got too close to a whizz-bang. Shrapnel. Out for the count for a bit, out there in the black, then came back in at first light on his own two pins. Time enough for the flies to do their work, though. No tea breaks for them, they just get on with it.' There was silence for a moment. Joseph could hear the slight wheeze in his own throat. Walter resumed, continuing to stare at the trowel in his hand. 'Moving with 'em, it was, like it was full of them cunning thoughts. How to swing it—'

Joseph interrupted – he could not bear the repetitions. It was like a scratch on a Decca gramophone.

'What *exactly* was moving with what?'

Walter touched his forehead with his thumb, leaving a knob of wet plaster on the skin.

'His brain. With maggots.'

'Walking about? With a hole in his forehead full of maggots?'

'Ay. It were like a damn fisherman's tub. Put that in your memorial book, if you want.'

Joseph shuddered involuntarily. Walter glanced at him as if waiting for a reply. There was no contempt in the glance, not even victory. Just plain matter-of-factness. That was the worst of it. Joseph rose to go, mumbling something about tea.

There was a soft, friendly grunt behind him. At the door he glanced back and Walter was bending over the wet heap of plaster, ready to scoop it. The way his trowel then sliced into the sludge was not deliberately done for Joseph, that much was clear – *quite* clear, surely – but Joseph surrendered himself to it as if it was. Its horrible sound made his whole project discreditable, in his eyes. He knew suddenly that words could revivify the slack awfulness of it all – the war, the moment-by-moment movement of it – as effectively as the mammoth's yellow rib in Cholesford church could bring the whole lumbering beast back to life.

Well, the sludge would never shape to art, that was the thing. Even the flat wall on which art might flower was no more the sludge than a man is primordial slime. The sludge was the war, oh yes, and that trowel sound was the real war sound. It was spew and mucus-rattle and slither of falling shells, all at once – the real war sound, that. A bullet in soft flesh could not have done it better. The disgust burst in on Joseph all at once, as voices do in half-sleep, and sent him almost tumbling down the stairs of the cottage into the kitchen, where a pot of strong tea and a nip of brandy revived him. He could write nothing.

What had Hubert said? Something about life being senseless. Now he had the very note of it. The very note.

He packed some bread and cheese and cycled out to a favourite lonely spot by the clear chalk waters of the Chess. The little river was running very low now, and he wondered if it would ever rain again. The drought was influencing his mood and this he did resent. He had imagined a soft green retreat, but the beeches were rattling with thirst and there was no grass anywhere that did not look scorched. The leaves in the south-facing woods were turning yellow weeks early, as if something had failed in the old dark ritual of the seasons. Perhaps Tammuz was angry that man no longer bled for him, or mourned his departure. In shadowy hollows, where cattle would cross muddy rivulets in normal years, dust rose under the hooves. Joseph thought of that deep clogged lane near London, when Baz and he had first come across Pitts; now they would be scuffing its hard top.

He unbuttoned his shirt and imagined himself lying stark naked, the sun still hot under the filtering boughs. Only the cock-sure or those with queer tastes would dare to lie naked in the English countryside. In Greece it was quite different. In Germany, too. He resented England bitterly, deep down. He would have to flee. To Germany, even. No, to Greece. Why not Greece? Desertion, that's what it would be. He would be caught by the Muses and put on trial in the sacred bell-tent and jabbed with morphia before the shots rang out. Like poor old Henry Billings, the Matlock chemist's son who had been shot for taking a walk away from the guns. Laughing, thinking it all a silly mistake, high on morphia – right up to the moment they pinned the cross on his heart. That's how his brother told it, at any rate.

Oh yes, Joseph reflected, we're in very low water, we civilised people. He could not flee England: he had to stay and fight, keep alert and furious. Greece would numb him. And Germany? He would not be avoiding things in Germany! But Germany was crumbling. Outside the beautiful dark forests, it was crumbling to bits. It had been kicked too hard by the victors. Triumph – no humility. There was the rub.

He lay on his back, stared at the leaves and the heat-blanked sky and considered Walter. He was too dangerous, behind that light, matter-of-fact manner. His neuralgic position was on the frayed end and might give him a fatal electric shock. The missing schoolmaster in the village had been invalided out of the army with shell shock, it was reported in the local paper. It was the heat acting on badly-knit nerves, his going off like that. Joseph saw the repaired nerves as melting in the heat and 'shorting' each other out. The whole memory part of the brain had gone dark, like Piccadilly Circus does now and again, or like theatres are said to do. The same could happen to Walter. Joseph was an amateur electrician dealing with a very complicated series of knobs and switches and flashing lights. He would withdraw his forces before Walter's matter-of-factness shorted out.

With that thought he fell asleep. He had not been sleeping well for days.

And it occurred to him in his sleep that he could go to Greece, if he wanted, by running into that wood beyond the stooks. There was the wine-dark Mediterranean just there, beyond the stooks. But he did not really want to, even in his sleep. England had to be worked through to the nub.

7

A Thumbprint

A FEW DAYS later he received a note from Baz.

I am taking a week-end excursion to the battlefields of Belgium, leaving for Ypres from Liverpool St this Friday (22nd) at 8.40 p.m. Do you feel like coming along? Agnes has pulled out – I think from female funk – but her ticket's booked. I wish to lay flowers on Hanley's grave. Call at chambers to let me know. Advance booking normally essential for these trips, I might add.

Joseph was surprised to hear Hanley had a grave; he had been blown to tiny bits, like poor Taylor's watch. Maybe somebody had gone out and collected the cogs and wheels, as it were. There were Great Eastern posters everywhere in London, advertising these tours. Joseph had even seen one pasted on a fence outside the tiny branch-line station in the village. 'Belgium and the Battlefields by the Antwerp Route', it said, with a rather grim photograph of a shattered sap-head and a broken tree. The trip cost £8.15s., which was rather a lot, and Joseph wondered if Baz was paying. The poster next to it showed a highly-coloured parasol on a golden beach, displaying the greater delights of Bexhill. Yet Baz claimed advance booking was essential for Belgium. The train companies were no doubt very pleased. For four years they had carried young men to their deaths and now they were carrying their grieving relatives. Good business, thought Joseph. Maybe it was the train companies who had persuaded the government to leave the bodies the other side of the Channel.

But he was keen to go, nevertheless. His cousin Roger, various other distant relatives and an alarming number of friends were lying out there, somewhere. His novel was stalled, terribly stalled, and he was avoiding Walter, who anyway was all but finished with the room.

Joseph had never visited the battlefields. These excursions were quite a new thing – the danger of unburst shells and tetanus from jagged debris had been too great before, so it was said. He imagined, however (though no one mentioned this), that the overriding reason was uncollected corpses. It would not do for Aunt Maud (we all have our Aunt Mauds) to step upon a rotting hand. He pictured a cold waste of wintry trees and mud, as in the posters: abstract and sinister. But it was summer, even in Flanders – waves of golden corn, hay-ricks, all that. He would have the devil of a job to think it back to what it was, to what he needed. It might put the setting awry, and he was having trouble enough with the setting. Some talked of cows grazing in fields and peasants threshing with flails, others of mud and slime and leafless broken trees. Often you got both together, the seasons all tangled up.

He did feel terribly conscious, all the same, of what he was missing of the great wilderness of the battlefield.

It was not a battle*field*, that was the trouble; the few soddened acres of Agincourt, the shallow valley of Waterloo – they were *easy*, pictures in a frame. No, it was the Front, a wriggling line hundreds of miles long – but Joseph kept picturing it as a dark chamber or a sort of sunlit stage, he could not get a grip on the vastness. Not even when he thought back to his own experience in the camps could he get a grip on this vastness: it was all confused hollows, not a sweeping line in view. He knew he must turn aside the imagination for a moment and go there.

Also, he needed to get away, take some 'leave'. His sheets of thin-lined foolscap had become a site of torment for him; he had never thought writing could be so hard.

He also wanted to get away from Walter.

The man had been behaving rather queerly since their conversation about Taylor and the flies; it played on Joseph's nerves. He was working on his notes in the garden after lunch on Wednesday when he heard a falsetto voice through the open window of the bedroom, shrieking that business about sciatica. He saw nothing at the window, the fellow was simply shrieking it to himself. It went on and on with the rhythm of a machine for several minutes, and then abruptly stopped.

On and on it had gone, in a sort of tinny squawk, exactly like a machine at the funfair.

So Joseph took *The Pickwick Papers* and some sketching materials along to the gazebo. He felt rather better there, well away from the house, in the company of Pickwick and friends. He sketched the manor house and a towering old elm tree (failing completely to capture their separate grandeur – they might have been a shed and a bush) and walked about a bit. He dared to peep in on the owl room, but there was no owl, not that day. He did not climb in, however: he just stared for a long time into the gloom.

On returning at about five, his flannels covered in grass-seeds, he heard the same falsetto shriek repeated in the same machine-like way. Perhaps Walter had spotted him coming up the avenue, but he doubted it – the leafage blocking the proper view of it from the cottage. He lingered in the lee of the hedge until the cries again abruptly stopped.

God damn my bloody sciatica!

On and on it went – but only in Joseph's head, now. Like a jazz tune, it was, scampering around and around in his head.

When Walter came down at five-thirty at the end of his shift, the proverbial butter would not melt in his mouth. His large, lugubrious eyes may have looked tired, but they were not deranged. The mask of white plaster made him appear clownish again. He discussed the weather with Joseph over a cup of tea and then left. Very matter-of-fact, it all was. Almost chirpily so.

At nine on Wednesday morning, he appeared as usual at the front door and was let in. Joseph had not slept well and felt unkempt and restless, and was slightly regretting his decision over the weekend tour. This was partly guilt; he knew Aunt Maud was keen to visit his cousin Roger's grave, and had frequently hinted, in letters, that her 'one surviving nephew' should take her. She had even sent him a Lancs & Yorks Railway's Weekend Tour leaflet.

Instead of going straight upstairs, as he usually did, Walter hung about in the little passage that served as a hallway.

'Do you need anything?' Joseph asked him, from the kitchen. Usually it was water, for the mix.

65

Walter came in and his customary stoop fitted the place – the kitchen's beams were not only low but hung with pots and pans, dried herbs and other rustic paraphernalia. He was holding his lunch wrapped up carefully in a cloth. A beer bottle was stuffed into the pocket of his overalls.

'Staying in, then, today, Mr Monrow?'

Joseph replied in the affirmative.

'Would you be available to be called upon at four o'clock?'

'Yes, why?'

'Want to show you summat, Mr Monrow. For your memorial book.'

'You'll be with someone else, then?'

'Ay.'

He tapped his nose. A secret. He seemed quite excited.

'Something to do with the war, obviously.'

Walter nodded.

'A wounded fellow?'

Walter pulled on one of his long moustaches, very thoughtful.

'Maybe.'

Then he disappeared upstairs.

Joseph took up his position under the plum tree and did his best to repulse the vague feelings of sadness and anxiety, the dread treading softly behind his shoulder, by working hard on his notes.

There was a vague antagonism, now, between author and novel. That really is the worst thing.

Nothing annihilates a young man's ambition faster than watching his elders achieve what he had hoped to achieve by dint of youth, and the book he had just read – yes, it had that effect on Joseph, it burned his innards right out just looking at it there on the blanket by his feet. The title, even: *Realities of War*. It was written by a jingoistic and very popular war correspondent for the *Daily Chronicle*, one Philip Gibbs. He had written the war up gleefully for the home front, then he had had some sort of Pauline conversion at the end of it. Out came the horrors and his own disgust. Pauline conversion – or opportunism? Joseph plumped for the latter. Not that this helped, not one jot. He was stung by the book, it drove right into his nerve centre and left him mentally paralysed. Gibbs had seen things, he had seen an awful lot. All Joseph possessed, on the other hand, was a fine anger, mildly moth-eaten lungs, and a certain skill with words. He looked at it there on the blanket, lying in its smart paper jacket, and felt totally slugged by the thing.

But Gibbs's book is not a novel, he repeated to himself. *Stick it.*

The book had really got him in the neck, though.

He whispered to himself – he often talked to himself in this way – *I'll write this novel, or I'll sell tin monkeys on the Strand.*

He never got into the real swing of it all morning. When Walter had gone off for lunch, he went up to the room to see how much had been done. He was startled to find the job almost completed. Steam crept about in the heat, puffed out from the damp plaster: it was like a dragon's lair or some sort of tropical den. Yet it was touching, too. Those tools carefully laid out. The neckerchief hung on the window-latch. Whiffs of shag tobacco and sharp sweat.

Gently, he pressed his thumb on the soft creamy plaster.

The lime stung his skin slightly. It felt terrifically illicit, what he was doing: the thumbprint made a mess of the whole enterprise. He had a desire, a very strong one, to mess up the whole lot. It looked so vulnerable, this wet, masterly work. Like taming a crocodile, to get this sludge onto the wall and flattened, trowelled out to this masterly smoothness! Like a muscular skin stretched over the rough old bones of the house, it was – all the shallow curves and faint hollows still perceptible under the slapped-up, almost polished smoothness. The thumbprint was a real blemish. It took away from the beauty of it. It was quite vulgar, even.

But he could not do anything about it, even with the sponge. He just made the most awful mess of it, a few square inches but indignant-looking, just next to the window and terribly obvious to anyone who came in. Yet he scuttled away like a naughty child. He never thought of leaving a note. He scuttled off with a picnic.

Coming back from the woods, he saw a badger. It was lame, missing a paw, lumbering away in fear and pain along the track. Shrinking from the daylight, it was. An ill portent, perhaps: no doubt one of the villager's traps was responsible. Yet it helped him get on with his writing in the afternoon, through the sounds of Walter working.

Nobody came at four. He had almost forgotten about it, only remembering at the last minute. Then he waited, quite strung up. Nobody. He clattered about in the kitchen at five, making tea, hoping Walter would hear. Still nothing. Walter had his own supply of tea, but Joseph took some up anyway.

'Is your chap coming, then?'

Walter had a stubborn look about him. He shrugged, though, and sipped his tea noisily.

'He might not come?'

'He might, he might not. It all depends.'

'Do I know him?'

The other paused, considering.

'Sammel,' he said.

'Young Samuel with the ginger hair?'

'Ay, that's right.'

He looked at Joseph, but still stubborn, intractable, pouting at his tea. There was nothing wrong with Samuel, bar the slowness of a certain type of countryman, a shyness. He lived with his mother opposite the garage and did odd jobs. He was always about in the village. He was in the woods quite a bit, too: Joseph would bump into him now and again, in the beech woods.

'Was he in the thick of it, then?'

'For a bit.'

'Has he stories?'

'Nay, but he's got summat else.'

The chap grimaced good-humouredly.

'Injured, was he? A wound?'

Walter tutted at that.

'Oh, I dunno. I dunno what you'd call it. If you want . . .'

And he gave a little quiver, all over.

Joseph felt he was fencing with a shadow. There was something he did not get. Then quite suddenly he knew what it was all about, and felt a fool.

'Does he want paying, then? To come?'

Walter blinked, but otherwise gave nothing away – except by remaining silent.

'Tell him,' said Joseph, 'to come next week, when I'm back from Flanders. I'll give him a shilling just for coming. Then we'll see about more.'

Walter nodded at that, and gave Joseph a wink.

It gave Joseph hope, all this. Every little stone helped. Walter's air of conspiracy was gratifying: there was even something almost sinister in the way he had nodded, with that queer little smile under his lime-powdered moustache. Something almost sinister – and impudent, too. If you wanted to see it that way. And Joseph did, no doubt about that.

8

Picturesque Postcards

He set off for London the next morning, planning to stay a night before the long journey. He tried to picture the battlefield: armies of labourers preparing cemeteries and throwing up houses from the rubble, and taciturn peasants ploughing the treeless waste. A great silence, despite all this activity. A sort of huge benumbed dumb show, with touring groups in black wandering about. Crosses all over the shop.

He would grasp the *scale*, would he not? It was a necessary pilgrimage. A rite, almost.

He got a room for the night in a plain boarding house in Charlotte Street. Baz had offered his floor, but Joseph was meeting another friend for dinner and fancied being independent. He was to meet Baz on the platform at Liverpool Street the following evening.

London was even hotter than the Chilterns, not surprisingly. Almost operatic, she was, in her infernal awfulness of dust and heat. He trudged about like a sweating foreigner, unable to locate streets and buildings which he knew well. They all seemed to have shuffled slightly to the left or the right, slipped in an extra alley, cheated him with an additional row of doors. A wind picked up in the afternoon which actually swept the heat closer against your face, bundled you up in it, hurled great masses of it in oven blasts, along with choking eddies of dust. People walked about with handkerchiefs to their mouths or gasped in doorways like stranded fish. The tramcars rang on the rails like wailing fiends. He avoided taking an omnibus; whenever one passed near him it swept a thick fug of confined flesh over his face, and on the top deck the passengers were grilling gently under their parasols. He sought relief in Hyde Park, its great trees autumnally tinted, the Serpentine scabbed with green algae. Naked urchins splashed about in it, screaming with joy. He tried to imagine the park in winter, a foot deep in snow, the lake iced up – but failed. Anyway, did it ever really *snow* in London, as it did up around Youlster?

The air was orange, but gloomy.

The blasts continued into the evening, developing into a continuous whistle and moan. A sort of blizzard, only with gritty dust and heat instead of snow and cold. Pedestrians hurried past with scarves around their mouths, like desert nomads. He had to keep his eyes almost closed, and was nearly run over by a dray. The cab-horses coughed and sneezed, their blinkers white with dust: they might have been statues, when stood still, until the whip restored them. And the paper boys were suffering too, unusually mute, huddled in the hopeless lee of street corners or at the mouths of the Underground – where a peculiar effect of air currents created a sort of miniature tornado, the stifling underground air rising to grapple with the fiery bursts of the overground stuff. He saw one pile of *Evening News* whisked up and scattered into oblivion like a flock of gulls in a storm.

The half-a-gale rattled the glass of the restaurant in which he was dining late with his friend. He had known Hadrian Ripley from school in Matlock; the fellow had made good in London as a history teacher in a posh private school. His fusty cover concealed an impish humour, which Joseph liked.

'I'll never go over myself,' said Hadrian. 'It's not history yet.'

'When does something begin to be history?'

Hadrian shrugged. He had a strawberry mark on his forehead the shape of Nero on a coin (or so he claimed; no one else saw it).

'When it starts to feel prophetic.'

'Really?'

'Takes an awfully long time for the voice to cry out of the wilderness. We don't hear it for ages. Everything I teach seems like I-told-you-so. Nothing, you see, is ever properly new. It only *seems* so at the time. It has its antecedents, though. That's history, the antecedents are history.'

'What about the business in Russia? What about the war? What about jazz, for that matter? Or modern painting, when you can't tell what it is even though it says, *Self-Portrait*? Or Mr Joyce?'

'Who's he?'

'A writer, like myself, only he writes in *collage*, the sort of Georges Braque of literature. *And* there's Monsieur Proust, who writes on his knees in bed without ever going out.'

'So? I feel like Monsieur Proust, whoever he is, every Monday morning.'

'Well, all that seems terribly new, doesn't it? If you tell me any of that has antecedents, especially the damn war, I'll be very content.'

'As soon as something does – that's it, it's become history. You only recognise the antecedents when the event in turn is history. You see? And that's not a syllogism, either. It's like the IRA – they'll all turn into King Brian Boru as soon this independence business is sorted out. You'll see.'

The wind sucked and blew at the glass. Dust and sooty grit spread in a fan around the door, blown in under it, as if this was the last building left standing in a desert.

They walked to Hadrian's club for brandy and a cigar, and were struck by the speed of the clouds scudding over the bright moon. The twirling veils of dust reminded Joseph (who had seen Ponting's photographs) of the aurora. Someone at the club had placed a thermometer under his silk hat and walked about for ten minutes at midday: it had registered 107°F. A member had collapsed and died at the Eton vs Harrow match two weeks ago, when it was up in the nineties on the pitch and the long stop had fainted. Nobody was looking forward to bed. The dust gathered like frost on the windows, although everyone's skin was grimy from it.

'Just like a sirocco on the northern shores of the Mediterranean,' said one fellow with a florid complexion.

Another shook his head. 'More like being in the Sahara just before the bursting of a sandstorm.'

'God at his most agreeable, at any rate,' said a young man with rather wild hair.

'London dust is a deal worse than desert sand,' Hadrian pointed out, knuckling a weeping eye. 'At least sand doesn't turn you into a negro minstrel.'

'Where's your banjo?' cried the florid fellow, sweat beading on his temples.

He started to sing, which upset everybody: it broke a club rule, apparently.

'Rubbish,' he cried. 'I will damn well sing where and when I want to.'

A brandy glass was broken. Joseph and his friend beat a hasty retreat, out into the night's billowing sail, the dark gritty canvas they had to walk against like embattled heroes. Shop signs and lamps creaked and strained, paper bags caught around their ankles, their eyes wept with grit.

'History,' Hadrian shouted, 'is a fistful of dust thrown against the blank wind!'

'Who said that?'

'*I did!*'

Joseph was a very bad sailor, and considered pulling out of the cross-Channel venture. Baz had left a message at the hotel in Charlotte Street, however, confirming their rendezvous and adding that the trip was on his slate – Joseph had implied he was short of the readies. He was embarrassed, but genuinely grateful.

The fact is, he *was* nearly broke, despite the simplicity of his life. He had not earned anything for months apart from the occasional shilling book review, had eaten his savings to the bone, and would have to consider hiring himself out as a harvest hand. He fancied himself as a harvest hand. He thought it would aid his intellectual work; somewhere in the novel there would be a harvest scene on the Somme.

He slept terribly. It was not just the moan of the Saharan wind down the alleys and the rattle of the glass in the gas lamps, nor was it the suffocating room itself, full of towering pieces of Victorian junk and a cracked mirror, nor even the racket of a London night after the hushed country version, but the thought that very soon he would be 'on the spot'. The spot, however, was dead quiet. At least, it was no longer crackling and bursting. That alone was pretty sinister, that loaded quiet. For anyone a bit fey, it was positively alarming.

He had the most awful dreams. He was in his old bedroom in Youlster; there was a fearsome knocking on the door and it turned out to be the missing schoolmaster from the village, the chap with the maimed fingers. The maimed fingers swooped down and he woke, sweating. It was the curtains brushing across his face, rippling like things possessed; the wind through the open window was blowing them almost horizontal. It reminded him of a silly scene in some haunted-house play before the war. They must have used a wind machine, with some poor chap winding a handle like billy-oh, but you are terribly impressionable at the age of ten or eleven and he had been petrified by it. He was not petrified in the bed and breakfast down Charlotte Street, it was more a case of discomfort and disbelief – the wind flapped the curtains over his face but did nothing to cool the room. In fact, the opposite was the case. The wind continued to be sirocco-like until dawn, when a certain normality came upon it.

London smelt terribly thick, even first thing: there was not the slightest suggestion of freshness. Drains, sour coke, fishy gusts, whiffs of something like hashed mutton, a sweet pall of rotten melons, omnibus fumes and soiled horse litter from the stables across the road – Joseph lay there and wanted to choke. Somewhere in all this were his public, his future public. His critics, too. His supporters and his enemies. Hard to believe, really.

He wished he were in Antarctica, lying on ice. Though wasn't it permanent night out there, now? Scott and the rest had died when he was still a boy, yet it seemed like last month when the world finally heard. His mother had cried, cut out the newspaper report, the photo of the little black tent filling the whole front page. Things got to her like that, for all her four-square side.

He sat up and smoked a cigarette, feeling rather shaky. This cleared the air somewhat. He decided that he would spend the day going to the cinema and seeing exhibitions; he could not be bothered to talk, talking with friends left him feeling faintly impotent.

The British Museum was almost empty. He spent a lot of time with the Elgin marbles, very struck by the furious horses. Or were they panicked? Oh yes – the last two thousand years had been a declination, however much we had scrabbled upwards now and again. Fundamentally the slope had been downwards – with a sudden severe steepness to it, like a fatal drop in a patient's pulse rate, over the last seven years. He wandered through the rooms, between the lovely fragments in their glass cases, cursing the fact that he was alive too late.

Baz was dressed very neatly, in a black three-piece suit. He was sweating, slightly fat in the jowls. A listless air about him, something of the undertaker, as they waited on the platform for the Great Eastern train. The other folk were dressed similarly, and Joseph felt a touch hearty and even vacant in his white flannel trousers and bright tie. He had even rolled up his shirtsleeves, holding his jacket over his shoulder and his bag in the other hand. He might have been about to go yachting.

The excursion ticket was third-class, but the trim in the carriage was velvet – a bright turkey-red. It belonged to another age, really. Joseph rested his head against its scuffed smoothness and stared at the photographs below the luggage rack: Ely Cathedral, the beach at Cromer, somewhere with lots of sky on the Fens. He had never penetrated this mysterious, melancholy east, he realised. Above his head, in one of the decklights of the carriage's clerestory, there was set a coloured transparency of King's College, the evening light setting it ablaze like a ruby. It gave him a momentary feeling of satisfaction with England: that this was, after all, the common aspiration – even in third class. It was a kind of hypnotist's trick, really: and he was lulled into trance by it. Unbelievable, the war memory was, in this smooth train with its English scenes lulling you into half-consciousness. He caught himself out soon enough, though, glancing at the other passengers in the compartment: all in black or wearing black armbands, they were, as if the train was a ghost one, as if it had already derailed and these were its phantoms. Mostly women, of course – who now and again raised an arm to touch hair drawn tight under a veiled hat. It would only take a stone, he thought, to smash the lovely picture of England. We are all cracked in some way by the stone.

He stared through the window at the rolling country, dusty as Spain. It was still terribly hot. Baz, too, had fallen silent. Joseph wished he had not come – he really felt quite awful, exhausted and hot and rather sick. Within an hour, however, they were pulling into Parkstone Quay, with the last of the light glimmering over the water: the wind had dropped, and the sea's inky smell excited him.

The *Bruges* was almost brand new, with a bright yellow funnel and electric coal fires in the public rooms. Joseph could not imagine these false coals lit: he could not imagine it cold ever again. Agnes had had a single berth booked for her and it was spick and comfortable, the taps in the basin gushing in a peculiarly satisfying manner. And *so* thoroughly pleasant the deck was, after the sweltering train. The boat revived him completely, in fact. Baz's stuffiness went, too; they talked on the deck until midnight, the moon scattering white light over the sea. Quite romantic, it was: but Joseph did not feel regret off his friend – that Agnes was not there to share the warm breeze and the moonlight and the sea. Odd, that.

He slept very deeply, lulled by the motion of the boat, and rose early. He stood on the deck with a rather rumpled-looking Baz, who had been sick. The dawning sun glinted off the snowcaps and the water was a very deep night-blue against the white foam of the wake; they might have been travelling between two isles of the Peloponnese were it not for the mourning crêpe rustling around them.

Joseph felt the freshness of the sea-breeze in his very soul – they really might have been bound on some great exploit.

'*Unhappy man, unbind this veil and fling it far from shore into the wine-dark sea*,' he quoted haphazardly, sweeping his hand. But there were tins and scraps of paper and other rubbish in it, all the same.

The boat's turbines slowed; they entered the smoothness of the River Scheldt and breakfast was served.

A good-looking girl in cream passed between the tables and Joseph pointed her out.

'There you are – Ino of the slim ankles, Ino herself. O *unhappy man* . . . Can't see any veil, though.'

She had some kind of shadowy mark on the edge of her chin, some flaw. Baz began to talk of Agnes. They were already engaged and were to marry very soon. Agnes had some peculiar beliefs.

'You know she has this hare-brained notion about electrical influence? It comes from her father.'

'I thought her father was a doctor.'

'He is. That's the trouble. He spent some time in New York where he fell in with some rum medical types and came back full of their theories. He's indoctrinated her with them. She's known nothing else.'

Joseph had found Agnes, the occasional times they met, rather overwrought and dark-browed, although he quite understood Baz's attraction: she had a slim waist and elegant features and played the violin very well. Her fingers were especially attractive. She saw the body, apparently, as a kind of nation communicating by telegraphic messages; the stomach is the galvanic battery that powers it. The electricity is provided by digestion, the breathing in of air, and the meeting of alkalis and acids in the mucous membranes. Joseph was sympathetic to this belief, breathing in the charged sea air. Yes, he was quite disposed to agree with Agnes. Baz then sighed and screwed up his nose, rather vexed. Beyond his head, beyond the great barges of the River Scheldt, Flemish fields and trees met the morning sun. Joseph felt elated, very glad he had come.

They sat out in steamer-chairs for the last half an hour, two in a row of about twenty passengers staring at the foreign views through the white rails.

Baz leaned sideways, as if to impart a confidence in his friend's ear. Which he did.

'The thing is, she has some odd views on, you know, the in-bed side.'

Joseph's ears pricked up. He felt a return to their old intimacy.

'Not mixing up our electricities, and all that,' Baz added.

'You mean she doesn't want to at all?'

'No no, I mean she wants us to have separate beds. We'll still, you know – but not more than twice a month, and then I'll have to go back to my room. It's an awful nuisance.'

'What, finding a place with two bedrooms?'

He was rather amused by Baz's discomfiture. He was even delighted, he realised.

'Seriously, Jo-Jo, don't you find it ever so – unnatural?'

'What does she think will happen if you do sleep in the same bed?'

'Keep your voice down, for goodness sake.'

The bibulous-looking passenger on their left was staying very still, his cane between his knees, ears all aprick. Antwerp was enveloping them in a smudge of wharves and smoke.

'We'll end up the same, that's what she thinks. When you, you know – *do* it – your electricals get all mixed up, and you have to keep away from each other to let them get back to normal.'

'Isn't it good to get mixed up?'

'No, you have to be different. It's more exciting.'

'Lights up Piccadilly, does it?'

Baz grunted in amusement. A young couple passed arm in arm, and the two friends stared with unusual interest.

'The funny thing is,' said Baz, 'married couples do tend to acquire each other's characteristics. Maybe that's why so many of them grow heartily sick of each other.'

Joseph had to agree there was something in that.

'You and Agnes are chalk and cheese, if you don't mind me saying. Mind you, if you shared the same bed, maybe you'd acquire nice fingers and play the violin rather well.'

Baz looked straight out. The wind was tugging at the ends of his moustaches and sending smoke from his pipe into Joseph's eyes.

'Nice fingers? Has she really?'

'Surprised you haven't noticed.'

'I never notice fingers,' Baz said.

He was staring at his own. They were rather pudgy for his height, but he had strong hands. Once, Joseph secretly recalled, Baz in a fit of pique had slapped his own cheeks so hard he had bruised the jawbone. How old had he been? Eleven, perhaps. He was unusual, underneath. Not many boys would strike their own faces in pique.

Antwerp was no less hot than London; the minute they left the boat, they felt it. It clamped to them with a smooth, fishy weight. The last part of the journey was a crawl. The train was a requisitioned one, Prussian, very old and painted a camouflage-black. It looked ready for the scrapyard: the copper and brass embellishments stripped to the last bolt, all the joints blowing steam, the long, old-fashioned chimney rimmed with soot. Really abased, it was. Inside the shed of a compartment there were signs in German everywhere, telling the passengers what they must or must not do. This amused the group, of course, and made up for the slatted wooden seats and walls, the lingering stench of shag, the hideous squealing of the wheels every time they were dragged around a curve. Oh, how the passengers enjoyed the abasement of the foe in that dreadful machine: they were really chattering, excited by it.

Oh, how the group laughed, trying to guess which little sign said *Do Not Expectorate*: they all seemed to say it, that was the hilarious thing, in German!

Flat, tedious country – yet foreign. Even the railway crossings looked different, terribly alien as they slid past, the odd person looking up. Joseph thought these people looked lost and pointless, but they were not: he had been too stuck down, too rooted, that was why he thought this about them. The names on the stations, the snatches of foreign talk, the plump red Flanders faces – it was all as exotic as China. Yet the route took them through the dullest country anywhere. He rested his head against the hard straight back of the bench but the vibrations gave him a headache. The good-looking girl in cream sat at the other end of the compartment between two formidable ladies in black, like a cake filling. Her eyes were closed, she was poised there with her head sitting erect on her shoulders, very poised and statuesque. Either she had a headache, or was praying. Her eyes opened suddenly and his own skipped away. Rather shy, he felt, there among the black weight of crêpe, the stink of mothballs and stale shag. He had not noticed her on the London train. Perhaps she had joined the boat from somewhere else. Ithaca, maybe.

One of the female passengers had transmogrified into their guide, wearing a hat with a ridiculous red ostrich feather in case they lost her. She hung onto the leather belt by the window and pointed out concrete blockhouses with a black-gloved finger – the first indication of the battlefield, these blockhouses. The train went very slowly over the canals, as if afraid. Yes, one has to be careful on these bridges, explained the guide: these heavy Prussian trains, these old bridges knocked about by the war. The passengers were almost holding their breath as they were inched over.

Baz and Joseph escaped her high-pitched illustrations and the fetid heat by standing outside in the corridor. Neither had realised that 'Tour' meant just that, with all the excursional paraphernalia one expected on a visit to the chateaux of the Loire or the pyramids of Thebes. The guides were mostly war widows, unpaid. This perhaps explained the strained enthusiasm of tone, like a Primitive Methodist preacher; Joseph found it unendurable. The glass was so grimy as to be opaque when the sun fell on it. They opened the window and the smoke almost choked them. Ah, there was something terribly half-hearted about the first signs of devastation, something belittling and truly ugly: like an oversized factory yard full of rubbish. Though it was mostly flat to the horizon, it had nothing of the epic sweep Joseph had anticipated. It was gloomy, sordid. Someone was cleaning up here and there, it seemed: there were stacks of things, almost neat, but they rushed past too quick to identify. And that is how he remembered the camp and the rear lines, now he thought about it: the litter, the heaps of rubbish in the nettles, the stench of latrines.

They puffed and ground through the village of Poelkapelle, stopped outside at the little grimy station with its blotches of geraniums and dusty shrubs in pots, shrouding the whole place in steam and sulphurous clouds with a great hiss. So superior, that tatty, Prussian train – such damaged pride! Joseph leaned out of the window and saw ugly wooden huts and even uglier convex Nissen types in tin: in between these – ruins. Real ruins made of stone, as if constructed like that. One which might have been the church, slates scattered all about it like tiny tombs. Of course he had seen ruins in France when the fever was still on, and had tramped between them in khaki, but now it was just a scar. Very curious they seemed, these smashed-up dwellings, without the war inflamed around them.

Further off, a few tents flapped in the dusty wind next to some hovels made up of old timbers and found rubbish: it was like a shabby gypsy circus. It was depressing, totally depressing. The people he glimpsed looked horribly poor, even from that distance. The way they stood, the shapeless clothes they wore.

'We're running along the old front line,' said Baz, once the train had jerked to life again. He had a scrappy little map in his hands, something copied out of a book. There were people in the fields, tiny-looking, flukes of existence. The map shuddered in the draught. Joseph's skin felt like greasy mutton.

'Dismal, utterly dismal.'

'First impressions,' said Baz, 'do lend themselves to that description.'

There were fields brimming with ripe corn, however – there a meadow of lush grass – and a grove of trees – the odd red-capped farmhouse. But there were equally large areas where nothing seemed to be growing but scrub, scattered with debris, enough to fill all the ironmongers' yards in Belgium. What appeared to be brickyards were shattered houses and factories. Worse, the wooden huts were all painted a dried-blood colour, a really horrible maroon red; some of these were hardly huts at all but huge and sprawling, low-roofed, very mean. A farmhouse was under construction at the spot known (they could hear the guide) as Cheddar Villa, and more blockhouses emerged from sheets of corrugated iron. Smashed trees everywhere, dead or with a little skirt of leaves. Joseph felt a peculiar misery spreading over him, like a rash. His light flannel clothes might have been coarse khaki. It was very like a troop train's cattle truck, this noisy Prussian devil.

Just before coming into Ypres they spotted the first cemetery; it occupied a large field and appeared to be a hive of activity, as if the war had only just finished. There were men with spades as well as knots of mourners, and heaps of flowers – the only bright spot, although the sun was shining.

'I suppose they're still finding them,' said Baz.

Joseph felt as if his soul was cringing, as if his complete being was cowering on behalf of everyone else, dead or alive or not yet born. The train stopped and started, pitching them both against the side. The natural state of the world might be an extreme violence, he thought, nursing his elbow.

'They're bringing order to the chaos,' he said. 'Much better to have it all neat and tidy, like a suburb.'

Baz raised his eyebrows at that. Almost laconic about it all. A silence.

'Awful job, it must be,' Joseph murmured. 'Moving cadavers.'

Then, a moment after: 'They must be rather gamey by now.'

'I say, d'you think they'll have shifted Hanley?'

'Depends where he was, I suppose.'

Baz produced a slip of paper from his diary. 'Clapham Junction, it says here.'

'*The* Clapham Junction?'

'Don't be a fool, Jo-Jo. It's a nickname.'

Joseph smiled wearily.

'Precisely. It's *the* Clapham Junction. Crossroads for suicides. No place to hang about. Which battalion of the Worcesters was it?'

'The 2nd.'

'Of course. Forgotten the date.'

'8 November, 1915.'

Silence.

'Do you imagine we'll find him?'

Baz pursed his lips.

'Back my life on it. He's my brother.'

Another cemetery, men in large moustaches sitting about under wraiths of cigarette smoke. Smoke in the distance, the plain between like one vast nondescript field.

'Maybe it'll never rain again,' said Joseph.

The smoke and dust were sour in his mouth.

'Makes you think of knights and archery, calling them battles,' he went on. 'Write about the slime in his letters, did he?'

'Hanley never wrote much. Not the expressive sort. Mentioned that his feet were cold and that the rations always arrived a bit damp.'

'Didn't really get on, you two, did you?'

Baz frowned. 'Brotherly love has nothing to do with getting on. We were very different except in the bits that rubbed up the wrong way. Yes, he made life devilish hard for me, sometimes, but he took me fishing and gave me my first cigarette. He made me a contraption out of wood, once, in 1913.'

'What sort of contraption?'

Baz looked at his friend as if he was teasing, which he was. Hanley would call Joseph 'Titmouse', for some reason, and would give him kicks on the shin under the table when he stayed at Baz's. Hanley must have been about thirteen when he did this.

'I was never quite sure,' Baz replied, in a grave voice. 'The point is, he did it.'

They were inching huffily into the station past rusty hulks of waggons and the shells of burnt-out engines, stranded among old man's beard and waist-high carpets of nettles. There were men tearing up the track around them, hoisting lengths of it onto their shoulders and walking thus in twos to a cliff of metal parts. Some of the lengths were twisted like liquorice. There was broken glass lying about and the station itself was in a dreadful state. Windows boarded up, like an off-season dance hall.

'The morning after the night before,' said Baz.

But the place was a bedlam!

Where was the eerie calm, Joseph wondered – the murmuring voice of horror? There was something sacrilegious in the din, the racket that met them the minute they stepped off the train, the sheer rowdiness of it.

Infernally hot, and terrifically noisy. His head swam as they were jolted towards the exit. But it was his soul that was jolted – by the unexpectedness of it. It was a real row, with some sort of gaiety in its confusion: mourning clothes looked quite out of order, here. And now the knot of passengers was moving through the streets like a black hat bobbing on a river. Aside from spots of khaki and the odd military truck, it might have been a gold-rush town in America. Whores and bars. Bars everywhere, some of them mere shacks parked in the rubble. Joseph was amazed. Workmen shouted from scaffolding, but there was little real work going on that he could see: after the killing, the shouting. Bottles of beer rolled at their feet, and the potholes were filled mostly with rubbish or tamped with shattered brick.

The new arrivals were dazed, instantly dazed. There were burly men everywhere, cock-of-the-walk types, and there were the women: loud, fearless, dressed as if for a stage show. One slouched smoking in front of a tent near the dinosaur ribs of the cathedral. She sported a Calamity Jane outfit – cream stetson, fringed buckskin, shiny boots, lips a butterfly of dark crimson. A sign on the tent said *Bar Wild Hickock*, with two crude guns in wood nailed either side. A frontier town. Donkeys grazed patches of grass where houses had been. In front of the old Cloth Hall – a welter of charred timbers and the odd patch of medieval gilt – canvas stalls sold lemonade and barley water, beer and sausages. A huge sign above a long stand announced, in English, *Picturesque Postcards and Souvenirs*. In an ugly dark swirl, impelled away from the red feather, clutching their bags and valises, the new arrivals swooped around it. Joseph felt disgusted and hung back a little, but was still dazed – dazzled, almost – by the gay abandon of the place in its devastation, by all these rowdy burly types seething over it as muscular ants seethe over crumbs. A waggon passed filled with metal bits, driven by a huge bewhiskered man in a blacksmith's apron. He was pure Thor, god of war and the anvil. The wheel's hub nearly had Joseph's bag off his shoulder.

And as for the picturesque postcards! Baz bought one for Agnes: a tasteful arrangement of mud, water, sky, dead trees and their reflections. How sardonically cruel that word 'picturesque', how bitterly it laughed at them! And the souvenirs? Joseph could not *not* marvel at them: twisted bits of shell on varnished wood, cartridge cases arranged into sprays of flowers, a tray of regimental buttons, wooden signs from the Front: *Hazy Trench, Schanzzeug Ausgabe* . . . Ah, yes, even he was laughing now, he was getting swept up – but he did so want to buy the trench sign that said, through judicious marks of whitewash – *For F—'s Sake don't F— about Here!* He did so want to buy it. Yet it was a 'souvenir', for tourists. Like a tin monkey on the Strand, a stick of Brighton rock.

He knew he should not have come: the war was finished, even its memory was finished, the nasty bits whitewashed out. There was only this gay abandon. Anything else – the moping about, the mourning clothes, the gleaming white memorials – all that was simply wrong, it was deathly, compared to this fantastic show of life. For life is ruthlessly busy, always busy. The whores slouched only because they were busy, in secret. The bars pulsated. The ruins were rather wonderful in their new life, under their tarpaulined roofs: they were not idle. The cratered streets were thronged by people excited by the impulsiveness of their lives; it had not yet settled back into the red box, the grooves of the usual machinery. He himself was dead against those grooves, that red box – his whole soul revolted against it. And there were folk from every nation, he could see that, standing there and watching in the wrecked, busy square. A large Hindoo fellow in a white turban, bare-chested, walked past shouldering a couple of pails on a pole. A platoon of Chinese chattered like sparrows nearby, and there were Africans, too – tall and bony, they were, strolling past in their dust-patched uniforms. Dragged out of a sacred Africa, they had been, into this nightmare: he saw that. He thought he heard Polish next to him, just snatches of it. Then Russian – definitely Russian. But it could have belonged to any of these types: up and down the crowd heaved, full of life.

Yet underneath it all he saw how desperate it all was, how solid the sadness at its heart.

They went on. It was not very far, but their pace was slow against the river swirling against them. The good-looking girl in the creamy dress, with the queer mark on her chin, distracted him again. She caught his eye over a little old grey-haired woman and smiled. When she smiled, her scar – for that's what the mark was, he saw, a twisty red streak cupping her chin – lifted more clearly into view. They passed a large wooden hall that called itself a picture palace; it was showing films – amusing ones it looked like – on every hour; people emerged from it smiling and laughing. But the laughter was glazed, somehow. It had no depth to it, no real vigour, no bloom. Joseph felt the senility of the human world, just there, passing the picture palace. Yet this – camping in the ruins – this was the future, he knew it. This was all that could be looked forward to, outside the red box and the price of eggs. If nothing else, he knew he had learnt this from Ypres. With the penetrating force of the first impression that holds firmer than anything after.

He had made such an effort, almost a superhuman one, to imagine the Front – the horror of it. Far worse, at any rate, than lugging his stove of a Blighty pack about, when acting out the soldier! He had put quite a strain on his mind, entering the thick of it in the cottage; but all those scenes were like a faint dream now, an obscure and irrelevant monograph. Almost shameful. He felt sick and giddy, and was relieved to find his room and lie a length on the bed. It was a rum place, the hotel. Rebuilt from about the second floor up, there were still scabrous patches of raw unplastered brick in the lower façade and the roof was only half-completed, the rest draped in tarred sheets which the wind rattled like a ship's sails. The buildings either side were a huddle of broken beams and the odd slab of creosoted deal. The place reeked of beer, wine and wet plaster. Apparently the previous owner had been blown out of the window and clean across the street by an *obus*, still clutching a bill. Which, their informant pointed out, was never paid.

Now it was run by a French couple, a rather trim pair with snubby noses and very black, oiled hair. It followed Gallic taste rather than Flemish, so the only carpet anywhere was a strip of threadbare coconut matting in the hall. Joseph liked this austerity: what a relief, he remarked, to travel in a country where economy and taste don't strike each other out. Baz found the hotel disgustingly spendthrift, with worn sheets and cockroaches under the water jug. So, apparently, did the rest of the group.

'*Two years ago*,' Joseph informed Baz, reading out of the little leaflet provided by the guide, '*a mounted soldier trotting in at the Lille Gate would have had a clean view to the other side of town.*' Baz knew this already, it was well-known, part of the general stock.

85

Yet the group's expectations were those of a weekend party in Llandudno.

It was the railway company's choice of abode, but Joseph doubted if there was a more salubrious one in town. Baz disagreed and went off for an hour looking for The Ritz of Wipers. His friend fell asleep, dreaming pleasantly of boats and painted women through the shouts and bangs floating up from the street and down from the roof – he being the *aurea mediocritas* on a bolster as hard and cold as iron.

9

A Botanical Outing

THE GROUP DEMANDED tea as soon as lunch was over, much to the owner's consternation, and it arrived in an enormous chipped jug. Alas, someone complained at the beverage's resemblance to heated water, and she informed them that she 'changed the leaves every four days'. When it was translated – oh, the grumbles! So shocking! An elderly monocled gent, who had just been comparing the weather favourably with Lahore's, expressed himself 'surprised' that the 'damn Frenchies hadn't learnt a thing or two from our boys before they got minced'. His neat little wife patted his hand and gave him a vast handkerchief to wipe his face with, from which the face emerged looking anguished, as if he had put on a tragic mask.

On cue, the guide passed round a sheet of paper on which they had to write the location of their loved one, and she spread a huge map on the table. Only half of them had any idea where the loved one was: Baz simply wrote 'Clapham Junction', which Joseph knew was hopeless – there were at least fifty little cemeteries within cadaver-bearing distance of the crossroads. The other half had apparently hoped to consult a register, or riffle through the cemeteries on foot, despite the fact that in most cases the deceased had been listed as 'missing'. Even if he was not missing, finding the spot would be fiendishly difficult since there were hundreds of cemeteries and hundreds of thousands of graves. And there was something about 'reorganisation', too.

Everyone was very disappointed. Even Joseph felt it, on behalf of the others.

The rest of the afternoon was to be spent gaining a 'general picture' from a motor-coach, while Sunday was the day for paying their 'individual respects'. How lost they all looked, in that bare neat dining room with its lovely creamy lace on the windows! Hard to imagine a man flying through them. What zany had brought them here, after all?

The handsome girl dressed in cream caught Joseph's eye again.

Yes, she was very good-looking, he thought – and not dressed in black. He wondered how she had scarred her chin; the effect was interesting, it made her intriguing, in a peculiar way. It set off her beauty. Her straw sun hat bore tiny leather flowers, bright yellow. She stood out from the dismal background of the group like a ray of sunshine in a cavern. Now he was, almost accidentally, next to her. They were right by the window. She was admiring the lace – from Bruges, she guessed. The sun slanted into it, making a long complicated shadow over the boards. Her own collar was of the finest lace, but made by her mother. Joseph thought of his own mother knitting her crochet, even in the shop – he had found something so tedious and dulling about it, though now he realised how precious this making was. Quite suddenly he realised this, talking to the handsome young girl there in the hotel dining room: how very precious this fine making was, and how it would not last. Not with the confused tearing burliness of life, the way it was going. The wars that must still come.

The heat had lightly cooked the polished floorboards: the room had a pleasant goldeny smell of timbers, like a ship. She was telling Joseph that her brother had been killed by a German aeroplane near Polygon Wood. She's from my neck of the woods, he thought – north Derbyshire, judging from her broad vowels, broader than his own yet elegant, not at all twangy. Maybe Manchester. She had a rousing sort of lisp, her tongue came too far forward – but it was attractive. It gave her an intentness. And her mouth never stayed still, it was always finding accommodation for the long plump tongue.

'Strafed, you mean?'

'No, it fell right on him.'

'You mean it crashed?'

'I suppose so.'

'That's proper bad luck. Maybe he downed it.'

'He was trying to get a telephone line to work, we were told. He had a leave warrant in his pocket.'

'Ah,' Joseph said, nodding like a veteran. He rather liked her, he really did. It was easy, talking to her in the woody smell of this neat bare room, from which the others had mostly drifted out. 'To hang about in the front line with a leave warrant in your pocket is asking for it, you know.' He had read about this suspicion. He was inclined to believe it. But he thought he had been a little flippant.

However, she gave him the most winning smile. Her scar lifted, it seemed to distort the edge of her chin, a thin rumple that affected him rather strongly.

'Where did *you* fight?'

He looked up at the ceiling.

'I had a bad time on the Somme,' he said, emitting a fine whistle as he breathed in. 'I can't talk about it.'

And so they did not. They talked about the Peak District instead. She was from Stockport. She was a student nurse in her final year.

They were herded into the motor-coach by the guide, her giant red ostrich feather already dusty and drooping. Joseph pointed out to Baz how a lot of the women positioned in front of what his (Joseph's) mother would term 'hostels of fugitive dalliance' were sporting ostrich feathers, and he musn't follow the wrong one.

'They're also sporting make-up thick enough to hang in the wardrobe,' Baz replied, not grinning.

Then he said, out of the corner of his mouth: 'Have you ever been with one, actually?'

Joseph chose not to answer that. He had no desire to know whether Baz had, though there had been a fair number around the camps.

The motor-coach was an ancient, open affair, only a few cushions away from a cattletruck. It growled out of the town by the Lille Gate (covered in scaffolding), nearly brained itself on a huge lump of concrete, then bumped along a road whose metalled surface had mostly gone. They held their hats and Joseph had to keep wiping his spectacles free of dust. What patriotic flunkeys they all felt, listening to the guide! There was a haze over the vast plain that might have been a gas cloud three years earlier. It was not just dust; the drought had sucked even the waterlogged Flanders fields dry, but the flood evidently lay close beneath the surface, emanating mist.

They passed the Hindoo encampment. Vast, it was. Horses and turbaned fellows wandered about between the white tents, and a few waved. 'The Relief of Lucknow!' cried the monocled gent, and everyone laughed. Then the laughs became embarrassed squeals as they drove within yards of one of these fellows; stark naked but for fronds of soap, he was pouring a billycan of water over his nape. His body glistened like a chestnut. He took no notice of the coach, despite the dust.

'Ah,' said Baz, 'that's the power of the heathen mind for you. Not even a blush.'

Flies kept settling on their sweaty faces, which (for Joseph) brought unwelcome thoughts of Walter and his matter-of-factness. Well, their little legs no longer felt sticky! And Samuel – he had forgotten the impending interview with Samuel. Suddenly, he did not fancy it.

The salient was flat and featureless, apart from the odd ruined tower, a windmill, the smashed trees – and lines of poplars here and there, clotted with mistletoe and miraculously overlooked – or perhaps they had shot up since. The guide indicated the ridge curving between Messines and Passchendaele, for which so many men had perished, but it was really no more than a wicked ruse. High ground! – Joseph wanted to laugh. Some of the smashed trees had tutus of green leafage, like prancing Palace Girls stuck the moment peace broke out. Most of the others were shorn of branches – prehistoric stelae, set up deliberately to some dreadful set of gods on a black tract of moorland.

'Grendel's passed over,' Joseph joked, pointing them out. And it really was as if some giant dragon had breathed on a vast forest: Joseph had actually imagined them all dug up and chopped to firewood, the Flanders trees. He had brought along his sketchbook but the motor-coach swayed all over the place. There were foxgloves here and there. Not much else in that line.

The wind smelt unpleasant: the *patron* had told them that cadavers were everywhere, just under the surface where the bottomless sea of mud began, and the heat was exhuming pockets of poison gas from the soil. Baz thought it a scandal that the fallen had not yet found a decent resting-place, and even Joseph was surprised. He could see harvesters at work in places, and the odd knot of fellows doing something or other in a cloud of dust. There was a lone man up to his knees in a hole, with a dark, twisted thing on a sheet of tarpaulin next to it; it was clearly a corpse, but no one said a word. There was only a kind of shiver of embarrassment running up the coach – and then it was gone.

Yes, the general impression was of barren ground, cracked by the heat and full of rusty rubbish in holes – a thoroughly *modern* wilderness! He almost wanted to set it to music, whistle a rag – oh so thoroughly, thoroughly, *thoroughly* modern! What he took to be ancient long barrows turned out to be bunkers, of course. He felt faintly ridiculous, as all tourists do, and consumed subtly by a subterranean guilt. They passed right beside the picked remains of a horse and he shook his head in inward lamentation; oh, how the animals suffer from us, their terror intensified by bewilderment!

A whiff of ammonia, like a dirty stables. Why the devil had he agreed to come? He bounced about in his seat – almost comical, it was. The coach jarred terribly, as if the driver was deliberately aiming for the holes. They were being punished.

This guilt, it was really something sick and ghastly, but it was not clean. It was not a clean, wholesome guilt, such as might provoke an outlaw to renounce the gun. An outlaw or even a cold-blooded murderer. Guilt, even guilt could be clean and unselfish, in this way, flowering out of conscience. But his was not so simple. He wished it could be. But it wasn't, not at all. There was something nasty and modern about his guilt, something selfish yet ill-defined. Just because he hadn't fought. And he *hated* the vileness of fighting, soldiers in their cardboard khaki, trampling over each other, flesh and blood – and maggots. He should be glad, very glad, that he muffed it. But coming here on this ridiculous, almost comical outing, as if to Llandudno Bay or Swallow Falls at Betws-y-Coed (where each year he would go, as a boy, when staying with his spinster aunt) – this had provoked an unclean guilt, remorseful and pocked with shame.

So he sat hunched in the horrible jolt of the coach seat, its metal already burning, and felt himself ready to weep, inside. The girl in cream was two rows in front of him, hanging onto her hat. He would think of her.

Shrapnel Corner, where they alighted for ten minutes, was an undignified crossroads whose potholes and outlying craters were yellowishly furred by grass and what looked like camomile. They pointed out other flowers – it was the first thing the group did point out, a real botanical outing. Joseph recognised some of them: forget-me-not, skullcap, clusters of rosebay willowherb, little eggs-and-bacon. Woody nightshade, growing forlornly where a wood had once sheltered it, now scrambling over a heap of old tins and shattered tree trunks in bright sunlight. And there were brambles, too, but made of rusty barbed wire, stuck fast to a sort of carved imitation of mud – though a particularly deep crater glistened like treacle at the bottom. All sorts of rubbish at the bottom. A fresh skull-and-crossbones sign on the edge put them off hunting in it for souvenirs.

Not that you had to *hunt* for them at all: it was more like walking a beach for pretty shells. One of the group picked up a regimental button and Baz found a squashed whistle. Joseph saw the heel of a wellington boot sticking out of a hummock but chose not to pull on it.

'The Aid Post here brought succour to the wounded,' the guide said in her high, sing-song voice, 'even though it was frequently shelled and rather muddy.'

A smelly porridge of slime. Now it was hard enough to kick.

Everything rock-hard, fossilised. Joseph raged inside. He noticed how pretty the girl's ankles were. Ino of the slim ankles, ay. They nodded at each other, the girl and he, but did not talk. It was an elaborate dance they were playing.

Someone tripped on a duckboard, stuck as things get stuck in ice.

'Duckboards were absolutely compulsory once the dykes had broken,' sang the guide. They drifted about, smiling sweetly, a kind of callousness in it. Then they poured back chattering into the motor-coach.

Which coughed and ejected a huge jet of steam in front of the ruins of a grand *château*. 'Bedford House,' the guide announced, brightly. 'An unscheduled stop.' A ripple of laughter. Laughter!

They had to set out on foot to various little cemeteries, which was a relief. Joseph felt better, walking, and he found himself next to the girl. A long narrow path strung between wheat fields led to the first one, but the path was too narrow for two abreast without a sleeve catching on the wire, so the girl had to go just in front of him and they could not talk. He felt this odd, solid affection for her, though he scarcely knew her, had never clapped eyes on her before that morning. She was very relaxed, almost sleepy, with a deep charge in her that flashed every so often in her grey eyes. She had a very fine, slim figure, really very fine under the cream dress and airy shawl, almost a dancer's boyish figure; understated, if too narrowly hinged at the waist to be boyish – and not moving at all like a boy. It fascinated him, this understated quality, almost secretive. And the fact that despite it she was thoroughly, ever so completely woman – this lit an interest that was almost philosophical in him, rather dry, though the kernel of it was moist enough: he thought about the gulf that lay between them, because of her womanliness. They might as well be a different species, earth and water, air and fire. And yet her form, as it moved, was not *so* far from the dainty sort a male youth can have.

So he watched the way her form moved along in front of him as if it had nothing to do with the girl herself, almost as one might study a marble statue in a museum. It seemed pinched by the wire either side, and a little powerless, almost drugged, the long ribbon of this absurd track through parched-looking arable seeming to drag it along behind the others (Baz easily the tallest, there near the front). He was looking at the girl almost technically, struck by the moment-by-moment solidity of her existence, when really it was so evanescent: no one else would recall it, not as it was at this moment, not ever. It was continually moving into oblivion. The shoulder blades were clear under the dress, she held herself very straight as she walked.

Marching along as if at a wedding, led by the rippling bright ostrich feather, sweating in the sultry heat, the slim creamy figure with its sun hat and thick coppery curls just a foot in front of him, Joseph felt a solid, new affection for the world in general, the people in it, and for this girl most particularly. But the procession was absurd. We must look quite absurd from a distance, he thought, imagining it: heads bobbing in a line over the brownish massed ears of the wheat.

The cemetery was a grassy square of about two acres. It was an island, really, stuck in the middle of what turned out to be one huge wheat field, not two. 'The end of the pier,' Baz called it.

The crosses were huddled up in one corner, a frightened flock of them. Elsewhere, scattered far from one another over the grass, were a few more graves, defined by wire loosely strung between four white posts. A small white cross lay at the head of each one. Lonely, Joseph thought. A desolate place to be asleep for good.

A wind had blown up, they had to shield their eyes. The nearest grave had a group of black-clad women and children around it, their big skirts whipped by the wind. They were carrying flowers made up into large wreaths. One woman ducked under the wire in a rather ungainly fashion in order to lay her flowers on the grave. All terribly amateur, haphazard. Joseph had pictured a sort of professionalism about the mourners, a sort of stiff statuariness. The group stood with their hands on the wire; as Joseph and the others passed near them he expected to hear sobs, but instead there was bright chatter. Extraordinarily bright. They were judging the effect of the flowers against the cross, as if at Chapel. He imagined a big, hearty fellow in the tomb, who would not have fancied any of this crying nonsense. The little girl, about four or five, was running about chasing butterflies.

But he knew, in the way that one can 'know' such things, that the dead man was not at all big and hearty. Scarcely a man, from the dates on the cross. A thin-shinned seventeen-year-old with a frightened stammer. The voices were suburban London, up in the nose and genteel. He was lying there, the poor lad, wanting them all to go away. Bewildered by his own extinction, looking down at his bony little hands, his crumbling boots.

Joseph felt he was beginning to bring home the goods. He made a note or two in his pad with his stubby pencil. And he had half an eye on the girl. He was too shy to make a beeline for her – she had managed to end up quite a way from him, near the huddle of crosses. Baz was near to her. He would go to Baz. He hurried across and almost twisted his ankle on a knobbly patch of ground; the ground was queerly uneven, some of the party had to be helped over it. There was a warm gust, the wheat rippling around them in its oceanic way, rustling and hissing like surf on coral. They were adrift on the ocean, marooned with their hidden dead.

The girl was bent over a rustling wreath. Baz and Joseph wandered up to her. She smiled at them in her easy, dreamy way. *To Bert from Mother*, said the wreath. The flowers were dead and the cross, made of grey tin, was bent over as if weeping. It was barely taller than the yarrow and white campion that had sprung up here between the graves. The wind blew scurries of dust around their ankles; the late afternoon sun was still burning on their faces. There was a stink of cordite in the air, or something very similar. Joseph, without speaking, tried to bend the cross back. He failed to, mainly because the tin was hot enough to fry an egg on. Maybe it had wilted. He felt comical and curiously out of breath when he stood upright.

'It does seem rather sad that Mother's so far from Bert, don't you think?'

She shook her head.

'The place is not important,' she said. 'He isn't here, is he?'

'It says he is. Look. *Robert Mulligan, fallen for his country aged 18.* That's Bert, all right.'

She pursed her lips.

'He's in the arms of Jesus,' she said, quietly.

He nodded, feeling a pang of disappointment. The dreaminess was shallow, after all. Its core was a barley sugar of Chapel stuff.

He was *really* disappointed, in fact. It was a blow – he was surprised what a blow it was. He felt like quoting H.G. Wells on God. The lisp was no longer rousing.

'Hang Jesus,' he muttered. He should have said it boldly, of course.

Baz had gone off a few yards, returning as the girl gave a sharp look. 'What d'you think that bang was?' he asked.

There had been a sort of concussion in the air, a tremor, but Joseph had hardly noticed it. He had not thought of it as a 'bang'.

'Our conveyance, probably.'

A white cloud, a rather strange one, appeared on the horizon. It was rooted to the ground, spreading out and heaving, rising higher, flattening out a little, then higher again. Almost beautiful, this white cloud was, billowing wide and high, almost majestic in its size and dominion over the flat land – a second fake thunderclap faintly echoing, dissolving into wind and the odd chirrup of a bird. A faint tremor in the air, as if a great bell had rung.

'Smoke,' said Baz. 'Something's blown up.'

There was another cemetery, and then another – scrappy affairs, really, a mishmash of different nationalities, including German, with the odd mourner laying flowers. They walked between the crosses, Ostrich Feather informing them of this and that, explaining it all away. The crosses were made from anything to hand: even lead piping, in one case. They were mostly black. Soon, all the dead would have their small white stone. Demure, clean, in a garden. The nations separated in their own little square of grass. Everyone was looking a little tired and sad, now. A mourner nearby was weeping in little bursts; it was quite agonising, listening to it. The crying would stop, then start as if following a decision, a thoughtful decision. When really it was without thought, just sheer agony. She was a youngish woman, too, in a neat rather fashionable jacket, clenching her fists. Her upturned face was drawn back in absolute agony, lips straining against the teeth, then the sobs burst out.

The group moved further away, almost shuffling as they tried not to look. Joseph felt the sadness in obscure waves, but sadness *itself* had tired him out, and for years now. He did not think many people had much of a residue of sadness left, these days – they turned to gloom, or empty frolics. Gloom and sadness were two quite different things.

One little impromptu cemetery behind a broken farm-gate had been shelled and many of the dead had been reburied several times, the guide said. Soon they were to be disinterred and reburied again, elsewhere. Listening to the guide, Joseph felt a sort of somnolence overtake him, a sleepy callousness. He saw black vaguely-human shapes thrown up in the air, almost balletically. It was all so revolting. The girl was avoiding him. Baz had found out her name. It was Tillie, Tillie Lainer. Joseph had never thought to ask.

They clustered about a huge crater with a precise lip, perfectly circular and hard; it reminded Joseph of a clay quarry, the type found behind brickyards – it seemed deep enough, though yellow slime hid the bottom. A thin strand of barbed wire ran all the way round: the girl was bang opposite. The familiar death's-head sign claimed that it was Dangerous to Enter, and you could spot the snouts of sunken shells. He felt a very tiny nudge of fear. He had thought such perils over, drawn like bad teeth. She was talking to Baz. Maybe she was right. Maybe the dead millions *were* all in the arms of Jesus, though the arms must be jolly big. A statement of fact, not holy fervour. He imagined her body, naked, as something pale and tender, rather like her mind.

But how could he know her mind? He scarcely knew his own.

She was smiling at Baz, showing white teeth. A flame of desire lit up in him, very sharp and hot – galvanic, he supposed. The gusts pulled at the dress sideways, moulding it to her right waist and hip and leg. A ribbon was flapping about, a little flicker from this distance across the bomb crater. She held onto her straw hat. The golden brown of a corn field behind conferred something of its ripeness on her, deepening her coppery hair. Baz was being wretchedly amusing, apparently.

Resentment, but nothing very deep. The pawing of a young buck, that's all.

He cleaned his spectacles on his tie and the tie caught on a barb of the wire, pulling out a thread. He had on quite the wrong shoes, too – white canvas ones. His feet ached, they were swollen. Some pretty cottages in the distance turned out to be hayricks. The odd thump and then more white smoke. Impromptu, perhaps: the local paper in the hotel had had reports of these accidents with munitions, it made nasty reading. The photographs of the victims – the odd small child, even – were of eerily dead faces, though taken when alive. Once someone is dead, they are dead in the past, too. They are always dead. Joseph's schoolmate, his best friend after Baz, had fallen down a lead mine some ten years ago, and it was as if he had never really properly been alive. Most of the human race is perpetually dead – now that was a queer thought . . .

Life is a sort of tiny outburst. Either side is this dreadful calm. This is what he felt about this place: it was like the dreadful calm of death.

And the guilt was *eating* him. Though his discharge papers were proudly kept in a drawer by his mother, when she had chucked so much else; especially matter to do with the shop.

He joined Baz and the girl – walking right round to them. She was dubious about him, he could see that. This made him swagger a bit, he was not sure why. This made him more attractive to her, he sensed. And she really did have something solid under the sweet-toothed religion. She really did have marrow. It flashed up in her eyes from time to time, and she had none of the round-shouldered, milky look of the unreflectively religious woman. She was something of a mongrel, he thought. She had come on her own, too, unaccompanied – she *had* been going to come with her aunt, but her aunt was ill. Not seriously? No, thank the Lord: dyspepsia, that was all. She'd always suffered it, the aunt, despite the powders, her *dyspepsia*.

Joseph nodded sagely. The lisp had struggled with the word, the plump moist tongue fumbling behind the lips. This girl should be running across fields barefoot in a shimmering Grecian shift, not recounting her aunt's maladies. This is what Joseph reckoned. She had finely-wrought features, she was undeniably pretty. She should not have to think about dyspeptic aunts, let alone mention them.

It was unavoidable, though. Life had so much ungainliness in it. War was just a species of ungainliness. The great mistake was that folk thought war handsome, because it went about in uniform knowing what it wanted, and they could sigh over it and feel titillated by sadness, or swelled up, inflamed by pride. The truth was, it was the ugliest, most ungainly specimen around. It reeked of dyspeptic thinking. Better to have let the Kaiser overrun everything, even England, he thought, as in the Saki novel he had read last year; yes, better to have given the fellow his 'United States of Europe', crowned by the Berlin eagle – the dear cove would have got fed up in a few years, or folk would have intermarried and the Prussian blood got thinned out. The Saxon was ours anyway. Anything rather than this. Baz was sympathising about the dyspepsia.

'We've got precisely nowhere for three thousand years,' Joseph said, out loud, as they walked along, after a brief silence. It was certainly a grim thought.

Maybe the other two reckoned it a reference to the treatment of stomach ailments, for it was left hanging.

A knot of men, digging along an old front-line trench, were prising out all things metal. A heap of their finds had already accumulated by the road, a scrap-merchant's pile. They called out to the party in French. Ostrich Feather hurried the others on but the two men and the girl hovered for a moment. The pickers were burly types with huge moustaches hooding their mouths. One of them threw down a spade and came over to them. He greeted them in a broad Cockney twang. He was joined by a red-faced chap carrying a shell on his shoulder as if it was a hod.

'Souvenirs, m'luverly?'

The Cockney was leering away at Tillie, who declined the offer. He was dusting off a German helmet. He wiggled his finger through a neat hole in the side.

'Got the bugger,' he joked. 'Five bob to you, Miss Bootiful.'

Frankly, Joseph would not have wanted it for the world. The man's fist and wrist made a miniature face inside it, without meaning to. His name was 'arry and he'd 'arried the Boche at Loos. He called himself an ironmonger and said that he'd made so much money in the last six months that he didn't know where to bleedin' put it.

'Down a dry throat,' his mate reported, with an Irish lilt. 'Only it en't mine, worse luck.'

They all laughed. Laughed yet again! You can't go without laughing for long, thought Joseph, unless you are alone. You would probably find something to laugh about in Hell, if there were other folk about. Tillie's laughter was, of course, as silvery as a brook plashing down Kinder Scout.

IO

Café de Paradis

IT WAS QUITE a hike they were on: the village of St Eloi was half a mile on a pitted road. But no one complained. It was a sort of penance, a dusty sackcloth-type pilgrimage. They were almost glad the motor-coach had broken down – they hoped it could be mended, though, since Ypres would be the deuce of a slog back. Someone remarked, very seriously, that the country reminded him of an area near Rickmansworth. He had thick round spectacles on and a determined mouth. Joseph wanted to laugh, picturing those tidy little villages around Rickmansworth! Well, the village they walked into here was rubble. Fantastic heaps of rubble through which they advanced with caution. They felt humbled, and weirdly cheap, as if life was cut-rate – even their own lives, their own deepest beliefs. So much cut-rate stuff, they were.

The Nissens and wooden shacks were set very close to each other in long rows amongst the rubble, like cloches in an allotment – in which families were leading their lives as if nothing had happened, some of them dressed for Sunday in their starchy best, tailored to the last button (though it was still Saturday). The older men's spade beards combed neatly, combed and oiled; the grandmothers perched on chairs under their white caps and black shawls as if in a cosy parlour.

And they greeted the party with nods and smiles. Not quite as Africans meet white men in remote villages but the Flanders version of it, all the same. It was like walking uninvited through someone's living room: the tin huts had no windows in the curved sides, the only light coming through the large door in the front.

Always open, that door – the heat inside must have been colossal, utterly gruelling. The people were generally seated at a table, making lace or playing cards or just smoking meditatively. There was washing strung up behind and wooden debris in front: empty grenade boxes, old pine stakes, the stocks of rifles. Some of the huts, even the tin ones, were themselves in a ruinous state, with filth everywhere and grubby infants falling about. It was hopeless. They had lost all dignity.

The generals and ministers drink champagne, Joseph said to himself, as if quoting from a poem. But he was not. He felt very angry, and hopeless. Baz's expression was unfathomably calm, if slightly curious. Underneath he was probably feeling absolutely gruesome, Joseph thought. He found himself biting his lip. All this was so wrong, it made him reel with the harsh wrongness of it, the way ordinary folk are wronged day in, day out, and not even for an idea. For what, then?

A smell of urine and rotten matter, enough to gag on at times – a hundred times worse than the sour pockets encountered in any English village. He glanced at Tillie, the other side of Baz. She had an anguished look about her. She was tender, and this place bruised her. She'd go running back into the arms of Jesus, he thought – and added, with a quick internal grin that shamed him: *lucky Jesus*.

A sprawling wooden hut with a roof of creosoted deal posed as the school; it was painted, like all the others, that really vile shade of dried-blood maroon, and had several broken windows. Next to it stood a shop, a long low affair topped by corrugated iron. Ostrich Feather made a point of showing them this unprepossessing place, as it had been raised thanks to funds from a women's guild in 'Blighty'.

'Sells nothing but plum cake and Typhoo tea, I suppose,' Baz joked.

He did not seem terribly affected, it was true. The others chuckled nervously.

They stood by the new water pump, which spat and dribbled rather thinly. Someone asked the guide if there had been any cases of cholera. She did not know. Though everyone was thirsty, no one drank.

They wandered about. Just ten minutes, they had.

'*Ricordo di Pompeii*,' said Baz, with a dreadful accent.

'Been there, have you?'

'A nice cousin sent me a *32 Vedute* when I was at boarding school – you know, one of those concertina things of views. I flicked through it endlessly, wishing I was there. God, I was miserable. I should have loved boarding,' he went on, 'but I loathed it. My mother, you know, dead and all that. *Ricordo di Pompeii, 32 Vedute.*' He sniffed a bit. 'You know, just saying it, I can smell that horrible dorm. Amazing. I can picture each view and in the right order, too.'

A curious, dreamy look came over Baz's face. 'Honour bright, I can.'

'No, now that really *mustn't* do as a comparison,' said Joseph, softly. 'Volcanoes don't think to obliterate.'

'Well, do *we* really think about it?' Baz said, as if suddenly nettled. 'None of this was *deliberate*, exactly. It was a scramble, all power and hot blood. Wasn't it? Even the Kaiser wrote that he wouldn't have wanted it, if he'd known. *Ich nicht gewolt* and all that. It was bigger than any one person, or any sort of thinking. A sort of volcano, that.'

Baz was a pacifist and the optimistic type. Joseph found this irritating, this refusal to recognise the darkness. The human race was fagged. Floundering.

'Life's a blank cheque, we can scribble whatever we want, only we choose to tear it up or make it out for thruppences,' he said.

Baz shook his head, leaning forward unnecessarily as they strolled between the wreckage. 'Not always. Much of the time we fill it with treasures. Saintly actions and brilliant ideas. It's not all *Sturm und Drang*, you know. Or the shadowy Freud stuff. Much of the time it really isn't. You can't be too jaundiced, Jo-Jo.'

'So this wasn't all done for an idea, then?'

Baz pulled a face. 'Look, what does it matter, actually, whether it was or it wasn't?'

'Put an idea into men's heads, they'll fight for it till they drop. Shaw says that, somewhere. It matters a great deal, I think.'

'Doesn't he mention hot blood, too? Cuff the Kaiser and all that?'

'The blood heats up anyway,' Joseph retorted. 'Even I felt it. It's a boyish thing, or an animal thing. But that's not enough to keep a big war grinding on – or is it? Strewth, maybe it is.'

'Do you know what Seeley, I think it was, said about the Empire? That we conquered and peopled half the world in a fit of absence of mind.'

Joseph smiled.

'Isn't that what they say about God and creation?'

A little further on, past the shattered hulk of the church, Joseph picked up a little wooden clog. It was split down the middle and worn at the heel.

'Perhaps we're all ill.'

'Pardon?'

'Perhaps we're all a bit dicky. The human race, I mean.'

'Oh, come on—'

'Why do you never look *straight at* anything? Look at this clog.'

Baz was flustered.

'I'm looking,' he said. One could imagine him easily in court, a tall upright justice in his wig, trying not to get nettled. I must watch him one day, thought Joseph, dispensing justice.

'A child's shoe,' he said.

'Perhaps it was thrown away.'

A snort. 'Oh yes, of course, one has to entertain all possibilities. Yes, perhaps it was just thrown away. Well, that's all right then.'

Baz was tremendously hurt; his eyes fluttered with it, his whole face looked pinched. Though Joseph's tone was not as sneering as it might have been.

'You mustn't always think you *feel* more than anyone else, you know, Joseph. As if that gives you the right to *own* it.'

'Own what?'

'The sadness. The bloody awfulness of it. It's very trying, when someone does that. Don't think I haven't spent a great deal of time thinking things over, since Hanley died.'

Hanley again!

Joseph placed the little clog on the lintel of a smashed house. A cart passed them, laden with planks. Baz did make him feel rather puerile – quite often his friend had this effect on him. They both stood silent in a kind of confusion.

'I don't think we should have joined up,' Baz said, suddenly.

'No.'

'I've often said to myself that we shouldn't have joined up, given in. That I'd rather have been shot for desertion. Like poor old Billings.'

'Really?' Joseph was genuinely surprised. They were both guilty men, then. This was the beast's final triumph.

'And I'm not blaming you, either. I mean, the accident business.'

This was the first time Baz had mentioned it, ever, in this way. He was turning his hat round and round in his hands. Joseph nodded.

Silence.

'Tonatiuh,' he murmured, as Baz was staring at his hat, his body awkward.

'Come again?'

'Tonatiuh. The Aztec sun god.'

Baz looked at his friend a little warily, then nodded. He had the most tremendous patience, in the end. Or at least, he *behaved* as if he had.

'What about him?'

'He got very hungry and thirsty, rising up and travelling through the sky and dying, over and over again. So they had to feed him a lot of beating hearts and blood.'

'That was completely different,' said Baz, anticipating as usual. Quite wrongly.

'Oh, but they believed it. Don't think they didn't. They weren't demented, they weren't doing it like Jack the Ripper might have done. And it wasn't just an idea, either. It was a faith. It was as damned real as a mountain. But we don't have a Tonatiuh, and that's the real mystery. We don't have a God, not to speak of. Not that terrifies us, anyway. He's more like a country deacon. Pitiable, really. Yet we go on feeding something, I don't know what.'

They stared at the savaged church. It was as if the sky had taken a great bite out of it.

Baz suggested, cautiously, that God was inside us, each one of us, and that's why He was a mystery.

'Nonsense,' said Joseph. 'That's simply like not wanting to discuss copulation in public.'

'I sometimes think English common law is God,' murmured Baz. 'An image of Him, at any rate.'

Joseph ignored this and looked up at the sky, its odd shadowy shifting that comes just before dusk.

'We're a mystery to ourselves, you know. We don't need God messed up in it. The old drunk.' He sighed, thrusting his hands in his pockets, stretching his back a little. 'I tell you what, a rain god would be quite welcome. I think we should all dance for rain. I think we should forget all our clever ideas and scientific knowledge and our filthy materialisms and self-serving laws and dance in all good faith for rain. Imagine how much happier we'd be, thinking that a little human dance might please our masters enough to send rain. I wish I was born to a race or a time when I could have believed that.'

He did a few little hops, more like a Youlster morris dancer than a heathen. Baz nodded slowly.

'Ye-es,' he said, rubbing his chin. He was not really reflecting; it was the signal for Joseph to stop. Baz had done this since he was ten years old or so, whenever his friend had gone on too much. He would go on too much in the fields around Youlster, the football idling in the tussocks. Baz was incapable of putting anyone down by wit, always had been.

He wandered away, hands behind his back. Joseph made a few notes in his pocketbook, rather aimless ones, while sitting on a broken wall by the obliterated churchyard. Baz had pointed out a sign used flat as a bench in front of someone's hut: *Shit House*, it had said. He wrote this down. Then he walked about a bit. He fell into conversation with a villager, a woman of about fifty, white-capped and clogged; she was knitting in a rocking chair on her 'porch' – it was marked out by shell cases sprouting geraniums. She spoke good French. She said that the biggest problem was where to put one's furniture, since the walls were curved. She said nothing about the awfulness of it, the horror of this degraded life in a place so poisoned, so bloodied. The sheer *atrocity* of it. She might have been sitting in front of a row of beach huts at Bexhill, except for the white cap. It was terrible, this mute acceptance. Moaning about furniture, that was all. Mild irritation. Joseph reeled, mentally. Yet he admired her, admired her quite a lot. What choice had she? What real choice? It was a sort of victory, the victory of the ordinary over the monstrous. And it's true, that business about the furniture: it must be a nightmare – everything must end up in the middle.

Yet he recognised that on another day she might have gnashed her teeth and wailed – remembering how it was, before, when the roofs were on.

The ruined walls had not tumbled, they seemed to hold themselves up, suspended. Civilisation had grown too sardonic to care, and time had joined hands with it, indifferent. Apart from a lick of scaffolding around the shell of the church and a couple of the houses, there was no sign of serious reconstruction. 'There's no money for it,' the guide explained. No money! There had always been money for shells, guns, for all the rest of it.

One hut had a sign above the door, *Café de Paradis*, but it was closed and they were all thirsty. Children were running about in the dust in front of it, playing tag and rolling a metal wheel rim as a hoop. Scruffy little imps. A tiny tot was kicking a gooseberry of barbed wire about. They did not know why it was shut.

'Maybe in Paradise they have a *Café d'Enfer*, which is always open,' suggested Joseph.

Only Baz laughed. Tillie frowned, and looked away. Joseph had a swagger about him, again, feeling the lick of desire all along his limbs. Even his toes felt wicked. She looked away and then walked on. He liked her crooked little scar, her frown, the way she walked. But it was not real, this desire – it was a passing flame. He had to refuse it; he was bound on a far greater quest, gloomy and mute with vocation. It was almost exasperating, this distraction.

In front of a huge lengthy bluff of rust-reddened shells, she looked at him again with dreamy defiance. He felt gloom curling off him like paint; underneath was something fresh. It was sheer youth, quick with health, that should not be brought down by anything. At any rate, it found a response in her grey eyes. But the shyness in him, the caution, was a kind of smoke, it shrouded the flame. He would always hang back, in tense situations, behind his spectacles and slightness.

'They're like antiques, aren't they?' he commented. 'Like Roman things, or Greek.'

She did not even glance at them.

'Oh, they're just keeping up the tradition,' she said.

The bluff of rusty shells towered behind her, dwarfed her in its shadow as she turned away. He lingered to take notes. It was far more powerful than her hugging Jesus, that bluff. Each shell was prodding, thrusting its sharp snout from between its neighbours, as faces do in crowds when royalty passes. You could almost see them jostle. Their tips ended, most of them, in a little ring, like the ring on a pig's snout. And they towered right up, ten, fifteen feet high – the cool shadow of a bluff, they cast. God knows how deep. He made notes. He thought about her and made notes on the precise look of a shell. Five-Nines, they looked like, soiled and blebbed with rust. On some of them was stamped the name Krupp. The faintest whiff of gas, which had his heart beating faster. Geraniums – the smell of the geraniums on the kitchen windowsill in Youlster, for instance, when the sun warmed them.

It was in him, the sickness of it. He did not need to make notes. His lungs and windpipe were scribbled on with the sickness and the madness of it. This big bluff of rusting shells seemed to him to be stood at the finish; the war had done in humanity.

He thought: I'd give anything to be back in Derbyshire, before it. The damp old woods behind Youlster with their Indian camps, the shrubby moors stitched in stone, the stone circles patient and silent and a bit shy under the rain, the broad vowels of the lead miners, the heavy lumps of lead swapped with his mates, the Silver Coach service that chugged him off to school and back each day, the stink of cows on his boots off the short-cut through Oddo. His father. The carpets and incense sticks. Great-aunt Winifred's in Drop Street: he, the great-nephew, sitting in her bay window all morning, reporting to her. Who had passed, and with whom. What they were wearing. While she crocheted in the shadows in her black tent of a dress, nodding. It was all gone, he thought. And he guessed that the older he grew, the less it would hurt him. He would write to Ma tomorrow, send her a postcard.

No – she'd tell Aunt Maud, straight off. He chuckled at that.

He hung back when the others made their way along a pitted track to the motor-coach, Baz drifting about the girl. There were at least twenty yards between him and them. He actually got a kick out of choosing to be alone, a kind of inner lift, almost spiritual. He understood hermits in their caves, their vivid refusal that was a kind of call from the beyond. Though loneliness was the worst thing, lingering in the soul and clammy as fog.

The group paused by an old tumbled-in trench and he paused in turn. All he could hear was a distant unrest of rooks, the birds no doubt circling for the evening. When the group moved on, he moved on. Baz was still next to the creamy girl, playing the gallant, bending elegantly down, gently listening, nodding, smiling. So decent and English, was Baz. The smoke from the explosion had formed a mist above their heads and the summer haze on the plain's horizon was turning a sickly red. The air sat on the face and felt humid, despite the dust swirling about – just a thin crust of dryness above a bottomless sea.

Better to have come in the winter, in really foul wet weather. The ground wanting you inside it.

Now the ground rebuffed you, sent dust up. There was a soldier's button stuck in it, as if the earth had been officially stamped. In fact, the more he looked, the more he saw, as with stars at night – glinting metallic bits and bobs, more and more of them. He might have been walking the high-water marge of a beach, but here everything was cemented in. Just where it had fallen into the prehistoric mire, just where men had lurched in raw cold through fog and soddenness – oh, that was quite impossible to imagine now!

He thought he saw a set of dentures, but it was only a part of a gas-rattle. A pilchard jar here, the edge of a tarpaulin there, as stiff as concrete. Another pilchard jar, with gobbets of something in it. The working parts of something giant, a howitzer perhaps, scattered like a diagram. Picket-irons to catch the foot on, webbing, eyeless goggles. The liquid world had frozen it all in.

He must come back here at night, he realised. For the scale of it, in the darkness.

He arrived at the point where he had seen the others pause. Beyond the tumbled-in trench, crossed by a couple of planks, he saw a sign with heavy Gothic lettering, very weathered, and scores of rusty iron crosses at all angles, their long shadows broken up by clumps of waving yarrow. The gold of the early evening glowed in there, caught by the neglect.

A German cemetery. Purely German.

A group of charred trees stood in the middle, their bark peeling off and the wood very white underneath, but otherwise intact and leafy. He crossed the planks and entered the cemetery, staying by the first of the crosses. Of course it was important to him to see the purely German side. The crosses immediately around him were wooden, already bleached and split. The careful, signboard lettering on the cracker-shaped cross-pieces – that was touching: *Sold. Heinz Schumacher, Sold. Willy Stramm* . . . Others illegible, vanished. Why had the guide not entered the German cemetery? What had she said about it? Had she said, 'Rejoice – *there's* a good few killed . . .'?

A figure rose from one of the iron crosses a few yards away – it made him jump.

It was a woman, not a decaying soldier. She had been kneeling; the evening light and the high flowering yarrow had disguised her. He felt somewhat embarrassed, as if he ought to have a better reason for being here. He stood uncertainly, holding his hat in front of him, giving the briefest of nods. He was not even sure she had seen him, since her full mourning included a veil: as well nod at the Sphinx, for she stood very still, head a little inclined towards the graves, her long, heavy skirt emerging from a short jacket and making her look leaden, really weighted by grief.

He wandered about discreetly, eyes fumbling over the stark, solid ironwork, over the alien names. *Hans, Karl, Friedrich, Siegfried*. The big German fair-haired boys under their iron swords. A few had rusty helmets propped on their crosses; meditative, they looked. Or abashed. He felt uneasy, standing among them. Genuinely uneasy, as if he had come into the enemy. It was the woman who made him feel this, watching almost closely. Though when he looked up, she was turned away slightly, not watching him at all.

He felt definitely that he should be out of the place. He had perhaps ruined it for her – the communion with the loved one. A bright patch of cloth flowers lay against one of the end crosses a few rows up. 'Weep, maiden, weep here o'er the tomb of Love' – he knew a smattering of Goethe's lines, not even a whole poem, and nothing in German. And that line of Goethe's was wholly out of place, here. Death here was not apparent, it was as stolid as iron. Love is never lifeless, not really, it can be revived by the slightest trifle – Goethe was quite right. But death!

The trees rattled their dry leaves – there were leaves already fallen, caught in the scented yarrow. Then a familiar bark of motor horn. The coach, a dark lump in the distance. Then another, crude: they were waiting for him. He was irritated, suddenly, by this impatience, this crude disturbing of the gravity of the place.

A rustle near him: she was coming over.

He bowed his head a little as she stopped, the other side of a cross. He could see the features moving indistinctly beneath the dark spotted veil as she said something in German. It had a shrug in it, almost dreary, it was as if she was talking to an intimate.

'I'm very sorry,' he said, fumbling a little, 'but I am – English and – I don't have the language.'

His apology sounded thin, piping. He was flushed, very hot in the face with embarrassment. A brief silence, in which her head did not move.

'No more do I,' she said, suddenly, from within her veil.

Joseph was astonished: it was almost imperceptible, her foreignness. Yet she was not English. One word, let alone four, can tell you this.

Only then did he see what she had said. He had nothing to add, save a quote from Wordsworth; it sounded mawkish, here. So he nodded bashfully, mumbled an agreement, and bit his lip. The coach horn blared again. She ignored it, so he did. To leave directly, on that instant, would be somehow disrespectful. As if he had just popped in out of curiosity – but the place was too raw for that. The light, slanting across, was caught in the tall yarrow leaves and flowers, dusting them yellow and gold. They both stayed very still among the gaunt wood and iron and the goldeny clouds of weeds. His thoughts fluttered about, like moths caught in a jar. Yet it was only a matter of a minute or two, this impersonal, respectful stillness.

'I lost my son,' she threw out, suddenly. 'And my husband. My husband died when he heard the news. Poof, just like that, his heart bursting. So the stupid war killed him, too.'

She was not looking at him, her head was turned to the side, it was not at all accusing. But it was so direct! And Joseph felt immense relief, as if a coiled-up spring had been released.

'Ah, I am very sorry,' he said, too weakly.

Silence. It felt derisive: he could not come up to her level, he knew this. He wished he could. But there was nothing to say. The dead lay all about, demure and without needs or desires. He was almost envious.

'And all to no purpose,' she said, finally.

Again, he was floundering.

'Well,' she cried, before he had lit on a reply, 'I need a cigarette!'

He felt her veiled glance upon him, and thought about Hubert Rail puffing away on the beach. He fished the packet out and approached her, squeezing past the cross, and she threw back her veil and took one. She sat on the nearest grassy hump, leaning against the upright of a cross. This surprised him, he was almost shocked. He lit the cigarette for her. He smelt brandy on her breath, leaning to her. Then he lit one for himself. She sucked on the cigarette as if it gave her sustenance, blowing the smoke out with a hiss, her elbow on her knee, her black shoes peeping from under her long, ugly dress.

She looked at him and smiled. She was about thirty-eight, he reckoned, with a face that was thin and rather ineffectual, rather worn out. Very pale, even in the reddish-gold light of a summer's evening – unless it was the leaden black around it that 'threw forward' the white, as Mr Douse would put it.

'Now we can go home,' she said.

'I suppose so, yes.'

She looked about her, her mouth pursed.

'It was not as I thought, actually.'

'No, not as I thought either.'

He was very glad of the cigarette, it occupied him – what an actor friend called 'business'. There were no fresh flowers on any of the graves.

'My son was hit here, they told me.'

'Just here?'

'Oh, maybe. Round about here, I suppose.'

She waved her black-gloved hand.

'How awful,' he remarked.

He pulled on his cigarette, almost twitching. Then he opened his mouth again but she interrupted.

'And you? Why did you come in here?'

The woman was studying him with a tired, dry look. He explained – what there was to explain: about the dead having no nationalisms.

'All men have to die,' she said. 'And there are many ways of dying. Even when you are not dead.'

Her accent – there was something odd about it, something familiar, but not German.

'Your English is excellent.'

'Thank you. My father worked in the German Embassy in India. I was brought up for a considerable time there. Calcutta. I had an Indian *aya*.'

Yes, she had an Indian lilt in her voice. She might even have black blood in her. Her eyes were dark enough, with a kind of bruised area around them. He dragged deeply on his cigarette and blew the smoke out in golden clouds.

'You must have been here,' she said.

'Well – in a way, yes.'

'Oh? You either were or you weren't, surely.'

The way she said 'weren't'– just like an educated Hindoo, that final drum-tap of the tongue. He thought of the *joss* in his father's shop, waving its many arms. Another wretched god!

'Or were you too young?' she went on. 'How old are you? I suppose you might be eighteen after all.'

'I'm nearly twenty-four,' Joseph told her, piqued. 'I was in France, not Belgium. I didn't kill anyone. Not many people wanted to, you know. Actually kill someone.'

A short, high laugh from her – ever so caustic. It grated.

'Quite innocent, are you? Oh, the English always are. I remember my father saying that, in India. They do not even *know* they are despots, he would say—'

'The guilty ones are the old men, not the young boys. It's nothing to do with being English.'

'The young boys? My husband was forty-nine.' She gave a contemptuous toss of her head.

'I'm very sorry,' he said, again.

She gave another brief laugh and looked down at the ground, the cigarette smoking in her fingers. The gusts of wind rippled the ribbons at her neck and tugged the smoke away. The wretched motor horn went again.

'Are they your people?' she asked.

Joseph gave a little grimace, as if to say – theoretically, yes.

'I think they are jolly impatient for you!'

There was a horribly large botfly on his knee. He gave it a slap with his straw hat.

'Are you on foot?'

She nodded.

'Would you like a lift?'

'I am quite all right,' she said.

Baz was appearing now on the path, hurrying towards them in his rather shambly way.

Joseph parted from the German widow with a handshake; her hand was floppy, like a doll's, but quite warm under the kidskin. Reticent yet appealing, as if wanting to be tugged. He assumed he would never see her again. The conversation between them struck him as somehow motionless; he reflected on it as he walked towards Baz. There was a lingering scent of peppermint on his hand. Baz was making silly jokes about 'fraternising with the enemy'.

'She was brought up in India,' Joseph said. 'Speaks English like a native. I mean like a Hindoo.'

'Who was?'

'The woman I was talking to.'

'Oh, her. Looked like a doll, the type girls cut out of paper and put paper clothes on. I was talking about the enemy below ground. Tasteless, sorry.'

A silence, then.

'Not a German, this woman?' asked Baz, in order to break it.

'Oh yes, or so she said. Lost her son and then her husband. Her husband—'

'By the way,' said Baz, 'Nietzsche said it before you.'

'Said what?'

'That the times are sick. The very word, *sick. A sick, weird period.*'

The motor-coach was turning over its engine, coughing a little. The others gave Joseph a rather filthy look as he got on – except for Tillie. There was an empty seat next to her and he bagged it.

'I was sitting there,' said Baz.

'There's one at the back.' It was next to the jowly harridan with the parasol.

'Splendid, splendid,' said Baz. 'What a gracious stinker you are.'

Then the motor-coach jolted into movement and Joseph had to give him a hand up off the floor. Tillie was trying not to giggle. The evangelical snag in her character seemed more absurd than ever, for she was even handsomer wreathed in smiles, her gloved finger pressed to her lips. Perhaps it was all a front. Joseph decided to flirt, almost despite himself.

'I hope you don't mind being deprived of my dear pal's company, but he is shortly to be married and I reckoned, well, how I ought to put him out of temptation's way.'

She frowned, as if not quite getting his drift. He felt stranded on an atoll of his own construction. He cleared his throat.

'How are you finding it?'

'Finding what?'

'This queer little odyssey.'

'I'm going to come every year,' she said. 'I've just decided.'

The motor-coach rattled and bumped over holes.

'Until I'm too old,' she added. 'Or until I'm passed away.'

She was very serious, oh yes – he could see her coming here in fifty, sixty years. Though the rest of it was unimaginable, everything else bar the graves and fields and the little old lady among them. And there was this powdery bloom on her cheeks – it was the dust, really – which made the old maid growing in her seem almost there already.

'I think your brother's very lucky.'

She turned and looked at him dead-on; he could have kissed her, although the coach was jolting her around a bit. He certainly had the desire to kiss her.

'*Lucky?*'

She seemed quite put out.

'To have you to remember him. It's the most any of us can expect, really.'

She ignored the theological impropriety, but blinked at it nevertheless.

'It's not a question of luck,' she said, 'it's duty.'

There was something, some little musty whiff that blew from her then, as if she had just crawled out from behind a chapel organ. Joseph pulled a bit of a face.

'I don't care what they call it, he's still lucky.'

'I'm a vessel to be filled,' she said. 'We all are. We just have to open ourselves up. He waits for us to open ourselves to Him. It can happen at any moment.'

He nodded blankly. Jesus and her brother *were* lucky. She got out her pocket Bible and showed him various passages, licking the tip of her glove before she turned the thin pages. As he leaned towards her to look, pressing against her slightly, he could smell sweat mixed up with the lemony tang of her scent. It was most agreeable. He noticed how smooth her neck was, rising in a curve from the lace collar. He forced himself to stick to admiring noises as she murmured the texts – he knew most of them anyway, they reminded him of Sunday school with Mrs Barber – until they stopped with a lurch and Ostrich gave out lemonade in small glasses. The lemonade was warm and flat.

'Well, for this much thanks, Miss Lainer,' he said, raising his glass. 'Here's to love and peace.'

'How do you know my name?'

'Extraordinary, isn't it? I guessed, and I was right.'

Her mouth puckered into a smile and he felt his chest contract around his heart.

'I'm Joseph Monrow, by the way. Jo-Jo to friends.'

'Hallo, Mr Monrow,' she said, and drank.

A drop of lemonade gleamed on her lower lip. Joseph had to calm himself down by chatting about his father's shop. She had not known it. Why should she have done? She was too young even now to buy carpets, Indian or otherwise. Stockport's a long way from Matlock, though her folk did take rides into the Peaks once a year, Kinder Scout and that. She put away her little Bible. He had half a mind to quote the bits he could remember from the Song of Solomon. Something was emerging in him, a sort of flower. It made his voice hoarse and he shut right up.

They stopped again at Hyde Park Corner, where a huge half-built rotunda gleamed in the ebbing light behind scaffolding and heaps of sand. The sand was hot to touch, almost scorching. The guide located where they were in relation to the 'battlefield', spreading the map on the ground. The group stood in a circle around it, Baz squeezing himself between Tillie and Joseph.

'One feels like a Saharan explorer,' Baz said. 'Most romantic eh?'

The wretch is sticking up to Tillie like mad, Joseph thought. It's hideous. But it's more hideous caring about it – I don't care a fig, how can I? I've only just met her and she's dotty about Jesus.

Yet when he looked at her, leaning a little forward beyond Baz, his heart was suspended for a moment, hovered like a bird in his throat. Just for a moment, a split-second even. That told him things, though. He was almost smiling at himself, but not quite. He was too overcome. He could not study it like you study a page. He just relinquished himself to the electrical charge – for the moment.

It was a very fine evening, very summery: you forgot the drought, once the sun was reddening, going down. The moon was coming up the other side, a proper harvest moon, corn-coloured and full. The group strolled in twos and threes through the broken wintry remnants of Ploegsteert Wood: a few, a very few, birds, flitting between the odd claw of a branch. Otherwise, quite still and silent between the ivy-clad stelae. As if the place was waiting for something, some savage rite to bring up the sap again. Joseph one side of Tillie, Baz the other. She was definitely inclining more towards Baz, Joseph could see that. His friend was saying all the right things. They had both lost brothers, for a start. The light was comfortingly burnished on the dead stumps.

'This is absurd,' said Joseph.

'What is?' asked Baz.

'*Why* are we here?'

They had stopped, because Joseph had stopped. Tillie inclined her head.

'You mean, in this wood?'

He spread his arms wide.

'An evening stroll in the woods. But why? These aren't woods.'

'Whoever said they were?' said Baz.

'Well, I didn't.'

Baz shook his head, perplexed. Joseph felt split between intense vexation and a low dull throb of passion. He let his arms drop with a sigh.

'It just seems – not good,' was all he could say. He was definitely mashed on the girl. He could not find the right words, inwardly breathless. It was exasperating, all this.

She touched his arm. 'It brings it back, that's why,' she said, in her soft lisp. 'It brings it all back, for you. I'm a nurse, or nearly one. I know what it did, the war. I'm still looking after your – your companions. For my sins.'

'For all our sins,' Joseph murmured.

He had lied to her, hadn't he? – and so now he was blushing.

Fortunately, Baz was out of earshot. Her hand left his arm. It had given him a faint electric shock. At least, that is what it felt like.

They motored back to town. He was bumping about next to the jowly harridan, who refused to engage in conversation. He knew she had lost a son at Clapham Junction, where Hanley had bought it, but he did not consider this a suitable topic. She clutched the top of the seat in front and stared grimly out, her whole face gravitating downwards like treacle on the side of a jar. He thought of Tillie's neck, the pale and tender smoothness of it. The coach took in a mile or two of the Menin Road to Hellfire Corner, before turning back towards town. He tried to picture Tillie's breasts, but they kept backing away in a sort of fog. They were beyond anything he could imagine: whatever he *could* imagine was false.

The old woman piped up, all of a sudden.

'What's the longest rope in the world, young man?'

'A hangman's rope?'

'Europe,' she said, lugubriously.

And turned back to the twilit bleakness, that was almost like a sea.

11

Vor Tau und Tag

B ACK AT THE hotel, the three made arrangements for dinner. They dressed, met in the salon, and headed for the Grote Markt. It was still hot. Tillie had changed into a calf-length frock on the same lines as the creamy version, only this one was navy with little yellow leaves: Joseph remarked on it gallantly.

'Six shillings post free from the model factory in Belfast,' she said, briskly.

He rallied, though.

'Well, my hideously swell evening jacket's a hand-me-down. Free as the wind.'

The dress was cut a bit lower than the other: you could see the knobs of her collarbone moving under the tender skin, the faint white tidemark where the relentless sun of the last few weeks had not touched it. A delicate Chinese shawl was drawn low over her shoulders and she had removed her gloves, showing fine, animated fingers. She's not a Chapel puritan, he thought. Just a touch enthusiastic. In love with Jesus: Jesus as her paramour. A few years back, at fourteen, he'd been in love with Mary Magdalene.

He took her arm to guide her safely across the road – the drivers of carts and motor-cars were mischievously in league, here. They hurried across between hubs and tyres and tinkling bicycles, frowning and smiling at the same time. From the fluid way she moved along beside him, he conjectured that she was wearing a lightweight corset. She removed her arm the minute they reached the pavement, but the cool touch of it lingered (Hubert Rail was quite right on that one, he thought). The crook of her elbow was bare where the sleeve ended – alas, Joseph's was not; he could easily have gone bohemian and sauntered out in his shirtsleeves, like so many of the working men around him, but he had wanted to impress. Baz wore a serge suit and stiff collar.

There was a restaurant opposite the cathedral ruins: it was shorn off just above head height, the few courses of new brick topped by a ramshackle roof in wood and tarred paper. The wretched state of the façade concealed a neat little place with lamps made of shell cases, the brass polished to a mirror shine. The tables outside were all taken and they ended up in a dark, coolish corner.

Joseph had a headache by now, too much sun or not enough sleep; yet he was vibrant with emotion, looking about keenly, excited by it all. The restaurant was full of burly types who in England would be supping on sausages and mash for sixpence in some brown eating house. Here the food was French and redolent with garlic – it turned out to be snails, to Tillie's horror. Joseph adored snails and persuaded her to try one. Baz tutted. She closed her eyes tight and chewed its gristle. Her lips glistened with oil; she pouted them in a mew of distaste and stuck to her omelette and chips. Baz was fawning on her, his face near hers, so Joseph turned the conversation to the engagement.

'And Agnes is a brilliant musician, you know.'

'I play the harmonium, but I'm not brilliant,' said Tillie.

'Really? I think you might be, deep down. Where are you planning to get married, Baz?'

'It's not decided. Agnes wants – oh, it's too complicated.'

He was rather thrown, was Baz, and drank in recompense – they whisked through one jug of hot-blue wine and ordered another. Tillie stuck to water, but there was no temperance speech.

Joseph knew better than to get tipsy, let alone properly screwed, in front of a sober girl you desire. He sipped at his glass and watched Baz become less and less attractive under the influence. His good nature was chafed away to its maudlin layer. Even his spotted tie was askew.

'I believe that everything went wrong when Scott perished. I haven't been happy since.'

'Oh Baz, I've seen you smile since 1912.'

'One man dying can't change the world,' Tillie said, 'unless they're called Jesus.'

How on earth, Joseph thought, could he be mashed on her? But the enthusiasm was like a feverish condition; it would pass. She was barely nineteen. He would release her from it.

'Do you like being a nurse?'

'Not very much. I don't like mess.'

'Duty, then.'

'Ay – duty.'

She looked at him with glancing, almost mocking eyes. He imagined her scrubbing patients clean, then washing herself hard, all over, with a big amber cake of Pears Soap. He could not imagine it well enough. There was something absolutely impassive about her, underneath the fluttery religion, the dreamy mockery of the eyes. It was this impassive beauty that had provoked the conceited Jesus side, he conjectured. The conceit was a mask. It hid the beauty of her natural face as well as might a pagan's solid mask of wood and straw in Africa. There were many ways of dulling appetites. Only in his case it did the opposite: it did not deflect him at all – it drew him.

Lucky Jesus.

'The fact is,' Baz drawled, 'God was against them. They shouldn't have perished in that little tent. In the white wastes. So lonely, all frozen. All I know is I haven't been happy since.'

'Baz, that might be something to do with the fact that in 1912 your mother passed away and you were sent south to boarding school—'

'I scarcely remember that,' Baz said. 'What I remember is Scott's little tent and the death of heroes and the white desolate wastes.'

He took a good gulp of wine. He looked as if he was about to cry.

'How old were you then?' asked Tillie, puzzled. 'You can't have been that young, nine years ago.'

'Just fifteen,' said Baz, 'when they died.' As if it was proof of something. And belched.

The babble of voices around them rose as more people pressed in: it was truly of all the nations. Tongues they could not identify, as well as Italian, Spanish, Polish, Russian. There were several Chinese and some Indian fellows in flannel suits. Despite his abstemiousness, Joseph felt light-headed; images of the wasteland they had just left swirled over Tillie's silken face, golden now in the lamplight.

'I hope this is a respectable place,' she said, pulling her silken shawl close about her. 'Is it respectable?'

'Oh, very, The Ritz of Wipers,' Joseph smiled.

'That's not saying a great deal, I don't think.' And did not smile.

She was flaunting herself a little, all that provocative, superior side: but she was also worried, he could see that. She was being drawn in. This was not Stockport: there were none of the same rules to apply.

And just then a noisy group of English fellows came in – northerners, too! They hovered by the bar, swaffing beer; her ears pricked up and she looked over almost expectantly. Joseph was terrified that she would know one of them. They might have been Derbyshire lead miners, from their accent and build and lead-coloured skin: dark grey, their faces were, eyes rolling about very white. Their booming voices established them in the dynamite line; blowing things up in a place where things had been blown up for four years. He listened keenly above the hubbub. They were *thee*-ing and *thou*-ing. He visited the outside loo (which was revolting) and hovered behind them for a few moments.

'I know what that big thump was about, earlier,' he said, returning. 'The one with a lot of white smoke. It was a premature explosion. It killed somebody, I can't catch who, I think maybe a Chinese sapper.'

'The war's Parthian shot,' said Baz, and raised his glass. 'Will it ever die?'

'How awful,' said Tillie. 'To think we saw the smoke. I'd have said a prayer.'

'What they ought to damn well do,' Baz slurred, his face flushed and glistening, 'is to get the *generals* to do it.'

'Not the Germans?' said Tillie. 'The German prisoners?'

Joseph gave her a sardonic smile. 'Chinese, Germans, Belgians – it's all the same, isn't it? Not English, at any rate.'

'I'm afraid so,' said Tillie, mysteriously. And left it at that.

The waitress told them, on being asked, that the German prisoners had all been sent home because they were too depressed to work properly.

'*N'y a pus*,' she said, in her Flanders dialect. They'd been content to see them leave. '*Les pauvres garçons.*' She left with a shuddery sigh.

'*Napoo*,' echoed Baz, his finger in the air. 'The only French our Tommies picked up, Tillie. It means, there ain't no more where that come from, mate. And even then they made it sound Hindoo.'

'I think she was in love with one of them,' said Joseph.

'Damn scribbler,' grunted Baz. 'Fabulator, Joseph Monrow.' His Derbyshire twang was back, underneath the clipped southernness.

'I? I a fabulator? I deal only in truths. Else I'd be fooling about in London, taking cocaine and dancing all night. Or go to Italy, maybe. Greece. Paris. Instead I'm in the Chilterns, quite near Rickmansworth, all alone in my damp cottage. Because I'm dealing in truths. It's cracking, by the way. The walls are cracking. I've had to get in a plasterer. But I labour on, oh yes. The knight errant in the middle of the wood. The Holy Grail of truth.'

Maybe the wine had touched him. He was not altogether serious, his wagging finger saw to that; though like a playfully choppy sea, he had calm blue depths of seriousness underneath. An unwelcome vision of Walter intruded. He looked down at the table.

'I didn't know you wrote,' Tillie said.

'I do.'

He suddenly shrivelled, he knew it, in her eyes.

'What were you thinking I did?'

She looked at him with her head on one side.

'Maybe a potter? A painter?'

Evidently, she had not thought about it until now. Baz chortled.

'I know what *you* are,' she said, to Baz. 'You're going to be a very red-faced judge who nods off all the way through the evidence and then wakes up for the sentence.'

Baz certainly found this amusing. Joseph was distraught, somewhere very deep down.

She tucked a stray curl behind her ear and nodded sadly.

'Yes,' she said, 'my dear brother was always talking about truths. Vital ones, usually.'

'So was mine,' Baz announced.

Joseph allowed a little caustic grunt to escape. Hanley was raddled before he was twenty, a complete dissolute: his truths were brandy, cigars and indecorous women. God knows how he got on as an officer at the Front, except that he was also a bully.

'My cousin Alfred was the most gifted member of our family,' he said.

'Where did he fall?'

'He didn't really fall anywhere. That was Roger, another cousin. Alfred stumbled a bit, probably. Then he came home and started seeing things, screaming at the dinner table and so forth. He's now in an asylum. I believe the only thing that calms him down is Chopin.'

'Chopin?' She said this with an air of faint distaste.

'Particularly the waltzes. You'd think it would be the Death March or maybe the Nocturnes. Even one of the Preludes. But no, it's the waltzes, the brightest glittering sort that make you want to dance. By the way –' he could see her face settling into a faraway sadness – 'do you like dancing, Tillie?'

He had been too sour in tone. He had to make up for it. She blinked uncertainly.

'The Devil can dance one to death.'

'Do you believe in the Devil?'

'Yes.'

'So do I,' murmured Baz, filling his glass.

She gave him an arch look. 'Then why do you drink?'

'I like it.'

'I think we ought to go back,' she said.

It was getting livelier in there, almost like a beer shop. She tensed, glancing around her. Joseph asked her about family, drawing her back. It wasn't so bad that she'd thought him a potter: bohemian, she really meant. Her father, whom she loved very much, was a part-time Chapel preacher and the manager of a small brush factory in Manchester. Her mother played the harmonium for the hymns. They were both part of some ash-grey Reformed persuasion or other with a redbrick warehouse for a chapel somewhere downwind of the old mills, from what Joseph could gather – straight out of *Hard Times*. They had never cried about her brother Ralph, they had sort of swallowed it straight and then started hearing his voice. He spoke to them during services. He was waving to them from the sky – they saw him on walks, waving to them. This had created scenes, resulting in their expulsion from that denomination. They now held meetings in their living room and were gaining an enthusiastic attendance. Other dead lads were now speaking.

Baz foolishly likened it to the Ouija board, which rather upset her. The dead lads only spoke during prayer and the voices weren't 'queer', they were angelic voices translated into the bodily realm. Had she heard Ralph in her head? No, she had not. Only her dad had. This gave Joseph hope. The business about the dead speaking through mediums was as common as salt, of late: even he reckoned that so many millions of young lives cut abruptly short must have had some effect on the ether. All those life-loving boys – they cannot have been content just to disappear without a trace, without a single trace, from one moment to the next. Some sort of hanging about must have occurred. Some sort of haunting. God, yes. Ectoplasmic clouds around the memorials. Bloodied faces smiling at you from shop windows. Shadows in the moonlight, whispers in the ear.

'Does Ralph talk about the life to come?' he asked, half-seriously.

'Not really,' she said. 'Not in any detail.'

'You see, I've always wondered whether they have tablecloths.'

'Sorry?'

'For the feasts on the heavenly lawns. But then again, maybe they don't have ants in Heaven.'

'I expect they don't,' she said. The way she said it, he felt crushed.

She looked about her. The place was a seethe of happy gluttony, but not offensively so, not like it might have been in England. As far as they could tell, only their northern compatriots were being offensive – about the 'Continentals', needless to say. It was an army habit, that. But it was all quick words in virtual dialect, no one else noticed. Joseph knew from her look that Tillie did not believe this thing about Ralph, deep down. She wanted to change the subject. He asked her why her parents had not accompanied her; again, that evasive glance.

'Ralph is on the celestial plane now. His death-place is irrelevant. Just so much slime.'

'So why are *you* here, then?'

She smiled uncertainly, her forehead creased in a little frown.

'I don't rightly know,' she said. 'I just reckoned that someone had to.'

'Pilgrimage.'

Her smile broadened, eyes aglitter. She absently rubbed the soft silk of her shawl between finger and thumb. 'Ay, that's right.'

She had worked as a factory hand in her father's place, tarring brushes. She had insisted on it – most of the men had gone off to fight and her father was taking on their womenfolk. Now she wanted to be a missionary nurse in Africa. The prospect was appalling to Joseph: she'd succumb to some ghastly disease within weeks. As she was talking, he could see her vivid features thin and pale and wither away, leaving only a pair of huge and bewildered eyes. It was too much. Her creepy enthusiasm had to be redirected. If she had been born out of the malign influence of her parents, she might have been an artist, a society beauty, a fabulous dancer. But she wasn't. What was she, then? Oh, she was a kid-gloved, simple girl – she knew nothing, really. He could not be *truly* smit on her, not to the great depths of proper love. How *could* he be?

There was a contempt in his denial; quite ugly, it was.

They left the restaurant and on the way out Joseph could see she was holding the men. It was almost lewd, the way she held them so innocently. But it did excite him. Baz did not notice, he was too drunk, too tall. All of a sudden, Joseph felt he was down at the level of the girl, that they were two dark little things scurrying along on the bottom almost gleefully while Baz was swaying about right up high.

They walked around the square, the girl between them: a very demure trio, very English, to the wilder stuff around them. Teeth shone in the lamplight, thick eyebrows, knotted sets of muscles. All this rebuilding struck Joseph as somehow passionate and absurd and barren. One knocked things down to build them up again, that was the human way.

He was talking like this, a bit excited. He felt terribly cheerful. It was the effect of the girl who had brought her redbrick chapel along with her and her queer persuasion, planted it in the middle of all this aggressive indecency. Exposed buildings, exposed people, stale cadavers lying beyond the broken outer walls, the lurid red of the sunset gathering into darkness, the heat beating off the rubble piled in heaps or not piled at all, still scattered. He could sense the girl's pale, tender body moving under her clothes and trembled with excitement as he talked, though his words hardly showed it. It was quite absurd, what he was feeling. He imagined himself holding her toes, for some reason, just holding them as one does any live thing – a duckling, say. Then there came a moment when they took off from the safety of the square, down a thin street without lamps. It was quiet, that was why they took it. The noise had bewildered them.

'Do you like walking out with men?' said Baz, quite inappropriately. He had sobered up a bit, outside. He was very serious – his seriousness broke through a load of drink, even.

'Oh come on, Baz,' scoffed Joseph.

There was an awkward silence. It was not such an odd question, though, Joseph thought. Things had loosened up and one had to debate it; it was like a social query. It would have been insulting a few years earlier. He wished he had not broken in like that. It gave him away.

'I've worked in a factory,' was her reply, eventually.

She lifted her head a little as if in challenge.

'Only dirty minds see any wrong in it,' she added. 'Or those who wish to keep the woman in the jailhouse.'

Baz gave a gruff, serious laugh. Always serious, always weighing up, an invisible ball in each hand.

The whole street was still wrecked but there were shelters in the wrecked plots, people cooking there. It was a secret life in the darkness, spotted with the glow of lamplight and little stoves on iron paws. Murmurs and growls and the odd harsh laugh. Faces and eyes. It was the queerest street any of them had ever walked, like an oriental souk. Above one blistered door there was a carefully-painted sign in German, *vor Tau und Tag*, perhaps a bar once. Why had it survived? Why had even the door survived? Tillie wanted to know what it meant.

'"Before dew and daylight,"' Joseph said, who knew poetic tags like this in quite a few languages. 'At break of day, really, but a prettier way of putting it.'

She assumed from this that he could speak the language fluently, but Baz ruined it by scoffing. Someone halfway down was playing a guitar and singing. Italian songs, maybe Sicilian. They stopped to listen in the shadows opposite, standing back from the street in the wreck of a bombed-out house with nothing left of the front wall but a window framed in brick. The bits and pieces might have been a city in miniature. It reminded Baz yet again of Pompeii, only there was much more of Pompeii left. He was talking about Pompeii as if he had been there, not just crouched over some postcard views. Joseph knew a few lines from the Schiller poem – he had been quite mad on Schiller at Oxford, had even tried to grow his hair as long and considered wearing a thin sword (he would have been arrested, however). He declaimed it standing on a heap of bricks:

> Is there life in the abyss? –
> Hath a new race (concealed till now) its home
> Under the lava? – Doth the Past return? –
> O Greeks! – O Romans – Come! –

Tillie found it amusing. He was doing quite well, on that score. Baz was shaking his head.

'I loathe Schiller,' he said. 'Romantic claptrap.'

In fact, Joseph thought, the whole place was more like the Roman villa some farmer had uncovered on the moors near Youlster; just a ground plan in orange brick, a slew of thick broken tiles. Or like somewhere in Syria.

It was hot enough for that, even at night. They sat gingerly on the remains of a wall. Baz whispered that it was hard to believe this was a stricken field, and burped.

'It was somebody's home,' Tillie replied, 'not a field.'

Joseph vaguely wished Baz would go off to bed. The full moon was shielded only lightly by a ribbed sweep of cloud, and it gleamed on their faces and the twisted remains of an iron bed. The window, sticking up virtually on its own, looked absurd. The singer with the guitar started on a passionate, almost angry song; they could not see him but he was very close, just over the street behind a wall of tarpaulin.

'Can we be in Flanders?' Joseph said, with an exaggerated sweep of his hand. 'That wet northern place of sturdy burghers and dry trade?'

'Sounds like Stockport,' said Tillie.

'Maybe it's changed forever,' said Baz. He started humming along to the song, strumming an invisible guitar, knocking a button off his jacket in the process. Joseph had never seen him so jolly.

But the ruins themselves were crumbling, one could see that. It would all be put up again. Waiting for the others in the hotel, he had read the local paper, complaining how hard it was to keep a ruin upright. Or maybe he had missed the sardonic tone in the clear-eyed French. To keep a ruin intact requires effort, skill and care, it had claimed. Yes, maybe it was an angry article, underneath. A faint whiff of lemons every time she moved.

There in the shadows, next to the Stockport beauty, in someone's wrecked home whiskered by weeds, he was quite happy with ruins. Possibility were what ruins suggested, along with the poignancy: in the uncertain moonlight and flicker of flame, they had the happy suggestion of Keats's faery castle. The music throbbed in his veins. Tillie turned to him once or twice and her lips gleamed in a smile. The gloss of hair above the pale sweep of neck, the bare forearms, the perfume of lemons, the soft brush of her silk shawl: oh, Joseph longed for her now. He had lost the foothold of caution. Now he was falling.

'The rose-lipt girls of youth,' he murmured.

Baz sagged, suddenly. 'I think I'm a little crocked up,' he said.

Then, like a miracle, he announced that he was going back to the hotel. With a bit of a stagger he bade the others goodnight and disappeared, negotiating the rubble with surprising ease. He was clearly about to be sick. It was a proper miracle.

Tillie had stood and made as if to follow but, springing to his feet without time to think, Joseph held her by the crook of the arm.

'You're off duty tonight,' he said.

She had tensed for a moment, her whole body tensed, and then relaxed. He felt terrifically bold and carefree, standing just behind her, the two of them alone and somehow illicit. Gently, ever so gently, he pulled her towards him as the guitar thumped and strummed. Her face was invisible, in deep shadow cast by the swinging curls of her hair, bobbed thick at the jaw line. A group passed down the street, carrying a burning torch as if in a carnival. The noises, the flickering light, the heat, the wild, mocking laughter: they might have been cast back five hundred years. The sense of the roughness of life, of endless possibilities.

It seemed to take just as many centuries to pull her towards him, but was a matter of seconds. She was face-on to him, now.

He stole an arm around her slim waist and, not feeling any resistance beyond the solid weight of her, applied pressure on the small of her back as one presses air slowly out of a lilo. Complicated, at first, her body was – and then mysteriously simple, as if a rebellious tangle of forms had turned shapely, fluid. She was breathing very quickly and it was loud in his ear. Helplessly stood as if about to dance a close waltz, bosom to thigh, they stayed like that for a moment.

Pressed against him, the whole hot fullness of her.

He touched her chin, where the scar was. She flinched, a tiny flinch. The scar was a little raised thread that he rubbed with the ball of his thumb.

'This makes you,' he said, very quietly.

Her face remained in shadow against the moonlight, and there was an aureole around her – alarming, almost – made by the frizz of her hair. He could not see whether she smiled or not, though he felt every flicker of her chin under the scar. Then her head moved forward and her cheek touched his, retracted a little as if scalded, and journeyed back again to rest there, smooth as kidskin. He was sure that his heart must be bruising her bosom. He felt excessively hungry for her – such a rage of an appetite! Yet he controlled himself with a quivering tautness, pressing himself a fraction closer to her, picturing the look on her face as one of absolute astonishment, even panic. Her cheek was hot and this heat stole straight into his loins and down into his calves, which were vaguely trembling as if he was attached to a generator. His left eye was lidded by various curls of her hair, which smelt sweetly of smoke and scent. He had forgotten how delicious it was to hold a girl close, above all when there was the imminent expectation that one might fluff it. The music wound its tendrils around them like ivy, they might have been a stone sculpture in an Italian garden. Half-formed, unfinished, all passionate intention. They might have been fused by some violent volcanic blast. His foot had cramp.

His lips slid onto hers.

Then the music stopped.

She shifted slightly with a small sigh, pulling her lips away, opening them as though surfacing from water. They had remained tight shut, pursed even! She was breathing even faster now, short sharp breaths that were akin to those of fear. He wondered if she was actually incapable of volition because of it, that his dominion over her was that of shock. Her Chapel swaying with the shock.

He tried to flex his foot in his pumps but the cramp stayed. The puffs of her breath had blackberry on them – the jet-black blackberry pastilles she had sucked on after dinner to remove the taste of the snail. Someone walked past with an oil-lamp and its rays caught the polish of her eyes. It was like spotting some sort of woodland creature, a goblin perhaps – he was quite startled. Still neither of them moved. Rose-lipt girls, he murmured again in his head, feeling no need to remember the rest of the poem. A fiddle started off somewhere near and then stopped.

'Let me be,' she murmured.

'I don't think so,' Joseph replied, without thought.

Then the queerest thing happened: he found his lips squashed against hers. *She* was kissing *him*.

It was a desperate thing, her kissing. He felt her teeth, she was more teeth than she was lip. It was furiously done. There was little pleasure in it for him and he found it a job to breathe. She pressed hard against him, his back against the brick of a shattered wall no higher than his shoulder blades and shaky – his elbow knocked a brick off. She was swallowing him whole, starting with his mouth: she had never kissed before, he thought. Yet the plump, moist tongue was filling his mouth, darting about in there, finding something. You might suck an orange that way. Another brick fell with a thump as he made fumbling attempts to undo her frock at the back, a fiendish device of ribbons and buttons, while his chest strove to work against the soft compression of her bust.

The warmth of her began to fill him: he enjoyed that.

Then her hands gripped the back of his neck so that he was clamped. She was making low sounds as she kissed, he could feel the vibrations of the sound on her tongue and the roof of her mouth. He clutched her as if for life and felt her teeth on his upper lip. The wall dropped a few more bricks, from the sound of it. He felt he might topple backwards, the whole wall with him. At one point she appeared to be sucking on his tongue like a boiled sweet. He fumbled with the ribbons and got nowhere, the slippery Chinese shawl caught in his fingers. Now he craved the actual tender flesh of her, he inwardly begged his hands to have the white nakedness under them, one of them kneading the thin crook of her waist. He did not even consider the indecency of it, a few yards away from the street, scarcely in the shadows. There was a cheeky whistle at one point, too.

And then he was alone, holding air.

She had torn herself away with a queer grunt, stumbled across the weeds and rubble and disappeared down the street towards the main square. Joseph wiped his mouth on his sleeve, took a deep life-saver's breath – and raced after her, towards a far-off glare of lamplight. Against it, her slender hurrying form was a shaky silhouette. Shouts and whistles followed him. He weaved between a group of couples arm in arm, all singing. Part-singing, it sounded like.

Catching up with her, he tried to take her arm. She sank to her knees, quietly sobbing, with an even more glorious aureole around her dishevelled hair. He felt ugly, inside – almost panicked by it.

'Go away,' she said.

'Why are you crying?'

She buried her face in her hands and shook it slowly from side to side.

He was not at all sure what to do.

'I think you can change,' he said. 'I think I can help you change.'

'How?'

'By – loving you. You are beautiful, you know.'

'Oh no,' she moaned. As if that was the last thing he should have said.

'It's not so terrible, being beautiful.'

He could see her in Stockport, going the same way as all the others: Chapel, children, a stolid husband on the board of this and that. Or spinsterhood, given the lack of men. Yes, he could see her as a spinster nurse, doing good, withering into charity and doing good. Discarded, in a way.

Her face was grey now, in the horrid light. Bruised and not very beautiful after all. Yet another sting of desire rose in him; soft and almost bestial, the way her body turned in his head. He touched his mouth, still wet from hers.

'I wish I was thirteen again,' she said, sniffing.

'Why?'

'Life had manners, then.'

'Manners?'

'You know. Life didn't come at you, in your own head. I wish – how it was, when I was a girl.'

'Well, it can't be.'

'I know.'

'I wasn't trying to hurt you.'

'I know.'

'Well then.'

'I'm going to pay for it, aren't I?' she said.

'For what?'

'Oh – for feeling like this.'

'In general, or right now?'

There was only a sigh in response. He felt himself tightening inside. There was something urging him on, some will that would not melt. It was not as if his feelings had turned to ash in his mouth: they had kissed, she had wanted him, he had not behaved like the pig her tears implied. No, not at all. It was coquettish, really, this behaviour. She was distressed, but more by her own confusion. It was the crack in the wall of her Jesus worship. Maybe her prayers were as ferocious. Catholic, Spanish Catholic even. Underneath the Protestant sheets.

His thoughts whirled. People passed, laughing. Like mockery, it was. Sheer mockery.

He bent down to her, almost crouching.

'You're a rare precious flower,' he said. 'I'd do nothing to hurt you. I wouldn't dream of it.'

His hand touched her elbow.

'Love has its own rules and manners, you know,' he went on. 'It's not all cosy, love isn't.'

'What *kind* of love do you mean?'

She sounded disdainful. Curious faces passed them, glimpsed in the flare of the gaslight. He sat on his heels, next to her. He was desperate for a smoke.

'Whatever is necessary,' he said, 'for us. Don't you see? There's—'

His hat fell off – her hand had brushed him away and struck his straw hat.

In retrieving it, a little startled, dazed even, he lost her — that is, she scrambled to her feet and sped off. He had time to notice a determined, set look on her face. There was something dropped at his feet — it was the shawl. A cheap thing, she wouldn't come back for it. He stuffed it into the pocket of his jacket as best he could and trotted along behind her, quite a way behind her, striding and then breaking into a trot to keep up. He tasted blood on his lip, from her teeth. She slipped along the side of the Grote Markt and disappeared into the hotel. He stopped and watched her disappear through the door from the middle of the square, feeling abased, paralysed almost. The town rang around him, echoing, as if everything was hollow, hollowed right out in its ruins.

He was properly abased, and angry at feeling that.

12

The Dressing-Room

H E TRUDGED ABOUT the streets, grinding himself into a deeper state of remorse and irritation. Tillie was a nurse. She must have handled men's bodies as you handle joints of meat. He should have pursued her, managed it much better. Her shame and bewilderment were all a feint.

And gradually his blood came up again, aided as much by the wild and dreamlike state of the town as by his thoughts. The walls were down. The hunger for love had replaced the more hateful appetites. He might as well have been in a moonlit garden surrounded by nymphs and cherubs, harlequins and drunken satyrs. The shafts of light, where they fell, were smoky, and the air smelt of drink, coffee, incense – and something foul underneath, some decaying or stagnant matter.

Faces emerged from the smoky coils, plunged towards him. On the edge of the town, near the outer wall, a circle of black fellows in a patch of rubble were talking animatedly, as if debating the future of the world. Sheets of tarpaulin or white cloth flapped in the night's gusts, gramophones gasped out dance tunes, people laughed and waltzed and squeezed each other in the shadows. A couple jittered about to an urchin clapping on an oil-drum beneath a sign saying *Field Cashier*. Occultish diagrams with exclamations in German. A huge dribbling slapped-up *Mutti* with a vast phallus chalked next to it. A wigwam of creosoted deal planks in which men played cards in the sickly glow of an oil-lamp; opposite, in a patch of scrub, a group of Arabians in long white tunics were sharing a hubbly-bubbly in silence.

He felt excited, now. This place was like the strange flickering village in *The Golem* – mesmerised by that film, he had been. He half-expected to see the golem itself, lumbering towards him with its clay face. He walked as if for the first time, as if unaccustomed to life. Come out of hiding, he was.

Coloured lights in front of certain doors, drifts of gay music. Gypsy, Jewish, Arabian – this would patch up the world again. 'Quick, O quick! and kindle – Kindle the votive sacrificial flame!'

He dived (hissing more Schiller) under some timber props into a cellar converted into a drinking-hole, a dubious place, furtive and somehow raging. It was packed, opaque with smoke, dimly lit by three or four gas lamps fluttering in brackets and swelteringly hot. It might have been a dugout, or a London yard in a pea-souper. The piano was being hammered in the corner on a stage made of old ammo boxes, the pianist's slicked hair bouncing up and down in rhythm. A woman in the dress of a Parisian whore of some twenty years before sang a song in French and showed her knickers in a drunken can-can. Joseph clapped and cheered with the others. Another girl, very young, marched around the piano in slacks that were torn in the seat, exposing a bare buttock. Men were tweaking her as she passed them, and Joseph took his part like an automaton, fumbling for the protruding white flesh. The touch of it – hideous, so plump and white and yet dirty-feeling, as if he had touched her innards! He was immensely excited, laughing now. It was all very Roman, yes – Baz was right. The girl with the bared rear went off arm in arm with a little chap in tortoiseshell spectacles, disappeared through a swing door at the far end of the cellar. Joseph ordered a café cognac, then another. He had to shout. He was his own man, shouting for his drink.

A laughing fellow with a huge moustache pulled the shawl from Joseph's pocket and put it over his head. Joseph snatched it back: it tore horribly, as easy as tissue paper. A thin cheap thing, he thought. He dazedly sniffed its lemony tang and stuffed it into his inside pocket. The laughing fellow bought him a beer then fell over, as if Joseph had struck him. Which he had not, oh no.

It was a rough crowd in that place, though, mostly burly types who had spent the day out in the fields, harvesting iron, explosives, human bits and pieces, whole cadavers. There were soldiers in uniform, too: a few British officers, some stiff-looking Russians, one American who turned out (on closer inspection) to be a woman, a Frenchman who might, judging from his uniform, have been top brass. The phantom of Tillie's kiss hovered on his mouth, inside it even: his cut lip stung when he drank and he drank too much. Something was abased in him. It was cheap stuff, the cognac he drank. He considered the women, rocked laughingly against one, who smiled and put her arm around him – and he nuzzled into her neck, scarcely noting her dirty teeth and raddled skin, found himself being led down a vaulted, gaslit corridor between low doors that looked medieval, with hand-hewn nails. Found himself like this again, as if he had blacked out, when really it was the consciousness of this one long journey that was coming and going. He chortled alongside her, drunkenly rapping the doors as they passed. He was as big as the golem. She held two fingers in front of his face, V for Victory, and he cheered and hurrahed. He sang the chorus of the Yiddish love song his father knew; joyously he sang it, thinking of his father. Barambarambaram. Yet he was arm in arm with a whore!

Who made the victory sign again, and so he nodded vigorously. They were in front of one of the doors, right at the end. Such a long journey it had been, down the corridor. He was laughing at it. She opened the door. He stopped laughing and blinked in surprise, swaying slightly.

Two girls were smoking on a large double bed, the bed-ends curling elaborately in rusty iron. They were naked, quite naked. Two fingers swayed in front of his eyes, again.

He took it in, nevertheless. There was female gear all over the shop, and the girls' flesh was yellowish and glistening. Two large candles were burning on a soldier's rusty trunk, stencilled in Gothic lettering – Leuchtkugel, it said. Looking incongruous, even sad: Leuchtkugel. The room's walls curved into a low vault, its big stones limewashed, scabbed here and there with damp. The girls smiled at him, missing teeth – not crones, though. One of them had a scar on her cheek like an extra dimple; the other was faintly pitted with smallpox. He hoped it was only smallpox.

Stopgaps, he thought. That's what someone called whores, at the camp.

They were not unattractive, with their up-to-the-minute bobbed hair. But their nakedness was sprawled, like models in a life class

– they looked condescendingly at him over their sprawls of breast. He would have found them more alluring in dishabille. A pair of tattooed butterflies had settled on the red rose of a nipple, the other girl had a blueish patch across her belly, like mould. Otherwise they were smooth and golden in the flattery of the candles, with long, goldeny earrings that flashed the candlelight. They might have been sisters, but the thought appalled him even through the fog of cognac.

'*Anglais*,' hissed his raddled companion – who promptly disappeared, closing the door behind her.

His heart thudded; suddenly, he was very nervous, his nerves had sobered him up, as if he had stepped out into a cold wind. The girls wriggled in a lewd fashion, open-legged, and said things that might have been English, saucy stuff made incomprehensible by their accent. They rubbed themselves, but absently, a burning cigarette in one hand and this imaginary soap in the other. The butterflies twitched their wings, the blue patch disappeared and reappeared, the earrings swayed. Then, as if at some prearranged signal, they began to feel each other, automatically, with automatic hands – almost callous the way they did it, not speaking now but humming, humming in appreciation. All the time they were looking at Joseph, stood there like a dummy, gazing on him in a vaguely off-hand way. Now and again they would take a puff of their cigarettes as if that other hand belonged to someone else, someone quite unaware of the lewdness.

Joseph blinked, stupidly. Something had mopped up his thoughts. He was almost without thought, caught in pure dulled simplemindedness. Pure vulgarity.

Weren't they supposed to come to him? But he was glad they didn't! It was a game, yes: he must watch them, be drawn in not by touch but by watching. Be winched up by degrees. Something, some vague memory of something said in the camp, told him that this was the expensive, luxurious option. As if not touching renders the whore more precious. All the cash he had was in his pocket, and it was scarcely enough to buy a meal or two.

A magazine photograph of Pearl White was pinned to the wall. Otherwise there was nothing but crumbling limewash and scribbles.

'*Nos corps te plaisent, p'tit Anglais? Hein? On te plaît ou pas?*'

He nodded, eager to please in his turn – the voice was stony, like a teacher's. The candlelight made lurid shadows across the rolling hills and valleys of their skin. There was so much of their skin, a whole long rolled-out desert of it! Yet underneath the tobacco and sweat and stink of candlewax, there was a marshy smell, salty, rotten. A strange hand travelled over each body, archly hovering between the legs, then rooting there in the thick, woolly patch. And emerging again with its play of fingers, letting the knuckles ride chastely up over the rest, absently, as if it might have been riding over blubber. His legs started to tremble violently, as they had done once when he was reading the lesson in Youlster church, standing there without a lectern, with nothing but a gulf of space between him and the staring, silent congregation. He leaned against the wall, his legs trembling of their own accord, almost in spasm with nerves. And nodded, grinning like an idiot. The room was tipping sideways like a boat, over and over again and quickly righting itself, quickly levelling before it sank.

He belched, suddenly exhausted.

Then the girl with the tattoo turned over and exposed her seat, waxy with sweat. He knew that something audacious was to take place, though in a sulky way – her smile had a tiredness behind it, a sulkiness. She lay on her belly and moaned, her fingers clasping the bolster's plump, shiny cotton – wriggled and moaned as the other hunched closer and drew her hand up slowly and almost gracefully between the fat cheeks. Drew her hand up again between them, between their waxy skin on which spots showed like tiny flowers, rather red and bloody, one as big as a boil. Joseph, his legs gripped by nerves, rested his head against the wall, from which flakes of plaster fell onto his arms. There was some filthy graffiti dating from the war, ordinary soldiers' stuff, and suspicious coppery splashes and spots – repulsive, these were, even now. He touched them, though, letting his hand slide over them gently. He knew what these *caves* were, not so long ago.

Dressing rooms. The dressing-room stink of antiseptic and blood, leaky oil-lamps, shit and piss and spew. Now it was a faint salt marshiness and hot wax, the cognac on his breath, his sweat-darkened jacket.

The girl on her belly moaned while the other one gave him the *tarif*, her cigarette still smoking. He only understood the half.

Absurdly expensive, it was. Now it was his hands that were trembling. He tried to stand apart from his lust. The whole thing – it felt like a conspiracy, a cellar conspiracy against the world above, which was hostile, flat and intolerable. He wanted to hide away his face, it was so open to the girl's indecent stare, her grin, her absent stroking hand. His legs had relaxed, but the nerves had crept into his hands. He really wanted to leave, but they were waiting for him to choose. Or simply to watch. But he could not move.

The earrings, in the dim light, looked oriental: he was on the golden journey to Samarkand, floating over golden sands. He felt faintly sick, and somehow found a rush-bottomed chair which swayed about under him. Their moans grew louder: maybe he was already paying, just to watch, just to watch and fumble with himself – so sordid, face to face with himself! And tight as a drum. God, he didn't want them to think he was no good. But his appetite had gone. He closed his eyes and thought about Babylon through a storm of images, as if hurrying through sleet to a lighted window: he thought of the sacred prostitutes before the temples of Astarte – their mystical mating, an honourable union with the Mother Goddess. But this wasn't like that: this was hidden, dangerous, snakes in a covered pit.

This was not his first time, of course.

He opened his eyes again, still tight. He could not speak. Tillie's shawl was a soft lump against his breast. He would go over and stroke them, that's all, like you stroked cats, running his hand over their waxy contours – but not callowly, oh no, he would do it with expert grace! And he was obstinate in his willingness to join in, though part of him only saw the half-mocking eyes of Tillie and was flush with shame, facing his abasement. He rose and stepped forward gingerly over strewn underthings, holding the fleur-de-lys knob of the bed-end for support – and was abruptly clamped by thirst, as by some exterior force. There was a pale blue jug next to an enamelled basin, near his feet. He picked it up with a soft grace and tipped its spout towards his mouth.

There was abrupt movement in the corner of his vision. The tattooed girl was wriggling on her belly like a worm, so that she lay the width of the bed, her feet towards Joseph; so very like a worm in the hand, her movement was. The other positioned herself on

her knees between the sprawled legs. This is a circus, he thought –
these are acrobats readying themselves for some quick turn. Then
the kneeling girl bent down and placed her face where her hand
had been, between the plump cheeks; she buried her face and then
emerged with her tongue stuck right out, grinning at him over her
shoulder. Yes, he was watching, and he was stirred, he really was!
Water splashed onto his jacket as he drank, grinning back like a
zany. She was kneeling, each knee set between the thin, sprawled
legs of her companion – and she placed her hands on the girl's rear,
palm-down on each cheek. He watched, waiting. She bent herself
slowly into a tight backwards arc that made sharp hillocks of her
breasts. She had a rash running under her left armpit, the colour
of the wooden huts. In the temple yards of Paphos, did they do
such things? Wouldn't he, perhaps . . . ?

'*Viens, beau gosse,*' she said, head screwed back towards him,
the voice forced under the grin, her teeth showing as if she was
in agony.

He nodded, still lapping the warm, foul-tasting water. He could
not have enough. The basin had a cloudy, yellowish liquid in
it – and he did not care a hoot. The water filled him. The
flame-quivering shadows made the place voluptuous. Now – now
he felt deeply caressed by it, by his thoughts and the lasciviousness
of the girls on the bed. By the stoniness, even, of the voice.

It was not his first time with a whore, oh no.

Quick, sharp and short, *that* time had been. A drizzly London
evening just after the war, a tasteful room full of nice china and
red drapes, smelling of Tiz foot ointment and gravy, as if sex in
England was odourless. Afterwards they had discussed the war and
the influenza epidemic over a cup of tea. He had even been provided
with a compulsory India-rubber sheath smeared with something very
like margarine. She had had a pale, oval face and brown slippers.
Between her face and her slippers was a mass he'd sunk into, oh yes,
but not enjoyed, not very much – not enough, anyway. Outside,
through the chilly drizzle, folk were going about in white surgeons'
masks, mouths hidden under lint taped to their cheeks, eyes fearful
of everyone else. The real plague-fear, that was.

The voice again, grating the words together like pebbles.

'*Qu'est-ce que t'attends, beau gosse? Alors, qu'est-ce que tu veux? Moi,
quand j'tronche pas j'suis malade—*'

Smiling foolishly at her, unable to speak, he saw, with a little shock, that the earrings were made of bullets. A single brassed-up bullet swinging from each ear. He did not remember them as being so long, so large. Machine-gun ammo, it looked like. Rather beautiful, polished up like that, sharp and shining. The end of war, he thought. It's the end of it at last.

He replaced the jug and unbuttoned his damp collar – an extravagant act, it felt like. The arched one wriggled her haunches hammily in anticipation, murmured something in English he could not quite grasp, but which sounded oddly Cockney. Then she wriggled some more. He wanted to giggle. It really was a most hammy performance, with the bullet earrings like something out of a Sinbad panto, or a fairground.

He had such a need to giggle! Five café cognacs, and he was ablaze and stupid with life's wonder, the rest blotted out. His giggling sounded like sneezes, as it forced its way through. No more war.

Her thinness – that was a wonder. You could see her ribs above the hard little belly. Her feet had scabs on the soles, their long toes crumpling up the sheet at the edge of the bed. Like a dirty tablecloth, the sheet was! They'd be eating off it tomorrow, Tillie and he! The girl's long dark hair fell loose onto her own behind – which she was now opening up with one grubby hand, grinning at him, submitting herself to him but at the same time frightening him with her blankness. There was something so utterly blank in her. The other girl was coughing on her belly, shaking the bed, then wiping her mouth on the sheet, darkening it in faint, pinkish streaks.

Joseph gazed on the gripped, exposed rear in wonder: it was a dark mine, somewhere whispering and dripping and dark. He would get lost in there, in the endless deep tunnels and workings of the woman: this faintly came through to him, through the fug of drink. He nevertheless stepped forward, so his shins were against the edge of the bed, and the woman was close enough to touch. But his hands were very heavy, hanging by his side, too heavy even to lift. The smell of the woman was very strong, very spicy, this close. She tugged herself wider, whimpering and moaning, arched right back now like a circus contortionist, her toes curling just in front of him, sleeves of grime in their folds. He heard the whimperings of the wounded, the poor yellow-fleshed men who had groaned and shuddered in here, swabbed and bandaged or left in a corner to dwindle to nothing – but there *was* nothing, nothing at all of that. It was finished. The men's withdrawal was complete. It was all woman, now – the moist, dark tunnellings of woman.

He, too, must withdraw, he thought, his shins pressed against the cold iron side of the bed, his hands like iron weights.

And he found himself in the corridor, as if he had jumped there. But he remembered, as if from weeks before, the rusty latch of the door opening under his fists. Down the corridor he fled, a queer silence following him. Then a shout.

He barged past a woman with a face like a carnival mask, nothing on but a cartridge belt, arm in arm with a stumbling French officer whose false moustache was dangling loose – and pushed his way through the rotating dancers in the cellar – and reached the street, cuffing his shins on the steep steps up. He was panting: the escaped convict. He felt giddy and sat down on the lintel of the pavement. The street rolled like a ship, while the dim lamp opposite flung itself away perpetually without changing its size an inch. He waved at it, feebly, as shadows of people loomed and vanished, along with their voices.

'Bye-bye,' he murmured, 'cheerio.'

The gutter had a little stream of effluent that sparkled as it flowed past his pumps. He buried his head in his hands and felt like spewing. He was really crocked. He wished he had never come to Belgium. The novel, the whole damn ambition of it, seemed of no more worth than the scraps of paper and crumpled tickets carried by the gutter. Sometimes life is too damn actual, thrusting itself forward in every impossible particular, and art withers. Oh, how easily it withers!

It had gone quiet inside. A familiar tune was playing. He hovered closer to the doorway. It was Chopin, one of his melancholic waltzes – he had struggled with it once himself, as a boy. Hated it, recoiling from its melancholy, that faint Polish melody Chopin's mother had sung over the pots and pans, the faint ghost of it there: it had dipped him into his own sadness. It had ridden up his arms like a rash, his own melancholy.

He wondered if Cousin Albert in the asylum played it, dipping his arms in its sadness, kneading it like clothes in the stream. The other fellows jerking their heads in that perpetual, terrible manner, as if banging with their foreheads on some invisible wall.

Joseph stepped down again into the cellar to have a peep. No one was dancing; one of the Russian officers was playing and everyone else was listening. Even the burly types were silenced, with the drunker ones rolling their heads from side to side. The thing is, he played it so very well, the Russian – with immense tenderness. He was steeped in its will, he was completely given up to its wiry strength and tender progress. Even his pince-nez suited it – even his black-gummed teeth that showed when he smiled, playing without apparent effort.

To Joseph's astonishment, the two young whores were at the back, negligees held to their throats in a vague effort at modesty, heads cocked in appreciation, smiling gently. He felt an abrupt surge of love for them, as you might for a child. The music made every living thing tender and beautiful and innocent. He wanted to cry out to them – thankfully he did not. Instead he sat on the steep wooden steps just inside the door and shut his eyes. The Russian played the piece three times without a pause. It crept into the garden of Joseph's dreams, for he had fallen asleep. He was woken up by the clapping. He had had the most delicious dream that had gone on for hours, snaked through by rivulets of enchanted music, but could remember nothing. People knocked him as they clattered down the stairs and the Russian officer was replaced by the slick-haired thumper. He made his way back up to the street and walked as briskly as he could away from the thumping, jittery Charleston, garishly new yet already so promiscuously used up.

The waltz's melody lingered in his head – all the way, in fact, to the sudden immense country of darkness he found himself in, walking right through the town gate without noticing. He had wanted the hotel, and sleep. He had gone very wrong, walking out into a country of darkness. A stilled blizzard of darkness.

The arched shadow behind him smelt of stone, like a tunnel. In front of him, thick low cloud, the kind that might be full of rain, had edged across the bright ribbed wastes of cirrus and obscured the moon. He looked out at the blackness of the fields as a sailor looks from a ship's watch at the blackness of ocean.

13

A Hole the Size of a Man

IT WOULD CLEAN him, walking out there. He felt hot with shame, degraded, when he thought of Tillie. The whores did not come into it, he had not been touched anywhere near the quick by them. But Tillie! – he grew aggravated just thinking about her, the shame turning into a hot sense of injustice, that she had swung to and fro like that, spoiled by her Jesus-worship, and made him look dirty, indecent.

He had half a mind to throw the torn shawl away into the night, he really did.

He stopped after a few hundred yards. His progress seemed terribly loud on the gritty surface. He knew where he was, he had gone through the Lille Gate and out onto the road they had first taken that morning in the motor-coach. There was now, he perceived, just a shimmer of blue moonlight over everything, enough to show the road directly in front. It was a dose of funk that had stopped him. The old fear of the darkness, of straightforward ghouls, of the shufflings of the dead. Something creeping up behind him – it was all he could do not to whip round. He wished Baz was out here. Baz was so sensible and straightforward that no phantom would dream of showing itself. The darkness was oppressive, the heavy clouds scurrying like a low, nightmare ceiling. The plain stretched out forever around him, while the town behind was a fitful glimmer, the lamps mostly extinguished.

'I must be barmy,' he murmured. He found comfort in the word 'barmy', its broad northern vowel.

Maggots, that's what it was. He had maggots on the brain!

– and he laughed, right out loud. The cognac had furred his tongue.

A countryside hush, its usual unlamped blackness. The very land itself in some ways to blame for being so fought over, as if it ever mattered who had what damn copse or ridge. The lop of the blackness against the eyes, until they clear to it, begin to see as animals do, begin even to listen. Rustles and squeaks. Foreign men, maybe . . .

Then he thought of Pitts and the letters, of Pitts's steady, obscene arguments on behalf of the war – cricketing similes, even! The black, thin ink trailing its acid. Likening the rules of war to the rules of cricket; one not madder than the other, both to be obeyed. All that word-rot. 'Objectively' done, of course.

And now even tragedy was diluted. An earthquake last year had killed 180,000 Chinese in one swift prod. Millions more had perished since the war – of the neutral, peaceful 'flu. What did any man's death mean, now – any man, woman or child? Nothing, or not very much. A little spurt of grief, then nothing. It disappeared into the massive flood of not-being, in the objective view.

But it had to mean something, every single death had to mean something, or the life preceding it would not – and the story of mankind itself, that too would be rendered futile. The Pitts God would look down upon it as its sole arbiter: uncanny, that. And Joseph could do nothing about it. Facing this wilderness, he could only hum Chopin's waltz like a drunken fool and walk on.

He came up onto a low ridge, he had no idea where. The wrecked trees were ogreish, bony-handed. Now and again there was a rent in the heavy cloud and the moonlight burst through, giving a sudden illumination of the scene much like, he supposed, the flare of a Very light.

It was awful, what it lit up for him. Worse, to his mind, than that which a soldier might have seen three years before. There is at least purpose in even the most futile battle – if only that of surviving it, or ending it.

What had Scott said, on reaching the Pole? *Good God, this is an awful place!*

Maybe Baz was right. Maybe that moment *had* triggered something. Maybe civilisation had followed Scott there, and perished likewise in the awful dead blankness.

Maybe we had to make our own South Pole, our own desolation. It was not enough to feel the cold inwardly. We searched for God, and found only a mocking flag, and desolation. Everywhere you face, now, you face north.

Yes, Joseph nodded to himself – this is truly the end of our journey. Now we will perish on the return. And he would take Baz's hand and congratulate him. Baz had perceived something deep, very deep.

He pressed himself forward, nevertheless. Now and again he tripped over some buried thing, and stumbled on. He could scarcely believe that he was passing by the same places they had seen from the motor-coach that morning. A time before the end of the world, that, full of light and company. He craved even Ostrich Feather as a companion, or the lugubrious woman who had made a rope out of Europe. His loneliness was a thick dead thing he hugged to himself, thinking of Pa and Cousin Roger and of his own dead friends, so *many* of them dead. They lived on, that was the trouble – his schooldays were still so close to him that he could not believe completely in this duck shoot. He heard the voices of his schoolmates quite often in the oddest places – omnibuses, pubs, the Tube, creaking branches in a wood.

He nearly fell into the crevasse of a trench – the shock of its crumbling, invisible edge.

He backed away, the blood ringing in his ears. The cognac was making him nauseous again, drying him out as it worked down, and his thirst returned. Ah, but he felt privileged, to be alone with all this. The last man. The only man, ever, in the history of the world. Adam in the garden. A garden in which everything is barren, blasted into hell.

Though a soft smell of camomile rose from where his progress was crushing its leaves; there was at least some life. He had turned off the main 'road' and was following a pale ribbon of a track, his eyes growing a little more adapted to the darkness. The track was a single broad rut: he was a gramophone needle in a groove. He heard at one point the proper sound of the sea, as if he was on a cliff or walking a shingled strand, and realised from the blanker bulk either side that he was passing between corn. It whispered in the warm wind and gave off sweet biscuity odours. Then the corn gave out, or at least silence once again descended, like some sort of lead weight, and when the moon burst through for a few moments he saw with a shiver that he was being watched by a parade of black crosses, the light glinting off their iron struts. It was very oppressive, they appeared to accompany him – over and over again the same crosses, when they were not the same, not really.

It was dead straight, the path. He did not think he recognised it. Bunyan's pilgrim would have approved, he thought. At the end of the path is a hole, into which we tumble. A hole the size of a man: that is the only fact no one can lie about. That old biddy was right. Everything else is invention. He stopped to light a cigarette. That's how the novel will start, he thought: *At the end of the path is a hole. A hole the size of a man* . . . Or: *At the end of the path is a trench. A trench the size* . . .

He drew the smoke deep down inside, comforting himself. His moth-eaten lungs were not really suited to it, it made him wheezier and husky, but he smoked for comfort, he could not imagine *not* smoking. It was a little, human thing in the great darkness, the glowing tip like a tiny camp fire on a prehistoric plain. And he had the most ridiculous notion that he might be 'potted out' because of it – it really prickled his spine, this daft notion. He really braced himself for the sudden whip of a bullet. He started walking again, wanting to free himself from the ominous crosses and this daft notion. The sky was coke-black above and almost aglow on the horizon, where the moonlight was spilling beyond the edge of the clouds. He could perceive the steady line of the horizon quite plainly; it might have been the edge of the known world, where you fell into the abyss, nipped in your prime.

The black crosses disappeared. He went on, nothing about him but wind and awkward shadows swayed by the wind: he tried to walk faster, stumbled and fell and scraped his palm. He sat on the path, sucking the dirt out of the graze, tasting the soured earth – something oily and metallic in it, oh yes. He had sworn out loud, and now muttered away to himself. He was irritated, very cross. The graze drew blood, was absurdly painful for a few minutes. His cigarette was lost somewhere in the darkness. He sat there cross-legged like a *joss* and promptly fell asleep on his own chest.

14

The Principle of Goodness

S HE WAS LOOKING down at him. He had dozed off and now
Tillie was there, looking down at him, a silhouette.

'Well,' she said, in a familiar but quite unTillie-ish voice,
'goodness gracious. Have you been drinking?'

The disappointment was immense. He blinked himself fully
awake. He knew her, ay, but from where?

'Yes, I have.'

His own voice was a little boy's.

'A lot?'

'Enough.'

'Are you sleeping out here?'

'No, I hadn't planned to. Just a little stroll.'

He cleared his throat of sleep.

'Like me,' she laughed.

'Yes, probably.'

She gave another brief, high laugh.

'Fancy meeting again!'

'Oh, it's not so strange,' he said.

But he thought it was, really. He had only just realised who she
was, from the high laugh.

'I thought you were someone else, actually,' he smiled, getting
to his feet.

'A ghost? I feel like one. I have been wandering about for ages
and ages. You are the boy I met today?'

'Yes, I think so,' he said.

His palm stung him.

'*Think* so? I hope you know who you are.'

'You might have met another "boy".'

'No, only you,' she said. 'I would like to meet my son, but I meet you instead.'

The woman looked at him in what he imagined was a direct manner. The face was completely in shadow from her hat, but the veil was off.

'I'm not clear – I mean, do you know where your son is buried?'

He was stretching a little, very stiff in the neck. She gave another short laugh, to his surprise.

'Of course I do.' She raised her hands. 'In the sky. Poof, up in the sky!'

He saw a glint of teeth from her smile. Maybe it was not a smile.

'Let us go for a stroll,' she said, in her mincing accent.

They did walk together. And even talked about the weather, how it had to rain soon and how the air smelt of rain. She stumbled on one of the logs of a corduroy, a loose one, and he caught her by the arm to prevent her from falling.

'Thank you,' she said.

The cloth had the feel of mothballs about it, faintly tarry. He let go of her arm, and looked at her, but she walked on. The aromatic sharpness lingered on his fingers. He saw a heavy cupboard, a sunlit German square with crenellated roof-lines, fat *Hausfrauen* rooting through trays of potatoes. He caught her up, slightly breathless.

She stopped for him. He looked at her again. Her face was fleshier than he remembered from that morning, and a sudden sweep of clearer moonlight confirmed this. Something formless about her looks. Something deeply ineffectual, as if she could not make an impression on life, almost no mark at all. Even her leaden dress denied her, in its ugly conventionality.

'You frightened me,' she said, in her level tone.

Her face was searching his, he could see the polished whites move in the sockets. Very gently, with her forefinger, she touched his cheek under the right eye, tracing it as if she was blind. Then his nose. It was as disconcerting as it was sensual, though there was nothing suggestive about it.

'Well, thank God,' she murmured. Her fingers dropped to his

lips briefly and he tried not to flinch. She was foreign, after all, she was not English. Her glove was scented, a touch of violet, but there was a sharp animal odour from the kidskin, too.

'I'm not a ghost, you see,' he smiled, when her fingers had left his chin. He was amazed at his own *sang-froid*. But his face burned all over. He felt a little dazed from the drink.

'He does not exist,' she said, quietly. 'Very well, very well.'

'Yes I do,' he said.

'Silly boy, of course you exist!'

She laughed. It made him feel small.

'I haven't understood.'

She looked at him. 'My son is dead,' she said.

'I see. No, I'm not your son.'

'Gunter.'

'Gunter,' he repeated, colourlessly. Something in his left eye made him blink. His cheek tickled.

'Thank God, the rain,' she said, wiping her eyes on a handkerchief.

It was the thinnest of drizzles, and tepid on the skin.

'Not exactly the monsoon,' said Joseph. 'More a holy sprinkle.'

He imagined the land as linen asperged by invisible fingers – and God ready with his flat-iron. He would have formed this image into words but she broke in too soon.

'Have you been to India?' she asked, over her shoulder, with her hands up, stretching them up to turn them in the flecks of rain. 'I would love to go back to India! Gunter, too. He dreamed of it. We would have gone together, run away together.'

'I read Mr Kipling instead. Less likely to fall sick. Drop dead.'

'Germany is jealous of your Empire, you know that.'

'I guessed it,' said Joseph.

She lowered her arms and walked up and down, hands thrust in the pockets of her short black jacket. A kind of grave mutter in the distance suggested thunder.

'Do you believe in good, young man?'

'What a question!'

'You English, you never think about things—'

'Oh, I agree with that,' Joseph cut in. 'But *I* think rather a lot, that is why I said it was quite a question.'

The crack of moonlight above the horizon was almost dazzling.

All he could see of her now was the smooth glistening outline of her hair. Another far-off grumble of thunder was abruptly nipped, as if told to stop. Their breathing, their scuffly tread – abstracted sounds, fluttering above the silence. He wondered if he was drunker than he thought. But he felt quite well. Odd, that.

'So? *What* is goodness? What is it? What *is* it?'

She was really relentless, she was almost squawking at him. He remembered a joke from university days.

'Something you can straighten your tie in,' he said, grinning.

She must have heard how his words grinned, but said 'I see' as if she had not.

They walked side by side, looking into the void at their feet that always, at the last minute, revealed the track. Joseph felt curiously blank about walking with her, curiously unbothered, as if it had been arranged beforehand. The soft precipitation blew like steam against their faces.

They reached the road, which slid off all aglimmer from the moisture. Without a second's hesitation she turned away from Ypres, deeper into the old battlefield. He followed her. They took a track off to the right, then another to the left. Everything was very stark and clear in the flood of moonlight, but he had no idea where he was. She seemed to know the terrain very well. There was no hesitation in her movements. They talked lightly, inconsequentially. About Germany, about England – nothing on politics, though: about social life, how and what people drank and ate, how the nations made their beds, how they passed their Sundays. Small cindery tufts of cloud passed low and quickly overhead, as if there was a train puffing somewhere near.

'Well, I dreamed of you, you know,' she let out quite suddenly.

'Really?'

'I dreamed of you, back in my home in Germany.'

'Are you sure it was me?'

'Absolutely. Unless you have a twin.'

'I don't.'

With a subterranean jolt, he thought of Hubert Rail.

'Then it must have been you. You have a peculiar face.'

'Peculiar?'

'Not ugly peculiar. Just peculiar for you. Your mouth. And your eyes.'

'What's wrong with them?' he laughed.

'And your spectacles,' she added.

He felt very self-conscious.

'Isn't everyone's face peculiar to them?'

She clicked her tongue.

'As soon as you came towards me, in the cemetery this afternoon, I knew it was you. And again tonight.'

'I see. It must have been a shock.'

'No.' She stopped and turned, putting her face up close to his. Again, the scent of folded fabric in long-shut drawers. There was nothing around them, nothing but suggestions of emplacements in the uneven shadows and black hollows, through which the sweaty night air puffed and whistled.

'Of course, I have just lied.'

'Have you?'

'I thought at first you were someone else, of course.'

She waited for him to say something. He refused to. He wanted to know where this poppycock was leading to, but preferred to let it run its course.

'I thought you were my son, in fact.'

He felt curiously indifferent.

'When?'

'When?'

'You mean the first time we met in the cemetery?'

His own words gave him a tiny sexual thrill; he had not meant to say 'we met' but 'you saw me'.

'Or just now, back there?' he added, matter-of-factly.

'No no – neither,' she laughed. 'I mean in my *dream*. I thought you were my son, walking towards me in this dream of mine. I was most disappointed when I reached out and saw, it was like a mist clearing – saw *you*, instead. You see?'

'But how – hang on, how could you know it was *me* in your dream, when you'd never seen me before, in *real* life?'

She made a noise in the back of her throat, perfunctory. Joseph felt he was playing the slow chap in a comic-hall act, that he was deliberately feeding her lines while knowing perfectly well what the actual state of play was. It was unsettling.

She turned away, without saying anything. He felt rather giddy as they walked on.

'Look,' she said, pointing.

And he looked. He drew his breath in, amazed.

About fifty yards away a tree was smouldering. Bright lines and glowing whorls crawled up and down its lopped-off trunk. The gusts of wind played on it as they might have played on the strings of an aeolian harp – only this was for the eyes, not the ears, brightening and shifting like burning soot on a fireback. It was absolutely sinister and wonderful at the same time, like some sort of enchantment or prehistoric rite. The tree was nothing but a tall smashed stump, but its whole length was alive with embers, flowing up and down, pulsing in the wind. It was as if its invisible body had opened up to them, or as if they had been blessed with occult vision.

Really, though, it was quite ordinary, on another level.

'It must have caught fire,' he said, plonking it down to this other level.

There was a sharp stink of cordite, and he guessed aloud that a cache of 'duds' must have been dealt with here, leaving the poor dead tree even deader, but with this curious charge of life.

'Did you bring me here especially?' he asked.

They were standing in front of it now, as close as they could get without being roasted. The tree was, in fact, on the edge of a huge crater. The moonlight picked out the crater's nearest curve in shadow, as craters are picked out on the moon. In the dark, they might have tumbled into it.

'No,' she said. 'But it – this tree – it was in my dream. You know? The same dream. As you were in,' she added, as if he might have forgotten.

Was he supposed to be amazed?

'And that is not normal, is it?' she continued, encouraging him.

'Maybe I was the god of the tree. The tree's spirit.'

'Oh, you weren't at all a god! You were just you.'

He blushed. This was all so peculiarly intimate – and he recoiled from this intimacy, really wanted to curl back in himself.

'Yes, but – you have to think of dreams as a way in which we go back to the old myths,' he said, softly. 'I think you were dreaming of – well, I was thinking of the old fire-festivals of Europe,' he pressed on, half conscious of how ridiculous he was now sounding, like a jejune student. But he did so want to deflect her intimacy: he could not stop. 'All those old rituals. For instance, Balder was burnt on a pyre of oak wood. And oak wood's sacred, you know. Or it *was*. Nothing's sacred now except for nationhood and – money. They call them – the midsummer bonfires in Sweden – they're called – or they *were* called – "Balder's balefires". I think your dream was really a nature myth. That's how we do it now, you see. Our nature rituals. Through dream and – art, of course. Art is the other way we do it.'

He looked at her. She seemed rather huge against the glow of the tree.

'You are a poet,' she said, with the slightest note of contempt.

Silence. And he was relieved, to be honest, to have his own voice so decisively curtailed. The heat pulsed on their faces, a further heat buffeting the tropic night, its glow playing over her skin. There were winks of embers at the bottom of the crater, and the sort of acridity that comes when you throw water on a vigorous fire in the hearth to extinguish it. The tree had evidently been soaked likewise, but not quite put out. Now and again a flame darted out from the wood like a little tongue, shadows converged and pulsed, shuffling the light into odd places, golden emanations that stroked the night around, then retreated. It made Joseph think of one of his favourite stories, a story by Turgenev – some boys scaring themselves around a camp fire in the middle of a vast Russian night with the sound of their horses . . .

'What else was in your dream?'

'Ah, that is hard to say.'

'Why?'

'You won't believe me. No, you won't,' she insisted.

'That's dreams, all right . . .'

'What do you mean?'

'They're only believable to the dreamer, is what I mean. They're silly to everyone else. Even nightmares. Even the pure terrifying nightmare.'

She nodded. Her face had more substance to it, was more effectual, in the soft pulsing glow of the tree. Inside the black sheath of mourning crêpe, her body nestled secretively. He was watching her out of the corner of his eye. Admiring her, even.

'What do you do? Are you a student?'

'No.'

'Then what do you do?'

'You mean, for money?'

'Yes.'

'I write.'

A silence. He felt very self-conscious, suddenly, of the bulky silk shawl inside his jacket, and crossed his arms.

'I put everything into it,' he went on. 'Bowels and head and heart. I'm a writer.'

He hoped it did not sound as absurd to her as it sounded to him.

'That's not bad,' she said, rocking her head to and fro.

'It's a species of neurasthenia, really.'

And he laughed. He wished he was back in the cottage. And then he was glad he was not – almost in the same instant.

'You're a poet, then?'

'No – well, not what I'd call a poet. I'm – writing a novel.'

He almost bit his lip with anguish, regretting this, that he had let this out – but it was too late.

'About the war, I suppose?'

He crumpled up, inside.

'Yes.'

This one little word – full of insinuations. His courage failed him. The novel was as vulnerable as tissue paper; the tone of her voice was like a knife. He stared at the tree; he could feel the heat wax and wane on his face. He wanted to burst out about the novel in a tremendous justification of it. That, too, he forced back down his throat. He kept quiet. He wrapped himself up very tight, inside.

'Everyone in Germany is writing the same,' she said. 'War, war, war. What have you done to your hand?'

'Nothing. Grazed it.'

'War, war, war. That's the only subject.'

He kept quiet. This was horrible.

'But yours is different, of course,' she added.

'Yes.' He did bite his lip, now.

She snorted derisively. 'They say that, also.'

'Do they?'

'*Ja, ja!*' she laughed.

She was being horribly condescending. He was genuinely upset. He almost burst into tears.

'I'm grateful to you for the encouragement. Thanks. Most helpful.'

His voice was thin and wavery.

'You are angry, young man.'

'No I'm not. Anyway, don't think you'll stop me. I know what I'm doing.'

'I am sure you do.'

'I do.'

'Good!' she cried, in a terribly good humour about it.

'I *know* what I'm doing, I do – that's the difference,' he added, relentlessly. The heat from the tree was like a bonfire's, now; sweat ran down onto his chin. He was desperate to relieve himself.

'Excuse me,' he said.

He trotted across to a vaguely-defined breastwork and clambered up and over its loose, dusty flank. The trench was in shadow and full of loose debris. He stood on the bottom and relieved himself, his head poking above the parapet. *God damn my bloody sciatica!* Ping! He looked along the trench, as black as tar, and felt men were watching him, crouched there in rows with turned-up eyes. They had never left, they were still waiting for the off, turned towards him with unseeing eyes as white as crocus bulbs.

Well, he thought, clambering up again – he *had* to believe in what he was doing: the novel, the shock of it, all that. It would *have* to create a scandal.

On the top he kicked his foot against the breastwork as if to establish its reality; loose grit made tiny scattering noises on the trench bottom. Yes, the whole business here was ridiculous, but ridicule diminished everything – even truth. He had to make something pure, caustic, it would burn right in. But he was nothing. He hadn't even fought, for God's sake! That was both his strength and his weakness. If he had stuck it out as a pacifist . . . but it was no good, he was a fraud, and shameful to boot. He screwed up his face. The black bottom of the trench might have been the infinite depths of his despair. But really, it was only three feet deep, this despair. He knew this. It was not despair at all, not really. It was disappointment.

He turned around and the woman, to his immense surprise,

had gone. Vanished. He scrambled down and hallooed, but not very loudly.

Well, he was alone on the salient and had not the foggiest where he was. He imagined himself stumbling out here forever in some sort of perpetual night. He looked back and took his bearings from the glowing tree. He was about fifty yards away. Writhing dragons in the form of black clouds were crossing the moon swiftly and silently, passing their shadows over the ground so conspicuously it made it difficult to keep steady. The wind brushed his forehead where the sweat was beading, scarcely cooling it. The spectres must be thick on the ground, all around him, here. Their pain seemed to be pressing on his head, crushing him down. A lot deeper even than sciatic pain, theirs was! Yet there was something grey about it, like old ashes.

He wiped his face with a handkerchief and made to turn. He already missed the woman.

15

The Dream

A ND THERE SHE was, directly in front of him, no more than five yards off, as if she had popped out of the earth. She was pulling down the hem of her jacket, smoothing the pleats on her long and heavy skirt.

'You should leave sweat on the face for as long as possible. It cleans out the holes of the skin.'

'Who says?'

'My father was a doctor. He wrote books. Do you want to know what else happened in my dream?'

'You gave me the most awful shock.'

'I was here all the time,' she said, pointing to a muddle of light and dark that might have been an old gun emplacement. Beyond was a cliff of darkness where the shadows were passing. Then the shadows sped right under their feet, alternated by stripes of an eerie glare as if some giant torch was at play, or a crazed lighthouse.

'It was a special night,' she declared. Now she was being laconic.

'What was?'

She ignored him, or did not hear. They started walking.

'You see, we are on a stream,' she said, 'all of us, carried on a stream, yet all we feel is the water moving under us. Isn't that so? Do you not feel it?'

He looked noncommittal. He was sleepy. The bits of Goethe and Schiller he knew did not really fit in, or he would have quoted something to impress her.

'If you dreamt about me, aren't I on your – this stream of yours?' he suggested, watching the path.

Then, after a brief pause, she said: 'I am a bit lonely.'

Joseph, too, felt 'a bit lonely'. But he did not let on. It was a very lonely place. It was lonelier than Antarctica, in its own way. It was copious with non-life, much more than Antarctica. Antarctica was simply frozen, it had not smashed the life that was already there. A few men with sledges, that was all. Here its non-life was countless living things – trees, animals, millions of people, flowers – everything except vermin and flies. He nodded, as if he was considering it all.

'There'll be others,' he said.

'Others?'

He nodded again. She was very distant from him, suddenly. Foreign and far away. There was a wooden beam, probably an old trench prop, visible on the side of the path, and she now abruptly sat down upon it. The burnt and glowing tree was a dim little pulse, now.

'Watch the nails,' he warned.

But there did not seem to be any.

'I like very much talking to you,' she said. 'Sit by me.'

He did so, gingerly feeling for nails. And this anonymous woman laid her head against his shoulder in a soft rustle of crêpe. It pressed against his shoulder, the weight of her head. It was considerable, this weight.

He stayed very still, rather stiff in his thoughts. He could have put his arm around her, but was paralysed by some sort of fear, a fear of getting into the wrong business, a scrape he would later regret. They stayed like that, very chastely, before she stirred a little.

'I suppose I must tell you,' she murmured.

'Tell me? Tell me what?'

A little pause. He was nervous.

'I never set eyes upon you before today,' she declared.

'I know that. Except in your dream.'

'Yes.'

'And?'

'He died on the same night,' she said, quietly.

Joseph felt physically restless, suddenly, but did not move, not a muscle. He took the news in dully, however.

'Your son, you mean?'

'Yes,' she said. 'I lost my darling, yes, that very same night when I was dreaming about your face.'

Silence.

'Don't be put off,' she added, mysteriously, with a hint of amusement.

Her hair was thick against his cheek and almost black in the moonlight. It smelt of smoke and something indefinably foreign to him – of strange, foreign childhoods without Bovril or bread-and-butter pudding or even cream custard. Chopin, yes, but not cream custard. Something both disagreeable and pleasant crept along his body. He made to put his arm around her but she lifted her head.

'Have I frightened you?'

'No. It's like a myth.'

He laughed, gently, a light laugh. His heart was thudding, all his blood was thudding right through him, toes to scalp. 'The god Balder, I do like that story. He dreamed of his coming death, didn't he, poor Balder?' He took a deep breath. He was babbling – that is what it felt like to him. 'Except that Balder couldn't ever recall his dreams, he'd remember the fear but nothing else. Just the fear, very pure and nasty. He had a brow as pure as the camomile's flower – it's named after him, in fact, did you know? Yes.' He trailed off, then picked up again. 'I do like all those myths of the Norsemen. Your story – it reminds me of them, those myths.' And quickly, to cover his confusion, because his arm was still up in the air behind her: 'Your son died, and then you had this dream about me? Why didn't you dream about – your son?'

He was tentative, his arm came back to him, his hands gingerly folded in his lap. He felt Tillie's shawl like the suggestion of a rabbit against his ribs. The woman shook her head.

'Of course not, why should I dream of him?' she replied. 'I didn't know.'

'You didn't know?'

'Two days after my dream, it was a – a Wednesday. *That's* when I knew he was lost to me. You don't believe it though, do you? Oh no.'

'Oh, I do.'

'No, I mean *one* does not believe it when a loved one is dead.'

'No . . .'

'It's the face. You see the face so clearly in your mind and you – you simply can't believe that it will never come back, this face. The way it looks at you, the way it is right for that person and nobody else. Can you?'

'No, I suppose not.'

She hardly mentions her husband, he thought. Didn't the news kill him on that same day? But no, it's all son.

'A lump,' she went on. 'A lump in the throat and you can't swallow it. Not ever, not for the rest of your days. I never forgot *your* face,' she added.

A little chill went through him, then. Though he was curiously numb about the whole thing. He wanted to see under it, into the motive; until then it was as meaningless to him as a book-keeper's entry. The moon shed a steel-blue radiance that made the salient seem ethereal – but it reminded him too of the blue light inside omnibuses during the war, their lamps shrouded against the raids. Maybe this is what Odin saw when he rode into Hel's abode, he thought: drear, mysterious, obscurely lovely. No red, no colour of life.

'It's still very hot,' she said, after a silence. She picked up her hat and fanned herself with it. 'Like Calcutta. But worse. There are no *punkah-wallahs* here. Ours was called Gabral, but he was a pure native. He had lost his nose, somewhere, and had not a tooth in his head. He called me *chota Bengali*. The little Bengali. He was an untouchable, but I touched him. I would touch the place where his nose had been. It had been bitten off by an angry *memsahib*, he said. I was very small, I believed him. There you are, I can see *his* face, too. Clear as day. Not like a painting – it is moving, these faces are always moving, they are always alive.'

Joseph felt a sudden craving for a cup of tea. His back hurt: it was clenched all the way up to his neck.

'Did you dream this too? Us sitting next to each other?' He leaned forward on his knees, resting his elbows on his knees. Shutting himself in. He felt a touch nauseous, again.

'*Der kleine Neuankommling*,' she said.

'I don't know any German,' he admitted. 'It wasn't a language one learnt when I was at school. We weren't even supposed to read Goethe, or listen to Beethoven. It was unhygienic, you see!'

'It means "the little stranger",' she explained, ignoring his drollery.

'Am I the little stranger?'

She took off a glove and started touching her own face, really feeling her own face, as if she was kneading it into life. Her fingernails glistened. 'Are my lips and my mouth very pure and sweet?'

'Sorry?'

He realised, then. He swallowed noisily, he could not swallow enough. *John Thomas tickled the feather*, he thought, in a loud internal voice – like a naughty little boy. He wished he had not hurt his hand or drunk so much cognac.

'Are they?'

'How do I know?'

'Because in my dream – we were sitting together, like this. And you called me *Der kleine Neuankommling*. The little stranger.'

'Did I? Golly.'

'And you kissed me.'

He gulped, quite literally – it creased his throat inside.

'But I don't know any German,' he said, helplessly.

His voice seemed to ring in his head, through the rushing blood.

'We women have two mouths, do you know that?'

'Do you?'

'Don't you know?' A brief little laugh, cut off short. She moved inside her black chrysalis. He could hear the bare skin rub against the fabric.

'Oh yes, I suppose you do.'

'So?'

He put his arm around her, so that his fingers cupped her upper arm, but she did not move. His arm started to ache. What was he supposed to do? In profile, staring out, her face seemed vaguely hostile. The blood beat in his throat. She refused to look at him. They might have been in a skiff in the midst of an ocean, and she staring out, staring forward into the steely nothingness of the swell.

Her lips moved. 'In my dream,' they were saying, 'you kissed them both, both of my mouths. It was a very nice dream. That is what I dreamt. You asked me—'

Her voice trailed away, embarrassed.

'Were we sitting here?' he whispered.

'Oh yes.'

He kissed her tenderly on the brow. He felt it was a good place to start. He felt very precise about it, almost cold. He knew without a doubt that his first copulation – the only term that sprang to mind – was about to take place. The time with the London whore, smelling of Tiz – that did not count, his manhood had been wrapped up and put in a cupboard, that time. This was *quite* different. Anyway, he did not care any more, he did not have to be head over heels with her. Or even aroused by her. He was aroused by the thought, by the sheer fear of it. He was quite calm under the notional, instinctive fear. One thing had led to another, it was all a bundle of logic – a real swirl but with a logic to it, leading to this. He pushed the thought of the whore to one side, along with the Ypres whores, and Tillie – Tillie was of another order, not even on this plane, she had fled right out of it. His hand pressed the woman to him, gently – rather too tentative, really.

There was a rustling noise from the trench and he looked up, alert as a sentry. The salient was nebulous around them, stretching to the absolute ends of the dead-flat earth. She waited. Supposing they were being watched? But there was no one. No people, no spectres, nothing. Just bundles of darkness. He kissed her again on the temple, brushing aside her hair, nestling closer, pulling her reluctant body closer to him on the trench prop. She was not yielding to him that easily, he thought: it made her more attractive to him, this fake resistance. It was a rite. A dance. And he knew exactly how it would end. The finishing tape was clear, and he was sprinting easily towards it. He would win. Nothing like with Tillie, he thought. There was a hair in his mouth, he had to pull it out as quickly as possible.

She did lift her face up, now. The lips, rather meagre, glistened and filled out. Her eyes darted over his, tiny flickerings. She seemed suddenly the most beautiful creature in the world, as clear and cold as a star in the night sky. She was his, that was the thing. He kissed her on the lips, a rather fumbling kiss, but she took it easily and softly. Her face was very warm, the skin smooth under his mouth as he roamed over her face; no matter in the world smoother and softer than this skin. He felt very powerful. He had kissed two women in one night and this made him feel all-conquering. The shawl inside his pocket was pressed between them: it was really of the thinnest, finest silk. It had all but vanished, between them.

'I think,' she said, surfacing from him, 'that we shall be doing what we did in my dream.'

'What was that?' he said, in a queer, quavering voice. He was removing his spectacles, which had misted up, placing them carefully in his top pocket with his free hand.

'Change this awful weather.'

'Oh? How?'

He was exultant, inside.

'By love,' she said. 'For love's sake.'

He was not quite sure what this meant.

'Will love do it, then?'

'In my dream, we brought the cool wind. And then the rain. Like India, after the dry season. Maybe I was thinking of India, in my dream.'

'What did we do, exactly?'

'It rained and rained so much. It was hot and dry, and then the storm came. So loud, the drumming of the rain on the roof. That was what I dreamt. Really, though, outside, it was cold, cold and grey, the trams and people hurrying along, very cold and grey and not raining at all. March in Munich.'

'Munich? Ah. That's where you come from?'

It was as if she had given herself away. It was a blow to her, he could see that. She had let it slip. She pursed her lips and looked down. Really, though, he was done with chat. His hands were roaming over her black crêpe. Rough, it was, almost flocculent, like running a hand through ash. His graze stung where it scraped against the fabric, but he ignored it. He felt her breasts under his good hand, surprising somehow, and squeezed there – and she sat like a sphinx, immobile, as he took each breast in turn in his hand and squeezed very gently. Very gently at first, then harder. It fired him up terribly, this did. Her waist was small, he felt around her waist. She had a womanly figure, the widow, under the sheath of black crêpe. It was surprising; he had thought of her as sexless, in the naïve, immature part of his mind. She was breathing quickly, eyes closed, her mouth slightly open, her throat exposed and very pale. Her breath smelt of peppermint, like her gloves. He stopped her mouth with his own.

They were on the ground, now. He had thrown his jacket down and there they had ended up, struggling with buttons and clasps. He unwrapped her like a present. Her ugly, heavy clothes came off very easily. The white skin was almost shocking, after the heavy black fabric. And she was burning hot between her breasts, although her shoulders and arms were cool. His shirt caught on his arms and he was a Laocoon, fighting the serpents of the cloth. He almost ripped the shirt, struggling with it behind him, balancing on his knees over her. She was very calm.

Then she gripped his shoulders, stilling him. Her breasts shone porcelain-white under him, uncorseted, the nipples blue and surprisingly large in the moonlight, the ugly jacket and long pleated skirt in a cindery heap by her side, next to the creamy underthings. He had thrown off the shirt and laid his head upon the breasts, heard the heart beating through the white flesh. Now he was looking down on her as if from a great height, his shoulders gripped.

'You have not said it,' she whispered. 'What you called me in my dream.'

'*Meine kleine . . .*' His voice trailed into breathlessness.

'*Der kleine Neuankommling.*'

He repeated it, as best he could, and laughed. Then he kissed her again, on each breast, as you might kiss a flower. Her breath roared in his ear.

'No-man's land!' he shouted, his head craned up. He really did not care. 'We'll have children! We'll have children here in no-man's land!'

He lifted himself on his hands, his hands either side of her cool shoulders, and looked about, exultant. The pain of his graze pressed against the ground was almost pleasurable, stinging like desire. His nausea had gone – the drink had burned right out of him. Her legs were forked now, white thighs forked and gleaming with a dark squared-off patch where they met. He was quite mad, inflamed with joy and desire. He saw the children tumbling out of the ground, creatures of his desire. He had scarcely ever thought about children, as an adult – let alone making them. But he must always be creating something. Nothing could be done just for itself, it must always have this issue, this created extra thing.

She was putting him inside her already. He watched, amazed.

He wiped his face and watched. The salient was very still around them, with its faint rises and falls and dim broken stubs of trees. It had stopped mizzling. Very still, it was. The earth smelt burnt, where the wet had grazed it, or perhaps it was the tree: something faintly bitter, anyway, in the heavy air, the pseudo-tropic night.

The woman had an even richer odour about her, very foreign and rich – almost sweet, almost as soft apples smell. Inside she was a warm, soft pulp. He drove in and out furiously until he ejaculated in a steady stream and, at the same time, as if from very far off, he heard her scream and whimper above his own sharp wheezes. It was almost as if she was imitating the wounded and dying snagged on the wire an inch away from them, or less. The dead opening their tattered mouths underneath the soil – yearning, chafing to be alive again, as alive as these two noisy strangers briefly among them.

16

Once Upon a Time

H E FELT THE charm leave him. For a long moment there was silence. He even dropped off for a moment. He lay there, listening to her slow breathing.

'It's still like Bengal,' he said, licking his finger and holding it up into a warm gust. She stirred next to him. Maybe he had been asleep for hours.

'Wait. You'll see. It will change,' she murmured.

'That's what everybody says about the weather.'

She sat up a little and stroked his hair, already dishevelled – it had grown quite long in the Chilterns.

'My darling,' she whispered, 'you and I – we have to be patient. The rain will come, the wind, very cool, very wet. Love will flood the world, but slowly, slowly. From this moment, now. Now it is a consumptive, the world, it is very sick, its lungs are bad – but we have filled it with love, with health. It will get better now.'

He nodded, stroking in turn her hair, her belly, her hips. He was floating in the cool flood of her thoughts. He was rocking, listening happily as to a wise mother, as lightly blown as a butterfly on a breeze. Yet he had to spoil it.

'Each time we are together – well, we can't overdo it, then. We'd better not or it'll be – it'll overflow!'

He was grinning. She turned her face away, suddenly.

'What are you talking about?'

His heart lurched, as if a trap door had opened under it. He blinked stupidly and drew himself up on his elbow.

'Well, would you like to? I would. Before it gets light—'

'I was such a good mother,' she murmured, quite to herself. 'I adored my son. Such a handsome boy.' She would not turn her head back, it lay on its side on the jacket, on the bulkiness that was the shawl; she was turned away from him. He felt his lips tighten. He began to feel mean-minded, irritated. He no longer desired her. She was no longer there to him; she had moved far off.

They dressed, very separately. She was far off in her own thoughts. He offered her a cigarette. They were back on the trench prop, as if nothing had happened. It was all very strange to him: he felt almost cheated. But as soon as they spoke it was as if their voices had been bruised; everything they said had this bruised quality. It was as if they had given something to the other that they could not have themselves. It was all very strange.

He got her off the son, though, by talking about the bad conditions in Germany, about politicians and powerful interests. Her voice became rather hard, rather lifeless, like a fossil of its living self. Its timbre was preserved in stone. It had all the fronds and curves and depths but it was hard, frozen into rock. He felt it might hit him on the head, strike him dead. She talked about the nothingness of Germany, the rubble of its pride, her German friends and their despair.

'There is too much feeling,' she went on, in this frozen rock voice of hers, staring out. 'We would be better off to feel nothing. Nothing. Nothing at all. As if dead. As if life and death have brought forth together a new form of life, a life that is too dead to feel. Don't you think?'

She looked at him. Nothing there, he thought. He wanted to run.

Something moved by her feet, enormous, a dark lump. She screamed and he had to kick it away, its sullen weight and softness against his toecap; like kicking away your own death. The rat – perhaps the same one – squealed and scampered off, a sort of rolling gait to it, very fat. Horrible. He hurled a stone after it, and another.

She was trembling, and he put his arm around her.

'I want to go back,' she said.

'Yes, there's a few more where that one came from,' he said, emptily. He was also trembling.

She broke away from him and bent down over the spot

where they had made love. She was scraping at the earth with her fingers.

'Have you a knife? I want a piece,' she said. 'All I can get is dust.'

'A piece of Flanders? Or a piece of me?'

She laughed. 'Both,' she said. 'This way I will have both. *Our* Flanders,' she added.

He produced his knife. She insisted on prising out a piece of earth herself. It was a small dry lump in her hand. She pocketed it somewhere in her dress without comment. He was afraid that if he said anything he might spoil the little ritual, something sacred in it might be mocked; so he kept quiet.

They walked slowly and steadily towards the Lille Gate. The dawn settled over the plain like a fine pale dust, dew or perhaps rain-beads silvering the weeds and grassy patches – *vor Tau und Tag!* It all looked horribly sombre, the great parched wetland – dragged out into the daylight like this, tattered and bleak, if suitably reddish for a few moments. She was almost asleep in his arms, her hair emerging from its night blackness into a deep reddish bronze. He felt tender towards her, and very grown up as he walked, very clear and fine. The uncooled air smelt metallic, rather cold and impersonal, like something made in a steel works.

They kissed again, lightly, under the gate. She would not tell him where she was staying. The new light revealed her rather cruelly: the creases around the eyes, the reparations of make-up on her cheeks, the lack of bloom. The ineffectual, thinned-out face. They made a vague mumbling promise to see each other the next day; she would try to call round at the hotel. He wrote down the name for her on an old Tube ticket.

'You don't know my name!' he said, almost laughing at the absurdity. 'In fact, I don't know yours!'

'We don't need to,' she murmured. 'Don't write it. Please.'

He handed her the ticket, *Hotel Régencia* crowded scarcely legibly around the big blurred *3d*, thinking how it balanced their future on its inch scrap. He was already thinking of a future: even of marriage! He saw them diving into a lake shadowed by pines, with hosts of their healthy children, laughing and splashing. It was strange, this vision – absurd, really. She pocketed the ticket in her jacket. Then she was looking at him, bright-eyed, as if just woken up.

'I can't find the enemy,' she said.

'Enemy?'

'The one to blame, you know. I can't find it. That is the whole awful problem. Do you see?'

He nodded. She seemed very bright, intent.

'I think,' he suggested, a touch wearily, narrowing his rather sore eyes, 'we must look – into ourselves. There's the enemy.'

She gave a contemptuous snort at that. He was surprised: he had thought it nicely judged. He felt very young, now.

'Well,' he pursued, mockingly, the words coiling out of his own hurt, 'it's either that or being a sort of – a socialist like me, blaming money, the whole economic—'

'Oh,' she interrupted, in a hectic tone, '*apart* from the bankers. Apart from the Jews and their furred wives with gold teeth. Too easy, too easy. *Everyone* blames them, like they have always been blamed for everything. My husband was *always* blaming them.' She gave a sharp sigh and asked for a cigarette. He lit it for her and she drew on it deeply. 'What will happen?'

'When?'

'Ah, you know! When – when we . . .'

She blinked almost myopically at him through the smoke.

'Yes?'

'Wouldn't he, perhaps, wish to stay with me always?'

'Who, me?'

She stroked his cheek.

'The perfect young English gentleman I met in Belgium!'

'Is that me?'

Part of him was horrified. She was mocking and serious at the same time: it was quite indistinguishable. Instead of replying, she gave her high little laugh and turned and walked away in her tent of a skirt with a very straight step, her heels clicking on the brand-new cobbles of the pavement even after she had turned the corner and disappeared, still laughing – flirtatiously (he thought), knowing that it was a performance, that he was watching her. She did not once look back, though. Just the heels clicking, that high little laugh, a curl of smoke from her cigarette – and then silence.

And as soon as she had disappeared, he touched his cheek and missed her. But he would not chase after her as he had chased after Tillie. He walked slowly and steadily to the corner. She had gone. At the end of the war he could have spotted her anywhere in any of the streets, over the waist-high rubble. He refused to hunt for her, though. A page from a newspaper blew along the street and wrapped itself around his ankle: English, the *Daily News*! He kicked it away and, missing her very much, went straight off to find a drink.

17

A North-Westerly From Iceland

T HAT ONE DANCING place still open, in the rue de la
Boucherie – it was certainly knocked about, though it did
have a roof on. Its shutters were closed, but he heard an accordion
playing a lively dance tune through the open door. That pulled
him in. It was not a rag, it was not the jittery Charleston – it
was something from long before the war, from the *belle époque* of
Montmartre, the gay nights in the windmills, the drunken singers
and poets, all that.

It was being played, this little battered accordion, by a very
old and blind Frenchman, who was kept going on generous
doses of Benedictine in a china mug. There was a scatter of late
merrymakers inside, all rather the worse for wear and too far gone
to dance, though they sang now and again to the better-known
airs. It filled him with a terrible nostalgia for a certain *idea* of
Paris, an idea with a vista of green roofs and waiters bending
over girls in dappled light. He would move there as soon as
he could. Every song seemed meant for him alone, though the
words were indistinct. He was given pitying glances by various
entwined couples, which pleased him immensely. His jacket was
as rumpled as an old woman's cheeks and his flannels were brown
with dust; he did not care a hoot. He laid Tillie's shawl on the table
and then folded it very carefully. The rosy silk slipped between
his fingers like water. There was a fine embroidered edge to
the shawl which reminded him of his mother's crochet-work.
But it was all torn, the shawl. It was a cheap Chinese thing, he
was sure.

Despite its gassy white brightness and the stink of stale perspiration – or perhaps because of it – the place suited his mood. He worked his way through a fat bottle of Cointreau and felt so happy to be alive he settled his head on his arms and cried.

No memory of returning to the hotel; he may have been helped.

Baz loomed above him at some unearthly hour, which turned out to be ten o'clock. The day was Sunday and the bells were ringing for Mass.

'Oh,' he heard Baz say, 'the risen man. Just in time for prayers.'

There was too much light: it hurt him. He had a raging thirst and a band of pain across his brow. He would have turned over and buried himself in sleep again, were it not for his consciousness, almost instant, that something marvellous had happened. As if the whole universe had changed its lodgings. He felt it on his naked feet, and then on his face. He leapt out of bed and made for the open window, entangled himself briefly with the lace curtains, then thrust his head and shoulders outside.

He took in lungfuls of morning air: great lungfuls of it. The sweetness! He could scarcely breathe enough in. He leaned out further, almost falling out.

A breeze from some magic isle was blowing gently and coolly over the town.

It all but quenched his thirst, as if borne from some ferny grotto in invisible flagons. It came from dreams of better things, but was as solid as ice. And wide awake, he was. He breathed in deeply, and felt the coolness in the tips of his fingers, the toes. It was a straight miracle.

'The deuce, Baz, what is it?'

'What is what?'

Baz was looking down at something on the bed.

'The weather! God, it's the new world!'

'What are you gibbering about? It's a north-westerly from Iceland or thereabouts, according to the meteorologists among the group. Isn't that Miss Lainer's?'

The shawl was tangled up in the sheets. Baz picked it up as if it was dirty.

'Yes,' said Joseph.

'It's torn.'

'Is it? Oh dear.'

'Why is it torn?'

'I found it on the ground, near the hotel. I expect she dropped it.'

The cool breeze was stroking his neck. He could not quite believe it. He and the widow had changed the weather – oh, there was no doubt in his mind about that. Anything was possible in the invisible. Anything.

By now he was quaffing copiously from the jug. Baz dropped the shawl and said: 'Shall I tell Miss Lainer that you've got her shawl in bed with you?'

'If you want,' said Joseph. 'Right now I need more sleep.'

'Been in your cups, have you?'

'Oh, I've been the angel, I have.'

Baz snorted contemptuously and left.

Joseph then slept deeply for a long time and awoke wondering where he was for a moment. He checked with the concierge: no one had called round for him or left a message. She gave him iodine for the throbbing graze on his hand, which made it look like a frightful wound. Feeling a mite delicate, he ventured gingerly out into the street and had a coffee and a ham brioche. The afternoon was advanced but the air remained delightfully cool and fresh. There was a bell tolling slowly and ponderously and he asked the one-eyed waiter why, in his most careful French.

'Och, for the dead,' the waiter said, in a perfect Scots accent.

He had been in the Cameronians, badly wounded in a 'show' at Messines, fell in love with a Flemish nurse, came back after the war and married her. A cousin of hers owned the café. He liked the life, knew a bit of Flemish, and scarcely needed French with all the 'foreigners' about.

'Terrible hot it's been, though. What we need is a good plump. You back for the memories, are you?'

'Sort of. Which dead, by the way?'

'The bell? Oh, the coolies.'

'The coolies?'

'The Chinko sappers. Ten of them killed yesterday in that accident, along with a couple of bairns watching the proceedings. Did you not hear it? The big bang? Made the wee glasses tingle in here.'

174

He nodded, thinking of the huge white cloud. 'I heard it, yes. I saw the smoke. That's dreadful. Especially the children.'

'Ay, they go dandelion-picking and end up in wee pieces. I wouldn't hoe a row of cabbages out there for all the skirt in Timbuctoo. It's a rum do, clearing up the mess. Leave it to the generals, I say.'

'So do I.'

'And I've told them, if they find my eye, och, I'll swap mon missus for it.'

Joseph was feeling as restless as a rook and wandered up and down the streets for a while, hoping he would see *her*. Not Tillie, but the other one. The idea of meeting Tillie embarrassed him. A lot of lively faces but none of them familiar. Everyone seemed to be very jolly with the freshness of the air: even a blind young fellow being led by the hand was grinning, turning his face aside as if to feel better the cooled air.

Then Joseph positively stumbled, whistling away, into the funeral procession winding towards the cathedral. There were two small coffins in white pine and a lot of distress in black, at least near the head of it. He took his hat off and bowed his head. It took an absolute age for the procession to pass him, exhibiting a diminishing sense of grief until the stragglers, shabbily clad, seemed unaware of what it was all about and were sauntering along, chatting merrily to each other, as if in a communion procession. He could not help it, he smiled ironically, a little ironic smile playing across his features – sharing with himself the thought that this was civilisation they were mourning, the whole doomed social state: and the stragglers, the shabby mass of folk, did not know it. They would stroll into the smash-up smiling and chatting, right up to the last twist of the rope.

He learnt from another stalled passer-by that there was a big funeral at the Chinese camp, with gongs. He was given directions and set off immediately. The place was just outside the town in a large field, not far from the Hindoo one, and had the same pointed white tents. He hovered for another age and was rewarded with the sight of flat-faced fellows carrying huge and very colourful dragon masks, but that was all. There were no gongs.

Still restless, he nipped back to the hotel for his sketchpad and carbon pencil. He had a sudden urge to draw. There were some members of the group in the hallway, but no sign of Tillie.

'Well,' boomed the monocle, 'missing presumed screwed, what?'

'Oh, I hardly touch it.'

'Then you're a feller with no stomach,' snapped the other. 'Unfit for decent society. Dead in Lahore without liquor.' He put a barnacled hand on Joseph's shoulder. He reeked of monsoons and brandy. 'But never do it on your own, boy. *Never.* That's my advice.'

The others simpered. Joseph went up to his room and hid the shawl in his bag. No Tillie, no Baz. He pocketed his pad and pencil and shot straight out again. He was heading for the area beyond the Chinese camp – promising, this area had looked. He was passing the camp on a wide track when one of the 'coolies' accosted him. He was a sun-darkened, almost withered-looking fellow, his peaked cap at an angle and his uniform shoddy. Lounging against a mangled, rusting tank, he was.

'Sah, you wan' shake han' wi' Gennel Haig?'

Joseph laughed.

'General Haig?'

'Shake han'!' The man shook an invisible hand. 'Gennel Haig! Yes? Come wi' me!'

'What is your name?'

'Me?'

'No, your name,' pursued Joseph, now finding himself following the fellow between the tents.

'My name – Mi! Mi, my name! Mi!'

This provoked more laughter between them, and Joseph liked it; he liked being ushered into this strange world of the Chinese fellows. The smell of their cooking – utterly strange! They nodded politely as he passed between the tents, and he reckoned they must hate him, really, hate the white race – not just the British subdivision – for making such a mess and then forcing their conquered subjects to clean up after it. But they nodded politely enough as he wondered at the big Chinese characters painted on the tents, and the narrow-lidded eyes, and the spiced aroma of the food. Maybe they didn't care about this life, he thought: maybe they were complete fatalists. And he stumbled on over the rough ground as Mi, beckoning furiously, led him right through the camp and out the other side. Somehow the man had acquired a lamp.

This was an untouched area, Joseph realised that fairly soon. A deadness, stilled deadness. Not a soul in sight. Danger signs crookedly placed here and there, and feeble attempts at wiring off, and twisted remains of tanks and trucks. Mi had stopped.

'Can we go in here? Isn't it dangerous?'

Mi grinned. His eyes were clear in the dark skin, like an Alpine peasant's. His ugly khaki jacket, his peaked cap: these did not suit him at all. Joseph wondered where the lamp came in.

'You go wi' Mi, no danger, sah.'

Joseph was sure he would have to tip him something; the fellow was too eager. The hotel people had moaned about the local thefts committed by *les coolies* – and especially the Annamites with their earrings and strange hair. But he was eager to see an area as yet uncleared. The ghosts would be very thick, here.

A straggle of blockhouses and pillboxes stretched away as far as the eye could see, some of them stoved right in, hammered to big chunks like broken pack-ice in a wild sea. The high white clouds had disappeared and the sky was a resplendent blue. Mi was almost running, now: he took the rough, broken ground as if he had been born to it. Joseph scrambled after him, panting, and caught his boot in some wire. Mi released it.

'Mountains? Are you from the mountains? High up?'

Mi nodded.

'Tibet?'

'Near, near.' He laughed. 'Gennel Haig, *his* han'.'

They went on. It was like a mystery story, Joseph thought: he was caught, now. The landscape was far more violently pitched and fissured, here: naked hate and violence. Quarried out, mined out, but to no plan: arid, dusty as hell. Stagnant pools lay in the deeper holes – he had to hold his nose, even with the fresher air. There was a drowned rat in one of them, repulsively bloated. Mi threw a stone at it. *Plop*, the stone went. It sounded very loud, and the ripples rubbed at the rat's black body and at the earthen sides of the shell hole.

This was the nearest he had got to the brute conditions of war, Joseph realised, as they sped off again. Nothing had been done to this sector; it was almost conceited in its deathliness, with only the odd patch of dry grass, the odd straggle of weed. And little swirls of dust rising and falling like queer flowers. He fancied he saw faces in the dried-up churn, like faces pressed open-mouthed against wet cloth. Folds that might be cloth or flesh, as brown as the dried mud. Features, hollowed eyes, shin-bones. But he could never be sure: everything had succumbed evenly to the earthen waste. Even Mi, his mountain peasant's squat litheness flitting over the waste, seemed at times no more than a moving clot of it.

They came to a curved sheet of corrugated iron. Mi yanked it to one side, revealing the stoved-in entrance of a cellar. He waited until Joseph had recovered his breath. They really had gone at a hell of a lick, given the ruggedness of the ground.

'Family – in China – very poor. Five chillen.'

Joseph nodded.

'You go out and clear the explosives, shells and so forth?'

He nodded. 'Whoof! Much danger. Many kill.'

'What about General Haig?'

'Here,' Mi assured him, pointing into the blackness of the cellar.

Joseph fished out a few pennies and Mi took them impassively. Then he lit the lamp. It reminded Joseph of a film he had seen at Oxford, about Egypt; the guide with the lamp at the entrance to the tomb, beckoning to the camera. The bespectacled archaeologist with his sketchpad. Faintly sinister, this parallel, he thought.

'Is General Haig in there?' he laughed.

'Gennel Haig!' the fellow cried, 'an' you shake han'.'

'Where are we, exactly?'

Mi found that question funny; true, whatever village or farm this fossilised quagmire had once been – well, it was now no more than this fissure in the ground.

He clambered inside over the detritus, Joseph following. The lamp fooled him with strange shadows, but the place was evidently quite a warren. It stank to high heaven: ill-smelly, as his mother would say. It was like clambering into someone's bowels. Very moist it was, with that high deep smell of damp. They went down a few steps and a tunnel appeared, just under the height of a man. Suddenly, he wondered if he was about to be murdered. What a fool he was – to be lured by a Chinaman into God knows what scrape! If the Annamites struck terror (the hotel owner had put it thus) into the hearts of the upright citizens of Ypres, perhaps there was a good reason. Perhaps Mi was an Annamite, after all!

But he followed Mi nevertheless, up the tunnel past two or three chambers with wire-netting beds, past mouldering sacks and barrels and a table covered in rubbish – tins, parts of guns, broken lamps, a chewed-up prayer-book – into an open area with a cracked ceiling of cemented brick. Airless! No natural light! Joseph felt a faint high shriek of claustrophobia starting up. Mi's lamp swung formless shadows out of the gloom. Part of the mole-hole had caved in – one side was a cascade of earth and rubble. A table had papers on it, half-covered in filth.

'Gennel Haig here,' Mi announced.

Joseph was looking at the papers. Operation Orders on foolscap, ration-lists, scribbled notes in pencil dated 1915. An HQ of sorts, at any rate. British, certainly. He had not thought anything was underground at Wipers, that it was all pillboxes and shell-holes and slime, but evidently this old Flemish cellarage had been put to use for a while, before the hellishness above had done for it fairly early on. Yet somehow it had not been flooded. Damp as hell – the only moist place in the world, it felt like – but never submerged. Freakish, that.

Mi was holding the lamp high. He looked like a conjuror in a pantomime. Water glistened on the walls.

'Close eye, close eye please sah,' he said.

Joseph closed his eyes uncertainly.

'Gennel Haig, hallo. Welcome. Welcome. Shake han'! Polite! Great honour!'

Joseph's arm was being pulled forward. He felt something oddly dry and hard enter the cup of his hand.

'Shake han' sah!'

He was urged to, and so he did. The graze on his palm stung against the clutter of dryness he was gripping. And then a sudden revulsion flushed in him, and he opened his eyes. The lamplight fell directly onto the thing he was gripping: ah, a human hand all right, shorn of its flesh, stuck straight out of the earth, out of a ragged scrap of khaki sleeve. Dry as a root, that hand, with something toffee-like on each knuckle. A Haig whisky bottle was embedded where the face might be, the label stained and yellowed. It was itself a primitive face, a childish mask. As if the thing might suddenly burst from behind the fallen earth and totter towards them.

'Good God,' was all Joseph could say. And he whipped his hand away as if it had touched flame.

Mi beamed at him.

'Gennel Haig,' he repeated. 'You see? Gennel Haig.'

He was pointing at the bottle, laughing now at his childish magic.

'Thank you,' said Joseph. 'It's a grand turn.'

He managed to find the air before retching. Mi was not bothered, not bothered at all. He was still laughing, in fact, his face wrinkling up around the narrow eyes. The fellow might be dead tomorrow, Joseph thought, wiping his mouth on his sleeve. It was only a turn.

Mi led him back to where a proper track curved away.

'Many chillen,' he said, beaming. 'Very poor in China.'

'So am I,' Joseph said. 'Here, don't move.'

He executed a quick sketch of the fellow and gave it to him.

'You'll be fond of this in your old age.'

It was hardly Mi, but he bowed and bobbed furiously. Then they shook hands and Joseph took off. He had made a bit of a joke of it, pumping the dry little root of the live hand, but he had felt like retching again.

He walked rather briskly up the track, keen to leave that untouched area behind him. The drink, the horror in the moist cellar – his nausea was only offset by the clearer air. He pictured Iceland and its north-westerly sweeping from the glaciers. He pictured last night, too. Oh yes. That was a victory, certainly. He had come through the dark mist and rung a great victory – not the mean modern type of victory but something wild and very ancient, a sort of rite, like the ancient fire-rites of Balder. That burning tree – it might have been an oak, after all. And the woman? Maybe she was deathless. Maybe through her he had partaken of something very ancient and very deep: the old, primitive, Aryan Europe of the great woods and gods. Yes, he did really believe he had been chosen in some way.

And then he felt faintly ridiculous, thinking of it like that, in that *Golden Bough*-ish sort of manner – going about with what Baz would call his 'mythometer'. He even laughed at himself –

chuckling right out loud in this still place. Well, he was not at all sure *what* he felt for the woman, on the ordinary level. He was certainly not in love – not with two women, at least. With one, perhaps? Then *which* one?

Each, when he thought of her, diminished the other. And that was a trick worthy of a conjuror, not of deep feeling! He did feel tricked by things, just at this moment. And there was no little coolie to put the blame on, either. He stopped to sketch a pillbox that had sunk in to its slit eye, a revolver lying just in front of it, among the debris plaster-cast in dried mud. A chess-game of light and shade, it was: but the chaos of it sunk him. He stuck to the shadows first but wrecked the highlights with fussy additions. 'Leave it to the paper,' Mr Douse would say, but he could not. The foreground scrap looked like a thick hedge, the revolver like an absurd little claw; very soon there was nothing left of it but a hole worn right through the thick cartridge paper by his rubber.

18

The Bones

H E MADE HIS way back on the main road between harvested
fields, passing a wrecked aeroplane cordoned off by wire with
a half-dug cemetery behind it. A huge pile of crosses was thrown
in a heap to one side and he made a few more feeble sketches. He
stared at them, amazed at how feeble they were. Further on, he
saw a commotion in the distance, towards Ypres – at least, a lot
of people were milling about in the road, raising dust. A truck
tooted and rumbled past, but had to wait until the crowd gave
it passage. There was a lot of folk in black, the women looking
particularly respectable with black plumes in their hats, the breeze
ruffling them grandly. A large shed stood to the left, raised up on
its own platform, up and down the steps of which a continuous
stream of people were passing.

He was curious and lost no time in joining the crowd. A sign
above the door of the shed said *Ossuaire*. To his surprise, he spotted
Baz and Tillie on the top step. His heart missed a beat. Beyond the
shed was a vast ploughed-up area over which a few official-looking
types were stumbling – stumbling *pompously*, waving papers. Then
other members of the English group emerged from strangers' faces
and he was spotted in turn. His heart sank but he waved anyway and
eventually mounted the steps to join Baz. Tillie smiled at Joseph as
if nothing at all had passed between them. His mouth went dry.
He thought of the torn shawl in his room.

'Slept it off, old man? Tillie and I were just wondering about
you.'

'I've been sketching.'

'Oh,' said Tillie, 'what a good idea.'

Her eyes sparkled. Joseph felt himself wrong-footed, rather than wronged.

'Let's see it, then,' said Baz.

They were having to pretty well shout above the noise: the steps made a frightful clatter and everyone else was nattering, too.

'I threw it away.'

'Threw it away?' Baz turned to Tillie and gave her a rueful smile. 'Artistic temperament, you see. What did I tell you?'

'What *did* you tell her?'

'I said you had an artistic temperament.'

Joseph loathed this sort of remark about artists, however lightly meant. It was the very lightness, the frothiness, that nagged him.

'With reference to what?'

Baz waved his hand ineffectually, as if brushing at one of the numerous flies about. It was as if they had all been blown here off the salient, like the people.

'What a shame,' said Tillie. 'I'll bet they were rather fine.'

'I hardly put pencil to paper. Defeated, you know. By the way, what's going on here? A big *fête*?'

Tillie shuddered. 'Don't go in, it's full of bones.'

'They're exhibiting the bits before they bury them in the mass grave back there,' Baz explained. 'Six hundred unknown chaps; French. There's every chance, you see, that someone'll be looking at the femur of their brother or son or husband or father. Whatever.'

'But they won't know it, even if they are,' Joseph pointed out.

'That doesn't matter. If they look at all the bones, then they can come out believing they *have* looked at it. Paid their respects. I went in and thought of Hanley.'

'But he wasn't French. In fact, he thought the French were a lousy flea-ridden garlic-munching—'

'Keep your voice down, will you?'

Baz looked quite upset.

Tillie said: 'Who's to know what's a French bone and what isn't?'

Baz nodded. 'Exactly.'

'You just told me that this was full of French remains.'

'It is, theoretically. They've been pulled from the French lines.

That's not to say that the odd Britisher or even German mightn't have crept in.'

'And I've shaken General Haig's hand,' Joseph muttered.

Tillie's eyes widened. 'Have you?'

He went in. The place suddenly grew to huge proportions, and echoed terribly. It was full of shelves, ranged up to the ceiling on either side with a double lot running down the middle, and these shelves were stacked with bones of every description, just like an ancient catacomb. There were a vast amount of grinning skulls, most disfigured in varying degrees, and endless white limbs. Scrubbed, spotless bone. Trays at the end held bits and bobs – vertebrae, foot bones, fingers. It was fantastically horrible, completely life-denying, pitted *against* life. One skull had a perfect cranium and jawbone, but in between was a splintered hole: no eyes, no nasal cavity, no teeth. It was as if someone had taken a huge hammer to it. There were men who survived such a wound, he knew that. Another skull had everything on it bar most of the jaw, quite chinless it looked. The rumour was that Kipling's son had survived like that, for a few hours at least, after a shell burst had caught him in the mouth. Dabbing with a handkerchief where his chin had been, and weeping.

He shivered and made for the door. The place had a strange, stricken fug to it, as if death was releasing some kind of primeval gas onto the unsuspecting crowds. The other folk appeared oddly jolly, pointing at the bones as if they were in a museum, nodding and smiling. Children tried to touch and were pulled back or smacked. It was a day's outing. It was hard to believe that any of these visitors were here to pay their respects to a lost relative – but, judging from their dress, most were. Perhaps it was all too odd, and when they got back home it would flood them with a nightmarish sense of the truth. Or perhaps they saw right through the whole business: the charnel house full of so many jackstraws, in relation to their own man. He was a few yards from the entrance, pushing his way past a stout elderly woman in an enormous hat, when he stopped dead in surprise.

She was here. *She* was here! With her back to him, partly silhouetted. Just for a second, through the milling crowd, he had spotted her against the bright light of the door. He did his best to hurtle, but only succeeded in knocking over a tot. By the time the creature had been soothed, and he had picked up his hat and apologised, the apparition (for so he thought of it) had gone.

He was terribly keen to speak to her. To walk away with her. Hang the others – it didn't matter. Even in front of Tillie, it didn't matter. He reckoned he had gone mad.

There were people everywhere, outside: Tillie's cream dress was easily spotted, but *hers* – hers must have melded into the general widowy black. She had been bare-headed, with that bobbed, curl-necked crop of coppery hair – but it was nowhere to be seen. He started to have his doubts. Silhouettes are always blurred and confusing. Had he recognised her shape, or formed it from another? Baz was indicating from the road that they should get a move on. A great sadness filled him, suddenly. He was very tired and rather hungry. The intensity of his experience last night, the actual glow of it, was wearing off. The hateful building weighed down upon him, everyone was a walking skeleton, X-rayed from their clothes and flesh – the place was enough to unhinge someone of a delicate mental constitution, and yet no one else seemed terribly affected. There was a camera on a tripod at the bottom of the steps, whirring away, and Joseph imagined himself as an enormous, shocked face on the screen.

'Where's Tillie?'

Baz pointed down the road. She was walking away with the others, about five or six of them. When she turned briefly, Joseph could see the way her scar set her off from the others, made her lovelier.

'Baz, don't let me tear you away from your pleasures.'

'Now now. That's not fair. I'm Miss Lainer's chaperone, that's all.'

'Did she, ah – how is she?'

'Without her shawl.'

'Well, I can see that.'

'Danced all night, did you?'

Joseph felt his nose sharpen. 'She went to bed soon after you did, Baz.'

'Oh, I didn't know.'

He seemed very pleased, of course.

'I had the most amazing stroll in the battlefield,' said Joseph, 'under the light of the moon.'

'Ah yes, the poet.'

'No, the lover.'

'Oh?'

'Or perhaps the lunatic.'

'I see.'

By now they were losing the ossuary lot, but Joseph dawdled enough to keep the others well ahead. Baz was chafing a little, he could see. The fresh breeze had dropped a bit. It was hotter on the wide road, with the sun beating off the white dust. He wanted to curl up and be alone somewhere cool and green and hilly.

'Where are they off to?'

'There's a little cemetery somewhere near this road where Mrs Harriot's son is supposed to be buried. We've had the most frightfully busy time touring the cemeteries. I never found Hanley's, but Tillie – Miss Lainer – she found her brother's best friend. The books are all in a muddle, we pretty well stumbled on it. She had a little weep and then we found this bod with a pair of shears who seems to know every grave in the place. He remembered seeing a Harriot in this spot half a mile from Wipers. My feet are utterly killing me.'

Mrs Harriot was a large, blotchy-faced woman who had complained vociferously about the tea the day before.

'I don't think I'll bother,' Joseph said.

'Bother with what?'

'Coming along.'

But Tillie had turned round ahead and was signalling to them. The group stopped and waited for them to catch up. Mrs Harriot looked even more disagreeable, like a stone statue lichened with age. She held herself very stiffly until they came up and then said, 'Gentlemen, would you do us ladies the honour?'

She indicated that the two young men should lead the group through a knot of fellows who were, in her words, 'decidedly raucous'. A waggon full of twisted lead piping was parked on the side of the road, its lathes white with dust.

'Fancy working on a Sunday,' Tillie commented.

'Fancy *imbibing* on a Sunday,' added Mrs Harriot, showing her teeth.

She was such a picture of disapproval that she cut a kind of swathe through the men, who were momentarily cowed behind their bottles. Continental drunkenness, this was: not even a whistle. The workers' waistcoats were dusted as white as the lathes.

'Thirsty work, you know, clearing up our mess,' Joseph said.

'Why *our* mess?' said one of the group.

'Humanity's mess, then.'

They turned into the cemetery. Amazingly, it had a row of young poplars at one end, in full leaf. Somehow, they must have survived the war as saplings. There was a variety of crosses, some German, some British, a little group of Newfoundlanders – and they each took a row to look for 'Percy Harriot', at the mother's command.

Joseph felt like a schoolboy, and paced up and down rather truculently. The whole situation was dragging him out of the magic circle drawn by last night's events, which seemed less and less real. He made for the poplars and stared up at them. Their beauty, the blur and rustle of the bright yellowed leaves against the blue – that was inspiring, it held him almost spellbound. They recalled the poplars at Iffley Mill, and that ineffable moment of certainty at the end of his first week at Oxford. Oxford! So long ago, that nonsense seemed! If he had had paints on him he would have attacked a canvas; if he had been a halfway decent poet he would have followed up the example of Gerard Manley Hopkins at Binsey. Instead he did as Mr Douse advised and took a mental photograph for later use. The trees' golden steeples imprinted themselves on his mind's plate so thoroughly that he could, years later, still pull them out of memory's drawer, bright as the day they were entered. The Wipers poplars. He was reluctant to take his eyes from them. They held him like candle flames.

'You won't find him there,' piped a voice, making him jump. 'He's not a bird.'

It was Tillie. He had been gazing up . . . dreamily, to her.

He nodded and smiled, slightly irritated. She smiled back. He thrust his hands into his pockets and continued to gaze up, more in earnest now, as if he was pondering something botanical. It was quite ridiculous: they were behaving like *ingenue* lovers, he thought. She was a funny sort, full of jokes but really deadly serious underneath, and at the same time wondering away at everything while she was also indifferent to it, because what properly mattered was God and His business.

'They're lovely,' she said. 'They're lovely trees.'

She held onto her little white bag as if it was the front rail of an omnibus.

'Quite lovely,' he agreed.

She stepped up rather coquettishly. Not that she was meaning to, he was sure of that.

'I don't care if I don't find my dear brother's,' she said. 'I should never have come. I know he's with the angels.'

He looked up again. Her voice had a light, metallic ring to it, very attractive, slightly *rauque*.

'He may be up there, for all you know, sitting in the branches watching us.'

'What?'

'I'm sure angels can come down to earth.'

'Of course they can. They intercede all the time.'

'Why didn't they in the war?'

She shook her head, gave a little twist at the waist.

'I don't want to talk to you. You're always teasing.'

'No I'm not. I'm just having a theological discussion.'

The others wove in and out between the crosses, like crows looking for scraps.

'I lost my shawl,' she said.

'Did you?'

'It was my grandmother's. Rather precious.'

'You might have dropped it last night.'

'We won't talk about last night.'

'All right.'

'*Easy*, isn't it?'

With this sudden rather venomous emphasis, that creased her scar right up, she walked away. The trees rustled and dropped some leaves. He brushed a leaf off his shoulder and started looking for Percy Harriot himself, losing his guilt and confusion in activity. The names were over-scrutinised: his eyes could have run along them swiftly, but refused to. They felt both very ancient and as new as wet paint. All of a sudden there was a fluster and a cry of 'Found it!' in the middle of the cemetery, only a few rows from where he stood, and he saw Mrs Harriot moving at surprising speed from the far end towards the victor, who had his white-sleeved arm raised. It reminded him vaguely of a game of cricket.

He reached the row at the same time as her. She bustled past him, her expression as stony as ever but her body moving with a terrible urgency, and the knot gathered there instantly separated to give her space. He came up softly, aware of the respectful silence, and Baz discreetly pointed at him. At the top of his head.

His hat! Joseph took it off.

Mrs Harriot stared at the cross, upon which her son's name was rather crudely etched and highlighted by flakes of paint, with a completely blank expression, as if the wood bore nothing on it but its patches of moss. Joseph thought the whole exercise rather a waste of time, and thought back to the previous night, to the white breasts and the blueish lick of moonlight, the warm soft pulp – instantaneously, with a sound that seemed to belong to no earthly creature, Mrs Harriot vomited a great high jet of bile which continued for many seconds in a steady stream all over the plot, gave a heart-wrenching howl, and sank to the ground, her large form shuddering all over.

Joseph, frozen in shock, thought she was dying, but she was not. It took at least half an hour to restore her to a semblance of her senses with generous nips of brandy, once the flask could be carried to her mouth. Otherwise, she howled and groaned and tore at the meagre grass with her hands, lay back against various arms in apoplectic tears, shouted unintelligible curses at whoever brought this about (man, Joseph thought) and then succumbed to a ghastly raucous moaning, a sound that had all the supportability of a knife on a whetstone.

Joseph was quite shaken by the end of it. They all were, it looked like. A doctor arrived with an ambulance and she was carted away to the hospital in town, accompanied by Tillie, bowed over her in white like – well – an angel.

Whether the woman ever recovered her wits, eventually, remained an unknown.

19

Gunter's Ghost

H E STAYED ON for a few days, travelling about in a bit of a
haze, not telling the others why. They had gone back in a
sombre mood, Baz rather miffed that his friend was able to take
a break from work, while he – Baz – was committed to whatever
a trainee lawyer does in his stuffy chambers. Joseph took a lift in a
lorry down to the Somme area and brooded.

It was also a wreck, the countryside there, but he could see
how it was all healing over again, the scar tissue of crops and long
white roads, chalk country, broom and pretty blue flowers. Then
suddenly you would have this chasm of a trench system, or a great
pit of a shell hole, and the usual rubbish of wire and old shells and
slabs of concrete, all whiskered by dry grasses growing through. It
was sadder and more beautiful than Flanders. It was the stuff of
poetry, even.

It was baking hot again, too, but dry with it – downland heat, the
air trembling in the distance over the rolling ground, very brittle
and dry. Even the harebells looked parched.

Peronne was as smashed up as Ypres, and full of types that might
have looked good in bearskins, and more Calamity Janes and thick
make-up and feather boas, and amidst all these wove the respectable
locals pulling neat little handcarts made by Miele – German, they
were! The ghastly Nissen huts were everywhere, and the maroon
sheds were clearly standard for the whole line. He walked miles
in the heat, over the downs.

Away from the new cemeteries and the gangs of metal-pickers,
the peace was only broken by invisible larks and the rumble of

shells being set off. He did not know whether they were set off deliberately – he did not like to think about it, about the children picking dandelions and so forth. Someone in the spit-and-sawdust hotel told him that the shells took folk every day, and often *nos gamins parmi eux*, but he couldn't feel anything – or at least, he brushed the feeling off, pushed it away.

At the bottom, he was infatuated. Maybe he was in love. Not with Tillie, not deeper down – it was the other one. He did not see how someone could be in love with a shadow, which is how he thought of the German woman – nameless, too. But this appeared to be the case. It was like falling for a stray, a night-bird in an all-night café in London, one of those perfumed mysteries with a muff who tells you she is a cinema actress and who asks to 'borrow' your cigarette for a moment, leaving her dark-red lipstick on it. He had very little money and ate mostly bread and thin stews, but he had lost his appetite anyway. Why did he light out for the Somme? He had this vague idea that he would find her there; he had exhausted all the lodging places in Ypres and drawn a blank: no guest, past or present, fitted her description.

After one night being bitten alive by fleas he left the hotel in Peronne and slept out in barns. The night air was so warm he hardly had to cover himself in hay. He made notes as best he could, sitting in abandoned trenches full of grass, peeping over the crumbling parapets. The peace, the silence – where there were not the metal-pickers and the odd group of real harvesters with their waggons, the peace was unearthly, it rang in the ears. Almost always dotted about in the distance were black figures, very black and bowed against the yellow and white. He kept them tiny by the route he took – it was easy, going where you wanted on those grassy slopes unless a skull and crossbones told you not to. He thought of Mrs Harriot, though, when he saw these grieving little figures, like emblems, little flakes of soot in the broad freshness.

Without his straw hat, he would have died of sunstroke.

He wandered about as light as thistledown, but he was heavy as lead inside. The strange thing was that in his dreams, snuffling about in the hay, the German woman and Tillie and the licking whore melted into each other, and this phantasm was somehow more complete and satisfying than any of them were singly. In these dreams he was much more devil-may-care than in his waking state, so he would wake up disappointed, ashes in his mouth (straw dust, really). He wondered whether he should not live like this permanently, a hobo, a Shropshire lad, filled with wanderlust and mendicant scraps, wandering Europe until, by sheer novelistic ingenuity and luck, he stumbled into the arms of Gunter's mother. But he knew that really she was gone out of his life. That was how it had to be: a memory. A regret, even. Your life shapes itself around the empty spaces of regret. He felt the grain of his life already starting to twist and flow around this regret, giving his life interest, even beauty, like an interesting piece of found wood.

Then one night, the moon very bright through the slats of a half-wrecked barn near the old Cuinchy sector, he woke up in naked terror, convinced that Gunter had come in with some loathsome wound. Yes, there he was. He watched him walk about a bit beyond the hay, near the shattered beams. Gunter's wound kept shifting, as if someone was smearing him in black treacle. Because he, Joseph, had the same looks as Gunter, he kept very quiet. It was Hubert Rail, really, pretending to be Gunter in Bosche kit. The moonlight striped his grey tunic and soft flat cap as he moved; he was all in grey, even his skin, and there was mud on his big plain cuffs. Every shift of Joseph's body rustled like a rat – it was just that aural likeness that saved him. When Gunter lifted his face to listen, Joseph could see that its expression was one of fright, despite the shadow across it. He was not frightened of Joseph, he was frightened of the rat, of the possibility of rats. Those little rats' feet stirring about, in for the kill, long greased tails dragging after them. But Joseph reckoned that if Gunter had known he was there, he would have overcome his fear of rats and advanced towards Joseph, where he crouched in the old cow-stall, and pounced.

Amazingly, Joseph fell asleep, watching the grey soldier prowl about.

Or at least, he found himself staring into a bright dab of sunlight, the air outside full of birds.

This nightmare bade him leave the wandering life (all five days of it) and take the first train home. The other passengers – mostly British – put their handkerchiefs to their noses and avoided his wild, unwashed gaze. From his light fur of straw and dirt, he enjoyed every minute of this attention. He imagined that he owned nothing but his body and mind, and how even that might dissolve into the earth and sky without undue struggle. The speeding landscape beyond the whirl of smoke belonged, however, to another time and place; his five days had existed very long ago, it seemed to him. He was hungry and light-headed, something the slow roll of the ferryboat only encouraged. He imagined he had arrived from the past, innocent of the present, and that if he felt in his pocket he would find the rough-edged coins of the darkest ages and their crude emperors instead of centimes and pennies. Even his fleas were ancient.

20

A Silver Curtain

LONDON SOON SORTED that out. She was a quivering mass of humid heat, like a brick and concrete version of the Burma jungle; there were black clouds piling up beyond the chimneys and the odd half-hearted purr of thunder. He had a sour cheesecake in a teashop called Guinevere's Garden, full of shingled heads and fancy frescoes of knights and damsels, and caused a brief stir.

He shopped for second-hand books and then went straight home on the last train. A red-eyed smooching couple in the carriage were reading the *Evening News* together, bemoaning the planned removal of the flower-sellers from under Eros, due to the squaring of the Circus.

'All a matter of omnibuses and fatter stores,' said a fellow with a long spade beard and a hearthrug rolled up on his lap. 'They want to remove Eros, too. Fair-square greed, I call it.'

Joseph nodded in agreement. No more violets, no more love! England struck him as loveless, wrinkled and loveless. Heart-broken, perhaps, but not admitting to it. It was as if he had been away years, not days.

Baz had been worried about him, of course, and he found a fretting letter in Baz's neat hand, posted for some reason in Swansea (what was he doing in Swansea?) and two cards 'from Ma' in his postbox. If he did not write twice a week, she would worry. Not for him, so much as for herself. As for Baz, he reckoned Joseph had looked 'rather queer' the day they left. He no doubt looked even queerer now. Also, he found a postcard from Tillie, which surprised him; it showed a view of the baths at Buxton, where she had stopped off on her way up. Her words displayed her mettle, by dint of the complete absence – not a quiver – of regret or blame: she merely told him that she had arrived safely and was 'fagged out'. Baz made no mention of her. Nor of Agnes, for that matter.

He was too tired to wash. There was no water in the place, anyway – he had drunk his fill at the pump opposite the inn on his walk up from the station. After chasing some hens out of the kitchen, and retrieving eggs from behind the washstand, he went to bed naked, without so much as a sheet over him, it was that stifling. All he unpacked from the bag was Tillie's torn shawl, which he ritually laid under his pillow. It smelt of peppermint, unfortunately – his toothpowder had spilt in his bag. Walter had finished the bedroom, done a good, smooth job, but the air in there was like a sour steam-bath. He would have to keep on sleeping in the study, for now. His dreams would mingle with his writing thoughts.

He thought of the widow. He had been hoping, the whole time he was away, to bump into her, even on the Somme. But he had not forced it. The rain had not come, had it? He felt faintly ridiculous, thinking back to that first fresh morning. Madness is a kind of ontological impudence; that is how it starts, anyway.

Somewhere deep in the night, he was woken up by the most enormous crumple of sound. He reckoned in his dream that it was a shingle-haired Prussian train crashing into some sort of purple edifice full of knights in armour with one skeleton hand apiece. There was another noise, too, like a lot of kettles steaming all at once, a long low hiss below the rumbling after-shock.

The hiss drew him to the open window and he stared out at a silver curtain, at folds upon folds of water. Gulfs of sweet air invaded the room, billowing about the little place as if sent from paradise or a lost childhood happiness, the whole land thankful for moisture, the woods exhaling their relief over the cottage, the sap itself that had just about dried out surging up again into the countless million dripping leaves and sad flowers.

And now there were trickles, water braiding down, pouring in thick ropes from the bent, ivy-choked gutter, shapes gleaming in the night made purely out of the downpour, carved out of wetness. It was very heavy rain, that. The claps of thunder shook the walls. The ink was blotched on his foolscap on the table under the window; but he did not close the window, he pulled the table back.

He went straight out into the garden and stood there, just stood there with his arms akimbo. It was as good as the waterfall near Youlster, where the beck drops twenty feet out of a granite scoop. It even got him shivering. The month of extreme heat was wiped out and done for. As was the sweat and dust of his week abroad. He took it, in the way you do in youth, as a ritual thing, a symbolic cleansing. The water streamed off his jaw like a Chinaman's beard.

Amazingly, his fixation on the German woman ran away with the dirt. Rubbing himself down in the kitchen, he saw her as retreating, distant even, in his consciousness. He felt vaguely condescending towards her. Yes, he thought, I can begin afresh. The air was fresh and his mind was buoyant: the week had been exceedingly satisfactory, all round. He had had an adventure abroad, a really passionate adventure of the soul – no, the body! He skipped about the kitchen, naked and cool, as the storm thundered and hammered and trickled outside.

It was as if he had forgotten about her promise, about the rain coming for love's sake. He had not really, but it was covered over by the sheer relief of the rain's arrival. It seemed such a detached, objective power, the rain, as it hammered down. Objective as pistons, as it did its job.

The rain, of course, found every leak in the thatch within an hour, and the upstairs floor became a pell-mell of crockery, bucket and bedpan. They made such a singing racket he slept downstairs in the parlour, curled up on the frayed settee between the chunks and flakes of plaster. He slept surprisingly well.

It was only the next morning, the rain still coming down steadily, that he wondered how the hens had got in.

There was no key to the cottage – he had not locked up – but there was nothing to steal apart from the furniture, and the best bits put together would scarcely come to three guineas. He scouted about, looking for a hole by which poultry might invade. Nothing, apart from mice droppings. Someone must have opened the door for a bit; there were hens everywhere in the village, they were always wandering up – even this far. Then he saw that the bread tin was empty, though the lid had been on. He had left half a loaf in for Walter's rabbits; they loved nibbling at it when it was dry as bone. Gypsies, he thought. Travellers. There were lots of them about – half the village seemed to be of that stock, in fact, to look at. He checked in the cupboard and, sure enough, his bottles of pop and Bass had gone, the nettle wine was open (but not much drunk, unsurprisingly) and Mrs Hamilton's cider was an inch of green lees. A hunk of hard cheddar had been reduced to crumbs.

He was annoyed – and then considered what *he* had been like when living rough those few days: a tramp, that is what he had been, seeking barns to sleep in and ramshackle places where a few centimes might gain him a crust, seeking them out with foxy, keen eyes. He was almost ready to beg by the end. It happens very quickly, the descent, the crumbling of custom. The rain was carrying on outside as if it had never been missed, and he was glad he was not out in it now. But the idea that the cottage was vulnerable disturbed him; he would mention it to Walter, and maybe the fellow could furnish him with a lock.

The rain eased off by the evening – Sunday evening it was – and he ventured out down the drive into the manor's grounds. The grass hung heavy, bowed with wet. The sun emerged just before dusk and the effect was stupendous: golden light, a flood of it, in cavernous rays through the trees and the light mist the rain had left behind, and everywhere afire with drops, necklaces of fiery jewels on leaf and branch and stem, red and violet and silvery-gold.

He got himself thoroughly soaked tracking through the heavy wet waves of wild grass on the manor's old lawn. Despite the fact that the storm had pushed it about a bit, he noticed other winding tracks – deer again, he reckoned. The mist was steam, really, but not humid somehow, just very sweet and pungent. He sat in the gazebo and tried not to feel lonely. The woods were ablaze with birdsong, all the birds glad at the same time, sipping at the rain and flourishing their feathers. He wondered how far the rain had penetrated into the parched land. And then he saw the island of Britain as a whole thing, lapped by seas, quite devoid of people, its earth sucking up the gift of rain and glad of it – the nameless land glad of it. No motoring signs or red boxes or roads to string them along, not even any rustic cottages or old crumbling mansions like the one before him, its dignified walls dark with damp again. No prices of eggs or mutton, no shingled heads, no trains, no books, no taste of coke in the fog. Just trees and gorse and animals and the sudden eventual roar of the cliffs. No deafening row of traffic, only that roar of the sea and an inland hush, all leaf-sigh and birdsong. A prehuman island whose time had to come, unfortunately, and be made a thing of, a paltry thing called a nation in which everything deep and good and ultimate is covered over, obliterated. For the sake of paltry desires with no more lasting value than a twopenny-upright down a stinking alley.

But he breathed in that sweet air as if he was up on Olympus. Did it rain in Eden? It was the drought that had unlocked the rain's magic. There are a thousand different rains, from the Irish type of grey vapour through Manchester drizzle to the solid wall of Indian monsoon, but it is what comes before the rain that counts. Everything before the war was lit like this, in people's minds. Golden, glittering, a far-off place. His childhood, too, he realised. Not that his childhood had much good weather, as it were; looking back on it, he saw a lot of grey patches, some confusion. There were wars before this last one, too: misery, massacres, all that. But something broke in the trenches, something deep, a very deep fracture. We would have to go about very carefully now, he reflected, if the fracture was to heal. He knew of a soldier who had broken his neck and somehow walked about completely unaware for months, until an X-ray examination spotted the dark streak. This is how we are, he thought: civilisation's neck is broken and we do not know it yet, we can still walk. But anything might jolt it to complete fracture, paralysis or death.

As he was murmuring to himself, he imagined he saw a head pop out of the grass, a wild-haired thing that might have been human. Then it vanished, back into the grasses it resembled, like the spirit of the grass itself.

The blink of an eye, it was. Wild, quite wild and almost human.

Pan, he thought. It is a sign. The spirit of Pan is what we need. And he felt a surge of electrical current pass through him from head to foot, out of the very earth itself. He stayed absolutely still for ages, until he knew he was back in the humdrum world again and needed a cup of tea.

This is what the rain did to him. It made the earth charged – and dangerous.

21

A Haircut

THE STORM CLEARED up on the Monday, and there was a fine clear air, washed from top to bottom. The garden shook itself like a dog and immediately started expanding, everything in it growing and expanding and thickening. He stood outside naked and felt the grass caressing his ankles, physically plumping up under him. It was almost frightening. Her thirst slaked, Mother Nature was exulting, dazzling him in the morning sunlight. Walter would have to come over with his scythe.

He had not yet supped at the pub since his return, he had scarcely eaten, the tramping had given him a queer appetite for unbuttered bread and warm milk straight from the udder. Or maybe it was the rain that had affected him. So he had not clapped eyes on Walter – but he would, he realised, have to see Walter today, pay him for the plastering. He felt a vague reluctance, allied to the Samuel business: maybe the planned meeting had been forgotten. He half-hoped so.

Footprints – he noticed footprints on the lawn, clear and dark in the beaded grass. They were not his. They wandered about a bit, then left by the gate. No attempt – unless the owner could fly – to come in by the door. He would have preferred that. He could sense what the fellow had thought: *he's back, I'd best not go in*. It chilled him slightly, seeing the thoughts in the footprints, the hesitation, the decision. The trampled grass already springing up.

They would not be back, now he was.

He was just settling to his thin-lined foolscap at ten, in the sunlit garden under the drying plum tree, when the postman arrived. He had a tricycle with a box at the back in which letters mingled with boots and shoes – a cobbler, he was, with a workshop at the farthest point on his round; you could give him your split boots along with your letters. The tinkle of his bell was something Joseph had found charming on first arrival, and now found irritating; it distracted him, it provoked expectation – and the fellow was a chatty old soul, huge, a huge pyramidal body that strained the tricycle to breaking point, a long white beard almost reaching down to the five long-service stripes on his tunic. Always merry, he was, and always talking. This is why he would hand over the post personally, if you were in. Once or twice, soon after his first arrival, Joseph had hidden, hidden away upstairs as the door was pounded and the bell tinkled. Mrs Hamilton had commented on this the next day.

'Unless you leave a note, they'll think you're passed away in there after three days. They'll bring the constabulary in to have a look.'

'But Mrs H., I eat here nearly every day.'

'That don't stop folk coming to queer conclusions. Mr Collins was seen regular in Upper Lane for two weeks after he'd passed away. Them dead 'uns hang about, y'know, for a bit.'

'Ghosts don't eat large suppers, as far as I've heard.'

'They steal food, ghosts do, from right under your nose.'

'Do they?'

'Not always gypsies, it isn't. They drink blood, too, do bogies. Harry Maskell saw a cheese thrown right across his kitchen, once – and Lily were three *year* dead by then.'

'But I might want to sleep in or go out for a morning walk. I don't usually, but I might want to.'

'Then leave a note. Folk gets accustomed to the pattern of your ways, see, Mr Monrow.'

Joseph did not like this at all: he had elected to be here for the sake of creative liberty, to be his own man – and instead the village constrained him. It was maddening. He felt snooped on, judged.

And here was Dan, the cobbler-postman, signalling to him from the gate.

He had two letters, one of them posted in Germany. The other was in the tight copperplate of Mr Frank Pitts.

'Bin off an' away, then, sir? Foreign parts?'

Mrs Hamilton had, of course, told him. The whole village knew. Dan's huge bulk wheezed its jollity, probing. An abundance of honeysuckle half-falling off the wall submerged them in scent as they talked. A letter from Germany – Joseph saw this instantly. His heart beat steadily. But she did not even know his name! He had forgotten that.

'I went to Belgium.'

'I see.'

The postman's jollity was benevolently coasting, with a little crosscurrent rucking it. A vicious little pull, just under it. You could see it in his eyes. That was what the war did.

'Interesting, was it, sir?'

'A mess, frankly. They've got a long way to go. An awful, depressing mess.'

He held the envelope in his hand and saw her breasts staring through it.

'I always tried to give her with a touch of dignity, you know.'

'Give what?'

'The informing letter. The one with the black edge all about.'

'Ah, yes.'

Dan took his hat off and held it against his chest. Behind him, under the towering elm at the corner, his tricycle had a pair of split clogs dandling from the handlebars.

'Like so,' he said, handing over the invisible letter, cap to his sloped chest, head bowed. 'And sometimes they ud crock up in front o' your eyes, even before they had opened it. I ud have to administer first aid, then.'

He produced, from his fob pocket under the jacket, a slim brandy flask. Joseph smiled. This man made a trifle of horrors. It was almost enviable.

'I hope not used too recently.'

'Mrs Pritchard's boy, in January. Never recovered from his wounds. No marks outside, it were all in yere.' And he rubbed his stomach.

'Oh dear, that is sad.'

'He *did* suffer, oh yes he did.'

And then, after a word about the storm, Dan was gone.

Joseph went into the kitchen and opened the envelope rather reverently. There was nothing, no card, no letter, nothing. Then he noticed a sediment of dark stuff at the bottom of the envelope. He tipped it out into his hand. It looked like dry earth.

He remembered the woman prising out a little lump of the earth where they had lain, where they had made love. The ghost of it was recorded in the creases of the envelope, but it had been crushed on its journey over. These pathetic crumbs were all that was left. It reduced the act in some way, made it rather vulgar. He tried to feel moved by it, by her gesture and the very real earth in the hollow of his palm, but in fact it repelled him. He could scarcely say why. Flanders earth, he said to himself, 'our' Flanders earth: sacred – and, well, poisoned. Literally poisoned. He blushed, thinking of what they had done in such a place. It came back in a very real way, almost icy in its shock, and he flushed to the roots of his hair. It was like holding the ashes of a man you had murdered – very queer, the force of his sudden shame. It was as if they had put a sticky thumbprint on the vast illuminated page of history. It was a big mistake of hers, this – rubbing his face in it, as it were. He wondered how she had found out his name. In her jagged script, it looked paltry, cowardly even: *Mr Joseph Monrow* . . .

He threw the earth-crumbs out of the back door and washed his hands. He could not face Pitts's letter, after that.

He tried to write. He was physically restless: his legs did not fancy being tucked under the table, after all that tramping. And his head was full of disappointment. He read through the account of Ted's death, with its Tennysonian petal and quiet gallantry; he ought to have been jeering inwardly but he could not, he found it moving. Yet he could not equal it, now; it belonged to a different time. And he could not even face looking through the notes he had made in his week away. He would only see how skeletal they were, how thinly approximate to the reality of things, how dutiful. He drew a little sketch of one of those neat Miele handcarts on the Somme that were full of potatoes or cabbages or furniture, only his was full of flowers, sweet-smelling white stock and star-like nasturtiums; and it was poised on the top of a comical little hill. It could run backwards or forwards, but either way it would go downhill.

A wasp tangled in his hair, but did not sting him. His hair was thick and rather dirty. He heated some water and washed it, lathering it up with a cake of Pears Soap. He had a fetishistic passion – that was the only way he could describe it – for the scent of Pears Soap. Its amber weight in his hands seemed to describe something from childhood, something very deep and far off and yearned for. Freudian, no doubt. He must, he thought, spend a half hour each day boning up on Freud – and Nietzsche. Not Frazer and the other lot. Nietzsche was important. As for Marx, the Marxians he knew put him off. And the Russian famine; though he found dark consolation in the idea of a single book causing so much trouble.

His wet hair lay lank and heavy on his head. He decided to get it cut. He breathed in the clean air, feeling it brighten his lungs, and was suddenly desperate for a cut.

The village barber was Mr Cox, known as Coxy, who also ran the garage, and the garage doubled as a wheelwright's. Within half an hour Joseph found himself sat on an upturned oil-drum next to the handpump that would now and again splutter petrol into a motor-car. A grimy bamboo-framed mirror was propped on a chair in front of him. It amused him that the mirror had the chair, not the customer. And he did not mind the smell of petrol: he even quite liked it, the slight burny flourish of Castrol in it, and the rich sweet sawdust from the wheelwright part always hovering behind. Coxy had 'cut the troops' during the war, and had only one style, which was spread throughout the village. Men *and* women. Joseph had, in fact, never seen such short-haired women anywhere, though Coxy would generally leave a heap of curls on the top for them. He had a wooden sign, a crudely-painted life-sized figure, which stood on the verge and pointed into the garage with scissors. Its haircut was like a giant bushy eyebrow, oddly. And Coxy would always finish one side of the head before starting on the other. Folk did look very queer, halfway through it.

Joseph *wanted* Cox's drastic sort of cut. It would clean his head up. And the locals had been looking a little askance at his thick black mop. He did not want to be noticed: he wanted to extricate himself from that, from the kind of subdued notoriety his solitary presence had already earned. Ever since he had gone down to the pub with his bedpan to carry some home-brew back, the local children had followed him about in Indian file through the village, calling him names – not nasty names, not even rude ('Walking Jesus', for instance), but names all the same. If he stopped and tried to talk to them they would scatter like peas out of a pod, giggling.

He had bought himself the kind of dull cotton shirt the local men went about in, and dull drill trousers, for when the weather cooled. He wanted to disappear, really. The straw hat was a problem: it was altogether too bohemian in style. It was strange, this shyness about himself. Most other writers flaunted their condition. But not him.

Coxy did not talk too much, just a few words on the storm and on the languishing drama of the missing schoolmaster, whom he referred to derisively as 'Twitcher Tom'.

'Oh, does he beat?'

'He cuts. And quite right, too. Never did me no harm, in my day.'

Coxy's hands had a permanent dark shine to them, like slate under rain; they fussed over Joseph's head, snipped and combed and shaved. The oil-drum was positioned just inside the main workshop, a curious place, vague and undecided: a buckled Bullnose Morris, the empty hull of Baz's motorcycle, rubber tyres and dark oily lumps of engines shared space with carpenters' benches, spoke tongues, felloe patterns and huge wooden wheels in various stages of repair. Shiny painted metal and creamy wood – these jangled, to Joseph's mind. Someone was hammering in the shadows, fitting felloes it looked like. A wheelless waggon right at the back, up on blocks, had been there ever since Joseph had arrived nearly four months earlier. Veering, the business was, towards some future no one could yet define. Yet sitting there under the brusque touch of George Cox, the road still soft and pungent from the rain, the trees surging and glittering in the last scraps of the storm-wind, the cunning little thatched houses giving nothing away of their inhabitants save the odd plain brown face at the door, Joseph could not believe that this would not be like this for ever and ever.

Ah, but there was something tragic in the felloe patterns opposite him, hung up in a row like old, unused swords in a castle. Something horribly wan about the slow hammering of the wood in the shadows. And he really started to doubt whether anything could stall it: the smash-up, the inevitable slide into a glazed subjection – of men to machines, as animals already were subject to men. And the consequent smash-up. Supposing the war had been fought here? He would be looking upon a wounded England, outwardly wounded as well as inwardly.

Joseph knew from Mrs Hamilton that Coxy had been a quartermaster in Field Ambulance during the war; it was rumoured that he would miscount tins of rationed petrol to spare a few for the officers' outings to the sea in a borrowed motor-car, and was rewarded in vintage brandy.

Joseph mentioned that he had been 'over' last week.

'I see.'

'Weren't you on the Somme?'

'Yes.'

'In what capacity?'

'Quartermaster, O.C. Field Ambulance.'

Coxy nodded towards the remains of Baz's motorcycle.

'Despatch rider out there, was he – your mate?'

'No no,' said Joseph. 'He bought it for a song last year.'

There was a leaden little silence, somehow disapproving.

'Used right up,' said Coxy. 'Burned out. A lot of punishment, them BSAs took. Sticky, that old mud were, weren't it?'

'Yes. It was.'

This was a fruitful lead, but Coxy was as spare as a needle with his replies. Joseph had the impression that his questions were bustling up and down a narrow alleyway. The stubbled head was an inch from his own, whistling through its nose, with a glaze over the features that might have been a film of motor oil. Walter passed on the road, leading a donkey, and Joseph lifted a hand in greeting, keeping his head very still under the blades scuttling over his head.

'Friend o' yours, is he?'

'I regularly sup at The Saddler's Arms,' said Joseph, brightly. He had not meant to sound like a suspect in a detective novel.

Silence.

'Keeping widows company,' said Coxy, half-suggestively. He looked up. The main street filled with a passing lorry, smoke rising and settling, a sudden sour gust like coal. He seemed disappointed that it did not stop: churlish of it. They could hear it banging off over the ruts gouged out by the storm.

'She likes me to read to her, generally Sir Walter Scott,' Joseph replied, not wanting to let the remark lie. He was blushing despite himself. This annoyed him. He did not like Mr Cox at all.

'Old Ted Hamilton,' said Coxy, chuckling under it.

Joseph frowned, his heart beating quicker. He felt curiously helpless under Coxy's hands.

'A friend of yours, was he?'

Coxy nodded at him in the mirror, pressing his head at the temples then pushing it abruptly down, exposing the neck.

'A friend to all and sundry, *he* was.'

'Killed in action, I believe,' Joseph said, voice muffled in his chest. 'Night attack—'

Coxy surprised him by bursting out into laughter – a grim sort of chortle, but laughter nevertheless.

'Action! Oh, you might say that,' he squeezed out. Joseph strained his eyeballs to look up. Through a fog of eyebrow he saw the man's face twisted in mirth.

'I was told he was shot cleanly through the head and – fell back in Walter's arms,' Joseph said, rather petulantly, head pushed up again. His heart was beating thick and fast; his own version of Ted's death ran through his mind like an actual memory. Terribly vivid, it was, in its soft Tennysonian glamour.

Coxy leaned towards the mirror, ghosting it with his breath. He was addressing Joseph's reflection. He looked about and then peered at Joseph's reflection.

'Fell off a choo-choo,' he whispered.

'What? Fell off? From a train?'

'Ay.'

'But how?'

'Blind screwed on pot brandy.'

'Oh.'

Coxy was very real in the mirror, through its grime. The very real face broadened into a grim smile, looking out of the mirror. 'Fell off a choo-choo, clean off onto the rails outside Rheims, tight as a nit, in his corporal's kit. Troop train, too.'

Joseph found it uncomfortable, seeing his own reactions in the mirror. He dampened them.

'Was Walter with him?'

'Not on the train, no. Why? Don't believe me, then?'

The scuttling scissors brushed Joseph's ear.

'I don't doubt it for a moment, no.'

'Good.' There was a cross little sigh. 'Because it's damn true, as George Cox is standing here. Beware the adder's sting. *Very* fond of a drop, was Ted Hamilton. Best customer in his own tap room. Dropped out the choo-choo at night and cracked his topknot smack open like a nut.' Coxy grinned briefly and jabbed the scissors at the mirror. 'Only don't go quoting me to the widder-woman. Fox among the hens. She thinks it was a bullet. Ever so heroic, like. Ever so *heroic*,' he added, taking up the cutthroat razor and shoving Joseph's head forward.

The red petal had burst into a mess on the rails. Joseph could see the mess, clear as day on the rails. And the one piece of writing with which he was pleased had burst likewise. It had lost its dignity. A ridiculous hot-house flower, it was, over-delicate and ridiculous: lotos stuff. Though the *real* death should have been laughable, in its absurd, careless reality. Well, it was; real life turned everything it touched to something laughable. He felt quite bitter. And even angry at the dead man whose face looked out from the snug's mantelpiece. Quite hostile towards him, he felt, for falling off a train like that, in the middle of a huge war. A 'choo-choo'! It did not help at all, knowing the truth. He felt the razor scraping at his neck, Coxy's fingers pulping the skin so that it hurt.

A large plum-blue motor-car drew up in a splash of mud. Coxy left him half-done and the vehicle gurgled down its happy gallons of petrol, the handpump wheezing and squeaking like an excited puppy. Drawn by the event, the fellow in the shadows at the back of the workshop emerged with his hammer and walked round the vehicle, admiring it.

It was Samuel, the ginger-haired lad Walter wanted to bring to the cottage.

Quite unmarked, Joseph thought. Nonchalant, perhaps a bit slow in the head. But nothing to show that he was worth displaying. Yet Walter had been gleeful, almost, about him. It was worth stumping up for. And Joseph, under his comic, half-finished cut, smiled at his own pun.

Coxy always filled the cars himself; though he had several lads working for him, he never let them do it if he was there. And he was ingratiating to the driver, hidden behind the glass of the open door. You could see that. He was properly bowing and scraping, his surliness vanished.

'Did you ever see such a handsome car?' he was saying. 'Four cylinder, three speeds, is it? And reverse? My goodness, sir. A very handsome car indeed, and brand new, is it? Shame about our roads, seems a crime to drive this about on our filthy roads what we have round abouts here, sir.'

Joseph could imagine Coxy greasing up to the officers. Accumulating his bottles of vintage brandy. No doubt he was nasty to the regular ranks, keeping back soap and cigarettes from the wounded, cutting everything to the bone and beyond. Coxy could, he thought, appear in the novel. A really mean-minded quartermaster trading in petrol and brandy. He must put in all types. The inescapable mirror of truth. Thus he shifted his hostility to the messenger.

Samuel, passing on his way back to the shadows, swinging his hammer, nodded at Joseph. He seemed a bit bashful, almost hurrying past, like someone who might at any minute be asked to sing a song or recite a verse.

The car drove off and Coxy came back to Joseph with some reluctance; it was definitely a step down. His combing of the right, full-headed side had a touch of cruelty in it, along with a stink of petrol. Joseph's head was almost jerked as the comb's teeth caught on knots. His eyes watered.

'Ouch,' he remarked.

Coxy mumbled something about stories.

'Sorry?'

'Nice auto, them Storeys.'

'Is that the name of the car?'

'Don't you know a Storey when you see one?'

'I know a story when I *hear* one.'

Coxy, whom Joseph could not see at this point, seemed to vanish for a moment.

Then he resumed with the scissors. Large, very sharp scissors, they were, and Joseph felt they were a little blasé around the flesh of the right ear. The joke had not gone down well. They clipped away. The rich, black hair fell in alarming quantities around the oil-drum. Then there was a lot of business with the cutthroat razor, and not just at the neck. He even had a go with Joseph's eyebrows, clipping them almost to the skin.

And when he finally looked at himself in the oval, framed mirror Coxy held up in front of him, Joseph realised he had earned a cut which even the army would have regarded as short. It displayed the contours of his skull, the bony knobbles of it. Coxy's rigidly blank expression had something in it that Joseph recognised from the unpleasanter officers: a silent jeering, waiting for a response they could smash. An expression you did not bother with, anyway. So he said nothing. Coxy would appear in the novel, complete with hairy ears. That was enough.

Now Joseph resembled the village children, whose heads had been shaved to the bone against summer lice a few weeks before, and were only just furred over. He could have been an escaped prisoner. It made him laugh. It really was funny. Another story. His thinned eyebrows were clownish. He had to see the funny side of it.

And the air found his head, quite cool. It seemed he had removed a layer of flesh, painlessly. He was quite grateful to Coxy, and paid him thruppence instead of the official tuppence. Coxy seemed to resent it, but did not insist on the penny change. Joseph felt he had won, in the end.

He started to walk back, bare-headed in every sense of the word, with quite a swagger. He did feel renewed. The long, puddled street held no fears for him, though it was no doubt all eyes from the houses straggled between the trees. The children were down at the pond, he could hear them, so only a couple of tiny urchins – gypsies, possibly, from the gaggle on the common – gaped at him. He stuck his tongue out and they squealed and stamped their bare little feet. He had a real spring in his step. Old men watched him from dilapidated porches, bent hands folded on canes, uncertain who he was. A hen scrabbled at his feet and ran off squawking, as if the sight of him had terrified it. By Jove, it felt good, having his thinking cap laid bare. There were very grand white clouds in the sky, and infinite blue between. It suggested heaven.

Walter was standing outside the pub, wiping his hands on a cloth.

'He can come up tonight,' he said.

And by saying nothing about the cut, not even a flicker of a glance at the head, Walter cast Joseph into doubt again.

'Do you mean Samuel?'

'Ay.'

'Alright. Come at six.'

Walter nodded, wiped his moustache on the cloth, and went back inside. Joseph was flat, punctured. The man had that effect on him. He hurried back, wishing he was wearing a hat.

The table in the garden was triumphantly shiny-wet, so he settled himself up in his little room. Dogged, he had to be. If he failed, he would go off and adventure in South America, like a Conrad character.

22

A Nervous Attack

H E WAS CUSSED. He could not have the Ted Hamilton character falling off a train, blotto. It somehow brought down the whole tone of the novel. So he kept to his old ideas, half-aware that they were mossy – mouldering, even. He felt cussed, though, really belligerent. And the new death was done in a few paragraphs. It started with a shell, then a machine-gun's chatter, then he thought of Tillie's brother and made it an aeroplane dropping out of the sky. The son-in-law was still in some way responsible. He still called him 'Walter': it was an intimate thing, and not just because it fitted him like a tombstone. Later, he would change it. Not now, though.

He read the drawn-out moment of the death, and found it utterly wanting, almost ugly. There was certainly no poetry in it, no nobility, he had got rid of the Tennysonian touch right enough. It seemed to grimace at him from the page, this new animal. It had no more truth than the previous lot, only a kind of sadistic delight. The aeroplane was actually comical, dropping from the sky like that. The character's name was Bob. Bob was wrong, very wrong. The village blacksmith was a Bob, that was the trouble perhaps.

So he called him Ted, like the original. Ted Hambling. Almost the way Walter said 'Hamilton', mumbling it in his northern twang. It was like finding the right little golden key to the tiny golden box.

And he rewrote the death scene in ten lines. Literally just ten lines, from scratch. It happened at night, during the return from an attack, in the fitful light of a Very rocket. A flare of light, with the smoke and dust misting it, a machine-gun spitting and sparking, crashing of bombs, Ted hobbling along through this misty artificial light. Then darkness. Then a second rocket fizzling up, and in the weird glare Ted spreading his arms wide suddenly, as if rejoicing. Then a third rocket, and nothing but a black lump on the parapet. Then darkness.

He was exhausted, after that. His stubbly head seemed to be full of a concentrated liquid. He fiddled with the paragraph again, just the odd words here and there. Then a touch more added, where it was simply too rigid, too bare. It was as if he had been in the thick of it. It was as if Ted had told him how it was. The drunkenness and the train was all Coxy, mean and vindictive. You could not trust Coxy, with his crooked reputation, his scissors, his nasty bone-handled razor. His mean, vindictive talk of 'choo-choos'. No, Ted had told Joseph how it really was, as if speaking from the photograph in the pub's snug; as if Ted had been able to stand back from his own death, stand in the trench and watch himself struggle out there in no-man's land, wounded in the foot – struggling to return from the attack. It was quite weird. His lips moving in the image of the photograph in Joseph's head, moving behind the huge moustaches. Telling him how it was. How precisely it was – but not how his son-in-law was responsible, not yet. Though now Joseph was sure that that answer would come on greased wheels.

He almost wanted to hide the evidence. He did, in fact: he placed a blank sheet of paper on top, and then a heavy dictionary.

It was the first wholly inspired moment since he had started this wretched thing God knows how many months ago.

He went down for a cup of tea and saw Pitts's envelope on the windowsill. He smirked, because he knew that it would not bother him to read the letter, now. He was feeling strong. He took it with his tea into the exquisite outdoors, into the washed air of a truly glorious day, with the fervent scent of every flower and leaf brimming in it, the scraps of wind now reduced to a gentle summery breeze. He really loved England on days like this. He saw it, on such rare days, as an island brimming with lushness, almost tropical in its green lushness, with deep shadows and lazy white paths and silken streams. All rubbish, of course – all that had gone long before the Romans, he had no idea how long before, possibly it started going with the first inhabitants, the type that scattered their bulky flints about on the moors around Youlster. Possibly *they* had started the rot. And then he tore open the letter.

It was very short, very sharp and short. It made his heart jump, as if he was reading an examination result.

Dear Mr Monrow, it said, in its tight purplish copperplate, very creaky and stiff, *I am in hospital recovering from a nervous attack brought on by your last letter. I see no point in continuing a personal correspondence of this sort, though I will not cease from holding to my beliefs in a steady, rational manner. I submit that your outrageous remarks regarding my person are the product of a diseased mind. I hope you find the 'cure'. Yours sincerely, etc.*

Joseph's mind was not so diseased that it could not feel a preliminary flush of guilt. Quickly followed, it has to be said, by doubt. The postage stamp on the letter showed the same place as the others: Chertsey, in Surrey. Maybe there was a cottage hospital in Chertsey, but a different town would have clinched it. As it was – he did not wholly believe Pitts. The man must be a proper nervous case, if it *was* true. All Joseph had said in his letter was that the man was a good friend of the worst tyrants, who also believed in the expendability of the individual for the greater cause, and most particularly with the savage tribes of old Germania, who also believed that fighting was better than peacemaking. Or maybe it was the suggestion that anyone who could look at the war 'objectively' was either sinister or had suffered from 'a Freudian disturbance in childhood'.

He could hardly think *that* a justification for turning hysterical. Though he reckoned that the Freud bit was shaving things close. It implied sexual disturbances to a fellow like Pitts – the fellow Joseph imagined Pitts to be, at least. A very cold fish, probably. Stone cold.

It quite spoilt the exquisiteness of the day, it really did. That and the sad little envelope from Germany. The post would not leave him be. It was an invention that claimed its price.

He did not burn the letter. Some obscure instinct.

The 'cure' – that was odd, from a chap writing from hospital. It nagged at Joseph all afternoon, that little noun in its quotation marks. He would rub his hand over his head, struggling over a sentence, and be shocked by the absence of hair – and think of mental patients — and that last word from Pitts would bob in front of him. Not *a* 'cure', but *the* 'cure'. As if there was only one for his particular disease, perhaps a metaphoric one. And what was his particular disease? To be a little over the top in trading insults, that was all. Or was Pitts referring to his — Joseph's — antipathy to war?

He saw Pitts in a stern hospital bed, his eyes steady with triumph. A nervous case, highly-strung. Probably middle-aged, balding, flabby. Very cold fingers. Or perhaps small and tight, like a tight little murderer, the type who poisons his wife and parcels her remains up in brown paper and string. Or maybe none of these. Pitts had no face, not any that he — the budding novel-writer — could make stick. The thought touched him like one of those cold fingers . . . that if Pitts chose to, he could come to the village — and Joseph would not know.

Actually, he had no desire to meet him. He had no taste for duels. And he knew that Pitts was the type incapable of making peace.

23

The Round Thunder's Word

WALTER CAME ALONG crack on six, by which time all Joseph wanted to do was go out. His own handwriting irritated him, let alone his words, his limping dragging phrases. The death of Ted flickered like a tiny beacon in a vast emptiness. All he wanted to do was to walk about quickly and efficiently before supper, get himself out of breath in the woods. But Walter came along at six, dragging Samuel in his wake.

The poor fellow, in his habitual shapeless leather jerkin, looked thoroughly nervous on the front doorstep. He had a wartime bandolier on his shoulder, its pouches filled not with cartridges but trapping paraphernalia, wire loops and so forth. His ginger colouring and foxy smell went with a flat, genial face that was oddly doll-like, the skin very porcelain-pale, almost Chinese-white, with little red veins painted onto the cheeks. (Joseph had already noted the paws nailed to Samuel's cottage door, opposite the pub.)

'Oh, Walter. Right on time. Come in, then. Recruited you, has he, Samuel?'

'Eh?'

Joseph had to repeat it, which made it sound silly. Samuel gave a surreptitious nod and then a queer little smile, his face blushing curiously over the white, albino skin, frayed and roughened in places by the time he spent outdoors, in the woods. He was a little older than Joseph, but looked and behaved younger.

He offered them tea or cider. Walter plumped for cider, Samuel for tea. Joseph felt obscurely irritated by this, heating the water. The air felt heavy, three men not knowing what to say, Walter touching the geraniums on the windowsill and Samuel shuffling from foot to foot. Joseph told them to sit down but they did not. Not until he did. So when he had done preparing, they sat around the table, awkward, Samuel stirring the sugar into his tea and blowing on it. His eyes were rather too bulbous and wet, as if set in glycerine.

'A fine day out,' said Joseph. He was sat on one side, Walter and Samuel on the other.

'Ay, a right shame to be dead,' said Walter, glancing at the open door.

A local saying, this, struck up methodically whenever the weather was fine. Joseph had used it in the novel, in the mouth of a ploughman sitting in a rain-sodden trench; he had thought it very cruel and droll. Walter saying it made him want to burst into giggles. Nervous, he was.

They drank in tentative sips. Walter talked of the local man who had brewed the cider. Walter did not like him, but liked his cider. Samuel nodded sheepishly, stirring more sugar into his tea. Joseph silently wondered if, in the end, anyone liked anybody in the village.

'Ay,' said Walter, 'nobbut should judge a man by what he makes, good or ill.'

Joseph was being stared at, by both of them, just for a moment or two. He flushed. Well, what did *he* 'make'? Nothing you could touch, taste, smell. You could hear it, if you read it aloud. He wanted to say this, as if they had denied it. Walter went on talking, though, his broad Lancashire vowels steady as rock. He was gaining ground, almost on his own territory here.

Samuel just had to sit and be. He nodded now and again, faintly. Apparently the only time the fellow had spent away from the village, since his birth in the paw-nailed cottage, was the war.

Of course Walter mentioned the wretched schoolmaster, who was still missing. It had become faintly irritating, this 'missing' business, as if it was truancy they were talking about. He reckoned – folk reckoned – the schoolmaster was 'bumped off'. And then Walter ran out of steam. Joseph mentioned the storm, the heavy rain. Now Samuel's head was thrust forward, cocked slightly, like an eager but puzzled dog. Joseph wondered if the fellow was slightly simple – and felt quite uneasy, out of his natural element, with these two establishing themselves, their tacky boots clattering each time they shifted.

There was a little silence.

'Plaster drying alright, then?' Walter asked.

'Oh yes. A very good job. I thought we could sort out the payment this evening, in the snug.'

Silence again, awkward.

Joseph opened his mouth to say something but was stalled by a shout – more like a yelp – from Walter.

'Sammel! Take tha spoon out o' drink!'

Walter pointed to his ear, for Joseph's benefit. 'That bloody din, you see,' he murmured.

Samuel took his teaspoon out, shamefaced. Joseph's mother was hot on that, too. It marked your class, she said. Folk who leave the teaspoon in the cup are either foreign or the dregs. Joseph had never been quite sure how thick these dregs of hers were, how far they went up the social scale. Quite far, probably. Just short of shopkeepers, probably.

'I'll make more,' he said, to puncture the awkwardness. He was waiting, really.

He put the pan back on the hob and fed the range with fresh sticks. He would let Walter make the first move.

'They say as we'll have electricals by th' end of this year,' the man remarked, watching him closely.

Joseph knew about this, but reckoned it was an empty rumour. They discussed it for a bit. He would have to buy more candles, he thought, and more oil for the lamp. He did not say, but he hated the high poles and their mass of wires, and the way a light bulb smashed a room into brightness, made everyone's face even uglier than bony gaslight did. Candlelight and oil-light were yellow and soft, golden almost, flattering to the skin, and left mystery in corners, allowed for darkness and mystery. But always the human mind must entangle itself in advance, or what it understood as advance. Nobody had learned from the war, from its industrial fervour, they did not bother even to look back except in a wretchedly sentimental way. There was no thought in it, no reflective decision to rethink everything from the bottom, scrape the pan to shining and begin again. Walter, for instance, was very excited by the prospect of electrical light in the village. You might have thought he had shares in it. Samuel said very little – grunted, really; his glycerine eyes set like dried fruit in sponge. Human progress was instinctive, the human mind was set on it as a dog's is set to smells, rooting out the nastiest smells, the filthiest – other dogs' piss and droppings most of all. The Enlightenment was no more than a way of setting this in neat type and numbered paragraphs. Modern progress was a mad snuffling about, in the end, right to the edge of the cliff and beyond. But Joseph did not say any of this out loud.

There was silence, eased only by the filling of the teapot. He put a tin of arrowroot biscuits on the table, apologising for the lack of a cake. He sat down. It was up to him, he could see that. It was Walter who was waiting.

'Well? You wanted to show me something,' Joseph said.

Walter glanced at Samuel. Joseph noticed that Walter's hands were trembling. As if at some pre-prepared signal, Samuel scraped his chair back and stood. He had been about to drink his fresh cup of tea, but the invisible signal did not allow him to, it had him upright in seconds. Strange, in a slow man: military, almost. His hands dangled at his thighs. He had on a pair of drill trousers which must have been sweltering in the heat, but countrymen seem peculiarly oblivious to such things. Joseph imagined he was about to give a speech.

Walter turned to his host.

'It's like this, you see.'

Joseph detected nervousness in his broad voice, something unsettled behind the apparent note of glee. Their faces were no more than a table's width apart. Point-blank range, Joseph thought to himself. Walter tapped his forehead with a thick-nailed finger.

'Taylor 'n' his maggots.'

He tapped his chest.

'Walter 'n' his ticky-bird.'

Joseph hadn't realised Walter had a heart problem. The man pointed at Samuel – at his belt, it seemed.

'Sammel 'n' his free 'n' gratis.'

Joseph could only guess at what the tag meant, with a sinking heart. The fellow had lost his balls! – the wound everyone feared as much as blindness or a knocked-up face. Walter nodded at Samuel, then turned his eyes back to Joseph. They were uneasy eyes. 'There en't just *wounds*, see. Wounds as are made by summat you can *see*, as comes at thee and goes bang.'

It was said with a dose of caustic, was the word 'wounds' – it made Joseph flinch, at any rate, thinking of the word stuck above his desk. Walter had seen it there, obviously.

'Yes, chaps off their chumps, and so forth,' Joseph agreed.

'Oh no, not that.'

'I don't mean – not even off their chumps. The damage can be very – quiet.'

Walter's eyelids quivered, as if the words were blowing on them. He shook his head.

'No no,' he insisted. Samuel had stepped back, away from the table towards the door. He was behaving like a soldier being given invisible commands. This was a rehearsed manoeuvre. It had the effect of a build-up: it made Joseph anticipate something vaguely hideous, though he was confused by all this 'unseen' business. Walter drew his hand over his moustache, down it, and it sprung back into shape, wiry and grey-brindled.

'Angels guard us while we sleep,' he recited, quietly and grimly, his eyes sliding sideways, then back to Joseph.

Now the man was smiling. His hands were tight fists on the table. He leaned forward, the war passing down his face like his hand had done, or like a shadow deep inside him. Perhaps this was a spurious impression, Joseph thought: perhaps he had only invented it.

'You see, wounds en't what you think, Mr Monrow. A bullet can pot out a chap and leave nowt but a dimple. If the skin be a young-un's.' He lifted his hand and measured with his thumb and forefinger a tiny space. 'Only that. A bullet's hole.'

Joseph had heard of this. It was like a magic trick. He nodded, his throat very dry. A friend had by chance seen a gentleman stabbed in Seville, right through to the heart, without a drop of blood being spilt, with only the tiniest little puncture in the white shirt. But a bullet was much clumsier than a stiletto. It was almost creepy magic, that.

'Save a bullet's summat that goes whizz through the air and bang, it aches, I stopped one in me shoulder, I should know. It aches like hell, eating you up. But there's other wounds, see, as you should put in your books.'

At first Joseph thought 'books' was 'boots'; it came out like 'boots' in Walter's Lancashire twang, as it had in the pub. Joseph felt shy – it was very odd. He tried not to look it, though, he tried to frown a little and look serious, appreciative.

'*Drop 'em!*' Walter barked. This startled Joseph into spilling his drink. He was aware of Samuel fumbling with his thick drill trousers, with the rope that served as a belt, and a nausea crept up on him, a really profound disgust at the whole business, as if the business was sexual. At school, as a new boy, he had had to drop his trousers like this, to be made a 'freeman' of – a foul rite, really foul, a second year had to spit on your penis three times and then you had to thank him. Really foul. It was a public school tradition copied by the others, and it shamed him even now to think about it, to think of the wretched business, the awful feel of it and the shame burning in his chest on and on, for years almost. He got up and waved his hand about.

'No, no,' he said. 'I'm not interested, not at all interested.'

Both men froze, Samuel's open mouth all surprise, or perhaps disappointment.

'What d'you mean, you're not interested?'

Walter's snarly tone was almost schoolmastery, it made Joseph feel very uneasy with himself, very young. He would have to fight back. His face was very hot.

'I mean, I think it's best all round if—'

'You brought us here, I'll have you know, young sir, in good faith . . .'

Walter was peculiarly annoyed. The 'young sir' was terrible, really terrible.

'I think it was at your suggestion, Walter.'

His face was really terribly hot. He wanted these men out of the close little kitchen, along with their sweat-and-fox smell. Walter just stared at him, fair bristling with annoyance.

'Can't take it, can you?'

Joseph sighed, swallowing back a bubble of fury. 'It's not that, Walter. I'm thinking of Samuel.' Though he had not been, not really. 'It doesn't seem right, you see. It just seems a bit – *sordid*, really, exhibiting him like this. It's my fault. I suppose it's my fault.'

'What do you think's the matter with him, then?'

Joseph pulled a face. Then he cleared his throat. Dammit, he would say what suited. 'Well, obviously he's had part, if not all, of his sexual machinery blown off—'

Walter laughed. Oh, how he laughed! He kept repeating the words 'sexual machinery' as if it was the punchline of the finest joke he had ever heard. It was unhinged, slightly unhinged, the laughter. Joseph merely shuffled from foot to foot, waiting for the gale to blow over. He was not so terribly angry now, the bubble had punctured – he was even smiling in a ghoulish, embarrassed manner. Samuel just stood, the inferior and rather stupid servant in an old play, holding up his trousers, waiting for instructions.

Then Walter snapped out of it, quite quickly, with a big sniff. His eyes were wet with laughter but the rest of his face drooped all lugubrious again.

'Well, Mr Monrow, you're wrong.'

'I'm very glad I'm wrong.'

He was rather exasperated. But he knew his obligations. It *was* his doing, in the end, all this.

'I said,' Walter hammered on, 'that there are wounds you don't see.'

'I thought you meant hidden by clothing.'

Walter was thoroughly unconvinced, shaking his head. Contemptuous, really.

'Here's a riddle,' he said, changing his tone but stabbing a finger in Joseph's direction. It was a new tack, and Joseph obediently folded his arms.

Walter recited, properly recited – stiffly, but in a booming voice, as if before folk in the pub or even on a stage, one hand on his chest and the other raised up, as if in a creaky old melodrama in the village hall. It was all very queer, somehow.

> My first is in th' slave which I make o' men,
> My second in th' death that I bring 'em to then,
> My whole lies on lips but I cannot be heard,
> Though my other name be th' round thunder's word.

Joseph, only half taking it in, clapped gently and then pretended to think seriously for a moment. Walter was grinning away. It was queer enough to see Walter grinning like that, without the booming verse that preceded it.

'I don't know,' he said, 'I really don't. No idea.'

Walter was happy at this, triumphant in a way, his brow shiny with sweat. Then Samuel's trousers fell, just like that. His hands had left them, his arms were folded on his chest. It was not deliberate, he had loosened the string more than intended. But he did not pull them up again. He looked a bit surprised, then held up his shirt that hid the thighs in dirty cotton. He tucked the flaps into his collar.

No undergarments.

Joseph looked, nevertheless. It would be more embarrassing, more awkward, not to have done – the man was so eager. Joseph was still surprised to see the testicles intact. Above them, nestling in a bright tuft of ginger hair where the penis should have been, was a small contraption fashioned from metal.

Joseph nodded, feeling a little heartless. He had always loathed medical contraptions. This one looked no less repulsive than the others, a thing of delicate butterfly nuts and rivets with a copper tube sticking out of it. It was like a miniature version of the iron mask in Hugo's novel – there was something medieval about it, something of the torture chamber, the world of thumbscrews and dangling iron cages. He wondered, heartlessly, if he was to show admiration or horror. Samuel was looking down like an engineer proud of his latest work.

'Ah yes,' Joseph said, 'that's bad luck, that is.'

'Bob's job,' Walter pointed out.

Bob, the local blacksmith, was a huge barrel of a man with hairy hands who mended bicycles in his spare time.

'Very delicate, too,' said Joseph.

Walter made a signal, rubbing his thumb and forefinger together. To Joseph's horror, Samuel started to unscrew the little butterfly nuts with his grimy fingers. It had briefly puzzled Joseph how the contraption was attached to the body, since he could see no belt or band around the groin. In fact, the penis was not actually missing – not all of it, at any rate. The metal separated into two parts on a tiny hinge, revealing a squat root of flesh topped with the nacreous shine of scar tissue. It was a penis without its glans, like the thick neck of a beheaded cobra.

Walter was eyeing Joseph keenly.

'Not quite an invisible wound,' Joseph said, a touch feebly.

The maimed young man stood there, helpless. He was not too abashed. Maybe he believed Joseph was a doctor. The 'doctor' took a deep breath and asked how it had come about.

'The clap,' said Walter. 'VD.'

He recited the riddle again, quickly, almost under his breath. *The worm that flies in the night*, Joseph heard his mind mutter.

'Wipers,' said Walter, 'it were in Wipers. Weren't it, lad? Right at the end of the shenanigans.'

Samuel nodded, forlornly.

'Big country, out there, as the hunters say,' Walter went on. 'Very open. But it weren't a bullet as got him, no.'

He pulled a face. The brief pauses seemed to hold something frenzied, but the speaker was very calm.

'One night in the bag, see. Skirt. Just one. Very dainty, but dirty. Bad luck, that. Still, one's better than nowt at all, don't you think, Mr Monrow?'

Joseph was very hot, very flushed.

'At any road, his John Thomas got to be a right mess. All them ulcers and stink, weren't it? The boys could sniff it e'en over th' trenches and all that muck.'

As if he had been there himself, smelling it.

Then Walter turned a touch conspiratorial, as a mother does with a doctor when her child's sick.

'He didn't know, y'see, as it were serious.'

He turned back to Samuel.

'What did you think, lad? Did you think it had a blasted little cold or summat?'

Samuel's mouth drooped.

'I dedn't know, Mr Monrow. I were jus' – puzzled. Raather puzzled.'

Walter guffawed. It was awful. He slapped his hands on the table and guffawed. Joseph did not know where to put himself. Samuel was grinning, though, as if the joke was deliberate.

Walter recovered, blowing his nose and wiping his eyes. He kept shaking his head and repeating 'raather puzzled' to himself in the way one repeats a punchline, as if not quite believing it.

'At any road,' he went on, finally, 'the doctors done the best they could.' He made scissors of his fingers. 'Chop chop,' he said, unnecessarily. 'Then Bob made that contraption for – well, it can't go pokerin' up or it'd tear, see. The skin don't stretch proper now, do it? If he starts to get th' Irish toothache, that thing starts to bite enough to knock the urge into next week. His Get Religion, we call it – don't us, Sammy? Tha Get Religion.'

Joseph nodded benignly. He had had quite enough.

'Ay. It's either that contraption, or it's never going within a hundred yards o' Maggie Hern.' Maggie Hern was the beauty of the village, about eighteen, very well-built with long hair like flax. Walter chuckled deep in his throat, dirtily. Joseph found none of this callous, however. There was affection in it. It's the way terrible things are folded in, he thought.

Samuel nodded forlornly.

'Never seed it afore,' he murmured. 'I dedn't know.'

He clicked the two parts back together, and tightened the little screws. He was about to pull his trousers up but Joseph stopped him. He had seen something extraordinary. He pointed to Samuel's belly. Something very strange there, really remarkable.

There they nestled, the two navels, one an inch above the other.

The stuff of freak shows, that was. Samuel was not a freak, though.

'Shrapnel,' the young man said, pointing to the lower one. 'First time I goed out there. I come back, then I goed out again.'

'And what be t'other hole, then?' Walter joked. Joseph had never seen him like this before. It was unnatural.

Samuel smirked.

'Where muh soul goed inside o' me,' he said, 'day I were born.'

Joseph's eyes shone. He was immensely excited under the mild, acknowledging smile. The two indentations were indistinguishable. He was invited to place a finger in them, like a doubting Thomas. He refused, politely enough. He gave a pound each to the two men for their trouble and Samuel left with a happy grin on his face.

Walter folded the note carefully and lingered at the door. Joseph was desperate for him to leave, but he lingered, making hints about the garden. The fact was, Joseph was very short of the readies, he really had to stretch himself as thin as he could.

But he mentioned the pilfering of his supplies and the invasion of the hens.

'It's a drat nuisance, Walter. I'll have to be buying a new lock and key.'

Walter narrowed his eyes. Nay, no gypsies or tramps in the immediate area, and the mere thought of a villager stealing was not even worth the blush of it. That appeared to settle the matter, though it hardly did at all. He left a little abruptly, as if Joseph had annoyed him.

As soon as that heavy tread had faded, Joseph shot upstairs with a candle (dusk had crept into the cottage at least an hour ahead of the garden), and scribbled down what he had seen. Not the clap business – the only record he made of that was the 'rather puzzled' line, the poignancy of which could not be missed – but that of the two navels.

Because he saw, albeit in an unformulated way, that this might be *the* key, the key image for the *whole damned novel*. He felt very grateful to Walter, and pleased with himself for angling for it in the first place.

The man with two navels. One a life symbol, one a death symbol – a living death, the living death of England, of the whole world after the war. Woman and life, man and death. He scribbled away on his thin-lined foolscap so eagerly that the table jiggled and rocked. Yes, the man with two navels. The point being – *no one could tell which was which!*

He felt a sense of triumph as he scribbled. The birth of innocence, the birth of experience. One nestling against the other, right up close.

Humming, he covered a page with his notes. So pleased was he with himself that he danced about in the little room, humming and shaking his fists with glee. Until there was a shock of something striking the window-glass. Little stones, it sounded like. He poked his head out of the window, rather breathless.

It was Baz. On his arm, looking up and smiling, was Tillie.

'What have you done to your *hair*?' she cried.

And then laughed, clapping her hands in front of her chest.

'I've cut it,' he replied, tartly. 'People do, you know.'

24

Four-Square Strength

IT WAS ALL quite ridiculous. They were getting married. In that blissful ignorance of obstacles or other people's feelings that folk in love own, Baz and Tillie had eloped, in a sort of way, and come rushing down to him, coming to the one person to whom the idea was crushing – asking him if he would be a witness. They had *spontaneously* thought of him.

How long had they known each other?

A matter of days. Ten, to be precise. Far too young, too. Baz, of course, had not gone back to London at all; he had accompanied Tillie to Stockport, staying in a boarding house so that they could see each other every day, in secret. It was madness.

'Why were you in Swansea?' asked Joseph.

'I wasn't.'

'I got a letter from you posted in Swansea.' He produced it from behind the geranium pot, where Tillie's card was also propped.

Baz laughed like anything. He looked rather odd, and Joseph only realised why at that moment: his moustache had gone.

'I gave it to a representative of a lingerie firm staying in the boarding house,' chuckled Baz. 'Black lingerie, too. He *said* he would post it in London. He must have forgotten and then found it after he had left the Smoke. I didn't want you to catch on too early, you see, seeing a Stockport postmark. That could only have meant one thing, couldn't it?'

Tillie laughed, too, at that.

Joseph asked about the missing moustache.

'It didn't suit him,' Tillie said. Baz's upper lip had not been bare since army days. She stroked its white softness with her forefinger.

Baz had the one change of clothes he had taken to Belgium and hadn't the faintest whether he was ever going back to chambers – officially he had the 'flu for the moment. He did smell faintly stale, slightly slovenly, behind the bright bare cub's face that love had given him. Joseph ground his teeth in anguish, out in the garden, in the dusky shadows. He had set the chairs in the long grass but Baz and Tillie were sitting on their own checked travelling rug on the lawn, drinking gallons of tea and finishing the arrowroot biscuits. Baz's voice carried right into the kitchen, where Joseph was kept busy filling the pot.

'Haven't you got a scythe, Jo-Jo? The rug's floating!'

'Missing, believed killed!' he called back. 'But thanks for offering!' He felt the accusation, though – the overgrown lawn as a symbol of idleness.

How had they got here? They had *driven down* in a friend's motor-car!

'I didn't know you could drive, Baz,' Joseph remarked.

'I can't,' replied Baz – and Tillie laughed like a drain, shredding grass-seeds between her finger and thumb.

Joseph inspected the motor-car pulled up crookedly by the front door, a very fine motor-car as motor-cars go, very green and curvaceous and smelling of leather and oil, hot still from the drive, dusty and hot and powerful. One of Baz's rich lawyer friends, he supposed, or a schoolfriend who did not have to work at all. He touched its hot flank and felt terrible, horribly dull and insipid. Sexless, almost. The two navels business was merely weird, all of a sudden, nothing more. The picture of Samuel's contraption swam about in his head in a sort of viscous oiliness. But he hid it all very well. He even congratulated them. They had created a great swirl of metaphoric dust and noise and he simply, rather selfishly, wanted them to go, to have nothing to do with them until they had calmed down and the stars had flattened in their eyes – in about a year's time, he reckoned.

But he did not say any of this, of course. He was not even sure they would physically hear him. They were inhabiting another world about an inch from his (his being the usual one that everybody else inhabited, of course) – and it was filled with music and laughter, an isle of strange noises and delightful lush foliage, great sticky flowers giving off scents of sweet flesh and musky hair. Ghastly, when you are not part of it and when it is not shut up in a book or a painting for your private delectation.

And Agnes, of the nice fingers and electrical theories? Poor Agnes had been told by letter. Dumped. Apparently, she had seen it coming, but she had taken it poorly all the same. Joseph reckoned her electrical beliefs had not helped her one bit.

Tillie was, like all converts, more extreme in her new-found conviction than he could have believed. She nibbled Baz's ear, swooned about him in her cream frock like a giant lily in a breeze, found everything he said completely fine and adorable. She looked almost pagan, but still talked about God and Jesus now and again – to whom she owed a personal debt of gratitude, apparently. And Joseph, against all the odds, found himself grinding his teeth in anguish. She had lit up, in her new-found adoration. The work was done: the Chapel brick had crumbled to dust and she was touched all over with fire.

He was, perhaps, actually in love with her. Not just drawn, no – but hooked deep. He thought of the pepperminty shawl under his pillow and blushed: if she knew the half!

They went inside when a summer squall blew fresh and wet through the woods and onto the lawn. Tillie needed to wash her face, and so forth. Joseph instructed her to stay in the kitchen for a few minutes and closed the door. The cottage only boasted the bucket closet, of course, and it was due to be emptied in a day or two. He buried the contents in the garden pit, washed it with rainwater from the butt and heaped clean sand in. He knew they would be watching from the kitchen: it served them right, slobbering over each other like that. But she did not turn a hair when he showed her where to go. He wondered if her family was, after all, rather ordinary, that the business about her father being a mill manager was a blind. He was almost disappointed. He wanted her to admire the simplicity of his life, the purity of it. For he could conceive, in his own head, of no other type of life for years to come.

He had nothing to eat in the house but a pail of potatoes and a hunk of cheese. The potatoes, a gift from Mrs Hamilton, were scarcely discernible behind their tentacles of shoots. He suggested they all sup at The Saddler's Arms. Baz cheered and said, 'Oh, that delightful old dear Mrs Havisham! Terrific! We'll go now!'

Joseph had never known Baz like this. Perhaps he had never really known him at all, until this moment. The bare upper lip looked faintly obscene, rather *too* white and soft.

'Mrs Hamilton,' he corrected.

He had the awful feeling that they wanted to stay the night in the cottage: which turned out to be correct. It was safer than a public place, they said.

Life was, in the end, about mating. They would mate and have children and grow dull to each other, and remember that time they dropped spontaneously on dear old, sad old Jo-Jo in his funny damp cottage in the depths of nowhere. Funny dear old Jo-Jo. Pity he never got anywhere, in the end, what?

Thus Joseph mused, almost enjoying the toothachy feel of it, pressing the spot until it hurt. Really, he ought to be throwing his cap in the air and bouncing along with them, flush with youth, as in a jolly modern novel or in one of those dreadful serials in the popular newspapers – no, in one of those he would be grim-jawed and dark of eye and shoot Baz, kidnap Tillie, and be hanged before the end of the month: Tillie weeping beneath the scaffold, naturally, between the advertisement for Beecham's Salts and the Chit-Chat column. Instead he was walking down with them to the village inn, quite sedately, feeling listless and fed up and a touch confused. The little boy somewhere inside him wanted to run off into the woods and cry. Really howl. Instead he was making conversation – the weather, for God's sake. They wanted to spend their honeymoon in – no, run off to – Spain. Spain sounded romantic enough and Baz had a friend with a *casa* . . . etcetera. Tillie had never been further than Ypres.

'Spain will be baking hot,' said Joseph. 'You'll melt into two little puddles of sweat.'

Baz squeezed Tillie's body against his as they walked down the steep little lane. It was ghastly. Even the trees seemed overbearing in the twilight. He was getting into a real brown study, was Joseph.

Tillie's parents had been left a note. It said that she had decided to become a missionary in darkest Africa. It was a lie, Joseph thought. Tillie called it a 'fib' but *he* called it (privately) a lie. Apparently they *wanted* her to become a missionary. If her father knew what she had actually done he would drop dead – he had a feeble heart, said Tillie. Joseph asked why she had not just 'fibbed' to their face.

'They'd have organised it all for me,' she said. 'They wouldn't have let me move an inch before buying me a dozen mosquito nets and a pith helmet. Though they're not at all well off.'

How, Joseph thought, can I feel *anything* for this girl? But he did. She had a real fire; even in Ypres it had flickered away just under her Stockport Chapel mask – and now the mask was almost transparently thin, the fiery spirit was in her face. He had not properly seen it before, this vivid look, very pretty to him in its dark vividness.

A glut of jealousy rose in him. He had to fight it all the way through the meal, which he scarcely touched. They asked him about the novel and he told them (his wiser half straining not to) about the fellow in the village with two 'navels', how that was the central 'picture' of the book. He was testing it on them, really.

They looked blank, both of them. Or they were too stupefied by each other to respond, intellectually. It did sound ridiculous, when he put it like this. Their blankness lacerated him. He wanted to disappear.

'Anyway, it never works when it's explained, just like that. It's always the same, explaining my work. It's like trying to dig up a tree and grow it in a flowerpot.'

'Oh,' said Tillie, 'then you've written it already, have you?'

'What?'

'The book.'

'No.'

'But you said it was like digging up a tree, explaining it.'

'Yes,' said Joseph, 'I did.'

Their eyes were very much on each other, during this.

'But you have – I mean, the tree has to be grown first, before you can dig it up,' she pointed out.

'It was a metaphor,' he said, lamely. 'Don't let's worry about it.'

He was impressed, however, by her nose for nonsense. It kept him on his toes. Her large eyes sparkled, they were very bright as she corrected him, found him out. Very bright and sparkling, those large grey-irised eyes.

As for the jealousy thing, Mrs Hamilton made things worse by treating Baz as a long-lost son and commenting on his fiancée's loveliness. Oh, it was awful. Poor old Joseph. He sat there and sulked behind the smiles and nods and jokes. He really was two people, inner and outer. He read no Walter Scott – thank God, the missus didn't feel like it, she was far too busy bowing and scraping to the beloveds. Walter did not show his face at all. Joseph just sat in the snug and sulked – not obviously (he was too proud for that), but secretly inside. He felt himself buttoned up to the throat in itchy twill, when he was not so at all, he was dressed very cleanly and lightly.

He even felt sympathy – an affinity, almost – with Tillie's pa. A real sympathy.

Out of respect for propriety, Baz slept on the settee cushions, brushed free of plaster dust and mould and placed on the bare floor in Joseph's room. The two old friends together in the same room. Tillie slept in the main bedroom, which Joseph had not yet gone back to sleeping in. But Tillie did not mind. She thought it was God's own. She even mentioned Jesus riding on a donkey, though what a donkey had to do with it Joseph could not imagine. The donkeys in the village were rather wretched old things, stuck away in lightless byres when they were not dragging things about, and the comparison irritated him; it implied Tillie was Jesus and his cottage was wretched. So he said how he thought donkeys were a deal better than motor-cars, and this provoked Baz into a sharp little comment on the way Joseph had always held backward notions, even as a boy.

'Even aged seven or so, he would tell me how he preferred pigeons to telephones. And do you remember, Jo-Jo, my father's spinthariscope?'

'No,' Joseph lied, coughing. The room was still heavy with the wet smell of plaster.

Tillie asked what a spintha-thingummy was.

Baz explained that it was an inexpensive little apparatus, a bit like an eyeglass, by which you could examine a particle of radium. The radium glowed and sparkled, it was very pretty, like looking at a miniature night sky or a firefly. Tillie said her mother took radium for arthritis, but did not look like a firefly. Baz laughed and went on, relentless: he said that Joseph had refused to take a peep into the spinthariscope and Pa was vexed, very vexed.

'A Luddite at the age of ten! Imagine!'

'Why didn't you want to have a look?' asked Tillie.

Joseph shrugged, pulled a face.

'I don't remember – a thing about it,' he said (though he did, very vaguely – the vexed father in the study, red-faced). 'Baz obviously does. It seems to have stuck with him all these years. I remember more important things, like the time I saved Baz from drowning in the river, because he wasn't a very strong swimmer. In fact, he couldn't really swim at all, at the age of fourteen.'

Baz grimaced at that.

'*Touché*,' he said, grimly.

He was stung: behind the sugary treacle of infatuation, he was vulnerable. This is why Joseph reckoned the whole business to be built on sand. Baz was essentially acting out of character: infatuation-love did this, yes, but *real* love just had the victim smiling benignly on everything, and most especially on disapproval. Disapproval positively *strengthened* real love, as it did deep religious faith. In fact, there was essentially very little difference between deep religious faith and real in-loveness. No, Baz's conversion was thin, very thin: it almost, Joseph reckoned, amounted to a desire to put his hand inside Tillie's blouse and squeeze. Once he had done that enough times, the rot would set in very quickly.

This was how he reflected, lying in bed. Baz and he had talked for a bit, after the candle had been blown out; Joseph had questioned him on the marriage business, but Baz was quite fixated on the notion. What about her fragile father? Well, she would resurface after a month or so, tell him she had returned from darkest Africa after contracting a tropical disease and was installed in London where she was recovering very well. She planned, anyway, to do good work in the East End. If she told her parents straight out that she was leaving not for darkest Africa but for darkest London they would no less approve but they would track her down; they were like that. Abroad, however – even the other side of the Channel – was to them as America was to Columbus before he got there: an unknown. Joseph listened to all this in silence. Finally he said, 'I hope you're not just tipsy on this thing, both of you. I hope you're not going to wake up with a wretched hangover.'

It was he who felt wretched, though. As Tillie was saying goodnight on the tiny landing, her face radiant beyond the candle she was holding to light her to bed, the bed a shadowy thing through the open door – the bed made up by himself with the rather threadbare spare sheets he had aired with a warm brick (no blanket, it was too hot for a blanket) – she had leaned forward and kissed him in a terribly sisterly way, only he was not her brother, he was someone who might, just might, but for a whisker (his own weakness and ineptitude) have been her lover. And the anguish had risen up in him again, along with a horrible, undercover desire – evilly grinning in his imagination – to snatch her from his friend. To elope from an elopement.

'And how are you going to take her Christian thing, Baz?'

'What Christian thing?'

Joseph stared up at the dim ceiling. The owl was going again, and a distant burble that might have been a nightingale. All they needed was a pea-green boat.

'Haven't you noticed? She's awfully keen on Jesus.'

Though now it was not brick, it was scarcely tissue paper. But he kept quiet about what he saw.

Baz grunted.

'It gives her a tremendous kind of four-square strength,' he said.

'A ticket on the Midland Railway to heaven,' murmured Joseph.

'What's that?'

'It closes a mind, Chapel stuff does.'

There was silence, then a rustle. Baz was leaning towards him. A dim creamy puff was his friend's face in the darkness.

'Listen,' he whispered, 'I know you're frightfully jealous, but I don't think you ever stood a chance. I didn't steal her, you know. I'm not saying we've discussed you at great length, but she did say she thought you were – brainy, that's what she said. Now you and I know that a fellow hasn't got a ghost of a chance with a girl who calls him "brainy".'

Joseph lay like a corpse.

'What on earth made you ever think I was mashed on her?' the corpse found its lips saying.

'Oh, just a little matter of an incident in Wipers. I saw you the next morning. You were quite out of your head, old boy. Quite understandable, of course. But you were tight that night, you know that. She holds nothing against you, though. She knows you were tight. You had her nice antique shawl in bed with you, do you remember that? You never gave it her back. I haven't mentioned it, though. Of course I wouldn't do that.'

'How do you know it was antique?'

'Oh, one can tell these things. Style and – quality. Anyway, she told me it was her grandmother's.'

Joseph fingered the shawl's slippery softness under his pillow.

'Why on earth did you come here?'

Baz appeared baffled by the question.

'Friendship, dear fellow. You're my oldest and best friend.'

'I apparently tried to pleasure myself with your fiancée. I'm apparently sick with jealousy.'

'She wasn't my fiancée, not then.' He was leaning forward even further, thrusting his face out of the darkness. His voice dropped to a sharper whisper. 'It makes me feel a lot closer to you, you see. All of us, us three, bound together in the most marvellous bond.'

'What does?'

'The fact that you've – wanted her. It's like a novel, isn't it?'

'Is it?'

'Don't you think? One of your novels?'

'I haven't written half a one yet.'

'Oh come on, you – you know what I mean.'

'Not really. You'd never have come down and taunted me like this, in a novel. It's much too contradictory. Instead, I'd have tracked you down and done something horribly bloody and dramatic.'

Baz laughed, disappearing back into the darkness. Then he said, all serious: 'I'm sorry you think we're taunting you. I really am.'

'So am I. Shall we go to sleep?'

'All right.'

Then, just as Joseph was dropping quite remarkably abruptly into sleep's soft abyss – 'I've completely misjudged it, haven't I? I didn't think you were really *serious*, you see.'

'What?' He was really annoyed, heart pounding. Baz was screwing him up to a night of insomnia.

'About Tillie. I thought it was just a game, in Wipers.'

'That's what they said about the war, if I remember rightly. Play up, play up, and play the game. Now please shut up and let me get to sleep.'

'Alright, old boy. But I really did just think it was a game, flirtation and that, you know. I just thought you'd be very glad and happy for us, in direct consequence. Tills and I first got to know each other on the train, properly I mean.'

'Tills? Oh my God.'

'You chose not to come back with her on the train, it was a free choice. You couldn't have been serious. You never gave her back that shawl, for a start.'

Silence. Joseph willed it, it was as thick as a wall between them. This 'serious' business was very Baz, very irritating, but he let it pass. And Baz shut up.

Joseph did not get to sleep, of course. He lay awake for hours, wandering through his beleaguered consciousness, biting his lip. Unconsciousness was an impossible trick his mind could not quite remember how to perform, like breathing underwater. He should have put Baz right off the scent, told him that, yes, it *was* a game, he was wild the next morning because of the German woman, nothing to do with Tillie – forget that damn old shawl. Now he realised it was everything to do with Tillie. The whole time he was searching for the German woman – whose name he did not even know! – he was really searching for Tillie, for his own feelings about Tillie (because he did find the physical Tillie, oh yes, he even *talked* to her, by the poplars). And why did she send him the postcard from Matlock, if she was with Baz? Perhaps Baz did not know about that. Come to think of it, the postcard was propped on the kitchen windowsill, next to the geraniums. Perhaps she too was searching for him through his best friend. Perhaps the whole business of coming down here was a ruse, an elaborate ruse, to bring her into his arms.

That was what the kiss on the landing suggested. Because, much to his surprise, it had been on the lips. Very chaste and tender, like a child's goodnight kiss, but it had been straight on his lips, that peck.

And Baz's theory about 'brainy' – that was so much four-square rubbish. In this busy new world, braininess was exactly what girls went for, along with a fast open-topped motor-car. At least he had *one* of those things.

And so he wandered on, in company with the owl and the nightingale, until he unconsciously allowed sleep to creep into the channels of his brain like a smothering oil – waking up rather late next to Baz's empty bed, in a blaze of sunlight and bird noise.

25

Dead Men

B Y AFTERNOON IT was covered again, dowdy and threatening rain, but they had walked by then, and lunched in a little place in a bigger village about four miles away, driven there in the motor-car with the hood down. Baz had the motor-car, Joseph thought, and *he* had the brains. Actually, Baz had the brains, too. There was the rub.

It was all so very odd, walking beside the couple – for couple they were, holding hands and generally canoodling in that fixated, self-absorbed way new lovers have. Not that it was as demonstrative as in the bohemian circles Joseph knew – they did not actually smooch, they only pecked at each other in a bird-like way, birds at worms – but by the standards of Baz's usual behaviour it was virtually incredible.

He hung back from them, pretending to appreciate nature. He was no natural history expert, despite his country upbringing, but impressed Tillie by pointing out a chaffinch, a dead grass snake next to an ant hill, a huge pink mass of jumping jack beside a rather dingy stream, and (a bit later) some plovers weeping over the corn. Tillie's bright laugh punctuated the heavy summer air. She was kindly, he thought, and warm and good. She had no airs, either – she was really quite ordinary, she had seen nothing of the wider world and had scarcely worked for herself, for money, living at home as she did, healing the sick nearby – yet she was like a precious gift unwrapped from a dowdy brown parcel. There it was: the gift. But it was Baz who had got to her first. Stolid, unimaginative Baz, who remembered his best friend's every foible.

He had to stop at times and pretend to be looking closely at something, or he would have fallen over with anguish. For years afterwards, strangely, he could recall in precise detail whatever he was pretending to study in the tangle of grass or branches: flower or beetle or bird. It was soaked in his anguish.

The rain had not really freshened things up very much, it had just dropped the absurd temperature to normal mid-summer figures. Endless clouds of gnats and flies bothered them and the mud had not yet dried, it was quite thick in places. It had cracked in the heat and formed plates, and then the rain had gathered there and created a particularly glutinous treacle, exuding a rather horrid smell. But the vast sheets of lofty foliage, the very high elms, the bright cataracts of beech everywhere, the great shadowy woods of beech and their underwater light – these were inspiring, and Joseph was almost proud of them, almost showing them off, these little intimate valleys and hills that made even Derbyshire look bare and bleak (though the pull towards the north was nevertheless very strong in him, he admitted).

They stopped by a farm, with a very dilapidated homestead and a mossy barn, and drank some milk. It was still warm, and Tillie got some ripe manure on her boots. Creamy milk lay on her upper lip as she drank from the can, and she wiped it off with her wrist, laughing. They watched the pigs. The toothless old woman who sold the milk talked to them in such strong dialect that they only understood the half.

'You see? London hasn't reached here yet,' said Joseph. He was obscurely proud.

They skirted Rickmansworth and passed between acres of lush water meadows. It was as if the drought had never been, though a labourer working in the watercress beds shook his head mournfully about it. Joseph pointed out the smoking chimneys of the paper mills along the valley.

'That's where it starts,' he said.

'What starts?' Tillie asked.

'The rot.'

'Paper, you mean?'

He chuckled. He was determined to be clever and humorous and a touch knowing. Sly of him, really – yet in another sense it was not calculated, it grew naturally out of the situation. Baz was talking to the labourer, a little way off. Joseph felt that it was self-conscious, this hobnobbing with the yokels.

She shook her head, smiling.

'*I* think you don't mean it,' she said, curling a lock of hair round her finger in a childlike way, a kind of throwback. 'I think you're rather pleased with being a poet.'

'Who said I was a poet? I'm a novelist. I'm not a poet. I tried poetry, but it's finished.'

'You mean you couldn't write it as you wanted.'

'No – well, that may be true, too – but I mean that poetry is finished as an art form. It doesn't answer to our times. It's too soft.'

'Mr Sassoon? My father reads him out in his prayer meetings, he treats them like prayers.'

'Is your father a pacifist?'

'He's a socialist and a Christian.' She gave him an arch look that answered his question.

Joseph was amazed.

'You mean, he talks to the dead and yet approves of Karl Marx?'

'Karl Marx is dead, too,' she replied, with a little laugh.

'They act as if he isn't, all those revolutionaries.'

'So? Everything's run by the dead,' she said. 'What rule isn't based on something dead? Dead rules made by dead rulers, yet we all obey. Like the war, we all obeyed, didn't we? Even the conchies agreed to be conchies. Tradition's based on a huge heap of dead things, isn't it? Only we don't know it. We don't *admit* it. You don't have to worship Mr Marx, you know, to be a socialist.'

'And Jesus,' Joseph ventured, ignoring her remark, 'isn't he dead, too?'

She was not at all upset.

'You know He isn't,' she replied. 'That's the whole point.'

'I don't know,' Joseph persisted. 'I've only been told it by my elders and betters. But to a revolutionary Marxian socialist, Jesus is definitely dead. Dead as a nit. So what do you say to someone like that? I mean, you can't be picky without admitting it, too.'

'Picky?'

'Picking which dead ruler is alive for you, and which one isn't. Or which dead god,' he added, a bit daringly.

She frowned and let the lock of hair fall onto her neck. Joseph was inflamed with excitement – as much intellectual as sensual. She could give as good as she gets, he thought. It was like the best game of lawn tennis you could imagine.

'Well, I can't *compel* myself to agree, can I?' she said, mysteriously.

Baz came over at that point, but Tillie's look lingered on Joseph just a fraction longer than it needed to, just enough to have him tortured.

He could have felt it with his eyes closed, her electricity. Even with all his faculties bunged up he could have felt it: like hair to a comb he was, pulled taut by it, taut and bristling.

He really found himself yearning for Tillie, at any rate. When she reached up once to fiddle with her straw hat he almost burned right up, he almost suffocated with yearning. But at the same time he saw how impossible the situation was.

The happy pair planned to get married in secret during the next month and Joseph would be a witness. He said neither yea nor nay but only: 'That's very hasty.' They were having lunch at a long table outside a beamed place with hanging baskets, medieval torture instruments and an AA sign. Baz's car was admired by a group of toothy types on a spin in a hired charabanc, members of something called the Cloak and Dagger Club – they all wore cloaks and black masks over their eyes and drank a lot, at any rate. (Presumably the daggers were under their frilly shirts.) Baz pretended the car was his own. The food was awful, lumpy, no better than railway-station fare. Tillie admired the thumbscrews on the wall; Joseph said they were made in Sheffield out of scrap iron from the war.

'Don't always be sarcastic,' she said.

'I'm not!' He was genuinely hurt, his voice went very high. 'It's the truth, I'm not being sarcy, I read an article about it in the paper. Folk are still mad on the Middle Ages, you know. They turn these out like—'

'Oh, never believe anything you read in the paper.'

She carried on admiring the things; and he admired *her* for it. Her cussedness.

When the bill came, Baz studied it very carefully and Joseph had to pay his own whack down to the last halfpenny. He had assumed, erroneously, that even English lovers were automatically heedless of parsimony, and that his meal would be paid for in return for a bed and having his day of writing smashed. Baz was taking his socialism very seriously, he thought – bitterly.

He felt very sore about this business with the bill, in fact, and at tea under a lowering sky on the lawn he made a point of saying he was out of biscuits. He was quite grumpy.

Then Samuel appeared at the gate by the side of the house, half-concealed by the falling honeysuckle.

'There's someone there,' said Tillie.

'I know him, Tillie, don't fret.'

He waved, too hot and bothered to get up. Samuel opened the gate and walked across to them in his shy, ponderous way.

'Walter said as you med need your grass cuttin',' he mumbled.

A scythe hung at his waist on a leather strap, like a Turkish scimitar. A phallic strickle, greased for use, dangled on the other hip.

'I do, Samuel, but not right now.'

'Oh, don't mind us,' said Baz.

'It's not you I mind. It's my empty purse,' murmured Joseph.

'Do cut it, old fellow,' said Baz, addressing Samuel. 'Or we'll never find our way back to the house.'

Tillie laughed. Samuel gave her a crooked smile, a missing tooth lending it great charm. The strickle dangled very obviously.

'I say,' said Baz, 'aren't you the lucky fellow with two navels?'

'It en't a navel,' said Samuel, stolidly. 'It were the shrapnel.'

'It only *looks* like a navel,' said Joseph, thoroughly embarrassed.

'How does it feel to be a character in a chap's novel?' asked Baz.

Samuel looked blankly at him. Joseph could have well-nigh throttled his friend.

'Didn't you know?' Baz went on, ruthlessly. 'Mr Monrow here has put your belly into his book. I think you should feel honoured, I really do.'

Samuel looked down at his belly, concealed as usual behind a worn corduroy waistcoat and thick drill trousers. Then he looked at Joseph.

'An' me Get Religion?' he murmured.

Joseph shook his head.

'Good God no,' he said, quietly. His face was burning. 'You can start cutting tomorrow morning,' he added, floundering now.

'What's that about religion?' asked Tillie.

'Nothing.'

'I don't want me Get Religion in no book, Mr Monrow.'

'It isn't.'

Joseph stood up. Baz was smiling coolly.

'I shan't be having it in no book, Mr Monrow—'

'Let's go in,' said Joseph, before Tillie could say anything (her mouth was open, ready). 'I'll see you tomorrow, Samuel.'

Samuel nodded, suspicious, an ugly shadow on his face.

'Can't we have a peep, Samuel?' said Baz. It was ghastly, the way he was treating the fellow.

'I en't a Red Injun,' Samuel replied. 'I en't one of they Red Injuns or one o' they bearded women.'

Tillie smiled.

'Quite right,' she said. 'Baz dearest, leave him alone.'

After Samuel had left, and they were in the kitchen, Joseph told Baz off. Tillie was in agreement. 'It's cruel,' she said. Baz shrugged.

'Why shouldn't I have told him?'

'Because *I* hadn't told him,' Joseph said.

'Why not?'

'One doesn't. It's not necessary. It won't be Samuel in the book, it'll be someone else.'

'I hope *I'm* not in there,' said Baz, darkly.

'Oh, everyone is, one way or the other.' Joseph enjoyed his power, suddenly. He was fashioning something secret and powerful, like a magician concocting a creature. He went out to the well and drew a pail of cold, stone-clean water. The handle creaked dreadfully.

'What was that business about Samuel's getting religion?' Tillie asked, when he returned with the pail of cold water.

'It's a euphemism, really. But I'm not telling you what it stands for. I've had my fingers burnt already.'

He gave Tillie a little, secretive smile.

She smiled back. Her eyes seemed to be straining against desire, glittering in her sunned face. She bent to the pail and splashed her forehead and cheeks, smiling at him. Her hair clung to her neck, wet and very dark.

Baz watchful in the chair, watching them both from under half-lidded eyes.

And then the lovers left, in a whirl of smoke and oil; left Joseph alone with his bothersome anguish. It would all end in disaster, he was sure.

They had roared off, triumphant, leaving him in the shade of himself. He had been diminished by their triumph, their contentment. Imagining Baz in her arms, their entwined nakedness, positively tortured him. And all he had to show for himself was a fellow with two navels. That was how it felt to him, anyway.

Tillie had lightly embraced him on leaving, like a foreign, a continental. But apparently it was what they did in her particular Chapel. It was a religious embrace. She had not kissed him. Just the hands on his shoulders and the light press of her body, affectionate, cheek brushing cheek, soft bosom against his. Baz looking on by the open door of the motor-car. Then her twist at the waist, that narrow hinge of a waist. Strong arms, though: they had arm-wrestled in the kitchen, elbows on the bareboard table, and she had given him what-for, laughing away. A real fight, she had given him. A nurse's arms, lifting crippled men up and shifting beds.

Then they had simply whirled away into their brilliant future, promising to 'let him know' when and where it would be, the wedding. It seemed almost improper, the way they went off together, shamelessly. He had not even agreed to be a witness, they had taken his pretend diffidence and shaped it the way they wanted it shaped.

A day of writing destroyed, too. Possibly more. He would have to set himself very firmly back in the rails until the end had been reached. He would write the first great War book if it killed him.

He took the minty shawl from under his pillow and buried it in the garden – a shallow hole in the old rose bed but it felt like a bottomless pit. That night, looking in the spotted mirror above the stone basin, he saw himself as very ugly, physically-speaking. It might have been nothing more than the fact that he was studying himself with his spectacles on, which was unusual. Not the fact that the spectacles did not really suit him, more that he could see his face clearly through them, cruelly so. Or it might have been the position of the candle, propped on a shelf above the mirror. Whatever, the effect was plain: he revolted himself, physically-speaking. He could not possibly understand how any girl could find him attractive, with or without his oval spectacles.

And he thought back to his week in Cornwall, to the effect Hubert Rail had had on him, to the stuff about senselessness and those bitter, pale-blue eyes jealous of his 'fortune'. A second-rate fellow, he had thought. Now it was quite clear to him, suddenly, that he had shielded himself from the truth through the weeks since: Hubert, his second-rate 'double', was physically repellent, effeminate, sharp-faced and weak and fluttery. This was how the world saw *him*, he realised – saw Joseph, that is. He had not really taken it in at the time, or not for more than a second or two, because he had chosen to believe that the fellow hardly looked very much like him at all. He had dismissed it – had he not? – as a silly frolic on the part of the more tedious members of the party. Now, however, he realised how his mirror framed Hubert Rail's face as much as his own. Skewwhiff, it was. Second-rate. He wished he had not torn up that wretched doctor's photograph, of course. Then he was glad he had.

He sat for ages in the garden, in the soft night air, listening to the night songs. He was bitten on his ankles, little red itchy bites. Then he went to bed in Tillie's bed, without changing the sheets. Her smell clung to them, lemony and dark. He buried his face in the pillow and breathed in deeply. A black hair lay on it, which he put to his mouth. He untucked the sheets and rolled himself up in them, disappeared into them. The experience was both agonising and delicious. He felt himself plump out again, lose the scrawny ugliness, the disgust at himself. He smoothed the sheets again and slept very soundly, as if wrapped up in her warmth.

The next morning, feeling much better, he saw how fresh and young he was in the mirror's glass, handsome even. Hubert Rail had fallen away – or the memory of him, the memory of the fellow's scrawny flutteriness, his dry, withered view of the world. Joseph felt *himself* once more. He would conquer heights. One day, Tillie would come running to him. He would not even have to search for her, to 'compel' her – that strange phrase of hers at the end of their discussion about socialism and God, about not *compelling* herself to agree, it sang in his head, turning round and about, thrilling him through and through.

Her soul would simply agree, and she would come to him. They would talk about Marx and God until their old age, seated under the plum tree. He looked out at the garden and saw them there, together, in their benign old age. Still handsome. She would never know he had buried her silk shawl a few feet from where they talked. It would be a secret sign of his love, of the sheer power of it – that he had tried once to banish from his presence.

He was standing there naked. He felt the fox in him paramount, that cunning tactical side that was almost instinctive. He smelt her on his naked body, standing in the kitchen with his cup of tea. On his hands, his arms, his legs. As if they had been truly intimate with each other, skin on skin. And he wanted to weep, because this was just as much an illusion as anything he was writing on the page.

But he continued to sleep in Tillie's sheets all that week, until her trace had been smothered under his own.

26

A Trip to Chertsey

O N THE MONDAY of the following week he received a bit of a shock. Unpleasant, it was, to come back after a short walk and find the back door open, and nothing touched but his sacred working table, where he had been working pretty flat out for five days.

The heavy *Chamber's Twentieth Century Dictionary* was thrown on the floor, broken-backed and a page torn out of it, so that it jumped from 'Quill' to 'Quiz'. Was that a message? – though it looked haphazard enough, the rip. He felt curiously shameful of it. The page itself was nowhere to be seen. The blank sheet he would ritually place under the dictionary was screwed up into a ball and lay next to his bed. His writing was exposed; with pounding heart he examined the exposed lines. He was quite convinced they had been read: they had that shamefaced look about them. Yes, they cowered there, all right.

And they really should have stayed hidden.

A bad time he was having. It was like a bad marriage, he could not come round to seeing the other's point of view. The 'other' was the novel, of course. It had its point of view, but he did not agree with it. This is how it felt, at any rate. It had this will of its own, this curious will. It wanted, really wanted, to be a cheap, vulgar little thing for Mr Smith's bookstalls – it would please the mass no end. But he did not want this. And they fought, it seemed, all the way. The author was up there with his tie straight, his spats clean, his hair razored, and the novel was a cheap little slut down in the shilling bookstall.

The death of the Ted character, for instance.

'Walter' heard 'Ted' cry out for help on the parapet, but did not save him, turned the other way. The stuff of tuppenny serials, that. Religious, even. Sickly. It had none of the grit of life in it. Yet nothing else suggested itself, not for days. Blank as an end wall, his side – no escape. He would stand at the door of the study and look at the table with the foolscap on it and the slut would be enticing him in. He had to run off into the woods for an hour or two, quite literally. He could imagine the paper rustling as it laughed, silently laughed at him, back there in the cottage.

He dreamt of squealing Prussian trains and fat little corporals in gear dropping off them like ants off a crust. He considered 'ditching' the whole idea of Ted's death and Walter's guilt, but nothing else took its place. It seemed to be the lifeblood of the whole creature. He just had to ratch it up out of the shilling bookstalls, into the giddy heights of poetry and deep symbol and universal meaning. He had to write something that he, the author, really craved. He alone. The rest would follow. The whole book would follow, and the mass would stumble after it. He could not follow the mass.

Then the breakthrough came.

It was something Tillie had said in Ypres about her brother that put a breach in the wall. He had been killed with the leave card in his pocket, she had said. That was asking for it, he had replied: chaps were suspicious about it, to carry around a leave card attracted bullets and shells, you had to get it and then scarper. Fast as your pins could take you. Otherwise you were *bound* to tempt fate, and fate is like a bloodhound, it sniffs out that sort of meat straightaway.

Off on a walk a couple of days after Baz and Tillie had burst in and out, he had snaffled it. Actually, thinking about Tillie's brother recalled a story going the rounds in the training camp, and he simply altered the story here and there, but not a lot. His version went like this; or this is what the page showed to anyone looking at it.

The Walter character is scared, dead scared. He feels unaccountably windy before a certain job – part of the ammo party, he is, carrying boxes up the liquid line. He is due for leave, too, in a few days' time, just after another fellow, a Welshman. Only this Welsh fellow was sentenced to a field punishment a month or two back (some trivial offence – burning lavatory seats for fuel in the beastly winter, Joseph decided) and, among other things, had been placed at the bottom of the Leave Roll. Right at the bottom, clawing his way up again for months. Only, the Captain has forgotten! Clean forgotten! And the Welshman – he is all packed and ready to go, literally saying cheerio to the others, heart thudding with the thought that he has got away with it, he can hardly believe it, it's the first bloody good thing that's happened to him in two *years*. Two years of stinking, bloody badness. And now he is going to see his wife and little girl in Aberystwyth, in his tiny damp back-to-back hole in Aberystwyth. But that place is paradise to him. He has thought about it every night for two years. Stood in it, in his thoughts – in that little damp hole of a parlour with his little daughter hugged to his chest, his wife beaming under curls.

Then he passes the Walter character. 'Cheerio,' he says, 'good bloody luck, corp. Oh, I'm a cushy bugger, I am.' He is on cloud nine, going home. He whistles louder than a cockerel crows.

And Walter, who is so scared, with the wind up, convinced he is going to be potted out that very day, remembers with a great hot flush that this little Welsh fellow received a field punishment a month or two back – that it's not this fellow's turn at all but his own! So he runs up to the Captain in the trench and tells him.

And the poor Welshman is recalled at the very last moment – he is already on his way back through the lines to the train, and he almost faints. One minute he was whistling like a lark, going home, dreaming of his green-eyed Wales, the next minute he is facing front again, blood and mud and madness, his brain all fuzzy with the shock of it. The Captain cannot do a thing to help. He hates the Walter fellow, at that moment. But orders are orders and the Walter fellow is already on his way home, off behind the lines like a rocket. So the little Welsh chap is sent up with the ammo and of course is dropped by a Hun sniper, leave card in his pocket. Dropped, stone dead, dead before he hits the gurgling slime.

Now, how does Ted come in?

Joseph was pleased with the next part. Very pleased. He had not had to scratch his head for long, either, before it rippled out like a glorious bright banner.

Vital it is to get the ammo up, terribly *vital* in that crazed military way – so Walter gets recalled just as he is off, he has almost got his boot on the leave train's footplate. Maybe this was the Captain's doing, the Captain's anguish at the death of the poor Welshman –

a kind of revenge, perhaps. So Walter is given the load of ammo the dead Welshman would have carried up.

Now here was the twist by which Joseph felt he had cracked the thing.

Ted comes back safe and sound from his trip up the line and sees his son-in-law with the ammo box, trembling like a jelly.

'What's up, boy?'

Walter can hardly speak. Terrible state. He has really got the wind up, now. Fate has got him marked down in big capital letters. And Ted feels *responsible* for his daughter's husband. 'Look after him, Pa,' she had said, 'look after my Walter.' So Ted offers to carry the ammo box himself, to go up the line again – though really he is officially due for a rest in the dugout, he looks like a ploughman on a very sticky day. And Walter, seizing at every straw, agrees. He is hardly in his right mind with fear.

So Ted carries the ammo for him, humping it up over the slippery duckboards – and is hit by a whizz-bang, falls dead as a nail with half his head blown off. *Right* next to the Welshman does our poor Ted fall, their hands touching, their blood mixing up in the sodden ground.

Oh, it meant scotching the present version of Ted's death, the one lit by the Very lights – a small sacrifice to pay for a top-notch solution. The Walter fellow was guilty through weakness, it was never straight neglect or murder. But it would have weighed on him like lead. He had done for two people, in a way. One of them his father-in-law!

And it was this story that was sketched out in the exposed lines, in full view of whoever had come up to his study. Very neat, not a scrawl at all. As legible as fresh paint, as his father would say.

Somebody angered by something, from the look of it. As if they had come prying and were angered by what they read.

His worst fear, of course, was that the intruder was Walter himself. And he felt like running for it, he really did. Bolting clean out.

He smoothed the bent pages of the dictionary. Shod with frostnails, that was how his mind felt. Every thought seemed to clatter. The ripped-out page with its missing words; it exerted some sort of authority over him, as sacrifices do.

Then he calmed down. He was not *that* afraid of Walter.

Anyway, it might not have been him at all. It might have been a cat, though a cat would scarcely have screwed up the blank sheet. And why screw up the blank sheet? If it *had* been Walter, he would have screwed up the libellous stuff. Unless he had not dared to, unless he was showing a kind of taunting respect.

So Joseph did it, instead. Screwed the page up, with its lies and fabulations. When he wrote it out again, 'Walter' was changed to 'Dick' and 'Ted Hambling' to 'Harold Abbot'. Strangely, it flagged, it was not the same at all. It was then that he realised, with a slippery feeling in his stomach, that invention was not quite his thing. He needed to hook it to reality, to something that *approved* his fabulation. This distressed him. Reality was like a schoolmaster, correcting his flights of fancy; he had to put his hand up, poke about for approval. He had to drag Walter in, and Ted, who existed only in Mrs Hamilton's tears and a dim photograph on the mantelpiece, and Tillie's brother – and even the German widow's quiet agony was dragged in as a bulwark. He was frankly *incapable* of free invention – through which he might strike to the heart of it, of the war that had smashed everything, and cracked our souls.

He had all the fury in him, all the rage; he only had to harness his rage to the wings of free invention as they swooped over the front line – and the novel would ripple out from his pen. But those wings were exactly what he did not have. He had paper wings, they got him nowhere. They bent and tore at the first gust.

Right down in the depths of his soul he felt doubt. From head to toe he was suffused by doubt, standing there by the little crude table. Somewhere between the owl and the nightingale, that was where he wanted to sing. The note of death and the note of joy. But when he read back a little, read those passages in which something like a style had been established – well, it was really an awful experience, he felt he was travelling through a comic, leering funfair for miles and miles. His own words were absurd, like leering mechanical faces in a funfair. They embarrassed him. And he felt the war slipping from his fingers, physically stealing out of the window like a great black cat, savage, terribly savage – and free to wreak havoc. As if, with this novel, these thin-lined pages of foolscap, he might have tamed it and saved the world.

Maybe he was going barmy, he thought. As long as he could use the word 'barmy', he was not. It was as safe and soft as his father's carpets and rugs, that word. It was a homeopathic fetish against the real thing.

And suddenly he knew what he had to do.

It took him an hour to find out whether there was a hospital in Chertsey. He went down to the Post Office, held the candlestick-telephone upright and waited. Yes, there was a hospital, a very small one. His heart beat with trepidation there in the Post Office: at any minute he expected to see Walter walk past – or actually enter. The place doubled as a second-hand clothes store and he paid for his calls over a heap of threadbare shirts. The plump postmistress, a gossip, was sorting through them and nattering, even though they were alone and he was miles away. No Walter, though. He ran back through a silvery shower of rain, relieved.

That evening he strolled down to The Saddler's Arms with an air of studied nonchalance and walked virtually slap-bang into the man in the tiny corridor between the snug and the tap room. Drinking, Walter had been – once or twice a week he would have the look of a man who had really soaked himself all day. It flooded off his skin, then. But it made him more forgetful than brutal. Right now he was fit to forget his own name; his consciousness was just a thin film that got him from one task to another.

'Hallo, Walter.'

'I'm to fetch th' mustard.'

'Good.'

Walter frowned at him, as if studying him through the surface of a stream. Joseph was really just the little fish, squirming about, sunning itself. But no fury in the look; just the innocent bewilderment of drink.

'Wi' th' ham-and-tongue. You put summat down to take it up.'

'Ay, you do.'

The little fish darted quickly away into the safe shadowy under-rock of the snug, where after supper it started on *Peveril of the Peak* over Mrs Hamilton's needles.

The following morning he took the train to London and clattered out again on the line to Staines. The sudden rush of it all, the abrupt plunge into people and rush and great noise, made him giddy. From Staines he took the local bus to Chertsey.

It was a very pleasant ride, along lush meads by the lazy Thames, and blemished only occasionally by a modern villa. He thought of King John, and of Harris, George and J. (not forgetting the dog) in their boat, sculling into the shady nook for supper: of the discarded lumber of his own life – and the lumber that yet remained on the mental level. Well, he was nervous. He thought about Tillie quite a bit, as they swayed along past the lazy green river. It was pleasant, despite his nerves.

He found the hospital after asking someone in the high street. It was a small, yellowish, Byzantine-brick affair stuck up behind some polished shrubs. It had a view of the river at the back. Rather expensive, no doubt. Rather smart, but still dreadful, still smelling of pine antiseptic and suffering. He went straight in and asked where he might find Mr Frank Pitts. He said he was a relative. Nurses flitted about, and squeaky trolleys and stretchers on wheels with starched sheets and wild-haired heads in them. He waited, his skin greasy from the train's smoke, not hygienically clean at all. The woman behind the desk was quite friendly, despite a sour pallor to her face. She had soaked up the place, he reckoned. Soaked up the sickness. She had a large watch upside down on her chest, like a nurse, with radium-painted numerals for the dark.

'What is he in for?' she asked, frowning, turning typewritten pages.

'Nervous collapse,' Joseph replied.

'Oh dear,' she said, abstractedly. 'It gets us all, don't it?'

He was suddenly feeling ready to collapse himself. The blood beat in his throat. He felt suffocated with nerves.

'There's no Frank Pitts here.'

She didn't call him 'sir', he noted. He was too young, to her. She was quite familiar.

'Maybe he's been discharged,' he suggested.

She was very slow, almost pretending to be stupid. She licked her finger and turned the pages, back, back. She seemed to be looking right back to the time of the plague. She shook her head and looked up at him over her ugly spectacles.

'No Mr Pitts has come in here, for the last six months. Not this year, not at all.'

She carried on looking at him, waiting for his next move, waiting to see if he, too, would collapse nervously at this news.

'Oh,' was all he said. Then: 'Is there another hospital in the vicinity?'

'Staines is the nearest,' she said. 'You could try Staines.'

'Thank you.'

Perhaps someone had visited Pitts in Staines and posted the letter in Chertsey, as Baz's Stockport letter had been posted in Swansea. In that case, the hospital might be one of a hundred. He went straight to the Post Office on the high street and tried to find out Frank Pitts's address, in case he lived in the town – the London post-office box might have been a blind. The postmaster looked him up and down as if he was not properly dressed, tucked his pencil behind his ear and gave him the thin little telephone book to peruse. Platt, Poulter and Pryce. No Pitts, at any rate.

There were three possibilities: either Frank Pitts did not have a telephone (like the majority of folk), or did not live in Chertsey, or was not really called Frank Pitts. Joseph felt baffled by all three – defeated, it is sad to admit. He was half-glad, half-sorry, that he would never be able to meet Frank Pitts face to face. He had looked forward to it and dreaded it in equal measure. A day wasted. He bought some baccy to console himself and located the old half-timbered pile where Cowley died: just a plaque, 'Here the last Accents flow'd from Cowley's tongue'. The street was very silent and still. As he puffed away on his pipe he felt a sudden love for life, a real euphoria in the warm sunshine. Pitts could go hang himself.

He got back to the cottage very late. By then the euphoria had dwindled to regret.

It had been a desperate idea. A youthful, luxurious indulgence. He had imagined it might unlock something in him, meeting the foe. Instead, he was left feeling the foe was everywhere, and absent. Yet powerful. He dreamt that night of the glowing tree they had seen on the salient, and Frank Pitts dressed in a hooded cloak, waving a terrible wand – a man's thighbone, really – in front of it. Tillie was with him – with Joseph, right next to him – they were proper lovers. But Pitts turned her evil, she came out in green spots, *hideous* she was. He woke up quite upset.

This was the last thing he wanted – that Pitts should gain a hold on him. He had a very strong reason to suppose that the man was a liar, now, but this made the fellow yet more sinister, even ominous. Worse, his defence of the indefensible, of the wickedest war ever waged, a holocaustic rite against the young, was somehow seeping in under Joseph's foundations – that was how he saw it, as foul-smelling water trickling in under his solid columns and buttresses, inching away at the sandy bed: and there was *nothing he could do about it*. The more he denied it, the more he heard the water trickling in.

And he could hear Pitts's laughter in the trickling water.

A letter from Baz arrived – scarcely a letter, more a note scribbled between his lovemaking. The wedding was planned for the end of the month. A secret, two witnesses only in a registration office in Clapham, their names stuck up on the board but who would ever notice? *Please reply by return of post if not suitable.* Like an order from a store. Hurrying along, Baz was, really hurrying along and heedless, driven by lust. Suddenly, Joseph felt the obligation of friendship drop away like a loose rock. Down the mountainside it went, rolling away into oblivion. Suppose he didn't reply? Well, they could drag in somebody off the street. It was incredible, to think of the conjoining of Tillie and Baz – that was the word he thought of, *conjoining*. It seemed to cancel out both of them, as far as he was concerned.

But his throat refused to join this game: it was as sore as when you want to cry over something terribly unfair, in childhood. He sat in the kitchen drinking his tea, with the letter in front of him on the table, and stared straight out at nothing, almost in shock. His desire for Tillie was unabated: he was quite certain that Baz was a halfway point. That, deep down, it was Joseph she was after. 'After' was wrong, too calculated, vulgar. Everybody in England was 'after' something, these days – money, flesh, the spirit world, cocaine and drink and dancing girls. A real debauch after the grim years of killing and grief, you could quite understand it, intellectually-speaking: but Tillie's vivaciousness was not part of that vulgar grab, that low material hunger. No, she was a gift, creamy-white in the blackness – Joseph had felt it instantly, the first time he set eyes on her on the ferryboat. A great precious gift. Her appetite was high, silvery, pent in only by the Chapel brick which he – not Baz! – had taken the first swing at. She was all sky and fleeting clouds, under the Chapel brick. And he, Joseph, had taken the first swing at it, dislodged the first brick from its cement.

But he had fatally hesitated. The German woman had thrust him off course. He saw the German woman, for a moment, as something sent from the underworld.

He shook his head. A tenderness for the German woman had stolen over him strangely as he had thought of her. It was very odd, but she was bound up with Tillie, bound up in the same tissuey stuff of his soul – as if they had been at one time or another his soul-sister, his lover, his wife, each separately in different faraway lives. He could almost conjure the places and times, vaguely Babylonian, sandy and baked-walled, oriental smells and sounds. And his present life was a mere cork bobbing about on the sea of these ancient memories, a vulgar little throwaway thing. His flannelled trousers and collared shirt seemed absurd – even his short hair seemed absurd, and the fact that he had no sword at his side (even Schiller had carried a sword). And the rest of his life stretched out in front of him as an absurdity, too, in which he must look upon Tillie in the arms of his best friend. Mocked and cajoled by the sight. And to think that he, Joseph, had had the gift proffered him, only to let it be whisked away, right in front of his eyes! Out of laziness, ultimately. Sheer laziness. The gods spoilt you only once.

He felt this ancestral right to the girl as something stamped on his soul. He was amazed by the depth of his jealousy, the sheer force of his disappointment. And funnelled into this modern body, this awkward modern influenza of a life (he kept smelling the antiseptic in the Chertsey hospital, for some reason, when conjuring the essence of this modern life), this ancestral right made the life seem trivial and absurd. Full of ugliness.

The poplars. That moment by the sunlit poplars. The gods had spoilt him: they had offered her a second time. But he had insisted on his cleverness, his trivial surface cleverness, and the moment had wrinkled up into nothing, quite vanished away. He hated his Englishness suddenly, this stolid side that failed to show him when he must leap like a fawn. No Englishman leaps like a fawn. 'There is no grace in us,' he murmured. 'We are quite, quite vulgar, heavy and vulgar and violent – heavy Saxon ugliness, that's us.'

'Though I am Jewish,' he went on, in a mutter. 'It's the Jewish side of me that craves the oriental sands. I am completely out of place here. Ancestrally, I belong to the East. I belong to Samarkand.'

And he looked about him, at the small cottage kitchen with its whitewashed, peeling beams and walls, its bareboard table and unpretentious farm chairs. Nothing could have been more English, with the green wash of the garden through the window, between the washed-out threadbare curtains, the broad sill set to geraniums and cress and a jam-jar full of field scabious that Tillie had picked, with the watery sun striking through the dainty square panes. Nothing more English than this homely box of a room, save that it was not cluttered enough, its clutter was books and a young chap's easy-going ways with tidying up. And he did not feel out of place at all, not superficially; he was almost incapable of imagining anything more homely, he had grown into it so much. He loved this place, even. He could imagine growing old here, growing a beard around his jaw and puffing on a short pipe – amazing, that he could picture it! Yet another part of him rebelled, stirred the dust up with a lot of hooves, restless and foreign-bound. It was confusing, thoroughly confusing. And all this steeped in the golden liquid of his love, as he pictured it. The golden elixir of it. Thoroughly confusing, ah yes.

'I'm in a right corner,' he said aloud. 'I need to break out.'

27

The Shadow

A T LUNCHTIME HE went off to the pub with the bedpan and filled it with cheap watery beer, walking back with it steadily and as steadily drinking his way through it in the woods near the empty mansion. Just sitting on the leafmould under heavy trees and imbibing. He began to sing. He laughed. He enjoyed his own merry company. He felt powerful and young. He talked to himself, and to the elves and dryads that he sensed were just out of sight around him, querulously looking on at this strange being.

He was incredibly unhappy, of course. All the little folk knew that, watching him. He knew they knew, too. That is why he enjoyed the afternoon so much. He felt it was a sort of ritual, and that he would always remember it as such. He dozed off sprawled in a hollow between a beech tree's thick roots, flapping dully at gnats.

When he woke up, still tipsy and not feeling all that dreadful, he again thought of his Jewishness. He lay there and mastered his headache and thought of his Jewishness much more precisely, how in fact he had never really *thought* of it before, never really considering it as something centre stage, as something principal in the play of his life. He was thinking rapidly, memories flitting past him like tiny winged things, like mischievous elves – memories of the morsels of Jewishness he had come across at home: old photographs of bearded rabbis in Russia, of plump families in leather chairs staring unsmilingly at him (their distant relative), of old books and letters and a lock of curled hair behind glass and his father's strange jokes and the odd strange term for things, quite ordinary things. But as far as he could remember he had never consciously known he was Jewish, the word had never passed anybody's lips at home – it was his schoolmates who had revealed it to him, in the normal rough repartee of the school yard.

And one day, when he was thirteen or fourteen, someone had got it wrong: someone had called him a 'half-breed Hindoo', because the decoration in his father's shop went with the carpets. This fellow actually thought he was an Anglo-Indian! Joseph had looked in the mirror and seen how, yes, that was eminently possible. Perhaps, he had thought, his father was just that, and not Jewish at all. Or could one be Jewish *and* Anglo-Indian? Could one be both? Why not, indeed? But he had never asked his father, not outright. He did ask, however, if any of the family had ever been to India.

'Ay,' his father replied, 'Great-uncle Albert on my mother's side lived there for many years, but I never knew him. I'm not even sure what he did there, as it happens. I ought to, but I don't. He came back very yellow, with a native woman, and opened a haberdasher's in Tideswell, as far as I know. He didn't survive long, though. I don't know what happened to the woman. I don't even know whether he was married to her. He always called his laundry basket a *dhobi* basket. I remember that, oh yes. I used to go over quite a lot, once a month at least. A *dhobi* basket. "Put your smalls in the *dhobi* basket, lad." Fancy that. Hadn't thought of it since, not till now.'

So it was quite possible, though he left it at that. He liked mysteries. He liked the idea of this exotic little mystery in his well-behaved family story. It had a very faint wicked smell about it, sweet and yellowish, while all his other forebears smelt of starch and mothballs and gunpowder tea.

He would read *Daniel Deronda* again, to see what you did with your Jewishness. He giggled to himself, despite his headache – and he remembered laughing out loud at a line in the book, a line about the Jewish race having fewer blockheads in it than the Gentile. And thinking of Eliot, thinking of her great winding rivers of words and people, he felt suddenly very small and worthless – as a writer. Against the great solemn predecessors, he and his ilk were jittery dancing-girls. The war was too big. It was over, but it was still there, everyone carrying it about with them. Either you ignored it completely (as you might ignore a continuous pain) – or you jumped about like a tiny puppet in its shadow, trying to embrace it. Nothing would ever happen again that was as terrible, save the Last Judgement – in which, of course, he was not a believer. And it *was* a shadow, it was not (now it was over) a thing of substance, a Goliath you could fell with a careful slingshot. It was not that at all. It was a shadow that fell over every action, every word, thus it was *anterior* to his own words, his own words were infected with it before they had even flowered on the page.

This tree, he thought, was infected with it, right to the last leaf. The shadow had lain itself right across England, across the whole wide world – even in the remotest African village, the remotest acre of forest where nothing but leopards prowled, it had lain its shadow. Even in the unpeopled pampas of South America. Even – and here he recalled what Baz had said about the death of Scott – even on the flat frozen heights of Antarctica, it had lain its shadow.

Joseph lifted himself up and sat with his face in his hands, seeing through it all at last. The beer was circling in his blood, he was still quite tipsy, despite his headache – and he knew then that a certain moment in his life had declared itself, a moment of change. He would be changed from now on. It wasn't too late, at nearly twenty-four: the drunkenness was a rite after which he would be subtly, subtly changed. Because he knew the enemy – the enemy the German woman could not find. Not surprising she could not find it. The enemy was the shadow that believed itself eternal and all-powerful, which lay upon everything from the moment the first bullet was fired in the war. And to defeat that shadow, he had to absorb it, he had to roll himself up in it and go about camouflaged in its colours (no colours, he thought, the shadow was colourless, a kind of viscous grey thing, a kind of transparent greyness) – at any rate, he had to take it in *homeopathically*, in minute quantities of conscious reparation. As a tree folds itself about a nail, absorbs the nail into the vast barky bulk of tree-ness.

He was, perhaps, the only living being conscious of the war's true nature. So he felt, at any rate. He had been born into this life with this purpose: to defeat the shadow. It was scarcely a conscious thought, this, it was more a sensation in his blood. This was the *modern* devil: not a red-painted creature in horns, nor even a sly voice willing you to perform wicked deeds, but the shadow created by men's actions. And the action of the war had been dense enough to form, not a flickering evanescent shadow, but a thick viscous thing that stuck, under which they all struggled, like flies – but not even as conscious as flies are of the stickiness. No one knew they were struggling in this sticky shadow, no one even countered it because they thought they had *escaped*. But they had not.

And in all this, the bright, sky-figure of Tillie refused to be blotted out. He was definitely in love with her. She was, in fact, part of the scheme of reparation, of renewal. Yes, he thought, he wasn't quite clear how, but she was a part of it. Without her, he was not even sure he could succeed. In the invisible together they would burn through the thick fibre of the shadow, they would find the root and burn it out.

He could scarcely bear to picture the names stuck up in the registrar's: Baz's with Tillie's. It made him feel sick.

He began to crave water. It was dusty and hot, even in the wood. He got to his feet and tottered a bit, until he found his step. He knew there was a stream running through the wood, further in. On the way to it, he wondered how the German woman fitted his picture. Had she been on the side of the shadow, after all? He thought of the crumbs of earth she had sent him, wordless, like a clue in a child's game. Was she playing fair, sending him such a thing? Had she played fair all along, indeed? Because he might read the clue in any way he wished. It was not a clue, really, but a sort of charm. He thought of the dark stuff lying in his palm like burnt crumbs of toast and how he had felt, looking at it. Really, it had thrown back at him his own thoughts. He had projected onto it his own deepest thoughts. That was clever of her. It was a sort of wax recording of his innermost mind, that little sift of no-man's-land dust; like the dust of the ground from which man was made – ah, so much dead earth until the breath of life was breathed into him, to become a living soul.

His own thoughts breathed upon it and he had cast it out into the garden, horrified.

No, it was a mistake to think of *sides* – he corrected himself, ploughing through bracken towards the stream, the sun hot on his neck when he crossed a clearing stacked with new wood, the sweet smell of sap pleasing him and the sun plumping him like a pillow – it was a real mistake, that business about sides, it was utterly wrong. He was still thinking in the war's terms – it was shadow-thought, that, to think of sides. The German widow was a confusion of shadow and light; they had made love in order, he reminded himself (saying it out loud, *sotto voce*), to banish the drought and usher in the new league of peace, of love, a storm of life-giving rain, a gleaming fresh slate.

Well, the rain had come right enough. But it had just run straight off the shadow, like water off a macintosh or a waxed boot.

He could not drink at the stream, though it was more than a trickle now; it was rather brown. The rains had stirred everything up and it had not yet cleared. He splashed his face – he was very hot and sweaty – and walked with his pitcher back to the cottage, feeling more and more dreadful. He had exhausted himself, thinking so hard. He felt he had poured all his mental energy into the ground, and there was nothing left for the book.

He felt bereft. The picture of the shadow, that had been so clear, was already broken into words, peculiar words like beads unstrung from a thread. They rolled about in his head as he ate some bread and cheese. He drank water and ate, feeling pretty dreadful. This would pass, he knew. He was still a bit drunk. And loneliness bit into him, then. He imagined himself sitting in a club in London with other young fellows and their laughing dancing-girls and talking, talking. Talking and laughing, the jazz music wailing in their ears. Morose, he felt, sitting there in the quiet kitchen with its peeling walls and beams. No better than a hen-coop. A sort of tomb. He became properly morose, which is the problem with drink: it lifts you up and then drops you very low, lower even than before.

He put his head in his hands and imagined Tillie walking in, run away from Baz and walking in with an anguished, needy look. No, not walking in – climbing in through the window, that was how he imagined her coming in. Planting her bare feet carefully between the geraniums and laughing as she did so, lifting her dress and laughing as he gaped in surprise, the odd broken geranium stem falling onto the brick floor as she climbed in. It was terribly vivid in his mind, as he imagined it. If only life was as easy to direct as a novel, he thought. 'But then novels aren't easy, either,' he muttered – and chuckled at that. Rather ruefully. It was as if the whole epic voyage he had endured in his head for the last few hours had wound down to this tiny landfall of ruefulness.

The sun-warmed geraniums sat there on the sill very patiently, though, all their leaves and flowers exactly as he had left them. And he envied them that. They travelled nowhere. Silently, silently, they inched up their sticks, but that was all. Oh, how he envied them. That vegetative, unthinking bliss.

28

A Right Bolt from the Blue Yonder

A DAY OR two later he did find one of them smashed on the kitchen floor. The clump of earth and the sherds and the broken plant. It was morning, quite early, he had heard nothing in the night. The window had been forced open. Nothing else had been touched. Perhaps there had been a wind, a sharp gust in the darkness. He chuckled to himself, thinking of the gust as Tillie in bare feet. He cleaned up and stuck a couple of stems of the smashed geranium into a jam-jar full of water. He would watch them snake out their roots, he thought, as he ate his breakfast. This is what his mother did with her geraniums – but his action he considered, oh yes, as much more *poetic* than domestic. It would help him get into the real swing for writing. There was nothing domestic about it at all, in the end. The key is to make all your actions, however trivial, poetic and meaningful. He thrilled to this idea. Then he thought of Tillie and how she would scoff at this, in her womanly way. It almost embittered him, thinking of it, of Tillie's high-handed bright laughter. The German woman would not scoff at it. Her deep, German consciousness would not scoff at it. He felt vaguely unhappy and confused, as if the smashed geranium had set something inside him awry, something that was growing rather slowly and blissfully inside him.

He stoked the fire and closed the iron door of the range with a clang. The sounds he made in his aloneness seemed as if someone else was making them, sometimes. Then, quite abruptly out of the air behind him, there was a sudden *Good evening!*

Oh, it made him jump so much – like a rabbit. The door was

half-open onto the garden but there was no one, though the voice had come from there, rather deep and strong. The thud of his heartbeat, that was all. It was not evening, either – it was ten o'clock in the morning. Then a shadow in the corner of his eye, in the window, flitting behind the geraniums. The voice might have come from there, through the open window.

He went outside cautiously, his heart beating furiously, and looked about. Nothing. Then he looked down, to the right of the door, where the clump of straggly wallflower bloomed against the brick and his ash-bucket was waiting to be emptied in the wood. There was a man crouching there, a middle-aged man with an untidy peppery beard, dressed in plus fours and tweed jacket, clutching a trilby. He must have crawled there from the window. He looked as if Joseph was about to hit him. A look of fear and confusion.

'Awfully sorry, got the wrong man,' he said – a smart, clipped accent. Pure clipped privet.

'What do you want?' was all Joseph could manage. He was that taken by surprise.

'I'm not a beggar, I've not gone a-begging—' and he gave a shudder.

'Look, do get up.'

He did not. The man stayed crouched, almost stubbornly.

'Why do you – what do you want?'

Joseph felt quite perplexed, slightly frightened. The eyes of the man were slightly frightening, light brown and fierce.

'Elimination!' he cried. He put his hands together above the trilby, praying in a gabble with his eyes tight shut. '*We beseech thee to hear us, good Lord, that it may please thee to eliminate all Bishops, Priests and Deacons . . .*'

His eyes popped open again. Joseph nodded, rather relieved.

'Oh yes, illumination. That's the ticket,' he soothed. 'Look, I don't think I can help you. I'm not—'

'What's three plus minus three?' the man cried, urgently. 'Quickly, come on!'

'Well, nothing. Zero.'

The eyes held him very tight.

'Tell me,' the man went on, in a harsh whisper, still crouched on his heels and clutching his trilby to his chest, holding Joseph purely with his eyes, that were terribly anxious now, anxious and expectant – '*am I still here?*'

Joseph was perplexed. The question flew past him, he had no chance to grasp it. It troubled him very much, not to be able to reply.

'Sorry?' was all he said, frowning, as if he had not heard.

The man's eyes were very pale and fierce. He straightened himself slowly, as if balancing china on his head. He seemed to sway a bit. Then he took Joseph's hand and shook it. A very firm grip, roughened skin. The eyes had tiny lime-green flecks in the brown irises.

'A final belch of fire like blood,' he intoned, 'Overbroke all, next, in one flood—'

His head was jerking to the rhythm. Joseph did not recognise the lines.

The man mouthed something, silently. It might have been 'doom'. 'It doesn't matter,' he went on, very loud and booming, 'if you don't know. I can't expect you to know everything.'

Then he scrabbled in his jacket pocket and drew out a crumpled, soiled sheet of paper. He held it in front of him like a songsheet.

'Quillet,' he intoned. 'Mote, mute, moon, then. Quint.'

'That's my page,' said Joseph.

'*Ve-ery* significant. All in counterpoint.'

He held the paper out towards the garden, squinting at it like a painter.

'That tree, for instance. Most significant. In counterpoint with this. Exactly aligned. That leaf. Everything in counterpoint. Goodness gracious. Are you part of the experiment?'

'No.'

'Quite so. Tra-la-la-la! Qui vive, you see? Astonishing.'

'I think I should have it back.'

'No!' he cried, crumpling the page to his chest. Then a sudden bark. 'Come on, come on, don't be slow, don't be slack!'

Without waiting for a reply and before Joseph could grab the page, the man stood up and ran off, just like that, in one monkey-like movement. A tall, lolloping stride that left a whiff of sourness behind it, a real whiff of the unwashed. A tramp, quite crazed, quite religiously dotty, but rather well-spoken and well-dressed for a tramp – though his clothes were pretty filthy, stuck over with bits of hay and seed, dried mudstains. Joseph was so much taken aback that he did not think of pursuing him, not at first. When he ran out himself, right out onto the manor drive and into the lane, it was too late. The fellow had gone. The lane was, as usual, empty, a heaving mass of shadows and greenish spots of sunlight. The potholes were as pale as cement, but it was not cement – folk tipped the ash from their ranges in the holes and ruts. Footprints in the ash, too: perhaps the intruder's. Running away from the village.

It was 'a right bolt from the blue yonder', as his father would say, whenever a big order for carpets came. A right bolt from the blue yonder. Joseph walked back slowly to the cottage, his heart thudding.

'Am I still here?' Now that was a question and a half. That really was. That was *the* question, when you came to think of it.

He had thought at first, madly, that it was Frank Pitts. But the man was too crazed for that. Or was he? Frank Pitts had owned to a nervous collapse – maybe he had discharged himself. Maybe – Joseph was making another cup of tea, to calm himself down with – maybe that was why Pitts was not in the hospital in Chertsey! Maybe behind his madness he was a deal sight more downy than he – Joseph – had taken him for, thinking him a mere fool. And then he remembered that the sour-faced woman had looked back six months in the book. No, Pitts had never been in the hospital, unless under an assumed name. Or maybe Frank Pitts was an invention. Maybe his real name was quite other. It sounded a bit invented, now he thought about it. The Frank and the Pitts together. It sounded almost meaningful, like a name in Dickens. Vole, Squeers, Pecksniff.

Joseph looked up at a shadow in the window, startled. It was a bird, hopping about. Every shadow would make him jump from now on, he knew it. Every damned flicker of a shadow.

He read Pitts's letter again. He did not like that last word, 'cure'. It snagged on something in his head, some dark underwater snag of fear. There was no doubt about it, the man had had a nervous collapse due to what Joseph had written in *his* letter. That was what the man claimed. Joseph had taken it as a lie, a part of the strategy, a defensive move in the campaign – to be followed by encirclement. But it may not have been a lie. It was probably true.

It could have been Pitts, yes. The face was somehow right. From what he could remember of it. A long head, quite gaunt, with shiny skin and dark-rimmed eyes and a long nose. The beard would have grown during his breakdown. The beard was not right, but that fitted the breakdown aspect to a tee. Maybe there was a lunatic asylum near Chertsey. He had not thought of that. They had had to build quite a few more, since the war.

Joseph actually shuddered. He would have to keep watch.

He got up and bolted the door from the inside. The bolt had to be knocked out of its rust, but it came eventually. It was a hell of a job ramming it home, because the door had dropped an inch on its hinges over the years, he had to lift it up to bring the bolt into line. He knew what he had to do, now, each time he left the house. He tried it out. He bolted both doors from the inside and left by the window, pushing the window to as best he could after him. But he could not lock it, obviously; the handle could only be pulled to from the inside and anyway he could never get back in if he did find a way, the doors were bolted tight! He almost laughed at himself, because he had actually tried to close the window, to lock it tight from the outside. He would have locked himself out!

The window looked shut pretty tight. A crazed man would never try it. And then, in a fit of inspiration, he drew a few tendrils of honeysuckle over the window, as if it was not usually opened.

He broke another geranium pot, climbing back in. But it left a space on the sill. He did not want to move all of them off the sill, because that would have been a clue. He resented all this, of course. He felt besieged; and an obscure boyish excitement.

He went up to his room and opened the windows, leaning on the sills and looking out of each one in turn. The cottage was smothered in vegetation, and he could not see very far beyond the old fruit trees that crammed their foliage into the limited space around. It gave him a sense of security, nevertheless, looking out from up there. It gave him a sense of power. The day was heavy, rather grey and heavy, there were a lot of flies about and the rampant vegetation gave off a thick sweet-rotten smell. Or maybe it was the mouldering thatch just above his head: he might be in Africa, he thought, it's that tropical. One of the sills was soft under his hands, a sliver broke off like wet biscuit; if he had wanted to he could have broken off the whole sill. The place was in a real state of decay. One day, if nothing was done soon, it would collapse and moulder back into earth, become earth again and indistinguishable from the plants that had pulled it down. They wanted the house for themselves, these plants. People grew them up their walls, all pretty, without realising they were tempting doom. He had never thought of this before. He looked at the thick-boled honeysuckles and ivies and the starry white clematis flowers with respect, and a touch of dread. He imagined the intruder climbing up their thick stems, like a terrible thin-limbed monkey. Joseph was powerless against him, in the end. He regretted not grabbing that page back. 'Quirk', he had read, and 'Quitch', and 'Quixotic'. The rest had died on him, like a list in an anxious dream.

He would go off for a few days. That was it. He was a fool not to think of it before. He would shut up shop and vanish. To London, of course. And then he thought: no, I'll go 'home', I'll go north. Ma will only whine if I don't go home soon. She'll whine and whine until I do, and that'll be at the wrong moment. Now is just right. He had a sudden eagerness, really a need, for the bare moorland, the windswept open moors with their crumbling stone walls, the lack of trees once the limestone dales were left behind. He had had enough of woods for the present. He really had. They were suffocating him.

He would tell people, let the village know he was going. Walter could keep an eye. He was glad it was not Walter who had come up to the study – he felt the relief in his chest, all of a sudden, as if he had avoided a bad scrape by a sliver. If this mad fellow *was* Frank Pitts, he would be after the novel, in the end. So he would take the drafts with him. About a hundred pages' worth, all told. To have those destroyed would be equivalent to murder, though to other folk they might be naught.

He shook his head, sitting at his desk. How *could* it be Frank Pitts? That was a man you never saw. Pitts was the type you never laid your eyes upon, not in a month of Sundays. This other man, this intruder – not Pitts, he was sure of that now. And he almost doubted he *had* seen him at all. It was such a sudden, brief little burst, like something out of the invisible. But the page in the dictionary was still missing, that was for sure.

Am I still here?

Now that really was the question. *The* question. And the way the dotty fellow had asked it, it was *meant* all right. Right through to the bottom, he meant it, sounding it to the bottom. It was more than religious or philosophical. It was a desperate enquiry, very desperate, and as real as a badly wounded fellow asking if he was to die – if that is what badly wounded fellows did (or did they just ask for water, like poor old gallant Sydney?).

He wrote the question out on a sheet of paper, big: AM I STILL HERE? It was, really, the question they were all asking, every nation was asking it behind the empty guff. It was Noah's question after the flood. Any catastrophe leads to that question, it is automatic – but it stays beneath the level of consciousness, usually. Way under it. You had to be dotty to put it into words. After the lights are put out, only the blind can see.

There was a sudden knock on the front door. His heart leapt and thudded. He was trembling. It was 'Pitts', or whoever the fellow was. He stayed very still. Then the knocking again. Everything was bolted. A long pause – rustles by the back door, perhaps, he could not be sure above the usual summer noises – and then he heard, very faintly, his name being called out, a sort of cry that sounded like his name but might have been a cry, almost an animal's. Maybe it was an animal's – there were so many sounds from the woods, creatures whose cries he did not recognise. Deer, vixen, probably badgers. Stoats.

Then the cry again. Was it 'Jo'? It was just like a yelp, from the front of the house. Very carefully, crouched like they were taught to crouch in the camp, he crept into the front bedroom with its damp chalky smell of fresh plaster and peeped over the sill. He did not open the window, of course, there were cobwebs on the hinges, it would squeak, give his position away. There was grime on the glass, the sun was exaggerating it, and he had to lift his head clear out of cover to see over the ivy leaves that crowded there. He was almost directly above the little porch, but whoever it might be was out of sight under its mossy tiles.

He waited, crouched there, cheek against the glass, ready to vanish on the instant. A moment later, he saw the top of a head appear beyond the roof tiles. A boy's scalp, very pale, hair razored for the summer. Before he ducked he just had time to note that. The boy cried again, 'Hallo?' And then added, rather lamely, 'Telegram!'

Joseph ran downstairs to open the door. The boy was the postmistress's son, about twelve – dressed in the old, outsize postman's jacket in which he delivered urgent items or relayed telephone messages for sixpence. He was immensely relieved to see Joseph. The boy handed over the telegram in an open envelope.

'I was working,' Joseph explained. 'In the garden.'

'I runned round and checked in the garden, sir,' the boy said, without turning a hair.

Joseph nodded unassumingly.

'You haven't noticed a stranger behaving a bit queerly this morning, have you?'

'A stranger, sir?'

'Ay. He's got a suit on and a trilby, long face and a beard, about fifty. A bit queer in the head.'

'A bearded fellow, eh? Know him then, do you, sir?'

'Not personally, no.' The boy was prone to cheek, Joseph remembered. Cocky type, the quick talker. 'It's just that he was hovering about the house just now. I think he's a bit funny in the head.'

'Warner, sir?'

Joseph didn't understand at first, he thought it was a name. The boy made the sound of an explosion in his mouth, then waved a finger by his temple, crossing his eyes.

'Ah, you mean war nerves.'

The boy nodded. 'Ten out o' ten, sir.'

'Possibly.'

'I en't seen no strangers at all this morning, sir. Worse luck. But I'll keep my eye skinned. Sir.'

'Thank you.'

He saw the lad off with a few pennies. He took the telegram into the kitchen, unfolded it and read. It was from Baz.

WEDDING TWO OCLOCK THIRTIETH INST SEE YOU THERE STOP

He felt himself go yellow in the soul. Suddenly, out of this sickly, yellowing part of him, he felt nothing for Tillie. She was not for *him*, after all. It took the telegram to tell him that: like an order. She was something abstract pushed the other side of his consciousness.

All he could recall of her, properly, in his yellowed consciousness, was the quick peck of her lips on the landing. That was all she boiled down to. All the rest – her voice, her presence, her look – well, he could not grasp it. He did not *want* to grasp it. Just that hard swift peck, not even the deeper kiss in Ypres or her line about not being compelled.

He waited for the yellow sickliness to subside. He almost leapt out of the cottage and walked very briskly and breathlessly along a chalk outcrop where the beech were leaning, their roots grappling out of the bare chalk into air. He saw in it a symbol of his own state. The yellowish view of Tillie refused to leave him.

But it did, quite abruptly, like grave clothes falling off a risen man. Later that day, when he had settled down into the words on the page, that peck grew a mouth, a nose, eyes, and a voice, and a body, and a full shock of hair. She flowered out of it, Tillie did. He could smell her lemony scent again – if it *was* scent, if it was not natural to her skin, to the hollows above the collarbone or the soft cool crook of each bare arm. He maddened himself with her imagined bodily presence. He knew what she would become, alongside Baz. And Joseph fancied saving her from that, picturing it: about as true to life as a tale of knights and damsels. He pictured her lying on the bed behind him, and then in the long safe grass in the manor's grounds – white and naked. Almost impossible to picture, this nakedness – it was too extraordinary, when you took the whole of her into account: her naïve liveliness and a certain streak of cussedness. Although cussedness was never it, he thought – no. And whatever he meant by this, well, it was not just the Chapel thing, it was more than that, it was a burly sense of her own right to be what she was and what she owned to, an intellectual right that lay right along her body, right up in her eyes. A certain burly strength in the slim body, that refused to lie down for him and bare herself, even in his imagination. And this made him yearn for her like nothing else did. She might have been a princess, and he a page, yearning for her as he did, in that way. And Baz? Oh, he was the evil baron, he was. He had to be knocked off his perch, oh yes.

And he laughed to himself, in his anguish, rubbing his hand over his furred scalp. He was too weak and full of goodwill to do anything about it, he thought. He was all milk, watery milk, a real milksop. The way Tillie had looked at him, he knew that there was a flame there, an attraction. But she had gone for Baz because Baz was a brick. Almost as four-square as her Chapel. That was what even the Tillie type of girl succumbed to, in the end. Even the proud type, who would not sell herself for anything, who would chain herself to railings before doing what a man told her to. It was because Baz was fatherly, in the end. Tall and safe. With just enough of a sense of fun in him to contest the notion that he was, frankly, a bore. That joke about driving, it was winning, a real winner. You could see Tillie melt. But it was a lie, too, it was surface: Baz had driven ever so carefully, he must have been shown at some time how to drive properly. The real product would have driven dangerously fast, not pottered down the lanes hugging the verge as Baz had done: grass caught in the spokes, sticking out like whiskers.

But there again, Baz had money. A career. And Tillie's eyes had glittered at that. What could he, Joseph, offer her, apart from his yearning? A damp room in a peppercorn-rent cottage for a few months, then an unknown beyond. An adventure. Talks about Marx and Freud and God. Myths, nature myths, the old nature gods – oh, that would be a battle. Battles, great battles. If she only knew it, she had it in her to adventure with him. No one had told her, though – not ever. Not in Stockport. Baz had got a catch all right, a romantic catch – not a safe, plump trout from a villa in the suburbs, but an original. Eloped with her, too, in a restrained sort of way. Very Baz, that.

He dug up the shawl and washed it in the pail. It smelt of earth, now, like a grave cloth. He folded it up and put it right at the back of a drawer in the main bedroom. He could not have borne it being buried any longer.

He tried to apply himself to the novel. He had written some grisly stuff, froth-and-blood stuff, quite shocking, but it was inert, somehow. It lay on the page as words, it had no independent being. He felt bitter, his blood bubbled sourly with it. A sense of quiet panic invaded him; he was neither one thing nor the other, he thought. He had neither stuck it out as a conchie nor made it properly to the Front. He had been cheated of each by his own weakness. Yes, he was a milksop. That was what it came down to. He was playing with other folks' pain and suffering. His heart thudded with panic, as if the long-headed fellow were back with an axe.

He needed to talk to someone, he was going rather queer here, stuck in these woods.

A week went past, slid past without him noticing it – flooded by sun, the smells of corn shocks and hot ricks and lazy water, long starry nights. Mrs Hamilton remarked that he had read three chapters of *Peveril of the Peak* but that she 'hadn't glued to it'.

'He wrote poems, didn't he, dear?'

'Yes. Very fine ones.'

'My Ted liked poetry. He'd read it out to me from the paper, each evening.'

Joseph glanced up at the photograph; no sound from the fellow on the mantelpiece.

'During the war,' she said. 'Afore he went out hisself. All helped, didn't it? Them poems.'

Joseph reviled them, of course.

'Yes. I'm sure they did.'

Walter's wife came in with Mrs Hamilton's cocoa. Mrs Furdew's laugh would sound through the door; she was all this laugh, there was little else of her that Joseph ever encountered. High-pitched, one with the boys. All bosom and laugh, she was, with a stooped slowness to her that warred with the rest. She seemed cancelled out, in here, away from the merriment.

'Cocoa, Mother.'

'Thank you, dear. We were just talking about y'father's love of poetry.'

'Ay?'

'The way he went were a poem,' she said, looking at the photograph and burrowing into her pocket for a handkerchief, 'with the rose petal on his brow. You could write a nice poem on that,' she added, turning her gaze on Joseph. 'A very nice patriotic poem on that.'

They were both looking at him, Mrs Furdew with a kind of impersonal contempt – as if her cancelled presence was projected onto him. And over the whole of poetry.

'I don't write poems any more, I'm afraid.'

He was betraying them, of course. The shame of it, of his moist secret pilfering of life, flushed into his face. The real Ted Hamilton was picking himself up off the railway track and staggering back with his smashed, sodden body, slowly making his way back. He wondered if the daughter knew, if Walter had told her. Coxy knew, the whole village knew – but maybe not the closest ones. The two women stared at him, as if in judgement. Then Mrs Furdew turned on her heel and left without a word, as if she had wiped Joseph off her boot.

'I expect you don't feel up to it,' said Mrs Hamilton.

'Reading?'

'Poems.'

'No, not really.'

And she began to recite the poems she could remember learning at school: solid English patriotism, full of God and vows and golden fields. Breathlessly they came out, in artless rote-learnt haste. While the smashed blacksmith staggered back, inch by inch, in Joseph's nodding head.

He changed his plans: he would go to London instead of his mother's. He would lift his mind up; high as a hawk it would go, talking to friends. He might even sound out a publisher he knew. He would go to galleries, the cinema. He would raise his morale and lift his mind up. Lift it right up into the clear abstract heights.

He worked for a couple more days with only brief breaks for a walk or a cycle. The weather became a muddle of clear glory and humid grey, even on the same day. But the writing went much better, with the breeze already felt in his sails. Much better. Mainly because of something he hardly noted, not right up in the visible mind: sneakily, creeping in under his decision to go to the Big Smoke and clear his blood, was this other motive.

To see Tillie – before she was irreparably lost to him.

It was as if this motive had been put in with a dirty finger, as his mother would say – a finger that was not his. At least, he scarcely admitted that it belonged to him, that dirty finger. The rest being scrupulously clean.

29

A Rattle

H E WAS ON the train before he had properly registered it, though it was the following morning, rather early. The third-class carriage was filthy, he noticed that: fag-ends and used matches all over the floor, ash on the seats, crumbs, a discarded copy of yesterday's *Daily Mirror* which he picked up and read. There were three pages of pictures on 'The Summer in Germany' – flaxen-haired folk bathing in the Ammer See, picnicking under trees, athletically exercising in striped bathing suits. The tone of the article was cunningly pitched, implying that the hunger and deprivation of modern Germany had somehow surrendered to these summer frolics, that there was something *immoral* about it – that we had not smashed them low enough, perhaps; it was a mean-minded, cunning piece, in its simplistic way. It made him rather cross. The ink was like grease on his fingers, the cheap furriness of the paper somehow repellent.

Oh, he was not used to other people's muck, to sharing it. He had really grown hermit-like and pure in his retreat, in his green woods. The other folk in the carriage seemed to be looking at him, swaying from side to side and staring out from under their low-brimmed hats. He kept his eyes mostly on the passing view: the country looked suave, somehow, with its low hills and silvery fields. The bunched little houses and big bay-windowed villas, the type advertisements called 'commodious, desirable', fled past – but the suave wooded hills were in no great hurry. Cars at a level crossing, honking halloos – people in them waving, as if they were royalty. And nobody here in the carriage waving back, even those who had noticed; just faint, satisfied smiles. The train could crush any old car, they seemed to be acknowledging. The odd vehicle on the white ribbon of a road – like a fly, ready to be crushed. Its tiny plume of dust in the early light.

Joseph hated their satisfied smiles. The world was tired of such smiles. The victors had had such a smile in the carriage at Versailles, he thought. Not the Americans – they had shown wisdom, foresight. But Britain and France had smiled and the Americans had bowed to it. And Germany was crushed flat. Never mind the summer frolics – she had been crushed into pieces, and the pieces crushed in turn. It was amazing, really, that the frolics went on regardless of the misery, of the shattered pieces, the dust that was all that was left of the former Germany. Goethe, Schiller, Heine, Beethoven. The proud, swaggering Germany of the poets and the composers. Nietzsche, too. And yet somehow folk went bathing delightfully in the Ammer See or wherever and spread their picnic cloths on the bank. One had almost to admire them, not begrudge them: he doubted the country would ever recover, and yet the athletic human spirit went on jumping and diving and vaulting, grinning with its hands on its hips at the Kodak.

And for the last part of the journey into London, as the train rattled along and the smoke and steam flew past the window and the rails shuddered beneath them – so strange, the hectic nature of it! – his attention turned to his memory of the German woman. That was *his* satisfaction, to conjure her white body beneath him secretly, without anyone else in the carriage knowing. Their tired, dull lives tramping on in their heads: work, work, work. The price of eggs, the red box, the lawn mower, the timid week in Hastings. He loosened his tie and sprawled a little in his seat. He felt very bold and young – that he would always be young. The others had never been young, with their tired eyes and lines and pinched mouths. He felt golden, like a youthful god. And the others noticed his satisfied little smile. They were not smiling, not now. It was as if he had defeated them.

London hit him like a wall, though it was cooler than on his last visit. Quite incredibly grimy, it was, soiled – everything he touched had a fine grey down of soot on it. Sheer dirt. He shared a growler cab splashed with filth from last week's storms to Piccadilly, where he rented a third-floor chamber up Clarges Street for a week – the same place, the place he knew from his first sojourn in London. It still smelt of dogs and Woodbines and sallow perfume, but the cooking was reasonable – breakfast, luncheon and tea served up in the room. Very private. It was also absurdly cheap. The landlady, Mrs White, used to boast that the prices had not risen 'for the whole of this century' – and she said it to him now, not recognising him with his hair so short. It was her one joke.

People, he thought, are like those automatons you can get to talk for a penny-in-the-slot. But this was also comforting, like the stale smells in the corridor and in the sparsely-furnished room with its threadbare, tasselled curtains. The loose sash window rattled to the throb of any motor vehicle passing below – he had to wedge the frame tight with a pair of socks. Yellowed, crumbling plugs of newspaper fell out: the window had not been opened for years, clearly. One of these newspapers was northern, the Newcastle *Evening Chronicle*, ten years old. Queerly fascinated, he flattened out its one big sheet carefully on the floor and blew the coke dust off it. The big train strike of 1911, in full swing – yet some fellow had made it down from Newcastle! The 'Space for Late News' was blank, the type coming through from behind: oh, but there was plenty of news to come, if only they had known. The rattle was still there: the trivial, sleepless rattle. While everything else had been smashed, or at least changed beyond recognition.

Ah, even his first proper stay in London felt a very long time ago – all of eighteen months back. He had expected the boarding house to be altered, somehow, but even the stale perfume was the same, and the dogs themselves, and puffy Mrs White's curiously clear eyes. All the same. Even when he told her who he was, she was diffident. It slightly upset him, to be honest. This had been his home for quite some time.

He had not planned to stay for a week, just for two or three days, but the moment he had stepped out of the train at Marylebone, into the coarseness and grimy sea of it all, it was decided. He could not say why: lurking in there, oh yes, hardly formulated into thought – more an instinct, a homing pigeon's impulse – was the yearning to see Tillie, to try for her, really try for her, before she was out of reach behind a piece of paper, a ring, Baz's grin.

But something else, too: a desire to disappear into the hurrying masses, to find sanctuary there. He saw himself as moving about among the crowds, faintly golden and glowing, a kind of redeeming angel. Hurrying men with attaché cases under their arms, anxious women hugging brown paper parcels; he would move among them like a redeemer, lightning in his hands, thunder in his voice. He sat there in his little stale room picturing himself as this redeemer and heard the bed creaking upstairs, rhythmically, faster and faster, urgent – urging itself on to go faster. Until it stopped, and there was a pause, and then a thudding of feet, the gurgle of the washbasin, thuds and squeaks. The house was mostly occupied by prostitutes – pleasant, chatty women of a certain indefinable age who seemed to be doing it out of choice, as others became teachers or bank clerks. He smiled to himself, sitting there on the bed: the city brought one cheek-by-jowl with others' intimacies, yet there was a sheet of black glass between. It saved you, that glass did. The thinnest sheet, yet it allowed you to remain untouched.

London was an ant hill, kicked into teeming business every morning. He was offering redemption from ant-existence, yes, that was it.

While at the back of his mind, scarcely admitted, like a mad aunt in an attic, the plot to snatch Tillie was stirring.

He took a walk through Green Park into St James's, among the nurses with their swaying perambulators and the hot, idling couples and the sinister-looking twitchy types with turned-up trousers all on their own, pretending to feed the ducks. There were days when he found people almost fascinatingly ugly and today was such a day: he lay in the sun with another abandoned paper – the *Morning Post* – but was drawn by the ugliness, the misshapen faces and bodies in their ugly clothes. He could scarcely stand it. He wondered if he would find even Tillie plain, in his present mood. He plotted nevertheless, because he suspected that until he saw her the world *would* look ugly – the other *people* in it, that is. The trees and flowers were beautiful, even here where they shared company with the thickly-strewn human race, with loose pages of newspapers and the throbbing noise and a sharp sulphurous stink of coke and something lusher, something rotten, like rotting melons. He was already pining for his cottage, the calm woods, the sweetness of the stooked fields. He felt its influence around him like soul-stuff, slowly fraying in this poisoned air.

There were quite a few folk with wreaths and blooms – heading for the Cenotaph, no doubt. He was not ready for that, not yet. He felt like crying, watching all these moving wreaths and sprays – for the whole injustice of it.

And slowly, slowly, the faces yielded themselves. Right until luncheon he sat, cradling his knees and watching the numerous faces pass. He had to know what each of them was, what they felt, he had to rummage into them and save them from their own terrible time, which was now, this moment, this day, too new and terrible. Otherwise they would float away forever and be lost, lost in the white nothingness of the Late News, the unknowability of the future. And they did float away, but in a *general* sense he was saving them. They were almost hallucinatory in their specialness, their specificity. The angle of their hats, the size of their noses, whether they were old or young, fat or thin, rich or poor, maimed or sick or blooming with health – this did not matter so much as what fixed their existence there in front of him as they passed on the path, or stopped, idling for a few moments as if lost what to do. And he did not know how to describe that element that fixed them so uniquely, even in their ugliness. It was there, but it had no form. It was everything about them, and yet nothing. Concealed, certainly, unreachable in words, yet he was seeing it plain, like an X-ray machine. It cried out as if in pain: I AM STILL HERE!

It was their humanness, he thought. Mute, pensive, even if their look was neither, even if they were chattering or laughing or canoodling. By seeing it, by recognising it, he was saving these people. He felt quite certain of this. He was passing them through his redeeming consciousness like threads through a needle, stitching a great pattern in the air.

His thoughts were no longer clayey, they positively flew; and he was sure now that he would succeed, that he would be a *great* writer, oh yes. He actually saw his readers in the people passing on the path; this is what will happen to his readers, he thought; for, in the invisible, the reader is taken through the writer's consciousness and saved – after a fashion. He felt annoyed with himself, then, for having taken a week off his writing. His nerves were taut, as muscles are for pulling a rope, ready and willing to write. But the rope was not there. It was almost agonising, pulling mentally on nothing.

He was exhausted, too, from concentrating so much on others. A soft depression crept up on him, after the taut joy. The sun sparkled on the little lake and he rose stiffly and took a quick turn around it before heading back to his room. There, lying on the bed after the luncheon – which was not good, not good at all, a slop of dumpling stew on a chipped plate – he felt blanketed by a depression which was deathly, really deathly. He had not a snowball's chance in hell with Tillie. She was completely unattainable, the other side of Baz – who appeared to him enormous, like the first time he had bumped into him in Oxford after those years of separation. Enormous, assured and strong.

Joseph's hand was stiff, cramped from his writing now that he was away from it. He only recognised the stiffness, now. With a deadly fatalism, being deliberately cruel to himself, he took out of his bag the hundred-odd pages he had so far written. He leafed through them, in a slow and deadly fashion, quite deliberately giving himself pain. It was like being thumped on the body with a leather cosh, not a sharp stinging pain but a blunt thud, bruising himself with his own self-doubt, disgust at his audacity. There was a bit of vanity in all this, of course. But the fact remained that the words on the page had as much force as a decorative frieze – plaster words, they were, for the most part. Far less to them than the black blocks of type or the smudged little phrases in the 1911 *Evening Chronicle*. Occasionally something stirred, leapt out for a line or two, the frieze wriggling into life – but only occasionally. Every ten pages or so! The two navels business had about as much meaning as a freak in a fairground show. And the death of the Ted Hamilton character – about as much excitement to it as a chunk of margarine. He would have liked to have cried, as a child cries or even as an adult cries after some terrible loss. He did not cry, though. He was dried right up. Humiliated by himself. He threw the pages onto the floor. If there had been a fire alight in the hearth, he would have burned them.

Without the cottage round them, or the woods – with just this scuffed, sad little room, the words died. As a tubercular child dies when taken off the mountain.

30

Singing Marie Lloyd

H E HEADED STRAIGHT out to the Cenotaph, by way of
the parks.

He had not seen it, had not *wanted* to see it since it had been
unveiled last year, that very grey November day of drizzle. Now
he dared himself to see it. Actually *dared* himself. Would he or
would he not buy flowers? He wrestled with that question all the
way there.

And then – there it was! Smaller than he had expected, of course,
somehow more modest, poking up at the bottom of Whitehall.
Until he came close to, when the monument reared up very
large and white. The flags were limp in the afternoon heat. A
heaped blanket of sprays and wreaths: he felt empty-handed,
though repelled. He felt as if he was inessential, standing there
without flowers.

A fellow in uniform was winding a barrel organ nearby, on
the Downing Street side; above the traffic's roar the music was
a piping wail. He had a dark leather mask across his eyes and
cheeks, out of which his nose protruded like a thumb. On a sheet
of card nailed to the barrel organ there was written: *Unemployed
Disabled EX-OFFICER. Matabele, South Africa & Great War. Family
to Support.* The fellow had shining shoes, his kit was immaculate:
with a service stripe and tie and flat, glistening hair, he was turned
out very neat.

A queer type of modern *capitano*, he was, with his comic mask.

The music stopped for a moment. Joseph walked down and
dropped a shilling in the tin.

'Thank you,' the ex-officer said.

'You ought to be playing right next to it,' said Joseph.

The man cocked his head, almost comically.

'What d'you say, young fellow?'

Joseph wondered if the poor fellow could see, after all – but the eye holes revealed no gleams, only a suggestion of raw skin that lapped from underneath the mask on the left side.

'The Cenotaph. Pity you don't stand right in front of it.'

'They wouldn't let me. And I wouldn't want to. They say it looks like a major-general's prick.'

Joseph laughed.

'I've never seen one – I mean not a major-general's, so I wouldn't know. But it's quite possible.'

A passer-by dropped a coin in the tin and the man thanked her and the music started up again – very jolly, as if it was jumping up and down, as if actors in half-masks might suddenly tumble out from behind it, whooping and screeching and making everybody scream with laughter. But of course no one tumbled out. It was all very sad and serious.

Despite the spotless kit, the man smelt strongly of latrines. He suddenly stopped the music.

'You still there? You? The young fellow from up north?'

'Yes.'

'Tell me, what do the people do, when they pass it? Do they spit?'

'They take their hats off,' said Joseph. 'To a man they take their hats off.'

'Prostrate themselves, do they?'

'No, they just take their hats off. Even the delivery boys. Even the folk on the buses.'

'What does it say on it? It must say something,' the man asked, looking up at nothing in his blind, intent way.

'*The Glorious Dead.*'

The man began to smile.

'It's right for them,' he said, 'it's just right for them.'

'The dead, you mean?'

'No no,' the ex-officer puffed, 'the fools what take their hats off as they pass and don't reach into their damn pockets.'

Joseph dropped a few more pennies into the tin and went back to the plinth. He had to shield his eyes, looking at the white stone in the sun. They had frozen it all here, they had taken that vast liquid mass of hurt and loss and frozen it into a white block of ice. It was a chunk of Antarctica burning white in the sun: he was amazed the flowers did not wither with the cold under them. Yet it impressed him. He had never seen anything so plain and white, so huge. It was a blank page on which you could imagine blood. It almost called out for blood: just a small bright splash of it halfway up. That would bring the nation to its knees.

And it was right at the heart of the nation, this emptiness.

Kenotaphion: the empty tomb. With the Union Jack like a silly napkin draped on its heights. And the resurrection? Well, in two thousand years we have come to this, he thought, touching its smoothness. From the cosmic cross of grief to this. A blank. Without beauty, without shape or form or decoration, in the old sense – just an emptiness with a bleached wreath of dead stone slapped on each side. Oh, it really was terrifically new and modern, this monument. He put his boater back on and bowed. Then he spread his arms, heart thudding right against his ribs.

'Life!' he shouted. 'Let life live!'

The traffic drowned him out, though. He left a bit shamefaced, glared at by a bristly fellow with three medals and an immobile leather glove.

He must see Tillie *tonight*, he decided. Not tomorrow or the day after, but *tonight*. He was chewing on some crumbly liver in a chophouse. Late tonight, without Baz.

Immediately, of course, time dragged. He trawled the second-hand bookshops up Charing Cross Road. As ever, their owners were mostly of a type: bearded, bowler-hatted, bespectacled, with a long loose overcoat, thin as a rake, rather miserable – that was the generic impression, at least.

By five o'clock, the dust from the piles of books had settled in his head. There were so many of them, too – books. Books and more books. He wondered how these shops could keep going on so much book-death and so few mourners. Feeling reckless, he bought a couple of old Thomas Love Peacocks in cloth of faded rose and a scuffed volume of Scott's poems for Mrs Hamilton. The first Peacock volume was signed: '*To Alan, love from Mother and Marjorie*'. It might have been a wreath on the Cenotaph's plinth.

The owner peered at it, half-blind behind his spectacles. 'Ah, an interesting book,' he said, 'I'd read it if I could, but I'm too old. Don't waste your time on all this modern rubbish, young man. These old books are best.'

'Well we have to have new books, don't we?'

'Do we? I don't know about that. What do we do with new books?'

'Read them, that's what we're to meant to do with them.'

'My word!' cried the queer old fellow, squinting through his bottle-glass spectacles. 'Haven't we enough to read already?'

'The old books don't talk about the war,' Joseph said, pleasantly.

'The war? Do you mean the Irish war? Are you an Irishman?'

'No, I mean the war that was supposed to end all wars.'

'And have you any objection to that?'

'It must be addressed,' ventured Joseph, rather weakly. The man was staring at him under low bushy brows, like a mad professor staring into a tube.

'My word,' the man said quietly, 'you wish us to look back from the door that leads out of the inferno.'

He was quite relieved, Joseph was, to step out into the great pulse of St Giles. Yet its vitality was artificial, even fatigued: the rush-hour omnibuses shoving into the maelstrom, their trackage filled up instantly by motor-cars, waggons, people, hansoms – it was all somehow enervated and terribly fatigued.

He beat a quick retreat through Soho back towards Piccadilly, buying an Eccles cake on the way in a crooked shop full of things for a penny. The roar was muted here in the middle of Soho. A group of boys passed him on roller skates and a little girl danced next to a barrel organ. But even these things were muted: it was as if the roar was gathering to sweep them away. There was a tyranny abroad, he really felt it: yet it was as invisible as poison gas. He was quite overwrought, thinking about it, clutching his books to his chest as he walked. If only he could smash it in some way: yet how could you smash poison gas? How could you smash a shadow?

Hours remained to him, leagues of hours before Tillie. He veered into the Royal Academy, needing to be swallowed up in the cool musty rooms and their dark swirls of oil – only to be accosted on the main stairs by a shrill voice. Toothy, somehow. You could tell that toothiness blind.

'Joey, my dear fellow, fancy meeting you again! Cut your hair, I see!'

The necktie, the old nickname, the bulging eyes: these were thrust at him, really thrust at him. It was a friend from Oxford days – scarcely a friend, someone on the fringes of his 'circle'.

'Now, take your time,' this fellow joked. 'Not school, not the war – *definitely* not that nasty scrap at Fuckuereuil—'

Heads turned – this was a joke Joseph had heard before. By some divine impulse, the name came winging to his rescue.

'Gerald!'

'No,' the chap replied. 'But at least you didn't say Gladys. Gladys would have been ever so tiresome.'

He carried on beaming, but in his eyes there was hurt. Joseph shook his head.

'My memory. I think it's old age.'

He had made a joke of it, but the fellow was hanging on – grimly, ever so grimly.

'All those Sunday sherries at D-D's, remember? It begins with A, by the way. A.C.'

The acronyms swirled in Joseph's head. He remembered queer old D-D, of course, the only don he had liked – but not A.C.

'I'm very sorry, you know. I give up.'

'You northerners. Heads made of granite, what?'

The chap gave a great toothy laugh. It was the laugh that brought the name running.

'Archie,' said Joseph. 'Archie Cauldswell.'

'Bang on!' He seemed relieved, as if placed again in the world. 'By the way, this isn't the first time I've seen you. I saw you last week. Longer hair, of course. But I didn't want to talk to you, you know, last week.'

Archie beamed at him some more.

'Last week?'

'You were *in blotto extremis*. Outside the Café Royal. Rum lot there, of course. Never thought of you as one of that sort,' he added, raising his thin eyebrows.

He meant, did Archie, the homosexual aesthete type. It was plain as day. Wilde, Beardsley, Beerbohm – already long departed, of course. Joseph shook his head.

'I was in Buckinghamshire. I've only just come up to London, this morning. I'm holed up in the country. You wouldn't catch me dead in the Café Royal, or outside it for that matter. I'm a hermit, these days, writing.'

Archie shook his head. 'You were there, old boy. Plain as day, I saw you.'

'I wasn't—'

'Don't mind me. I won't telegraph it. Half the world's blotto, if you ask me. You were singing that Marie Lloyd number – how does it go?'

'Absolutely no idea—'

'A passable rendition but God isn't she awful these days? My *mater* remembers her, for God's sake, back in the last century. Do you like this jazz thing? American, I hate it.'

Joseph ignored the question.

'Marie Lloyd's a much better bet if you ask me,' Archie went on. He was one of those types who were sensitive to their own but not to others' hurt. He simply did not notice. 'Music's gone pear-shaped these days, don't you think? What?'

'Keep off the beer, Archie, or whatever it is that makes you see things. I've only just come in from Buckinghamshire.'

He left Archie stranded, gasping a little. Then at the top of the stairs he heard the fellow calling out.

'Don't have a twin bro, do you?'

Joseph turned round. Archie was challenging him, diminutive on the stairs among the furred types, the smart shingled hair, the trim beards and neat little gloves travelling up and down the stairs.

'No, of course not,' he called down. And he pictured the white face of Hubert Rail, sucking like mad on his cigarette as he stared out at the sea.

31

A Corner of England

THE CAFÉ ROYAL! Yes, it drew that sort of sucking bee. The only place in London that did, when he thought about it.

It was faintly amusing, this idea of himself as a louche drinking type, singing Marie Lloyd in front of the Café Royal. Well, a writer's reputation soared if he put a few pellets of cocaine and dirty-mindedness into his dull scribbling life. That is what got you into the Café Royal throng; nothing easier, in the end.

He left the RA feeling mean-minded. He could not even recall Archie beyond the fact that he had once lent Joseph a bright-red necktie for a party. He regretted his passing fib about meeting his publisher: it made the real thing seem impossible. As well climb the Cenotaph without ropes as find a publisher to publish you, unless you were part of the throng. But to be part of the throng, you had to have a book under your belt. And to have a book under your belt . . .

That was the trouble with going to galleries: they were glorified clubs, you always met somebody who knew you. He did not want that. Others did, they thrived on it, but not him. It was why he had hardly ever stepped inside a place like the Café Royal: you were no longer absolutely free – not to be your own man. The chatter, incessant, of artists and writers and musicians completely cramped him, as if he was in a cage. Cut-glass accents, most of them. Shrill and cut-glass. Like Archie. He always felt underbred, because that is how they felt about him, he knew it.

And if we fell to the Bolsheviks, those types would *all go*.

He stood in Piccadilly in a bit of a daze. A tramcar swirled past, deafening him with its sudden clanging. Time seemed to be flowing like treacle, he was terribly impatient – but he knew he must wait until very late, until Baz was certain to be clear out of the way. Meanwhile he must kill time; he could not face seeing anyone or doing anything, not even the dark of a cinema house, yet he could not face his room, either. Simply existing so near to Tillie without seeing her on the instant – this chafed at his mind, his jaw clenched tight in a kind of anguish. He felt a need for sweetness and bought a packet of barley sugars and a chocolate bar in the confectioner's on the corner, then stood outside the shop and slowly, slowly let himself be drawn mentally into the bustle, benumbed, slipping into the great tide of the modern masses. It was almost delicious, letting himself be wrapped up in that senselessness. *Come, let us go*; it whispered. *Come, let us go.*

He returned to the boarding house much too late for tea and Mrs White's buns, and lay rather disconsolate and frayed on his bed, feeling horribly similar to the younger chap lying eighteen months ago in the same house. The bed above squeaked, but not rhythmically. Not all clients went the whole hog in the usual way, apparently. Yet the washbasin gurgled.

This faintly excited him, even amorously so. Best not to see the 'clients'; that would deflate the pressure, straight off. The 'girls' took all types, as long as they were respectable. Mrs White would never have owned to running a whorehouse – not in a month of Sundays. She had tenants and they had visitors, that was all. A free country. These girls were worlds away from the two in Ypres. Those two unfolded dimly in his memory like figures in a bad dream. He had been drunk, that was it. Drunk, if timorous. He *could* be drunk and wild, like Hubert Rail, if a touch timorous with it. Ay, yes.

Someone was singing. Or it might have been a gramophone. Twilight crept about the room. Clarges Street still throbbed, though, and his socks had fallen from the window onto the floor. The sash frame rattled like a tiny drill. Then he saw what had changed: the house was running on electric. The old gas fixtures had gone, the bulbs sat under their shades like onions. He found a rubber switch near the door and the lights, two of them, came on. No faint stink of gas. It was a bit dim, though. None of the white ferocity of gas. None of the mystery and warmth of flame, either. And silent, utterly silent. Deadly, in a way. It was silent, but it could burn you to cinders, or at least shake you until your teeth rattled. He switched off the light, let the dusk stroke the room into contemplative gloom, the window pulled right up, open to the night. It was better that way.

Though night did not seem to come. It strained to come – then it did not, not quite. There was an artifice of light that blocked it. The stars were hidden. He had forgotten that; the modern banishing of the night.

It was easier, thinking of Tillie in the sulphurous gloom. Plotting.

It was nine o'clock, suddenly. He was hungry. The room choked him. He could not be inside a moment longer, he would be throttled by it. He sprang off the bed and left the house almost at a trot, bursting into the street. His limbs were full of fire, now.

He walked all the way to Judd Street, stopping only for a pint of Bass in a careworn old pub in Soho. A group of Irish men and women were being nasty about some Jewish trader in Whitechapel. And in Whitechapel he had once seen a Chinaman from Limehouse jeered by the Jews. And the English sneered at everyone, blanketing them with sneers. Sneering little despots, were the English, lording it over half the world. He watched the Irish men and women jerking their heads about, imitating the Jews, and felt the disgust in his expression.

And he wondered if he would always be a critic of life, detached in this way, listening in with a faint, self-righteous disgust. The beer settled his hunger somewhat. An oily-haired man at the bar was discussing, in a loud suburban twang, the Collect of the Day. And this made Joseph think about writing a poem – a tiny stir of inspiration: the man's talk was like a church overshadowed by a gasometer. It sounded almost jokey, this picture, not fit for a poem. And so he noted nothing down. Anyway, he was too nervous for that.

He knew Tillie had lodgings in a boarding house for a month, a brisk stroll from Baz's rooms off the Strand. He remembered her, when she was down in the cottage, telling him the street, an amusing name – Sandwich Street. But not the number. It was just off Judd Street, that was what Baz had said, 'two minutes' walk from St Pancras station'. As if there was a convenience in that.

So here he was, suddenly, very near – but without the number.

Two minutes' walk from the girl he was utterly mashed on, yet paralysed by circumstance. And out of breath.

Not at all! He walked up and down Sandwich Street with vigour. There were two boarding houses, one with *Vacancies*. It was slightly shabby, black and nondescript, from what he could see in the lamplight. He asked in both of them for a Miss Lainer, without success. When he tried to describe her, they clammed up, these redoubtable landladies. She would have changed her name, of course! A girl looking quite like her came into the second one and gave him a wink above false pearls, her dress fluttering its hem around her knees.

He would just have to wait. Anyway, he did not want to alert her straightaway – or Baz, for that matter. At one point or another she would appear. Baz would be with her, of course, but if there was a good hiding place . . . his heart began to thud; the short, straight street had very few places to take cover in.

There was a church halfway down. Next to it was a shrubby patch behind some railings, a place where folk tossed paper and fruit skins. It was a few houses down from the boarding houses, and on the opposite side. He waited until the coast was clear – a cab clattered up without stopping, an old stooped gentleman in a silk hat walked the length of the street – and climbed over the railings.

It was in shadow, this little no-man's land, and he found a place behind a shrub where, even if someone were to walk right past, he would be hidden. There was a disagreeable smell, something like horse dung mingling with the sharp stink of cats, and the earth was curiously damp between the few straggly weeds, curiously bared and damp. There were flies too, gnat-like creatures which settled on his skin, and old rags that had quite probably lain there for decades.

So! – this was his refuge. He felt kindly towards it. It was a forgotten corner of London – of England, for that matter, totally forgotten and yet definite, framed by brick and iron. About the size of his study in the cottage, he reckoned. And he smiled at that. The shrubs were greasy-feeling, downed in soot. There were small chunks of glass scattered about which, held up to the streetlight, turned red and green – old stained glass from the church, no doubt. Maybe this was an ancient burial place – a plague pit, even. You could not find a more dreadful little place to have your last rest in, if that was what it had been used for. Yet he was fond of it. He smoked through all his cigarettes, cupping the glowing end in his hand to conceal his position. He wished he had brought a pipe.

He had many false alarms. At one point a couple walked up from the far end who not only resembled, in silhouette, Baz and Tillie, but who stopped outside the nearest boarding house. But it was only to light a cigar. And in the flare of the match he saw a middle-aged couple, quite sour-faced, too. Growlers and hansoms came and went, and a long yellow motor-car, then a haughty and very ancient vehicle that sounded like pots and pans falling off a shelf, and three bicycles. Several people emerged at different times from the boarding houses, getting him terrifically excited, but proved duds.

By eleven o'clock he felt almost ill with boredom and suspense. The disagreeable smell was on his skin, now, he had soaked it up. A scrawny cat had appeared and licked his hand with its harsh little tongue. He felt worthless, tramp-like. This is how a tramp must feel, all the houseless beggars. He craved his room – any room. How could he speak to Tillie, now? He would be soiled, smell of cats and decay. Tomorrow he would snap out of this madness, look up his friends and go to a concert in the Aeolian Hall, have a drink in the Café Royal, cadge dinner somehow – maybe at the Savage Club, where he knew at least two of the members.

He didn't *have* to talk to Tillie tonight. He simply had to locate her dwelling place. He had a whole week to talk to her in.

No, the sooner the better. It would not take one meeting, he would have to see her again – and again. If she told Baz, then all was lost anyway. If there was a *glimmer* of hope, he would stay right up until the wedding day. He would sit it out.

I am still here, he thought.

32

Tillie at Home

A COUPLE STOPPED right at the end of the street. There was
what looked like a meeting of faces, then the woman came
on alone, the man watching. As she dipped in and out of the
streetlamps, her shadow wheeling over the road, she became Tillie
Lainer. Joseph clung to the railings like a furious, caged animal.
She was definitely unsteady on her feet, quite definitely unsteady.
She was dressed fashionably in a wet-silk tube of a dress which
fell as she walked into deep, illogical folds and shadows. It was
the kind of modern dress Joseph disliked: he did not like the way
these dresses hugged the limbs and yet flapped loosely around the
knees. There was something smoothly dark about them, something
almost corrupt, in the drooping shoulders and chests of fashionable
women, their white calves and ankles. While the rest of them
clumped about in heavy, mannish mourning.

He scarcely recognised Tillie. She was already corrupted.

He waited until she had disappeared into the furthest boarding
house and the man had gone. The man was, of course, Baz –
though he had been an obscure whitish form, more movement
than shape, from that distance. The street was now empty. It
was well past midnight. Joseph felt his disapproval rise in him,
bile-coloured. Tillie – drinking? Or had she danced herself into
giddiness? Either way, he disapproved. It seemed frivolous, empty.
In his reveries, he would go for long silent walks with her, make
love in long grass, talk of many things: it was all rather intense and
forlorn.

He approached the boarding house as silently as he could,

without looking as if he was on night manoeuvres. Anyway, he was conscious of his white outfit: no camouflage there! He had torn his flannels on one of the railing's spikes, climbing back over. He could feel his flesh through the tear, his damp thigh. It was a blessed nuisance. He stood in front of the building, eyeing the tired porch, the grimy black brick, the subterranean-looking windows. Then, miraculously, one of these lit up, on the second floor. Electric light, rather dim. He saw a wavering shadow and then a hand through the yellowed net, the curtains twitched across. They did not quite meet. The sash window was pulled down halfway.

There were no pebbles around, that was the trouble. He could hardly call out: he felt like a fellow who had wandered onto a stage by mistake, only the lights were not yet up. He sensed the audience out there, waiting for the slightest sound. Every window held them, their ogling faces, all the way up and down Sandwich Street. She might scream, bring the faces to the windows and the bobbies running.

He was almost bewildered by his desire and helplessness. The glimpse of that hand had inflamed him terribly. Now she would be undressing in the naked electric light. Her pale, tender nakedness, unsteady on its feet. She would have to sit on the edge of the bed, tugging at her stockings. Feeling the cool silky bed-cover on her seat.

He heard a popular song jinking through his head. Perhaps he had invented it. *Oh oh oh, no other girl like her, she's such a free bird, she's my moon.* He almost wanted to jig about, right there in the empty street.

No pebbles or gravel around, only match-ends and what was either a black wig or a lump of horse droppings. He thrust his hands into his jacket pocket and found an omnibus ticket, five cigarettes, and a small bag of barley sugars.

He threw a barley sugar at the window but it missed, falling back with a click on the kerb. He retrieved it – there were not too many left in the bag – and tossed it again. There was no sound at all – he guessed it had flown through the open half of the window and struck the curtains. He imagined it flying through onto Tillie's lap and grinned. He was really quite enjoying himself, though his heart was thumping fit to bust. He threw again, taking careful aim, just as someone appeared from a side alley. It was a drunk, muttering to himself. Joseph melted into the shadows of the boarding house under the black-stockinged pillars and waited for the drunk to pass. Slowly he passed, swaying and belching like a music-hall clown. A curse, a really foul, despairing curse, and then he was gone, leaving a faint whiff of rum and urine.

This time the barley sugar hit a glass pane with a ping. He waited. The electric light burned on. He threw another and it struck again. It was surprisingly loud. A shadow on the curtains, then a hand, then a face looking out through the glass.

It was Tillie. He had been half ready to disbelieve it. It was her, though, sure as day, her face framed in coppery hair, looking out suspiciously – he guessed suspiciously, though he could not be sure; apart from anything else, his excitement was steaming up his spectacles.

She was, as far as he could see in the dim light, dressed in her nightgown.

He waved dramatically, as one waves at a ship. The sash window – the bottom half – was pulled up. Her head appeared, leaning out. Her hair fell loose on her bare neck and shoulders. The nightgown was a flimsy affair, he could see that.

'Tillie!' he whispered, as loud as he could. A real stage whisper.

She just stared at him for a moment. He had no idea what more to say. He had not planned it at all. No Romeo speech came to his lips. So he just said: 'Hallo!'

She called down, softly: 'I told you no, Hubert.'

A great tower crashed down in his head.

Hubert?

'I'm not Hubert. I'm not flaming Hubert.'

There was a brief silence, in which her form became blurred. He should have taken off his spectacles to wipe them, but he could not make such a gesture, such an ordinary gesture. A vein seemed to be beating in his nose, a hot needle rammed into the bridge.

'What do you mean?' she said, eventually.

'It's Joseph. It's me.'

Another silence. He brushed his cuff across his lenses without taking them off and she was distorted by the smears.

'Oh, you'd best come up. Number 5.'

He mounted the dark stairs in a confusion of despair and excitement. Number 5's door was ajar, Tillie waiting inside.

The place was small, divided from a larger room into bedroom and sitting room and bathroom – but badly so; the shapes, the proportions, they were all wrong. The ornate plaster fan around the old central gas light was cut through by one of the walls: it was a little nightmarish, somehow. The sitting room had no windows, only a fanlight into the stairwell and blood-coloured panes on the door.

'Why not put the bedroom here?' Joseph wondered aloud, stood awkwardly by the one easy chair. Tillie had shown him round as if he was expected. There was not much to see. The rugs were worn through in places to the cord backing, the bedroom ceiling stained with damp. There was a grinning electric fire filmed with grease and dust. They were both breathless with embarrassment, and she was definitely a little tipsy. 'The bedroom should be here. You don't need windows to sleep.'

'Tea?'

'Thank you, I will.'

The room was lit by a single lamp on a shelf, its shade patterned with hunting dogs. He could not quite believe this: Tillie making him tea, alone with him after midnight. She heated the water on a little army cooker set in the hearth, filling the room with a paraffin smell, hiding her scent and the general mustiness. Neither spoke for a bit. The floor creaked every time he moved.

'Do sit,' she said, and cleared her throat. She had thrown a dressing gown over her shift but her hair was tousled and her feet were bare. She has very nice feet, he noted. A high arch, elegant toes. A dancer's feet, really. A sylph's. A sylph's with a lisp.

'You've made it snug very quickly,' he remarked.

'Thank you.'

He sat on the edge of the chair, elbows on his knees, hands dangling down. Her parents – he assumed her parents – stared at him from an old porcelain photograph above the fireplace. He must either go at it straight, this Hubert business, or lose it altogether. She did not really want him here.

'Nice situation, too. Quiet, handy.'

'Thank you.'

'Yes, it's near everything that matters, as landlords say. It's nice to see you again.'

'Kind of you to say that, considering,' she said.

'Considering?'

'That you were burst in on like that, in your cottage.'

'Now I'm doing the bursting in!'

'Oh, I hadn't gone to sleep yet.'

Everything he said, she treated as a kind of compliment. She was in fact rather servant-like, doing the tea for him. Her scar cupped her face like a little faery hand. She was being dutiful. She must be used to queer types at all hours, up in Stockport, with her queer table-moving parents and their elated, staring eyes.

No, she's being the nurse, he thought. She was kneeling now, weary-looking, tucking her hair back; the water beginning to boil in the pan. He imagined it tipping over and scalding her bare feet.

'You thought I was someone called Hubert,' he said, scratching his head.

She kept quiet for a bit. Then she yawned, trying to hide it.

'Ay,' she said. 'And I thought that he was you, the first time I saw him.'

'Hubert Rail, then.'

She nodded, and looked at him. He only then remembered that he had come here to take her away from Baz.

'You were out with Rail tonight?'

She nodded again. Her expression was unfathomable: not defiant, really, certainly not shy. More obstinate, as if they had been arguing for hours. Quietly obstinate. He studied his knees. He had been on his own too long: all rusty, they felt, the working parts of conversation.

'Know him well, do you?'

'Pretty well.'

'Since when?'

'Last week. You know I really did think it was you?' she said.

'It wasn't. I'd have remembered.'

She went straight on without smiling.

'The light was very bad, they'd shrouded all the lights like in the war, it was a nice effect, all blue. That's why, I suppose. At least, that's why I went up to him in the first place.'

'Where?' Though he knew.

'The Café Royal.'

'Oh, there. Ay.' Shrewdly, he kept contempt out of it.

'Last week. I called him Joseph, said I was surprised to see him – you – but you're not at all related, are you, you're not twins?'

'Not that I know of, no. Unless we were shipwrecked as babies.'

'Sorry?'

'Nothing.'

'It was the poor light.'

Her hair glinted thickly as she moved. 'Really,' she went on, 'I don't think you look like twins at all. Many folk *resemble* each other. Especially when he took his spectacles off, he wasn't you at all. Though he has the same voice, the same movements. He *suggests* you, that's what it is. I told him that I didn't think you were twins. Wouldn't you have the same colour eyes? You're quite different, from different stock completely.'

He was glad, and then wondered if he ought to be.

'Let's not go on about it,' he said.

He sipped at his tea. The milk was slightly sour, clotting on the top. But he drank it anyway. His hand shook, bringing the cup to his lips.

'You've got a snail on your shoulder,' she said, with a little laugh.

'So I have.'

'I thought it was an epaulette.'

He plucked it off, the viscous body almost pulling out of the shell.

'Now what to do with it?'

'Don't throw it out of the window,' she said. 'It'll break.'

'What do I do with it, then?'

'I could keep it as a pet. Call it something.'

'I did that as a boy,' said Joseph, feeling the current run between them, his heart swell with longing and love. It was bound up with recalling their childhoods; she seemed to have been there already, in his childhood, running right through it.

'What was its name?'

'Mine? Oh. I forget. Hang on.' He thought hard, holding the snail between his thumb and finger. Its body emerged again, searching for ground, the feelers growing from nothing then disappearing again into the viscous mass when his finger touched them.

'It was my playmate, anyway,' he said. 'I made a land for it.'

'A land?'

'An island, really.'

He felt embarrassed about this, suddenly. And his much-loved snail had died, drowned in the bowl of water among the leaves and branches set in an old crate with *Mazawattee Tea Calcutta* stencilled on the side. He put the snail on the floor, in front of Tillie's feet that were tucked under her shins. She was seated on a cushion by the brick hearth. He felt like bursting into tears.

'There you are,' he said. 'There's Roderick.'

'Roderick!' She laughed. 'Was that the name of yours?'

'No.'

A pause.

'Tillie's living with Roderick,' Joseph said, with an attempt at a rueful smile. 'It'll get them talking.'

He glanced at her then, not very casually. She was looking down, watching the snail. Hiding her face, he reckoned. The snail was sliding towards her, feelers waving. His heart was thudding all over.

'Hullo, Roderick,' she said.

She smiled at Joseph, quite openly, candid as clear sky. He felt himself sliding down a chasm of love. No, it was love rising up around him in sea-green waves. But he would have to be cold to it, if he was to know what was going on. He would have to shut his ears from the sweet music. He would have to attack, front-on.

'Does Baz – where does Baz come, in all this?'

She blinked a little, looked away.

'Is it your business?'

'You know why I think it my business.'

'Not really.'

'Oh, come on, Tillie.' He was insisting now, he could feel it, a hard masculine insistence that made him shrink inside.

'No, I don't.'

'He's my friend,' he said. 'And secondly—' He swallowed. 'I think that I'm – you know my feelings. I mean about you. I like you – best. Out of anyone. Out of anyone I've ever known, ever.'

He could not use the word 'love', oh definitely not.

'I know,' she said, and sighed.

'Well?'

'Well what?'

He was slipping away, he had lost the grip on it.

'You know *why* I came to London?' he said, rapidly.

'Why?'

'You don't know, do you?'

'No idea. Why should I know? That's your business.'

He snorted, despite himself. The dankness of the church plot was on him. He placed his tea on the floor, the cup tumbling over loudly in its saucer so that he had to right it. And then he just sat there looking down, his elbows on his knees.

'Well, I think you know that.'

'Do I? I don't. I can guess, though. You're – in love with me, is that it? You came to see me, is that it?'

Her candour was appalling – it boxed him in walls. She would not talk like this if she felt something for him, surely.

'Do you always say things, in *front* of people?'

'What do you mean? I'm just getting things straight. I'm tired.'

'It leaves you indifferent, then? That I've come to see you.'

'No. I just don't like it.'

He was closed in darkness.

'You like Hubert enough, though.'

His voice was bitter. But he stopped there, for the moment. A faint shriek sounded from somewhere in the house. A London noise, shrugged off, like the inner rumblings of the Tube.

'Well,' said Tillie, 'I did think it was you, and so did Baz, in the bad light – but we were ever so – *surprised* because you were behaving in a way that was not you.'

'And what isn't me? I hope something really – ugly. Like being a drunken idiot and singing Marie Lloyd—'

'No, he was telling jokes.'

He stared at her, open-mouthed. She was stabbing him, mentally. The room bore down upon him, full of night, full of hunting dogs, acrid.

'I mean,' she went on, seeing his hurt and surprise, 'he was the centre of attention. Everyone was looking at him and laughing. He's a very fine mimic. He's a show-off, really.'

'I see.'

'And he pretended to be you. He led us along a bit.'

'Oh dear. Made a face like a gargoyle, did he?'

'He wasn't rude. He just didn't let us know who he wasn't, that he wasn't you, in the bad light. He answered to Joseph, you see. He'd even – his hair was shaved off. For the summer, you see. There's a lot of lice about, he blames the war, you all brought it back—'

'He was out there, was he? In the war?'

She nodded. 'You should see the sketches he did, sitting in the trenches and sketching.'

'Good, are they?'

'More than good. They're upsetting. Nobody would ever exhibit them or put them in a book. He's tried but – well, nobody wants to. And yet it's just what he saw, what happened – just what was around him, whatever he saw. Very straightforwardly copied, really.'

Her eyes were shining.

'He played us along, you see. When we asked him how the *novel* was going, he said "Oh, pretty badly", just as you would. And Mrs Hamilton – we asked after your Mrs Hamilton and he said she was doing *famously*, that was it. Those very words! That wasn't very you, though. You wouldn't have said *famously*, in such a gay way. Anyroad, he played along for – oh, about an hour. Then Baz found him out, accidentally, and we all laughed. It was a joke, you see. Then he didn't really look like you at all, not under it all. I think it's the spectacles. Afterwards, Baz said he'd known all along but I don't believe him—'

She giggled, suddenly. 'He even knew about your fortune, Hubert did.'

Joseph took off his spectacles. 'I haven't got a fortune.'

Her elegant, precise mouth crumpled into a mew of disapproval.

'Oh come on, now. You're going to inherit a huge fortune.'

'I am not.'

'You said, in Cornwall. Hubert told me. He's come up here to see if you're related.'

'I am not. It was a joke. There was no shipwreck, or whatever. There is no fortune. This isn't the Gaiety Theatre, you know.'

He could not believe that this wretched little joke was shuffling back to him in this grubby, malevolent manner. She frowned in disbelief.

'Is that's why he's in London, then?' he snorted. 'Why he's up here?'

She nodded. He could not believe it. He tried to think back to the beach, to remember what exactly he had said, what Hubert had said. But he could not, not exactly. There was only Hubert's taut white face, half-smiling at him.

'So he says,' she went on. 'He's been to Somerset House and that. But he doesn't think you are. Related, that is.'

'We're not. That was a joke, that fortune business. I make jokes, too. I'm—'

He didn't want to tell her he was broke.

'I'm a poor writer, and that's it.'

'Oh. I'm glad.'

'Why?'

'He's quite worked up about it. *He's* a poor painter, you see.'

'Ay, the Cornish Constable.' He snorted. 'Tillie, have you dropped Baz for this – this—'

'For Hubert?'

He nodded, smiling grimly.

'I prefer to call him by another name,' he said.

'Don't.'

'Only I can't think of one that's – polite enough.'

Silence. He was very much out of his depth. She had no Chapel left in her. It was rubble. He felt very lonely, as if left behind. He had unfastened from the world while in the cottage, drifted off. He could no longer paddle back. He had thought Tillie was part of *his* world, but no – she was singing and dancing on the huge liner, doomed like all the rest. She had been snatched from him. He wanted to build the Chapel up again in gossamer soul-stuff, seal her in, protect her. Then together they would sail through to their own heaven.

'So Baz is off the board, is he?'

She frowned. 'Not exactly. Maybe.'

'Has Rail made love to you?'

He had the frankness of despair, now. And blushing furiously with it, remembering the kiss in Ypres.

'Yes,' she said, without any hesitation, 'he has kissed me.'

The meeting of the faces at the end of the street.

'And you didn't mind?'

'No.'

She was very candid, very clear. His face was burning.

'I see. And my best friend doesn't know?'

'You had better ask him.'

'You've broken off the engagement?'

'Yes.'

'When?'

'Yesterday.'

'What did Baz do?'

'Cried, on the steps.'

'Which steps?'

'Oh, some church. I don't know London churches. I said a prayer for him, afterwards.'

Joseph ran a hand over his mouth, cupped his face like a bowl.

'Well, that did the trick, I expect,' he said. 'Poor old Baz.' Secretly, he was rejoicing.

'It might not be forever,' she insisted. 'I don't like being rushed into things—'

'You want to be free.'

'That's it.'

She stared at him very firmly, very obstinately.

'How did you get your scar?' he asked her, suddenly.

She smiled. 'Why d'you ask?'

'Because I bet no one else does.'

'Oh, some of them do. I fell off a bed.'

'A bed? Not a brick, then?'

'A brick? Why a brick? No, a bed. When I was three. I don't remember anything about it. It's ugly, isn't it?'

'No, it's very beautiful. It sets the rest off. It makes you different.'

'Oh, that's what Ma always says, to cheer me up. More tea?'

She was infuriating him, now. He stood up.

'No, I won't.'

She cupped her chin in her hands, waiting. She was waiting for him to go. His mind was a fog, a complete blank in which emotions writhed, or loomed like buses. It was tiredness, and a recognition of failure. He held his boater to his chest, biting his lip. She was watching the snail. It had reached her foot, was touching it with its feelers. She was smiling, flinching at its touch.

'I'm not going to marry Hubert, by the way,' she said.

'How do you know?'

'I'm not going to marry at all.'

'Oh.'

'Why should I? Queens have to marry, princesses and that, but why should we be always marrying? The man I loved best in the world is dead.'

His heart skipped a beat.

'Who was that?'

'My brother, Cecil.'

He nodded, sorry for her in an abstract manner. No doubt it would deform love between man and woman for a generation, this mass sister-grief for brothers.

'So he makes jokes, he makes people laugh.'

'That's not all there is to life.'

'Baz is paying for this room, is he?'

'I'm paying him back, of course. I've got a post at the children's hospital. They're short, you know. All that influenza.'

'The war.'

'Oh yes, the war. It drags on in the wards, you know.'

'And outside. It'll drag on forever, like a curse.'

'Oh, not forever. Everything heals in time.'

The snail was on her foot, now, on the curving instep. 'Look,' she said, pointing, 'Roderick's visiting me. He does tickle a bit, though.'

He had to get out. But he would die, shrivel up, if he left now.

33

A Very Hot Fire

H E WOULD BE frank. Anything less was tommy-rot.
'I'd better see Baz,' he said. 'I'd best be loyal.'

'Yes, maybe you had best see him.'

Her scar was really rather disfiguring, he thought, it confused the line of her chin.

'You see,' she said, 'it's all a question of what we want. What do we want? That's the question.'

'Is it?'

'What do *you* want, for instance?'

A flush again enveloped his face.

'You know already,' he said.

'The novel?'

The novel was suddenly a contemptible thing, almost ugly, like the black lump in the road. He could not be frank. It was beyond him. He would write her a letter, confessing it all. She was looking at the snail on her instep, wincing a little; she was fonder of the snail than of him. It had left a little trail of slime on her skin.

He shook his head.

'The novel's something else,' he said, vaguely. He looked at her straight. 'I think you know exactly what I want.'

'I don't, because *you* don't,' she said.

'What? I know what *I* want.'

'Do you? I mean, do you really?'

He wanted to be in Hubert's shoes, that was what he wanted. He wanted to lie in Tillie's arms; he wanted to be with her for the rest of his days; he wanted his Ma to say, *our Tillie*. And only then did he want to write the great War book (but this felt grey after the other desire, pale and grey). He gave a big sigh, rather demonstrative.

'Oh Tillie, isn't it – it's clear as day, isn't it?'

She drew her feet up carefully and hugged her knees like a little girl. The snail was like a huge wart on the bony top of the foot.

'Actually, I don't have a clue what I want,' she said, balancing her chin on her knees. 'I'm open to suggestions.'

Now he was confused.

'Jesus, I thought Jesus—'

'Jesus is rather stunned by me,' she said. 'He really doesn't know what to say, for the moment.'

She's not all there, he thought. She's dotty, after all. A great disappointment welled up in him, and a fierce undertow of relief. She was tapping her chin gently on her knee, her lips rumpled like a child's, pondering. She was becoming very childlike, losing ten years just like that. Yet her breasts swelled from the cotton to touch her updrawn thighs, her hands were a woman's, her feet too. She was a mish-mash of solid woman and unfinished child.

'What if He tells you to stop?' he said.

'Stop? Stop what?'

She was frowning at him, blearily, as if woken from sleep.

'To stop going out with Rail, of course.'

She made a curious sound in her throat, a kind of chirrup.

'Is that what you think?'

'Think what?' And his heart rose in hope.

'That Jesus might bother himself with such things?'

'Well, all creatures great and small,' he said, cleverly. He was very pleased with himself, though his hope was smashed.

'I think you'd better go now, Joseph.'

It was the first time she had used his name. He nodded slowly. She was looking at him very steadily, the lamp picking out gold in her hair, the fine clean threads of it. He had thought of mentioning Rail's red-rimmed eyes, his suspicious 'treatments', for some time. He could not. His voice would come out all dainty, he knew, and she would tell him about her lover's war.

'Don't get in too deep,' he said. 'That's all I want to say.'

'I can manage myself quite well, thank you.'

She was not going to get up, to see him out. She was hurt. He placed his hand on the door knob and turned it; the blood-red pane shivered. His longing for her had not been quelled, not at all. But over this longing was this film of coolness, of mental cleverness. The scar taunted him, he saw that. He was quite sure that had she not been marked in that way, by that little scar, he would be able to forget her, to put her aside; the scar, however, made her irreplaceable. It was not really the scar alone – that was just surface, like a surface explanation of uniqueness. Yet the scar was the little claw that held him, very deep. There would never be anyone else like her. Jesus probably *was* in love with her, after all; He would have her for Himself, soon.

A gust from the dank stairwell rushed up, it was almost straining to suck him down, away from her, into the welter beyond. He stood there on the threshold, where the linoleum began. It was blackened by feet, curling and swelling muscularly; it disgusted him, to see such ugliness, such low detail, in everything. Tillie had no low detail, that was the thing.

'Thank you for the tea,' he threw out, without turning to look at her.

'Tell Baz I'm sorry,' she said.

Joseph thought: she looks upon me as Baz's friend. Just that. He nodded, very small inside himself, very shrivelled and weak.

'Alright, if you want.'

'I do.'

'Yes,' he said, 'it's better to know what you want.'

The black stairwell smelt faintly of cats and boiled fish. Haddock for breakfast, grisly mornings in London, work, work, work. Oh yes, there was something very underbred about modern life. Linoleum was especially underbred.

He turned to look at her. She was stood up, now. He had not heard her stand up.

'These sketches of Hubert's,' he tried in a thin, colourless voice, 'they're very good, then, very strong?'

'They're like a very hot fire,' she replied, mysteriously.

Yes, he knew what she meant. His effort was a little gas flare, compared to the true work. His own sketches on the salient: the revolver like a claw, the feeble, fussy lines and shadows, the paper worn right through by the rubber – these all flashed into his mind like a light-bomb. It was the same with his words, his writing. He gloried now in his sense of defeat, properly gloried in it, staring back down at the black stairwell.

'Goodbye, then,' he said, eyeing her sideways.

'Goodbye. I'm sure we'll see each other again.'

She was so sweet, so deadly sweet. Smiling, drawing him in.

'We're not on the same train anymore,' he said, quietly. 'So I doubt it.' His voice caught in an echo on the stairwell, and was hollowed right out.

She looked rather crestfallen. That, too, was drawing him in. She stepped forward and gave a sudden cry and at the same time he heard it, the cracking sound. It was the snail: she had crushed the snail under her bare foot.

'Are you hurt?'

'No. Silly snail,' she said. 'Poor Roderick.'

She was looking down at the snail. Its fleshy muscle was moving under the broken bits of shell, glistening and swelling, frothing slightly as if angry.

'He's still alive,' she said, touching the plates of shell with her finger. The snail writhed ponderously. 'I'll look after him. Do shells grow back?'

'All depends,' he said. 'Put it in a cage and sing to it.'

He left abruptly, fumbling at the green glow of the switch by the stairs and descending quickly as the timer creaked and groaned. He did not like what he had just said; and he did not even know what he had meant by that business about trains, not really. He was so tired out he could hardly think four-square. Voices drifted in and out of his ears like smoke. He stumbled down the stairs, slipping on its loose linoleum runner, and positively ordered himself out into the night air.

It was one of those voices that was giving him orders, instructing him. It was telling him to use the sketches. It was an excited voice, almost babbling. It told him how Tillie had been a decoy – the real bird was this business about the sketches. Yes, everything had been leading towards the sketches. There had been a few exhibitions of unofficial war art, but nothing dangerous, nothing too shocking. Thick charcoal sketches of men in bandages, of dugouts, of men smoking or just fagged out, indistinguishable from the lifeless subjects, the proper cadavers and bits of cadavers. Sensitive pencilled renditions of rubble, ruins, trench mess, coils of wire. Paintings, too: torn white chalk and puffballs in the sky and weary men in ooze, very detailed – right down to a botched nail in a duckboard slat. The rumour was that the Germans had the shocking stuff, coarse and satirical. Whores with fat thighs around black squiggles of pubic hair, drunk generals vomiting, soldiers spouting blood from their stumps, blind Berlin beggars. A bit debased, it was generally thought. Prussian crudity. No – it was honesty, Prussian honesty: all the copper and brass stripped off. Humiliation and anger. Much better to lose a war than to win it: then war is exposed, belly-up, for the white-fleshed horror it is. At least Germany, he thought, would never make the same mistake again. But England? Oh, England would charge into it at the drop of a sabre, right into the bombs and machine-guns and gas.

Joseph walked quickly, his nerves up, the nasty images bobbing about in his head. At first only cats were out, their brief enormous shadows under street lamps. He thought he had the city to himself. Then, crossing Russell Square, he passed the late-night revellers with scarves and capes, beggars shuffling in doorways, the odd tough he gave a wide berth to. And a few rooms still glowing. Bloomsbury intellectuals, he thought, staring up at an open window where figures flitted before a lamp, a low swarm of conversation bearing down. It was after two. Little peals of laughter. Politics, books, painting, sex gossip. How he despised them! They cast their net over the whole business of creation – how instantly it was turned by them into 'atmosphere' for their soirées, their weekend parties! He made a crude gesture he had learnt in the army. His knuckles gleamed in the street light.

Corset Underclothing Umbrellas
Developed & Printed 3 Hrs
50 Tons Rags

Words could not be kept down. Like that strange odyssey of Mr Joyce's that everyone was talking about – which would never be published now, he supposed. He had read parts in an American magazine and found it confused, then he had emerged into the street and it had affected his mind – he experienced everything in a stream of tiny curious details, even the January cold on the hairs of his cheeks became vivid. So it must have been truthful, in its own way. Contagious, too. Men would not kill each other if they noticed such detail: the flakes of sugar pastry on a mouth. What had he noticed about Tillie? He had not been looking properly. He could only picture the linoleum. Strange minds we have. He should have mentioned the shawl. He had thieved it, really. Her grandma's precious shawl.

He passed the great temple-bulk of the British Museum and turned into Holborn, past dead theatres, beneath giant winking electric bulbs. On the corner of Shaftesbury Avenue there was a coffee stall. It blazed its yellow light, its raised shafts like two horns with the OXO sign for eyes – a strange wheeled creature of the night, almost absurd. Under the flap stood three or four people, as ever; winter or summer, the coffee stalls always had their three or four people. He felt hungry, all of a sudden, the smell of sausages and coffee wafting on the gusts. Yet he passed on swiftly – really hurrying past it. The group, the usual mixed bag, either overbred or underbred, was watching him; he heard the sausages sizzle in the quiet. One of the fellows had a silk hat and white gloves. He felt very numb, very alone, leaving the stall behind. Its faintly illicit air, its kindly blaze, the squat chimney spouting smoke: London sleeping for miles all about. Yet he could not face the people, their fly-by-night readiness to chat, to share gossip and secrets, to flirt with you through greasy lips. And as soon as he was out of sight of it, he regretted not stopping, as a sailor regrets not making a landfall at a tiny island. He thought he heard laughter – maybe he looked queer, ticking along hurriedly up the big silent street.

At any rate, not stopping there seemed very much connected with his failure with Tillie; it seemed to be all *him*. He would always go hungry, he thought. Right until his dying breath, he would always refuse himself. He could almost taste the sausage in his mouth, and the sharp, bitter coffee. Yes, he could taste them. As sometimes he could taste the gas that had nearly done for him, a mouthful of chlorine – as if a bubble had been released from the dark mud of his soul, bursting full in his mouth.

He was almost alone, crossing Piccadilly Circus – builders' rubble and spill from roadworks in front of the poshed-up Swan and Edgar's, a broken sign saying *MPAN*, the lingering stench of hot tar, trampled flowers and petals around the fountain where the wrinkled, red-faced flower girls had sat all day behind their huge baskets, and would do for eternity. This, he thought, is the hub of the world; square it and remove Eros and the flowers, and the world will fly off. Did he want it to? Perhaps. Yes, perhaps he did. He felt quite privileged, having the place almost to himself. He could contemplate shoving the world off its course somehow, here, just by willpower, some strange symbolic action at the hub. Books did that, sometimes, but very infrequently. Marx's had, somehow. The Bible.

Those sketches of Rail's. He could use them. Their very hot fire.

He leaned against a squat slit-eyed postbox, immobile yet flinging its contents from the hub to the farthest points of the globe, spinning and spinning and flinging them out like ink drops: *LONDON & ABROAD* one side, *FOR COUNTRY LETTERS* the other: the whole world, that was. He thought of his 'country' cottage, then, with a curious nostalgia. He wondered if that mad fellow was even now ransacking its meagre contents, and whether the fellow's mental problems were due to the war. But the war was not responsible for every damn thing: he had to be careful of that.

His footsteps echoed in the silence of the summer night. A dog howled – really howled: the dead hours when dogs do such things.

He was quite light and high-stepping in his head; ideas began to come, quite thick and fast, as he circled the fountain. There would be a sketch for each chapter, the chapter arising out of the sketch – you did not need a conventional story, stories were probably finished anyway. During the war a fresh-faced, eager fellow could go out to the front line and be killed within half an hour, ten minutes even – or two! There one minute, napoo the next. Another might survive four years. Never any *reason* to it, no ground plan. Homer had Troy, Shakespeare had Agincourt, Thackeray had Waterloo, Tolstoy had Borodino, but the modern author – he has only unreasoned machine-mess, machine-anarchy, machine-futility. Nothing begins or ends, there. How do you make a story from that? He laughed bitterly, quite loud, looking up at Eros whose bronze leg was still impossibly cocked, the wings catching the red flashes off the huge electrical *BOVRIL* sign on the corner. And then felt a stab of regret, as if the launched invisible arrow had struck him after all. A lone cab whirred past, coughing and whirring. No doubt he looked thoroughly sozzled to its occupants. When he thought of Tillie, he did almost reel with hurt, like a drunk.

He walked slowly down Piccadilly, shoving away the hurt by thinking, furrowing his brows with the effort. What was it Tolstoy had said? 'The one essential thing, in life as in art, is to tell the truth.' The true great book of the war, he realised, would be unreadable; it would drive the reader to distraction, cut-up bits and torn pieces, the sympathetic hero killed by a shell within five pages – that would be honest, the only honesty worthy of its name. And the boredom, the tedium of waiting, of *not* being killed, only injured or maimed or disfigured or turned barmy: three hundred pages of tedium and nerves until the last sentence descended into gibberish. The book would have to be a great splash of blood-words, a great ooze of pain and grief. And love? Love would be the equivalent of a coffee stall with its night-time sausages and coffee: a temporary shelter, a comfort, the mole hole of a warm dugout. Which in the morning, in the harsh day of reality in the world, is wheeled away.

At the corner of Clarges Street there was a beggar rolled up asleep in a threadbare blanket, hands poking through torn mittens, a bottle clasped in his arms. What I need, thought Joseph, is a revelation. A thunderclap after which everything might come clean. He gazed down on the beggar, filled with useless compassion. He pulled out his purse and left a shilling on the flat cap that lay beside the coat. The coin shone in the headlights of a passing motor-taxi – flashing briefly and then seeming to vanish. The sharp stench from the beggar reminded Joseph of certain places on the salient. He thought again of the German woman; was that a revelation? He could make it one, in retrospect. You could make anything a revelation, in retrospect.

He walked down Clarges Street, the first hint of dawn more in the cool wafts of air than in any touch of light. A market cart clopped and rattled past, heaped with some green stuff – spinach, probably – and he watched it as it turned into Piccadilly, soil and horse-leather and dark shag floating in its wake. Coming to life already, the new day was, lifted from the tombstone of the dead hour of night – he was almost afraid, thinking of the relentless march of the days, the lamps flickering out and the bustle up and at it again. He felt again the weight of failure – and alongside it, as if born from the ribs of failure, a massive sense of what might be achieved, of what he might yet do. His youth like a weapon, not a weakness.

They tried to wipe us out, he said to himself, standing by the window in his room, flung open to the night. The grey filter of dawn was leaking over everything – the brick, the sills, the gutters, the roofs, the straining chimneys, the surface of the road and pavement down below, empty of people or traffic: well, this is the revelation, he thought. They did not succeed, and we are still here. I am here. It was as if he was directing the light, flooding the world with it, a world which at that moment was inimical to him because it was filled with evil, with evil intention. At that moment he really felt a power in him to change this state of affairs. He could see the tiny form of the beggar on the corner, rolled up in the doorway of the confectioner's, and willed him to rise and take his blanket, willing him with a stare of pure love. Never mind the beggar did not stir at all. The light coming up quickly, ushering in the new business of the day, the sudden exhalation of carts and vans and loaded hand-barrows and people – here and there, not many, but just beginning, like an emergence after a great deathly sleep of centuries: it was as if he had directed all this, every detail. As if he could return it all to night by closing his eyes and willing it back, back into its deathly sleep, immobile and safe.

There was a curious noise, a sort of moaning or humming, through the open window. It was almost frightening, in its eerie strangeness. It grew louder. It was rather like the moan of a Zeppelin that first time he had seen one pass overhead, like a squat silver cigar – and yet this was animal, it was not a machine moan, and strangely familiar to him. It was a moment or two before he caught what it was with his eyes, before he set the sound and the sight together and made sense of either: passing the end of Clarges Street like a momentary flood, a grey moaning river passing down Piccadilly in the first light of dawn, was a flock of sheep, moving from one park to another. The noise rocked down the smaller street as if a sluice had been opened. The shepherd with his curled crook, the little busy black-and-white dog, the grey foaming backs of the flock, hundreds strong, moaning and shivering and bleating, flowing on and on. And then nothing: only the carts and vans and the early-rising folk on foot, flitting past the mouth of the street.

That, too, could be my revelation, thought Joseph. The shepherd leading. Lambs to slaughter – or to salvation. And he found himself praying, offering his life-force to the Saviour, using those very words: 'life-force' and 'Saviour'. An invented prayer that he immediately felt shy about, and yet too superstitious to deny.

34

With Baz in a State

'HALLO, YOU!'
'Joseph. What the blazes are you doing here?'
'Concerned for your welfare.'

'What'll you have to drink? Have a very dry sherry. Sherry do? Finished the Madeira, and the port. Yesterday. Honour of Sir William Grant.'

'Who's he?' Joseph asked, finding the leather chair under a cape and a squashed hat and various documents. Though he was not really listening.

'Don't you know? Finest judge ever, so they say. Would fuel himself on a bottle of Madeira and a bottle of port before bringing judgement. Plus a large dinner. I tried to call you, but you were in London, obviously. You were here. Sir William had the clearest and most rational mind in the history of the law, yet he never skipped his dinner, his Madeira, and his port.'

Baz's hand trembled, pouring out the sherry. The office in Lincoln's Inn Fields was tiny, its walls lined with pastel-coloured files and leather-bound documents in heavy mahogany cases – very stuffy and dark, it was. Baz's desk was a riot of paper and files. And the occupier was dishevelled, with red-rimmed eyes. Joseph had tried his attic room above the optician's in George's Yard off the Strand, but the landlady said that Mr Beardow had gone to work, like all good Christian souls. He had stood in the narrow little Yard among strewn handbills, hearing faint rumbles and surges of song from the Royal Adelphi next door, while the landlady's squeezed white face glared down at him.

'So, I saw Tillie,' said Joseph, sipping at the dusty sherry. He had expected to find Baz sobbing, a broken man.

Baz blinked at him.

'Did you?'

'I gather, um – the engagement's off.'

'Yes.'

No longer blinking, Baz had a very fixed, death-mask look about him. Joseph knew this look.

'I suppose you must feel – pretty bad about it.'

'A bottle of Madeira, a bottle of port. Not quite full bottles, I have to say.'

Part of Baz was not present; the suffering part. The tiny office did not have room for it, with its coloured abstractions of legal matter. Yet the hands trembled.

'What did she tell you?' Baz asked, nevertheless.

Joseph told him – about Hubert Rail, mainly. He wanted Baz to give him Hubert Rail's address, assuming it was known. Last night, in the few hours he had slept (waking to the terrific clash of midmorning), he had dreamt of straining against a sloping deck on which the sketches were scattered – slipping slowly into the sea, they were, out of his grasp. What he had seen of them in his dream – extraordinary, really extraordinary. Like something by Goya: fierce, cruel, horribly truthful. Though now he could not picture them at all. He said nothing about this to Baz. He only told him about Hubert, not Hubert's sketches. Baz, of course, already knew about *him*. His face became tortoise-like.

'I'm a blank, Jo-Jo. A dud. I'm not broken, I'm blank. I feel nothing.'

A clerk came in and out with papers, a husky fellow in his fifties, very ill-looking with a runny nose and brown blotches on his cheeks and a lifetime of smoking behind him. Men were labouring at legal business all around them, squeaks and behind-wainscot murmurs, all hidden in their offices. It was quite beyond Joseph: he felt he had been trained for nothing, that life would always be a mystery to him. He could scarcely boil an egg, let alone make bread. He played with a rusty paperclip, craving to do something outrageous and brave, something to do with mountains, high white mountains – the Tyrol for instance, he might cross the Tyrol in snowshoes, scale glacial peaks wearing a frock coat and panama, something really outrageous and brave and mad . . . And Baz droned on about the case he was working at, dragging in this other world of bizarre little incidents that flowered poisonously and ate up people's lives and livings – certainly a bizarre matter, this one, involving a marble, the sloped floor of a ham-and-tongue shop, and a customer's badly-broken leg.

'It will set a precedent, if we lose. No ham-and-tongue merchant will ever let a child roll a marble between his legs again. The world will change. But it was the sloping floor that did it, really. That's what we're banking on. We tested it out. The marble *definitely* rolled back into the middle where the customer's foot found it. It wasn't the ham-and-tongue merchant's fault. It was the floor's fault.'

'Or the Earth's fault,' said Joseph. 'Round, isn't it? It's never flat, not anywhere. So I've heard. It slopes.'

'Does it? Golly. I thought the damn thing was flat. Science will save us, I suppose. Trouble is, the judge won't accept it. Judges believe Galileo to be too damn modern.'

Baz's humour was as dry as the sherry. It crackled like brown paper. It hid everything, wrapped it up out of sight. Joseph felt in the way, here. His feelings of hurt were somehow in the way of this elaborate game of stiff papery dryness.

There was a silence. Baz was eyeing him curiously.

'Hang it all, Jo-Jo,' he said, 'if you hadn't looked like that damn feller—'

'Sorry.'

'Not your fault, of course.'

'Oh, I see, well that's a relief,' said Joseph, a touch mockingly. 'Look,' he went on quickly, 'you're better off away from her, Baz. I think she's dangerous.'

'Do you?'

Baz looked almost happy.

'Well, I think she has psychological – problems may be too strong a word. Certainly she's deep, too deep for me. This Jesus obsession – I think it's her father, a projection of her father.'

'And who the devil are you to know?' Baz cried, laughing a little madly.

'Quite,' Joseph said, crisply. He retracted very fast, at that.

Another silence. The air in the room was thick with a vellumy scent, rather sweet, above the ugly metallic sourness of ink. His foot knocked over a pile of documents, tied up in ribbons of faded rose.

'Leave them,' said Baz rather airily, waving his hand. 'Plenty more where they came from.'

Joseph tidied them up, nevertheless, though they would keep sliding off each other. 'Where does he live, by the way, our splendid Hubert Rail?'

'Café Royal, as far as I can see.'

'Ay, full of public school fops pretending to be Dada.'

'Why their fathers? Their sisters, more like.'

Joseph laughed. '*Dada*, Baz. Chaps dressed up in Cubist masks reciting nonsense poetry, the urinal as a work of art. The deluge. All art is senseless, like nature. It'll reach England properly when it's a puddle and we'll still be outraged.'

'Is it that Continental bolshevist thing—?'

'Some of them are bolshevists. I don't see how, though; unless the politics of reason is that of pure unreasoning destruction. Maybe it is. Ours is. Look what our bourgeois politics did—'

'I don't think nature is senseless,' said Baz, 'it's just bloody hard.'

'He must lodge somewhere, some miserable garret somewhere.'

'Oh, probably.'

'You're not interested?'

'No. He can go to hell.'

Joseph realised then, from the way Baz's face puckered up, that his friend was extremely wounded, after all, by Tillie's defection. Someone was hammering nails; builders outside were shouting to each other, metal clashed as if far below them, inside the earth. Joseph had only just noticed this noise.

'He can go straight to hell on a one-way ticket, third class,' Baz added, staring into his glass. 'He can go to flaming hell. Or Paris. Why can't he go to Paris and commit suicide like everyone else?'

'Between the miracle and the suicide, that's where we find ourselves.'

'Who said that?'

Joseph shrugged. 'Folk who read a lot of Dostoevsky.'

'Love's a damn flaming nuisance,' Baz sighed. 'I'll never get over it. I'm right at the bottom, right now. Even this glass marble case – we're going to lose that, I know it. And Hanley's bench is broken.'

'Broken?'

'The wretched boys jump on it, I don't know why. Its seat's all cracked.'

'The spirit of Hanley, that: *he'd* have jumped on it. Burnt it, probably.'

Baz poured out more sherry. It was snug in his office, after all. They lit up a couple of Baz's Turkish cigarettes, advertised as having been smoked in the harems of old. The tobacco was pungently sweet. If only, thought Joseph, the office was indeed a harem, full of smooth brown flesh.

'How's the book, Jo-Jo?'

'The charm's off,' he replied. 'Either I lie and tell a story, or I do something nobody will read.'

'Oh, tell a story. We all like a story.'

'The war killed stories.'

'It's the peace now, Joseph. You can tell stories of love. And betrayal. And treachery. All that. I suppose it all seems very – trivial to you, this love business.'

Baz twitched at his own openness, downed his sherry at a gulp. Joseph nodded.

'Yes, it does,' he lied. 'It's tiny, but there's a lot of it about. Then you realise it's all there is. A great mesh of love, made up of lots of tiny loves.'

'Truly? You're not being – you're not teasing?'

Joseph drew his mouth down. 'I don't know. I try to make sense of it all, but it comes at you so quick. I should go Dada and drop cut-out words on the floor and publish the results on human skin. Do you want to be a good person, Baz? Do you believe in good?'

Baz nodded sagely, drawing deeply on his Turkish. He blew the smoke out.

'Yes, I do,' he said. Though Joseph did not believe him – he had not said it from the inside, not really.

'Would you then define good for me?'

'Not doing anything that you would not later regret,' Baz enunciated, as if remembering a lesson.

'That's tommy-rot,' Joseph said, softly. 'Old men regret their youth – that they weren't a damn sight wilder when the going was good.'

'Do they?'

'You will, Baz, you will.'

'Should I be wilder? You're not wild, are you? Maybe being wild is good. Maybe even whores are good. But you're not exactly wild, are you, Jo-Jo?'

It stung, that did, but Joseph tried not to show it.

'You can always be wilder, there's always more place to be wild in, inside,' he said. 'There's no limit, really. Complete freedom, inside. All that stops us is the blank page.'

Baz was lost, from the look of it. He stared out of the grimy little window, from which there was nothing to see but a blank cinder-coloured wall. The invisible builders hammered and yelped. His frame seemed to be buckled by the tiny scale of the room, the heaps of papers, the documents and lowering book cases with further papers heaped on their high tops.

'Anyway, I think I might give up writing,' Joseph said. 'Talking of being wild.'

Baz frowned, turning back.

'Really?' Ah, there was something lightweight about that 'really', as if Joseph had said he was to stop drinking.

'It's hopeless. I'm no good.'

'You were very good at school.'

Joseph laughed, mercilessly. Baz shrugged.

'Don't see what's so funny.'

'I'm not brave enough,' he said. 'Like in the gas chamber.'

'Oh, that. Listen, if the brick's proper quality the house'll hold up. That's what my grandad used to say, the builder one. Tillie and I – we went off for a weekend to the country, you know, to Berkshire. A village, new houses near the brick kiln, lovely rosy brick, not vulgar and nasty at all. Built from the earth around them. I thought that was interesting. Lovely rose-coloured brick.'

The familiar-looking clerk came in and out again. His fingers were bent with arthritis, the nails yellow. He puffed in and out like a little train, a sour-smelling cigarette smoking between his lips.

'He's a pain in my neck,' murmured Baz, after he had gone. 'But he's been here since Magna bloody Carta.'

'No,' Joseph continued, 'it's nothing to do with bricks. I'm too timid. I haven't got the spine.'

He was thinking of Hubert Rail's sketches, the absolute *absurdity* of the idea that he might use them! Ah, how the same idea could come and go in different outfits: kingly robes one minute, fool's cap-and-bells the next! As if ideas were never really naked at all. Oh, to have the one naked idea—

'I'm not a born writer. I haven't got the spine,' he insisted – over-insisted, really. *Fishing*, his mother would call this sort of talk. *Don't fish, dear.*

'Oh God, we've had enough of bloody spine,' Baz said, waving his free hand about. 'Give us being timid any day. Don't fret about y'flaming spine. Write from being timid. Make *that* strong. That's what we conchies used to say, wasn't it? When we *were* conchies – brave enough to be, enough spine. Us frightened womanly types. If only we *had* stuck it out and won. If only we had been – had *believed* in – in your good old timidity. It's timidity saves lots of little animals. And big ones. Most creatures, really. Deer, mice, rabbits, birds. Leopards, probably. Ears and smell, fear – that's the product of timidity. One day us two'll write an article on timidity, we will. A scientific philosophical thing. Science will save the day. Drink to that. Our amazing essay.'

He tossed back his sherry with a flourish. The northern twang was emerging again in his speech; the more emotional he became, the more it emerged.

Joseph looked around him. 'Absolutely everything is legal business here,' he said flatly. 'Absolutely everything.' He was faintly irritated by Baz's counsel: it seemed flippant, not really to do with writing, his own anguished state.

'So?'

'It must distort your view of the world. Doesn't it, distort it? Everything argued out until it dies into a heap of dusty foolscap. Everything crisp and clean, no crisis, no mess—'

'My dear chap, it's *all* crises, in here! Legal business is but the manifestation of crisis – lots of little people's crises! If I, who am in crisis right now at present, were to shoot bloody Hubert bloody Rail dead, that act – that morally defensible act's final manifestation would be as a – a dusty file in Chancery Lane somewhere, or here, right in this chambers, long after – long after we, everyone involved, had all rotted away to nothing. To dust, as a matter of fact. Actually, the thought consoles me,' he added, nursing his glass. He was a bit tipsy, it seemed. 'It really consoles me, Joseph.'

He looked up. 'Get your bricks right, old fellow. Dig 'em out of home earth.' He had tears in his eyes. 'Dig 'em out of your failures.'

They went out for sandwiches and consumed them in the 'Fields', sitting on the square's immaculate lawn. The grass was almost garish, unnaturally bright and green against the dark buildings – and it was very soft, the blades springy, almost decadently soft, with grimy little birds picking at crumbs and legal people scattered all over it in their black gowns, smoking and guffawing. Smoke drifted lazily across the bright sun, cars whirred and honked invisibly all around, the trees threw a mosaic of shadows over everything, and tiny metallic bits flashed.

'This is peace,' said Baz, lying back with his hands behind his head. He kept his eyes open, though. Red-rimmed and still as if in shock. What Joseph thought was a butterfly transformed into a slot of sunlight on Baz's brow.

'It's not right,' said Joseph, 'to call it peace.'

'Well it is, whatever you call it, it is.'

'We've still got it in the bone, the war. It went too deep. It's still in there, right in there, inside. Right in the marrow. Even those who are getting born, now, it's in them, too.'

He threw crumbs for the sparrows: jittery, urban-looking creatures.

'Dandelion-picking,' he added in a murmur, as if to himself.

'Oh, look, it could have been a lot worse. Imagine what they thought in Carthage, after the Romans had flattened it. You know they sprinkled it with salt, just in case? Very thorough, the Romans. Dear old General Scipio, with his fire and hammers. Not a stone left standing. And then heaps of salt, just in case. At least cities weren't flattened in ours, despite the Zeppelins. *Urbs antiqua fuit, Tyrii tenuere coloni, Carthago, Italiam contra—*'

'I prefer,' said Joseph, sitting up on his elbows, 'what comes just before. *Can such great anger live in the hearts of the gods?*'

He waved his hand about, rhetorically. Chalk and pipe tobacco and the smell of camphor on Frankie Robinson's jacket rose in his nose: far-off schooldays, the other side of the war, yet awkwardly close, too close really—

'Good old Virgil,' said Baz, emptily. 'As long as there's Virgil, there's hope.'

'What are you on about, Baz? What's a dead stuffed Roman poet got to do with anything here, now?'

He was crouching, half-turned and crouched, as if to receive a blow with an axe. His friend made a mysterious, snuffling noise.

'Don't shout, old feller.' He was staring with round, bleary eyes through the mask of leaf-shadow on his face. 'Don't shout. I'm liable to fall to pieces.'

'That's your fault for going barmy,' said Joseph, tearing at the trim blades. 'By the way, she said she was sorry. I forgot to say that. Sorry.'

Silence from Baz.

The drift of cigarette smoke, guffaws like soft explosions, the shadow-fretted sunlight, an abandoned newspaper lifting and falling. A heavy pall of legal stuff hung in the air over the square; it made the air thick. Joseph felt dreadful: cut off from it all, a little pointless. The confident, guffawing barristers in their black robes: they belittled him.

'You know,' said Baz, in a high, slightly mad voice, 'I must tell you that it might have been you, after all. It ought to've been, really.'

'What do you mean?'

His nerves anticipated something momentous, while his mind was quite deadened to it.

'I just want to say that – I think Hubert is you really, in her mind. That's the whole trouble, you see. Except that Hubert is better because he's – clean, he hasn't disappointed her.'

'And how did I *disappoint* her, Baz? How am I – unclean, then?'

Baz sat up. He was wringing his hands, it seemed. Joseph's fingers went on picking at the warm, decadent grass, in which match-ends nestled here and there – even here, on this perfect lawn.

'She has a very stout view of life, you see.'

'I see. Does she? For a slim girl.'

'And you rather forced things. I didn't. I simply flirted with her in a gentlemanly manner.'

'I see,' said Joseph.

Baz looked as if he wanted to say more, but could not. They were playing impromptu cricket further off. The ball was an old tennis ball, a dog's plaything, they were hitting it with rolled-up newspapers or perhaps rolled-up documents, priceless vellum documents. Joseph smiled. He wanted to tell Baz about the German woman. The ball rolled towards him over the flat lawn. He stretched rather self-consciously and threw it back. He felt hearty and self-conscious. The ball bounced off a tree: it was a bad throw. The lawyers were contemptuous, he was sure. The whole world was contemptuous of everyone but those the newspapers heralded as our saviours. Utter crooks like Horatio Bottomley, for example. Everyone knew he was a crook, yet he was hailed like a Caesar, his damn newspapers were read by the ton. Everyone else was treated with contempt: it was a real struggle to keep your head above water, above the ocean of implied contempt. A tall thin lawyer bent to the ball and pitched it with a hearty yelp. In that moment, Joseph despised him. He did not know him from Adam, yet he despised him. He could have taken a machine-gun and enfiladed the whole lawn. He enjoyed the sensation of this fury in himself, as he lay there mildly stroking the lawn's warm flank and wondering if Baz was right.

'Well, it's very nice of her,' Joseph said – into Baz's silence, like a knife-thrust – 'to think of us so *morally*. Do you think she drops all her men just so, on a sort of *moral* basis? And picks others up in the same vein? With a prayer on her lips?'

Baz frowned. 'Hubert Rail's hardly moral at all. I believe he takes cocaine. He's a regular cad. He's a painter but I believe he acts, too. Continental cabaret, probably. He'll ruin her.'

There was a pause. Yes, Hubert probably did act. Hubert and Tillie retreated in his mind, dwindled physically to small figures on a far-off stage. He thought how he must go to a play, before he left London. Real stages made people seem larger, not smaller.

'A regular damn cad,' insisted Baz.

'Maybe I should write plays,' Joseph murmured.

'Plays?'

'Maybe a novel isn't right. Maybe what I should be doing is writing a wild, a really madly wild piece for the theatre, about the war. In masks.'

'You'd have to pass the censorship lot.'

'So does a novel.'

'It's a bit late in the day to change now,' Baz said.

'It's never too late, why is it too late?' Although in his heart he had no intention of changing, he was still thrilled by this new notion, and sat up for a moment. 'The novel's finished, as an art form. It's the play that'll count. Folk like to watch things. The novel's finished.'

'You're extrapolating the general from the particular,' said Baz. 'That's a lawyer's game.'

'What do you mean?'

'*Your* novel's finished, that's all. Or you think it is.'

'I do think it is. There's a chap in the novel walking about with a wound in his head, you can see his brain, actually *see* it, and in his brain there are maggots—'

'Impossible.'

'Walter Furdew told me that one. It's fact. It happened. I'm putting it into the novel, I wasn't going to but—'

'He's pulling your leg.'

'I don't think so.'

'Oh,' groaned Baz, 'I'm lovesick, I've got maggots in *my* brain.'

'In the play, one of the characters—'

'Maggots in his brain?' Baz cried, half-laughing.

'Why not?'

'How would you do the maggots?'

Joseph thought about it. 'Pellets of blotting paper, the way we did maggots at school. Anyway, that's the make-up people. That's their business.'

Baz's face was mocking. 'Stick a few dancing-girls in to do the Maggot Waltz or the Brain Shimmy. That'll have them flocking.' Then he leaned forward. 'Nobody needs the truth right now, Jo-Jo. All they want is *The Golden Moth*. That's all they want.' He looked at his fob-watch – an antique touch that somehow depressed Joseph. 'I ought to be running along, you know.' He lay on his back, stretching his arms behind his head. 'Five minutes shut-eye. I didn't sleep last night.'

'Oh God, Baz, it's *such* a bloody battle,' groaned Joseph.

He also lay on his back on the lawn. The grass felt waxy in

the heat, under his shirt. It would be autumn in a month; it was like death coming – the cool wet winds, the endless sour fogs, the winter. He had got precisely nowhere after a huge mental effort over the spring and summer. He had imagined, back in April, finishing the book by the autumn, had almost smelt the autumn fruit-pulp sweetness and the feeling it would give him of completion, of bottling success and achievement in the still-room of his mind. Now he felt a crumbling sense of nullity. He almost felt old, but not wise with it. Degraded, too. The love matter – Tillie, and the German woman – these crumbled likewise as he considered them. Must he always be disappointed? Must England always disappoint him? It did seem bound up with England, his disappointment – even the German woman, she too seemed bound up with England, the way he was considering her, the way he had converted her to debris, a crumble of soil in an envelope.

He heard light snoring and saw that Baz had nodded off. The ball-playing lawyers were taking a breather, leaving their ball under a tree. As he watched, the sunlight flickered uncertainly and dipped behind a white ceiling of fog-like cloud, the whole square darkening as if someone had drawn a curtain, growing remote and somehow chill. Joseph shivered, even. And it was at this precise moment that he recognised how all he had was his writing: take that away and his soul's house would fall down. The sole illusion to be broken was that it might ever be easy.

Baz had stirred. He was looking up at the leaves, as if considering something. He scratched the back of his neck and sighed.

'Well, and then there was the *Fräulein*,' he said. 'Where Tillie was concerned.'

'What *Fräulein*?'

'The one who came up to us at the station.'

'What? Which station?'

'Wipers.'

Joseph found himself staring with a stupid look.

'Baz, what are you on about?'

'The *Fräulein*. Your *Fräulein*. She came up to us at the station, heard us talking English I suppose.'

'And?'

Baz was being oddly brutal – callous, almost, a lawyer's dogged callousness.

'This *Fräulein*, she said how you had been just too marvellous. Those very words, I record them precisely.' His finger was up, making the point to the jury. 'Just too marvellous.'

Baz rose onto one elbow; his eyes glittered – a real touch of malevolence, there.

'What on earth are you on about, Baz?'

'Your conquest.'

'What?'

He felt disgust rising in his mouth. A man walked between them holding a gramophone under his arm. Baz leaned forward, his glasses turning opaque in the fall of sunlight, flashing and opaque, concealing the glittering look.

'"Just too marvellous", she said. With her hand on my arm. Then she walked away. The one you met in the cemetery. Something about the weather, of course, very polite – and then she walked away.'

'Why did she say that? Is that all she said? Was she looking for me?'

'Oh, I don't think so. She seemed rather exhausted. The bells were ringing. And the station, you know – she had to shout. Actually, to be honest, she shouted it.'

'How did you know she was German? She doesn't even sound German.'

'I recognised her from the cemetery. I don't forget a face, you know. Not for a few days, anyway. Looked just like a paper doll, I thought. Not uncharming.'

Very callous and brutal, in his lawyer's way.

'And what did Tillie – how did she – did she say anything about it, after?'

'She's not platonic, you know.' He faintly quivered with embarrassment, did Baz. 'I mean, she picked up quite clearly what the *Fräulein* was on about. Once we'd decided she wasn't dotty.'

'Well, what *was* she on about?' Joseph asked, with heat.

His blush deepened. His hand on the grass – it was also on the smooth belly of the woman, moving slowly towards the thatch of her groin. He might almost have gasped at the private audacity of it. Ah, he could not bear the fact that Tillie knew.

'Oh, my dear fellow,' said Baz, apologetically smirking, 'we are all broken wands, now.'

'It was not sexual,' snapped Joseph. 'Why should it be sexual? That's dirty minds working, that is.'

'Come on, Jo-Jo,' said Baz. He was shaking his head, mocking.

'We made the rain come, that's what she meant by *marvellous*.'

'Danced for it, did you?'

'Seriously, Baz, we were working on the invisible. I do believe in the invisible . . .'

Joseph was speaking very quietly and rather hopelessly now, into the grass.

'I'm afraid it hadn't rained by then,' Baz scoffed. 'There was that Icelandic north-westerly, of course—'

'Exactly. It was cool, and then it rained a week or so later. It rained an awful lot, too. It broke just at the right time. She knew it would. And with it, you see, comes the new era of love and peace and – so forth. Goodness. Plain goodness.'

'Well, it sounds ominously like the sermon at Harvest Festival,' Baz joked, stretching out again on the grass with his hands behind his head. The sun caught the stubble neglected on his upper lip. 'The harvest completely dashed, rain dripping off the stalks, and yet you're supposed to give thanks.'

Joseph said nothing. He knew it was hopeless, explaining to Baz. He might as well have Frank Pitts in front of him, for all he was getting anywhere. Baz and Frank Pitts might as well be the same person, for all he would ever get anywhere, explaining what had happened, and what might yet come of it.

35

Doubles

JOSEPH LEFT BAZ in a kind of sullen daze and made straight for the Café Royal. It was, anyway, very close to his lodgings. On emerging into Holborn he all but collided with Baz's clerk, who was returning on roller skates. It was very incongruous, the sight of this mawkish, ill-looking fellow in the act of roller-skating. The man wiped his nose on a large white handkerchief and apologised.

'But it is so convenient,' he said.

'I'm sure. Well—'

'If I could, I would skate all the way from home. But it's a bit far, Chertsey.'

The clerk's face took on a distorted, tragic look – but a chortle came out of it. Positively squeezed out of the gruesome face, with its highwayman's mask of dark ill-health around the eyes.

'Chertsey?'

'Yes. Do you know it, sir?'

'I was there the other day.'

He was promptly expectant, and the clerk flattered by this interest – in his mournful way.

'Not many people go to Chertsey,' he said. 'The meadows are very beautiful – the ruins of a once-great abbey stand there, you know. It makes you think of that line in Shakespeare, what is it, I can never remember lines—'

'Do you know someone in Chertsey by the name of Pitts, Frank Pitts?' Joseph interrupted. Passers-by jostled them, omnibuses roared. The two were straining to hear each other.

The man frowned. 'No, I'm afraid I do not. Mind, I keep myself to myself. I don't know many people.'

Fumes from a wheezing coal lorry enveloped them as they spoke and the clerk coughed, wiping his lips with his handkerchief.

'Our Master Beardow, he is very unhappy this morning. Snapped at me twice. I fear he has had a blow.' He glanced at Joseph rather hopefully.

'*O tell her*,' recited Joseph in a laconic drone, with his hand on his breast, '*brief is life but love is long, And brief the sun of Summer in the North*.'

The clerk nodded slowly. His eyes gleamed from their dark hollows. He kept himself very steady on his skates and bared his head, as at a graveside.

'Well, it is the lot of all of us to be unhappy, sir. At least once.'

Joseph made his way to Regent Street. He wondered how the German woman had looked when she had spoken to Baz and Tillie. Very indiscreet, it all felt. Clearly she had been looking for him. It had all spilled over and messed everything. Everything. He felt very sore about it, really.

The Café, spread uxoriously along the curve by Air Street, always struck Joseph as intimidating, and this irritated him. It was London's one bohemian hang-out that was not seedy. It was, of course, expensive. He had no doubt that he was to meet Hubert Rail at some point in the day, or night – he fancied the fellow could be sent for by minions, as happened in shilling shockers. The money would not be wasted, he thought, perusing the luncheon bar's frightening prices. He would have a coffee in the Domino Room and sit it out: this was the nub of his plot. Where all the art crowd went, the Domino Room. Mr Eliot might be there – his poems were all the rage, very modern – and Joseph felt nervous again. How could he sit it out with a coffee for hours, if the likes of Mr Eliot were there? Royalty, too. And then he never recognised anybody, even the very famous. It was at times like this that he felt about fifteen, not twenty-three.

He wished he had a book. His clothes were rumpled, the tear in his flannels had been stitched that morning but it still showed; it was like a tell-tale scar. The types going in and coming out were not the dishevelled bohemian types, they were smart, the type that eye doors at parties and sport motor-veils. Shallow types, but not shabby, not at all shabby. Brilliant, clever talk but very shallow. Sleek. Only one was eccentric, got up as a corsair and apparently sporting red boxing gloves. Probably French. He did look terribly silly, coming out into the drab London crowd. Fancy dress, in the end.

He entered on a deep breath and made his way to the Domino Room. A waiter nodded and smiled over the tables in an over-friendly manner and he wondered if he was being mocked, if his nervousness was like a placard saying LAUGH AT ME. He was very stiff and awkward, very self-conscious, working his way between the laughing, chattering tables to the Domino Room, a piano tinkling like a sing-song gossip under it all. Eyes caught him and he saw mockery in them, while the lips continued to move over other matters. It was quite a dead time, between lunch and tea, yet there were still more folk than he had anticipated. Except in the Domino Room. This had the air of biding its time, waiting for the onslaught later in the day.

He sat down at a marble-topped table, feeling under his hands the red plush of the velvet seat. There was a group of three murmuring in the corner, conspiratorial they looked, smoking and glancing at themselves in the mirrors. They were elegant types, the two men and the woman. They seemed infinitely older than him, and taller, yet they were young. He felt like a little boy, and this infuriated him. They might be very well known, he thought: although he was indifferent to coteries, it frustrated him not to know who was who.

He was glad of the dimness in the room, and the quiet. The piano had been playing what sounded like a harsh jazz version of 'Old Mother Reilly'; in here, though, it and the chatter were a muted hum. The waiter came up, the same waiter who had thrown him the over-familiar, mocking smile: a youngish, stooping fellow, with the look of a heron. To Joseph's great surprise, the waiter's hand stole surreptitiously onto his left shoulder, then down his back. The hand rubbed Joseph's back in small circles. He could not speak, though his mouth was stuck open.

'Hallo, beauty,' murmured the waiter, his eyes roaming over the room, not looking at Joseph at all. Above the eyes hung a pair of thin, painted eyebrows dancing against the smooth skin, its smooth polish like wet soap.

It had never once occurred to Joseph that Tillie's confusion in Sandwich Street might be repeated in the Café Royal. This oversight struck him in later years as astonishing, a kind of grotesque feebleness in him. What was not feeble, not feeble at all, was the nimbleness with which he faced the discovery. All he had to do was shut his gaping mouth and remain passive.

'Hallo,' said Joseph.

The hand left him. Their eyes met. The waiter's head was cocked to one side on a rubbery neck, his smile crooked.

'You're very quiet today,' the waiter said, in a soft, tender tone. 'Early, too. What have you been up to, you in your awful suit?'

Joseph smiled, vaguely. It could have meant anything, that smile. A terrible feeling was coming over him, poured over him like treacle; he wasn't *playing* Hubert, he was *being* Hubert. It took no effort at all. To be a queen – an ambidextrous queen, at that – required no effort at all.

'Oh, rolling about in the hay,' he said.

'What fun. With your nice little bird, was it?'

Joseph found himself nodding, though he was repelled.

'Can I have the next turn?' murmured the waiter, his pencil poised over the notepad, the serviette dangling clean and crisp from his forearm. But his eyes were suspicious, his pencilled brows puckered in. He had a cadaverous face, but polished, very clean. This waiterly intimacy was very strange.

'You know I'm playing rugby tomorrow,' he said, unexpectedly.

'Are you?' Joseph was genuinely shocked.

'So surprised?'

'Frankly, yes.'

He kept the smile flickering, studying the menu. Hubert would not study the menu, he thought. He put it down.

'Well, I am not all I seem,' said the waiter.

'Ah, *c'est ça*,' replied Joseph, automatically.

'Over at Camberwell, we're playing, if you want to give me a cheer.'

'You must be joking,' said Joseph, 'I would rather watch a bear scratching his bottom.'

He felt curiously evanescent, free to say whatever he wanted.

The shallow, witty self had grown his hands, and they were fluttering about ineffectually. It was glorious, being Hubert. It reminded him of the time he had played Mistress Quickly at school, with whalebone stays and absurd breasts stuffed with cushions. He had found something wonderful in the absurd game of being a woman. His very heart had changed.

'Quite!' the waiter shot out, a touch ironically. 'I'll say!'

'Just a coffee,' Joseph said.

The waiter did not move, did not scribble anything down. He was looking hard at Joseph, the pale brow clouding.

'Have you been nibbling on the white stuff?' he murmured. 'Naughty wretch.'

'Oh, just a little.'

'You'll feel better soon. You're not quite yourself, Hubie.' And he walked off, in his heron-like way, leaving Joseph with a feeling of hurt. It was a few minutes before Hubert crept out of him, and even then there were traces left, little green puddles in his soul.

'Have you seen *The Golden Moth*?' he asked the waiter, when the coffee was brought. 'On at the Adelphi.'

'No. And I won't.'

'Why not?'

'I loathe dancing-girls who show their midriffs,' he replied, screwing up his face demonstratively.

Joseph shrugged. No, Hubert would never shrug. He realised then that it was Hubert who had played the waiter last time, in Cornwall. He wished he could play this game every day. It felt like being let out of prison for a few hours. The waiter went off, suddenly busy. Maybe Hubert had slept with this fellow. Maybe Hubert really was a regular bugger as well as a skirt-chaser. Desire spilling over like boiling milk into both camps. It appalled and fascinated Joseph, thinking especially of Tillie; yet he stirred his coffee coolly, the others glancing at him now and again as if in admiration. He felt very strong and unique, sitting there as Hubert Rail. The world had shifted slightly and revealed new landscapes: not even sexual ones, more metaphysical. London spread through the window like a glittering shop window of treats. He was no longer scared by it, or bored. It hung there for his delectation. And a further barrier dropped – he felt it removed like a shadow, as when the shop's shutters had come off in Matlock each morning, when he was helping inside: nothing must be made an end in itself, or it is dead. Nothing is an end in itself.

He repeated this in a murmur, like a mantra. *Nothing is an end in itself.* Yet once the initial lightning bolt had flashed, the meaning became obscure again, just out of reach. He felt it had more meaning, more final meaning, than he was giving it. Hubert would have been able to explain it. Then he grinned over his coffee, the steam caressing his lips, when he saw how he was making the phrase itself an end in itself. He thought: there's nothing that's an end in itself, when you think about it. Not in nature. Only machinery – no, not even machinery. Even the war had obeyed his new law, though the damn politicians had treated the war as an end in itself – the end being victory, as if victory mattered more than human lives! And where had victory got them? And as for defeat – not even political revolution in Germany. That, too, had been squashed.

The others were looking at him – one or two more had come in, rather dull-looking shingle-headed girls, sugary somehow, and very thin. He grinned and murmured to himself, as you were expected to do in such a place. The knife-edge between genius and madness. One of the girls was giving him a wave, crooking her fingers and wobbling her invisible hips. She had a big nose and painted rosebud lips.

'Hallo, Hubie! I didn't see it was you!'

He waved back, coolly, from the other side of a meditative glass. She respected it, and turned away with a curious ripple in her body. Hubert seemed to have immense power. Very quickly, in a matter of weeks, gaining by his newness like a new jazz dance. It was because he was free, Joseph recognised. He had recognised that freedom even in Cornwall: the disdain, that business about the senselessness of the world, that cool, embittered superiority that might heat at any moment into wit and laughter. The charm. That was what he found himself covered with: charm. Yet it was all being thrown at him by others. He simply had to sit and not think beyond the next moment.

He imagined, very clearly, as if he had done it already, picking the girl up by the seat, his arms wrapped around the upper thighs, and hearing her squeal. She was so light. He found himself rising from his chair, heart thudding but helpless to stop himself, and going over to the girl. There were two girls, one with a glossy curl at each cheek. He stood there, playing at being Hubert, staring at them pensively. They giggled and told him that he had the worst clothes ever. He frowned, pretending to be cross. It all seemed to flow logically and senselessly at the same time. They asked him why he looked ill, each saying half a sentence like a double act in a music-hall. He said nothing, just stood there looking at each of them in turn with a light smile playing on his lips. Then he bent down and pulled the large-nosed girl out of her chair, light as gossamer she was, pulling her by the wrists. She had a strapless silky dress on, like Tillie's the previous night, sexless and yet arousing, shocking even in comparison to the girls of his boyhood – and she squealed, and he picked her up easily by wrapping his arms around her thighs and lifting, lifting her up.

Everyone laughed as he carried her around the Domino Room. 'Hubert! Hubert! You nasty rotter!' she cried, unconvincingly, gripping his furred scalp. She knew, really, that this was an event she would recall as an old woman, the madcap days after the war – oh, he was giving her a sweet moment of recollection, dancing about with her, his cheek against the hot fork of her legs, feeling the bump of her underthings through the corrugated red silk, the faint ammoniac smell of her.

He plonked her back in the chair and the group in the corner clapped, then turned and chatted on as if this was not a terribly special event: very cool about it, they were, almost superior, with their cigarettes in ivory holders, their long-fingered hands. He felt very wild, wilder than them, wilder potentially than anyone not certified insane. He was panting rather wheezily, though. The girl was snorting and giggling into her hand, her friend grinning with a cigarette smoking in her mouth, like a worker.

'Hubert, you are too much.' Then she was adjusting her dress. 'You hurt me, you know.'

He had an urge to go further, to lift her dress up and bury his face in her bony thighs, guzzling her there. He very nearly did this, but something stopped him. He stood there poised for several long moments, right on the edge of doing this dreadful, very wild thing, panting inside himself from carrying her about, his heart going very fast, but saw the worried shadow on her face, her recognition of his strength and power over her. That recognition shrunk him inside.

He kissed her ceremoniously on the knuckles, very gallant, and the other girl, too, whose hand was like cold meat and heavy with rings, and went back to his table. He had not said a word throughout. He was trembling, now. Whether from the thrill of it or from fear he could not say.

The waiter had come back, was serving the girls tea. The three of them glanced at him and laughed indulgently. The waiter came over.

'You know the charge for carrying off women, you Hun?' he said.

'New Hun or old Hun?'

'Oh, they're both the same, my dear.'

Joseph paid, not liking the waiter any more.

'You *are* being unfriendly, Mr Rail,' was all the waiter said, pocketing the shillings – and appeared to recoil a little as Joseph left, brushing past with a nod. The girls waved goodbye. He touched his hat, that was all.

The Café flowed past him with its chatter and plush and tables and he emerged into daylight, blinking as if he had just woken up. A smell of Condy's Fluid from a bucket and the swabbed pavement by the door failed to hide a sourness of sick. The other side of drink, he thought, the shabby side of the stage set. He walked away quickly, as if at any minute he might meet the real Hubert. He did not want that now: he did not need Hubert or his damn sketches.

When he considered Tillie, he was confronted by a sombre set of shadows. It bewildered him: he could not decide whether she knew of Hubert's openly ambidextrous nature. And then he thought: yes, she does know, but she has fallen violently in love with him. It is her wish to save him. And it thrills her, slightly. It might have thrilled her to know that I had monkeyed with a woman so soon after our kiss, he considered – but it did not. Or maybe Baz made sure it did not. Maybe there was a betrayal, there.

Really, he was bewildered. These were scraps he was throwing at the fog. He had no idea, not really. She was too curious. Perhaps everyone but him was a curious creature: hybrids, shiftless in their depths. He passed a billboard with *Jesus Saves* emblazoned upon it: someone had added *To Buy Anthracite*. That was about it. He had very much returned to his own earth-bound self.

He flushed suddenly, halfway down Clarges Street, when he

thought of his behaviour in the Café. He felt no pride in it at all. He just grilled to the tips of his ears, wanting to hide behind his hands. And then he realised how feeble and slow he had been: he might have deliberately ruined Hubert with some outrageous act in his name; lifting the girl's dress and guzzling under it, that would have been a start! He might have really smashed Hubert's name for good, if he had had his wits about him. If he had plotted his moves properly and stayed cool.

36

Returns

H E HAD TO leave London early – he was desperate to leave. He woke up the next morning with a wild energy that compelled him to return to the cottage, to the thin-lined foolscap. As for Tillie, she had somehow passed beyond him; also, he did not like the idea of Hubert and this phantom fortune business. The man would know soon enough about his visit to Tillie's and then the Café Royal, and would react. It was this reaction that Joseph half-feared. He imagined, in clinical detail, Hubert breaking into the room and killing him with a gun, in his senselessly logical way, and then pretending to be Joseph Monrow – for the sake of the phantom fortune. His mind was cluttered with such tuppenny serial stuff; it bothered him immensely, because it interfered with his own imaginary task, which was of a much higher order, oh very much higher.

The landlady made him pay to the end of the week, pleading regulations of the house and her lonely single state: it nagged at him all the way back – or at least until the last red villa had been swept away and the fields and trees took over. He read a few pages of Thomas Love Peacock, his mind bouncing off the words without effect. He had the fidgets. He would have preferred an Erskine Childers – a good mystery yarn, anyway. Could *he* write a Childers-type yarn, if he wanted to? Probably not. Could he write a novel at all? He smiled to himself, watching the smoke whip past the window as the train clattered round a bend. Probably not. It was not like building a bridge – not everyone thought they could build a bridge as everyone thought they could write a novel. But deep down he felt it was his destiny, this writing business. He felt eager and strong.

' . . . as by thy special grace, preventing us, thou dost put into our mindes good desires . . .'

His lips were moving with it, though it was in his father's voice. A good desire, this novel. The train rocked past the hedges and woods, lulling him into somnolence.

He was very glad, however, to arrive at the little country station, with its scent of trees and hay. It really felt as if he had been away years. It was squally weather, a first hint that summer would not last, and the huge beeches swayed and rustled, losing leaves; the storms had revived them, but not thoroughly. Autumn was still precocious in its colouring, and the lanes had their fair share of leaf-drift. The air was so sweet he sucked it down through his open mouth.

He washed his face under the squeaky pump in front of the pub. Mrs Hamilton's daughter was sweeping the front step and they talked for a few minutes very pleasantly. He would offer the Scott to her mother this evening, he decided. He was eager to get to the cottage, which seemed to house his energy in some way. He strode down the lane and saw the huge elm on the corner, the mossy hump of thatch beyond the open gates of the drive, the upper windows, the skewwhiff porch – oh, a great love for it all, he felt. He fairly bounced up to the door, whistling 'Old Mother Reilly' – only remembering that it was bolted at the last moment.

He went round to the back, to the kitchen window hung over artfully by tendrils of honeysuckle. Oddly, it was already open quite a few inches. The wind, he thought. He pulled it open wider and climbed in, placing his feet carefully between the geranium pots, laughing to himself about this whole performance. There was an odd, sweetish smell that was unfamiliar. His eyes accustomed themselves to the light and then his heart near came to a standstill: even when he saw who it was, sitting there at the kitchen table, he could not quite believe that it was not a figment. He must have looked suitably impressed, though; he just stood there, blinking like a dolt. The scrape of a chair brought him to his senses. She had risen from the chair and was smiling at him, her hazel eyes looking back at him and smiling. There was a long pause – really only a matter of seconds.

'You did not expect me.'

'No,' he managed.

'I wrote to you—'

'But there was only a – a bit of earth.'

'That was in case you had forgotten me, that time. I wrote to you as well.'

Something stirred violently in his guts, like ferrets in a sack.

'I never got it.'

'Well, the card was never posted.'

'Ah, I see. How did you get in?'

'As you did. The window was wide open. Do you mind?'

He shrugged. He did, really. He had not left it open like that.

'How very glad you are to see me,' she said, brightly.

'I'm sorry. Hallo. Would you like a cup of tea?'

She nodded. During this time neither of them had moved. He put down his bag and made himself busy at the range, which was not lit. Nothing was where he had left it. He was giddy with shock, almost nauseous with it. This was really quite dreadful. His lungs felt as if they were tiny; he had to sigh to catch the air.

'You've been here – you didn't come today?'

'I arrived here yesterday. I decided to wait.'

'You slept here?'

Her eyes rolled upwards. 'Up there,' she said, 'there is a most comfortable bed.'

It was bewildering. She was so calm and self-possessed. He felt a brief surge of passion, then it was tidied up somehow, while he was making tea. She was polite enough not to make tea for him, at least, in his own house. Stouter than he remembered – perhaps because she was wearing a thinner dress, a rather loose lemon-yellow one, which exposed her stoutness. The same ineffectual face, as if it might pale into mist: but not plain, either. It was as though the face had been beautiful until a certain definite moment, when a hand had foxed it.

'How did you know where I lived?' he asked, poking at the fire in the range, with a pretence of normality. Look, this is my life in England, everything seemed to be saying. He was very self-conscious about the least action. 'Did you go to the hotel?'

'Yes. You had just left. They didn't know where. I copied your name and address. J.T. Monrow.'

'Yes. J for Joseph, T for Taylor. Family name, Taylor.'

'Joseph. Not Joe?'

'No, never. My mother thought it common.'

The kettle whistled. He poured the boiling water into the teapot. He took several moments to find the lid and almost dropped it.

'Have you eaten?' he asked, having to clear his throat to ask it.

'Dry sausage,' she said, with a low chuckle. 'It lasts for a long time. In Germany there is not much else to eat.'

'Really?'

She shrugged.

'You came all the way from Germany?'

'I got a lift back to my home from a charmingly stupid colonel, in his car. Then after a month I caught the train and the boat. I sold my house. I had always wished to see England. London – it is very thrilling to see London, you know. The Houses of Parliament, Madame Tussaud's, the Strand.'

'Is that why you came to England, to see the sights?'

'Oh no, I came to see you.'

He felt a surge of panic.

'I see,' he said, very dry-mouthed. 'Why, exactly?'

'Why?'

'Yes.'

She studied him carefully.

'I had to. Now I am here but you don't like it. You haven't even kissed me.'

He smiled, but his eyes were panicked. This is mad, he thought. Really dreadful. It was like finding you had a wife, a stolid weight of wife.

'Are you going to kiss me?'

'Nay, not yet,' he said. 'The tea's settling.'

'Is it all over with us?'

'I'm making the tea.'

He forced himself to kiss her, after a stiff silence – setting a cup in front of her then bending down stiffly and setting his lips against her neck, then her mouth. It disgusted him, her dry mouth. She was not the same woman. Years had passed, it seemed. Her eyes were closed as he kissed her. His were open behind the oval spectacles, which he should have removed. He had not the faintest idea what to do. Her hand held his neck lightly but firmly. Her mouth tasted of plums. There were plums, he then noticed, on the table, in a cracked bowl.

'Have your cup of tea,' he said, when he had done kissing her. He poured it out. 'Did anyone see you, in the village?'

She shrugged again. This maddened him. He sat down with his tea, turning the chair sideways on, facing her on the same side of the table. He had to be strong.

'Why are you here?' he asked.

'You're looking after me very well. Please take a plum. They had dropped off your tree.'

She laughed lightly and pushed the bowl towards him. He took a plum and ate it as she watched him; the fruit all but burst as he bit it, and he had to wipe his chin without making a face. He felt a fool. He went to the cupboard and unearthed the tin of biscuits. At least the unhinged fellow had not been in. That was something.

'Thank you,' she said, taking one. He was irritated by the chomping sound it made in her mouth. She looked at him steadily, still watching him, and took small sips as she chewed – a habit, Joseph remembered, his mother had particularly frowned upon. He drank his tea.

'You don't want me?' she said, simply.

'It's all rather – a surprise.'

'A nice surprise?'

'There are nice aspects to it.'

'And nasty, too?'

'Look, I know – I don't know what to think. I've got to get on with my novel,' he added, feebly. 'My work. I've got to concentrate on that.'

It sounded preposterous. He was annoyed that he could not feel passion for her, even the simplest physical desire. The very faintest pulse of general desire, yes, but of a boyish order. He would fondle her breasts and expend himself in her and then want nothing more. There was no soul anywhere, no love. The thought even shamed him, that he might consider making love to her again. She was nodding slowly, rubbing her hand over the bare boards of the table.

'Watch the splinters,' he said.

Her hand stopped and she turned it over, as if expecting to see splinters in her palm. 'Yes, it is very difficult to be happy,' she murmured.

This maddened him, too; there was accusation in it – as if the power of love – but how could he possibly enter into a contract like that? She held her head in her hands. It struck him only then that she had made a long journey and that this automatically obliged him in some way. He wondered why she was out of mourning: it struck him as ominous.

'You met my friends at the station.'

She looked up, puzzled.

'The next day. In Ypres. Why did you do that? Why?' he pressed. It was like pressing on a tender bruise. 'Why did you go up to them then, at the station?'

'I expected to see you there, of course,' she said.

He nodded. Of course it was quite obvious, the way she put it. 'You went to the station deliberately?'

'For you, yes. The hotel told me the time of your train. But you didn't return with the others.'

'No. I went to the Somme.'

'It was cool, the next day. Did you notice? And then the rains came. Like it used to come in Calcutta. Did you notice that?'

'I did. They came a week later, though.'

He swallowed his tea and stood up. He stood leaning on the table, on the tips of his spread fingers

'Why did you say that, to my friends – that I was "just too marvellous"? What were you trying to – to say, really?'

She looked almost dismayed.

'Did I say that?'

'Yes. "Just too marvellous." As if you were saying that about the sexual part. I'm sorry, but that's what they must have thought. I mean, what it must have sounded like, it's not that they've got dirty minds. Anybody would come to that conclusion, if you ask me. You have to be careful when it's not your language, you know. Did you know that, when you said it?'

'The sexual part?'

'That's what it must have sounded like, when you said I was

341

"marvellous". It's called insinuating. Did you know what you were saying?'

'Oh, you English. I think – I was being metaphysical.'

And she looked off vaguely, towards the window. 'I wanted you to know, Joseph. How marvellous you were, metaphysically.'

'And the sexual part, that was metaphysical, too, was it?' He *would* keep on, he could not stop himself. Beads of sweat were tickling his nose.

She did not turn to him, she kept looking out at the garden, rather blindly. 'Oh, the sexual part – yes, if you want. They were your friends, the tall boy and the pretty girl. But no matter. If it has upset you to know it—'

It was she who seemed upset, her voice deep and rather broken. Her eyes were wet, she had to blow her nose. There was a silence of a minute or so, in which she kept fumbling at her face with the handkerchief.

'I'm sorry,' he said, placing his hand on her back. 'I'm sorry. I'm a proper pig, sometimes.' Then he paced once around the kitchen, thinking.

'I am sorry, truly. Look, would you like to go for a walk? If we meet someone, I think it best to say you're my aunt from India. Don't say you're German. You don't sound very like a German, anyway.'

She laughed shakily at that, through wet eyes. She looked much younger, laughing.

She slid her arm into the crook of his elbow while they were walking down the rough drive. It was good to be out of doors. She was imagining, aloud, the fine carriages that must have rolled up here; he told her about the last occupant who had died of influenza, his friend's grandfather – a recluse, his body not discovered for two weeks. He told her about the owl, too – and they climbed the broken steps and peeped in gingerly, but it had gone. He suddenly felt rather blindly happy, showing her around, feeling her weight on his arm. He could not think beyond this moment. The long grass behind the manor had burst its seed and looked rank. He explained in a matter-of-fact voice that these were once stepped lawns descending to a lake, but the lake had long filled up and was covered with trees – where the silver birch were, he pointed out, a light green cloud of birch among the dark oak. It seemed to both of them a symbol, this rankness – of decline, obviously, though neither of them ventured to say the word outright. He felt easy with her: her intelligence shone through. Not saying the word 'decline', for instance; it would have been vulgar and obvious to say it. The sheer oddity of walking with her, the German woman, through the manor's rank grounds faded in his mind. Neither of them commented on the oddity of it; they were dislodged from the normal run of time. It was exactly as it had been on the salient, only with trees and hills and daylight. Her touch had again crept over him – there was something restoring about it. Yes, he definitely felt straightened, in her presence.

He wondered, as they sat for a while in silence in the gazebo, under its mat of heavy, blown briar-rose, if this was love – if he was partially in love with her in a deep way, in a way quite different from his other love that was hooked by a scar. Looking at her sideways, at her rather blurred profile, he felt no pull towards her physically. Yet he was very glad she was here. The trees whispered rather sombrely in the gusts: there might be a storm, he thought.

'Can I ask – this seems ridiculous – I presume I'm allowed to know your name, now?'

She smiled, continuing to gaze out. Old man's beard, twined among the loops of the rose, dropped little fluffs on her lap now and again. She twirled the plumes in her fingers.

'Marda,' she said.

'Marda.'

'Yes.'

'A very nice name. Is it German?'

'Does it matter?'

'No. It might be Indian, that's all.'

'Possibly. My father was *almost* a Parsee. One can say, anyway, that he preferred the teachings of Zoroaster to those of Jesus.'

'My friends called you the *Fräulein*.'

'I am flattered. Or maybe they believed I was a dried-up fig of a governess.'

She let the seed go and it floated off. The gusts were quite cool but the air was thick. There were midges about.

'Seasonable weather,' she said. And then laughed.

'Why are you laughing?'

'I never knew what it meant. English people said it all the

343

time, in India, but I never understood what it meant. *Seasonable* weather.'

'It means the weather is right for the season,' he told her.

'Oh, I know *now*,' she said, laughing at him, 'but I didn't know *then*. It sounded like the opposite.'

He could see her, suddenly, as a little girl in India, perplexed among the pith helmets and the *dhobi* baskets. He put his arm around her. She smelt of violets, she had traces of violet powder on her bare neck above the loose lemon-coloured dress. She leaned against him. He felt very complete, even though part of him, deep down and primitive, was faintly repelled by her physical presence. There were very fine lines of age around her eyes and mouth, but these struck him as rather beautiful. It was more the slackness in her neck which repelled him, the heavy leadenness of her body. Her tired, ineffectual face. It was worn quite out, that was the trouble. Maybe, he thought, it will bloom again, given the right touch. But even as he mused he felt a faint disgust: the thick violet scent, the dryness of her hair against his chin, the way she was throwing herself on him. Another son at her side!

And then suddenly he knew why she had come and he flinched, his whole face burning in panic. She felt it, and pulled herself away. Quite rattled, he was.

'Have you a cramp?'

'No, I'm sorry. Listen – why exactly did you come?'

'Here?'

'Yes. I think I know why, you see. I'd rather you told me right now. I must know, now.'

'*Why* do you think I have come?'

She said this, in her odd sing-song way, as if he might genuinely enlighten her.

'I think—' He rubbed his thighs madly, very nervous.

'What is the matter?'

'Look, you waited a month, then you came.' He was not sure about the timing of it, suddenly: on certain female matters he felt very ignorant.

'So?'

'Why did you wait a month?'

'I must sell my house.'

'Was that all?'

'Yes,' she laughed. 'Why? Did you want me to come straight-away?'

'Well, you wouldn't have known then, would you?'

'Known?'

He half-looked at her, keeping his eyes down. He felt absurdly embarrassed and ignorant. 'That you were in the family way,' he said, catching the voice of his mother in it, a certain puritan twang. He clutched his knees, his neck gripping itself.

She appeared perplexed. 'You are like Tristan in the *Walküre*,' she said. 'In a very poor performance I once saw, when the fellow's trousers were too tight for him.'

He shook himself out of his crouch and got up and walked about in the long rank grass, his arms tightly folded. She frowned, perplexed.

'What do you mean, "family way?"' she asked. 'Having a baby inside? Is that it?'

He was relieved. 'Yes yes,' he said, rather madly. 'That's it!'

She threw her head back and laughed.

'Oh, my boy,' she cried. 'Oh, my dear sweet boy!'

He was alarmed. The old gazebo rocked as she laughed on its rusted bench, and clouds of old man's beard flew in a little blizzard. The wrecked grounds took her high laughter and deadened it. A faint echo off the blank walls of the manor house behind – it made him glance over his shoulder at its blank and shuttered face.

'What's funny?' he said.

She stopped laughing and wiped her eyes on her wrist.

'My boy,' she said, 'dear Joseph, excuse me, it is so funny.'

'What is?'

'It is very late to be worrying about that,' she said, looking up at him.

He felt ashamed.

'We had gone upstairs to change,' she said, half to herself. 'It was about six o'clock. The man came with the army telegram and the maid gave it to my husband. I was in my little dressing room. I heard a cry and a thump from the bedroom. My husband was lying on the floor. The news had killed him, he was not in a dead faint. Of course immediately I took the telegram out of his hand and read it and something – tightened too much inside me. Apparently I didn't cry. I was just ill. For quite a while, stupid and ill. I have never quite got better, inside. That's why I laughed so much—'

'You're barren,' said Joseph, quickly, almost like an order.

She lifted her face towards him.

'It's a horrible – abyss. All the time, just under me.'

'Yes. It must be.'

He felt very young, as if his age was a reproach.

'So,' he said, 'I caught a cold.'

'Have you?' She looked concerned.

'It's an expression. It means I've been an awful chump.'

'I see.'

'So?'

'So – what?'

'Why *did* you come, all this way? You came a long way to see me.'

'Do you hope that I am going to turn – go back?'

Joseph tousled his hair in anxiety, though it was rather too short for that.

'Very difficult,' he said, 'it's all very difficult.'

'Anyway, I am probably going to kill myself.'

'Oh no, don't do that. Why do you want to do that?'

'Oh, because there is nothing to live for. Nothing but this – abyss.'

She said the word hurriedly, as if she was pulling away from the edge, as if saying it might drag her down with its vertigo. He felt numb. The air was a little chill and wet, rather depressing. The sun came in and out across the manor's rough front, its tufts of grass in the walls making peculiar shadows.

'Is it because of me?'

'No, you cannot blame yourself.'

'You're no longer in mourning?'

Over the lemon dress was thrown a large blue shawl: he was glancing at it. She pulled it tighter.

'I have decided not to be,' she said. 'Like a sick man decides to walk around the garden to feel better, though he is too weak to do so. But if he does, he feels better.'

'Why isn't there anything to live for, then?'

'When you're in mourning you don't think of anything but the past. Now I'm thinking of the future.'

'And there's nothing in the future but this abyss?'

'Nothing.'

She gave a little laugh.

'Oh, there'll be *something*. There'll be life and death and misery and *ein Hauch von Frühling* – a bit of love, a bit of joy. There'll be the usual things, only maybe a bit worse.'

'Did you come all this way just to tell me that you want to kill yourself?'

'I didn't know until you walked into the room and saw me.'

'Then it's all my doing,' he said, his body shuddering a little.

'I made no predictions,' she said, a little awkwardly. 'Don't blame yourself. I just came.'

Joseph walked away a little, into the long grass. He felt like being very good, saintly even. He felt this very strong desire to overwhelm her with his goodness. He felt Tillie watching him, equally overwhelmed by his goodness. Meanwhile, Marda was leaning with her head on the side of the gazebo, half-hidden from his view by the loops of old man's beard. He would surprise them both with the maturity of his goodness. It felt like an heroic act, as if he was coming over the abyss on a thin plank towards her.

He came back and sat down next to her. 'I'm going to marry you,' he said.

The instant he said it, he thought himself a fool. And she laughed, waving her hand at him as if waving away a fly. He dangled from the plank by his hands like a cinema clown.

'Don't be so silly,' she cried. 'You don't mean it. It is because you are very young and want to impress me. Anyway, who believes now in marriage? No, I will go back to Germany tomorrow.'

'But you've sold your house?'

'Oh, it is the beginning of my new life. I will have my *own* house, now. You can buy and sell a house for nothing, in Germany. Money is dying, nothing is taking its place. We see the future by the light of a match, that's all.'

He looked at her. Her expression was rather queerly ecstatic for an instant. 'That's good,' he said. 'That's very good, to start again with your own life.'

She said nothing, just stared out at the rank thickness of grass, its seed heads bowed in a confusion of stems. She looked very lonely, sitting there, very lonely and out of place.

'And you won't kill yourself, will you?' he added.

She was crying, without touching her face; just sitting there and staring out with the tears squeezed forth of their own volition and making their way crookedly down her face. He held her hand, rather lightly.

'Will you, now? If you do, then the beastly war will have won. Death will have won. Old indecent Death, he'll be laughing at us.'

She nodded. They sat in silence for a few minutes, just sitting, with his hand very lightly on her knuckles, very demure. Yet he had the sensation that his hand was pulling her back from a desire to go out of this life completely. They could appreciate this life deeply and slowly – just sitting there rather like old folk sit, or the ailing, among the drifting plumes of old man's beard. You don't often let life happen around you like that, in all its greenness and natural business, without interfering in some way, he thought. It was as if he was showing her just what a blank it would be, to kill yourself. Better to be utterly paralysed and in the garden of life, than moving about healthily in the blankness of death.

So after quite a few minutes they rose together, as if sated, and walked into the woods further down.

Joseph did not know them well, surprisingly. They had never been on his walking itinerary, he had established that very early and stuck to it like an animal to its run. The leaves were falling sparsely but continually, much too early it seemed – though he could never remember, from year to year, what happened when. For a time they were lost, tramping through bracken and sticky swollen tubers in thick shade. She lifted her dress above her knees and her stockinged legs seemed to him very abstract, white and smooth and abstract, cutting through the bracken: he could not imagine that he had lain between them, that he had found in them a flooding-over of warmth and desire. They were being very chaste with each other, he thought. It made him feel oddly grand and noble.

Then the wood stopped and they came out in a field he did not know, bounded on each side by tall hedges of bramble and more woods crowding up the low hills. He saw she was laughing at him, because he was looking perplexed. She laughed easily, he realised; it was almost a neurotic reaction. The field had just been reaped, and bound sheaves leaned against each other like drunks.

'I love this,' she said. 'I love being lost in England. I always thought it was not possible to be lost in England. But it is possible. Lost in the woods like poor little Gretel.'

She checked her stockings for ladders and brushed out her dress, covered in cuckoo spit and seeds. The bracken's spores had made her cough, and now she coughed again. The open gate had a dirty piece of paper on it, stuck onto a botched nail. Joseph went closer to look.

'My God,' he said, 'we're being aligned.'

'Sorry?'

'Counterpoint.'

He showed her the crumpled, stained page.

'A page from a dictionary,' she said. 'What does it mean?'

'It means that the mad tramp who tore it from my book has been this way.'

'Mad?'

'Definitely,' said Joseph, pocketing the page carefully. 'If you don't believe everything around you is in counterpoint. He got into the house. He's been pilfering my supplies. That's why the doors were locked.'

'Is he dangerous?'

'Oh no. It's us sane ones that are dangerous.'

They walked between the propped sheaves. The smell of the cut wheat was deliciously sweet and crisp: the sheaves looked very vulnerable and he glanced up at the squally clouds.

'Cluttery weather,' he said.

'What is that?'

'Seasonable,' he grinned, putting his hand out to catch imaginary drops. 'It's attracted by the smell of reaped corn.'

She did not understand. There was a gulf of language between them. For the first time – as he was gesticulating – he felt a sudden dull thudding pain in the palm, the one he had grazed on the salient and which had never quite healed over. He wondered if it was poisoned, if his blood was poisoned fatally by the corrupted earth. If its devil had got him after all. Gennel Haig! Yes, that was it. The fatal infection of his touch.

At the other end of the field there was a gate and a further long field, half-harvested. At the far end of this field they could see a group of three or four men standing beside a reaper-binder. He recognised the buildings beyond them; a farm he would pass through sometimes, bicycling.

'We can make it back to the cottage from there,' he said, pointing.

'Don't worry after me. I am very happy, you know.'

'Good, I'm pleased.'

They would have to pass the group; he felt shy of country folk at work in fields, they made him feel idle. He had planned to help with the harvest, he was nearly broke, now he felt it might be too late. They made their way over the cut half of the field, skirting the sheaves. As they approached, one of the labourers walked towards them, waving his hand.

'Live around these parts, then?' he shouted.

Joseph replied that he did. The man came up touching his flat cap and said, 'You'd best take a peep.'

'What is it?'

'Come wi' me,' he said. He seemed excited, in his earnest way, behind his big seed-flecked moustache. He told them he was a part of a hired team. 'En't familiar with folk hereabouts.'

Joseph followed him, wonderingly, and Marda followed Joseph.

'What is the matter?' she asked. 'I can't understand what he says.'

'I don't know,' said Joseph, 'maybe an accident.'

'Arn murders hereabouts, of late?' the man called back over his shoulder.

Joseph's heart began to beat faster. 'Maybe you should stay here,' he said to Marda. 'Oh dear.'

She ignored him. Joseph had the impression that they were coming up to the other three men very slowly, almost sauntering. It was really because he was very nervous. The men glanced up, rather blankly. They were stood in a rough circle where the reaper-binder had reached; the uncut corn rustled behind them in the gusts. Their leather waistcoats and flat caps were all they had in common; one was stumpy, one old, one long and thin. The thin one held the horse-team's harness; the three horses dipped and lifted their heads in a cloud of flies and the chains clinked like irons.

Joseph looked down at the reaper platform and saw a thick bundle lying violently twisted and confused in the revolving slats, pressed against the cutting blades. A leather shoe was lying against the gears on the binder cage and the torn white shreds of a cotton shirt were visible in the unsheaved stems of corn half-pushed into the binder. There was a faint, disagreeable smell over the richness of the cut wheat. Joseph began to make out the flung arm of a tweed jacket, the leg of a plus fours, and a pair of soiled underthings. There was a black trilby at his feet which he recognised immediately; it was just as he thought. He looked inside the trilby for a name. *Extra Quality. Lincoln Bennet & Co. Sackville Street, Piccadilly, London.* He had passed that shop only yesterday.

'Know him?' asked the first man.

'Yes, he came to my door. He's pilfered food from my cottage. He's a mad fellow, a sort of tramp.'

Joseph lifted the lapel of the jacket. There was a silk label monogrammed *T. E. Jonson-Lois.*

'That name rings a bell, I must say. Dammit, I know that name. I'll take these to the police. I hope he's not been done away with.'

'Mebbe us shall find out shavin t'other haaf,' said the old labourer.

'Mercy me,' said the thin one. 'I hopes not.'

'Caw caw caw, I can it see it all,' intoned the other, flatly.

He pulled a large hessian rag off the back of one of the horses and handed it to Joseph, who bound the clothes up in it. Then they got back into business with the reaper-binder, leaving Joseph and Marda to walk back with the bundle. The clicking noise of the machine was faintly threatening, the horses snorting and coughing through the clouds of chaff dust. Marda said she had not understood a word, the men's dialect was so thick. They walked through the rick yard onto the wide track home.

'I preferred it when it was all reaped by hand,' said Joseph, 'with scythes and rakers. There's no poetry in a reaper-binder. Nothing *biblical.*'

Marda laughed.

'Oh, someone will write a marvellous poem to a reaper-binder, one day,' she said. And she laughed again, a brief and slightly hysterical laugh that sounded very foreign to Joseph, just there on the rutted track with the sharp-smelling bundle in his arms.

37

The Reaper-Binder

M ARDA WENT STRAIGHT back to the cottage while Joseph
dropped the bundle off at the Post Office, requesting that
the police be informed. The bundle sat happily with the other heaps
of second-hand clothes, though Joseph advised the woman not to
open the rag. The ammoniac smell came through it anyway, filling
the room.

'Do you know a Mr Jonson-Lois? he asked.

'Jonson-Lois? Mr Tom Jonson-Lois? That's our schoolmaster as
went missing,' the postmistress said.

'Good grief. These are his. If he's not been done away with,
then he must be wandering about somewhere, naked.'

'Well you don't say!' Her eyes were glittering at the thought of
it. 'Mr Jonson-Lois in the altogether! Did you ever imagine such
a thing!'

Joseph felt very bad, not having identified the poor mad fellow
quicker. The postmistress called the police and within half an hour
the whole village knew that the missing schoolmaster's clothes,
including his intimates, had been found in Mrs Allsop's field.

At least, it was half an hour after the call, the lugubrious
policeman having taken details, that Joseph emerged from the
Post Office to find Samuel walking beside him. The man's face
was very red, and sweat gleamed in little drops on his nose: he
had been to the field and back, to see for himself.

'Very queer, innit, Mr Monrow, our Twitcher Tom losing
his togs.'

'More sad than queer, I think.'

Samuel walked slightly ahead, with a hunter's light, long stride. He was almost loping along, in fact. Maybe, Joseph thought, it was to do with the contraption, his 'Get Religion'. He admired Samuel at that moment.

'Look,' said Samuel, showing his palm, 'still see the marks where the bugger thrashed it, afore the war. Never did me no harm, mind.'

Joseph saw no marks. 'It's not *very* queer, at least,' he added, 'if he was not in his right mind.'

'Queer enough,' Samuel said. He ran his tongue around his lips. He appeared to be accompanying Joseph all the way to the cottage. Then he laughed.

'What a thought, eh? Old Twitcher Tom going about in his birthday suit!'

And he laughed again, freely.

They entered the steep sunken lane as a hare loped across the road at the far bend. They talked about animals. Samuel knew the devil of a lot about the local creatures, mostly invisible to Joseph – mere rustles and calls, a kind of discreet haunting around the cottage, they were. And yet the fellow trapped them in wire snares; mysterious, this love for the creatures he maimed.

They stopped by the pair of rusty gates, as if they were closed. The great elm shook its terraces high above them.

'Thank you, Mr Monrow.'

'Thank you? For what?'

Samuel's pale face glistened. He glared at the ground.

'They don't care about it, see,' he mumbled. 'They say as it were my fault I'm only half a mannie.'

'When do they say that?'

'It do get on top of me, sir, sometimes. Then they say as it be my fault, for going that time with a bad girl in France.'

'Bad, was she? Oh, I don't suppose she was bad, not really.'

Samuel looked up the rough drive, surprised. Joseph turned. It was Marda, walking towards them from the cottage.

'Ah, my aunt from India,' Joseph said, quickly.

Samuel touched his cap as she approached.

'It was the schoolmaster,' Joseph announced.

'The schoolmaster?'

'The missing fellow. The togs in the field – the clothes. The mad one.'

He was nervous; Samuel was shifting from foot to foot.

'This is Samuel,' added Joseph, as if they had talked about him at some point.

'Hallo, Samuel,' she said, with a sweet smile, proffering her hand. Samuel looked at it in amazement. It was as if he was listening for something, bowed forwards and straining to hear. Her wedding-ring gleamed – Joseph had not noticed it before. Then the hand was retracted. There was a moment's dense embarrassment, a kind of breathlessness over which the elm swayed and sighed.

'Samuel,' said Joseph, rather uselessly, 'is a great expert on animals.'

Samuel scratched his nose.

'Are you?' said Marda.

'Oh, I dunno,' he replied.

'The schoolmaster went mad, poor thing?'

'Yes.'

'And now he's naked. Well, it is probably very healthy for him.'

Samuel grinned, showing missing teeth.

'Naked as a babe,' he said, grinning away at her.

'We should all be naked from time to time,' she said. 'Like the savages. I go naked quite a lot in my home, in the day even. It is healthy. It lets the aura stretch out. One returns to zero,' she added, raising and lowering her arms, smiling vaguely.

Samuel was grimacing, now. It was as if what she had said was painful to him. Joseph wondered what more she might say; perhaps she had no idea how simple and narrow in their thoughts these folk were.

'I draw the curtains,' she went on. 'I don't let anyone see me.'

And she gave an obscure giggle, like a girl – not like a woman at all.

'Just as well,' ventured Joseph. 'Right then, we'll go have some tea. See you later, Samuel.'

'Mr Monrow.'

'Yes.'

Samuel was stricken; at least, he seemed moved by some interior thought that was flecking his cheeks and glistening around

355

his eyes. He moved away a bit, beckoning shyly. Joseph followed him.

'Mr Monrow, I *en't* half a mannie,' Samuel hissed. 'That's the thing, see.'

His eyes flicked downwards. Joseph looked. There was only the man's thick drill trousers and the clumsy mud-stained boots.

'What do you mean?'

'It hurts. Like a rabbit in the trap. I can't git away from me own trap.'

Joseph waved at Marda to return to the cottage. He felt sick with compassion – queer, that. He wanted to embrace the pain of the world, just for a moment, the pain sighing like the huge elm sighing above them.

'Then take it off,' he said.

'They says as I can't. I'll bleed meself dry, they says to muh, when I gets the Irish toothache.'

It was uncanny: Joseph knew exactly what to say.

'Gentle does it, then. You take it off an hour a day and think of my aunt walking about naked. When it hurts you give it a dash of cold water. You go a bit further each day. Then the day will come when you'll be perfect and manly and it won't hurt and you'll throw your trap away. But you know what, Samuel?'

'No.'

'It's called sympathetic magic. You can't go trapping and maiming and shooting, now. You have to stop that for good, or it won't work. Let the badgers and rabbits and so forth – let them live in peace. Let them go their way and you'll go yours.'

The man's eyes shifted uneasily.

'Aye,' was all he said. 'Thank you, Mr Monrow.'

And he turned away down the lane with his odd, lolloping stride, leaving Joseph standing by the gates, very warm and cock-sure.

Marda was sitting in the garden. She looked unwell and suddenly older, huddled on a chair in the garden.

'What was wrong with your friend?'

'Samuel? Oh, he was – just something about – goats.'

'Goats?'

'Whether I want to buy a goat.'

'A good idea. Milk, cheese. Is he a simpleton?'

'No, not at all. He knows a lot about the woods. Animals.'

He made tea and told her about Jonson-Lois. The postmistress had said he was a legendary thrasher; if a child started to write with the left hand, the poor creature would have to bunch the fingers on it and Mr Jonson-Lois would bloody the tips with a ruler.

'Oh, that is normal,' said Marda.

'It's not normal, it's only what is done,' Joseph corrected her. 'If you live in a madhouse, then what is done is only normal in terms of the madhouse.'

'Do we live in a madhouse?'

'Yes.'

'I agree,' said Marda. 'Yes, I do think that.'

Mr Jonson-Lois would have walked into the field as a man walks into the ocean. Maybe he thought it *was* the ocean: that was why he stripped naked. Maybe he ran and dived in, naked. The reaper-binder would have to proceed cautiously. He could smell the harvest on the air; it made Marda sneeze. He realised, thinking about the schoolmaster in the corn, that it was he who had made the tracks in the long grass behind the manor. The Pan apparition, too – that must have been him. Joseph did feel disappointed, at that. He started to picture Marda walking about her house, naked – and then through the long grass behind the manor.

'You know I do the Tarot,' she said.

'Do you?'

'And the Tarot directed me to England.'

Joseph's heart sank. He felt he had made a fool of himself in front of Samuel; it was like soberly looking at yourself after a tipsy night. He had talked out of turn. It would be around the whole village soon enough, muffled in laughs.

'Did it tell you anything about the next chapter?'

'Oh, I turned up the Fool,' she said, 'and lots of hearts.' She gave a little, hard laugh.

'It's all sham, you know,' he said, 'it really is.'

'Sham? I don't know this word.'

He thought about it, gazing up at the leaves rattling in the squally gusts. Really quite cool, the air was.

'It's a pretend thing. False. It makes you feel spiritual when there's no spirit in it at all.'

'Is all divination "sham", then?'

'Probably. The next moment is unknown, yet to be born. The

357

page hasn't even been written. That's the problem with books, with stories in books. The next page has already been written. They're sham, too. Novels are sham – the great modern book of life is sham, too.'

He felt slightly breathless, wrapping himself up like this in his bitterness.

She said nothing, looking down at her hands. She had, he noticed, very elegant and long-fingered hands. She was faintly smiling.

'We Germans think science – we think science is the future.'

'Oh, that's just more childish magic, science is.'

'Ah yes, we Germans are very proud of our scientists. We will lead the world, you know, with our science.'

'That means you will lead the world.'

'Yes, we never needed war to lead the world! But we're so childish, too. We thought we had to use guns. *Wir Barbaren*,' she added, in a murmur.

'Yes, you'll lead the world without guns, right enough, you Germans.'

There was a brief pause. He considered the hundred pages in his bag: he must unpack. He must not lose all faith in his work.

'Yes, you're right, we're so childish,' she said again, looking down at her thin, elegant hands.

'We're *all* childish, you know. I mean, all nations are. Now you've learnt your hard lesson, well, you'll be the most adult, all you Germans.'

She shook her head. 'No, I don't think so. We're too angry. Anger is very childish.'

'You're not angry, then, about your son and your husband?'

She shrugged. 'I am too broken to be angry. Too sad.'

Silence.

'Another cup of tea?'

He went inside and made another pot. He had to snatch at moments on his own. He looked at her from the kitchen. The afternoon light, rather sallow through the cloud haze, fell on her form as if it was in the way: a foreign body. He felt pity for her, seeing her so foreign-looking, so unlikely in that ordinary cottage garden. He rubbed his neck and wondered if she really meant to leave tomorrow. He felt vaguely bewildered, wondered how on earth he had come to the marriage proposal. The memory of it made his stomach quiver. It was as if her sense of destiny was gigantic, much too big for him. She had dissolved the energy that had impelled him back from London. That was very strange, to have that energy dissolved so completely.

He checked the bucket closet; he had left it fly-strewn and smelly, this cupboard-like room with the tiny cobwebbed window, but she had evidently scrubbed it clean and he felt ashamed. It made him feel as if she was nursing him in some way. He felt his manliness start to dissolve. He took his spectacles off and knuckled his eyes, as if knuckling himself into firmness.

He slipped upstairs with his bag. The little study felt strange to him and at the same time familiar, like a younger cousin who has plumped out in your absence, become a woman. Vaguely threatening and strange and yet with the same voice and smile and eyes. He stood in the room and absorbed it. The ink-pot in its broken saucer, the books, the interesting stones, the notes to himself on the writing table, the various charms collected on walks – the jaw of a shrew, a rust-barnacled key, curious bits of wood on the windowsill: ah, these almost infuriated him with their implied promise. The blank walls, whose rough limewashed plaster he had found beautiful enough in itself; the absence of any curtains; the green-hued views; the old box bed – he had been left behind by it all, in some way. And now the sheet of paper with *INWARD WOUND* and *England* written on it . . . oh, how that embarrassed him: it hung on a nail and had a cobweb running across it, a drip had streaked it down the middle. It was like a withered bloom.

He looked into the other room. There was now only the faintest trace of damp plaster in the air; her bags were on the floor and her personal articles were spread about on the bed and the little rush-bottomed chair. Her violet perfume had obliterated the damp smell and the smell of Tillie: she had spread fresh sheets on the bed. She must have poked about until she found them in the cupboard at the top of the stairs – the sheets were shiny in places with age, threadbare at the edges. The bed was made very neatly, with a book on the pillow: *Der Golem*, by Gustav Meyer. The cover showed a hideous face, more robot-like than the film. She had settled in, the night candle almost a stub. He sat on the bed for a moment and wondered why this did not bother him, now. He even feared her going. And yet he could not envisage her staying. It was very taxing, his confusion.

A thick squirrel-skin coat lay on the end of the bed, stinking of mothballs: she must have imagined England as cold, even in late summer. Or perhaps she thought she would stay into the winter. He stroked its smooth pelt, thick enough to bury his fingers in. He gripped it in his fingers, squeezing.

He checked in the crooked chest of drawers: the shawl had not been touched. It did look a sorry thing.

'I'm sorry I don't have a car,' he said, back in the garden and pouring out her tea.

She gave a curt little laugh. 'Why, do you think I'm not happy just where I am? Do you think I need to take a spin?'

Joseph sat on the rug near her feet and wondered about supper: he would take her to the inn and play the same 'aunt' game. It would be a lark.

And after supper? He dared not think of that. He could not imagine them chastely sleeping in separate rooms, yet to go with her again would reap terrible consequences, he was sure.

He glanced at her and caught her eye. And he flushed scarlet under his olivish skin. She looked away, poised and ambiguous. He cursed himself for turning scarlet. The air had become thick between them, viscous with their inability to voice certain thoughts. He knew that each would bring the other on, just by thinking about bed. He swallowed nervously. Her faint violet perfume wrapped itself around him each time she shifted in her chair. He would have to be very strong, very strong indeed. He would have to keep the door to it firmly shut.

'You must write your poem,' she said, unexpectedly.

'What poem?'

'To that machine in the field.'

'Oh yes. I must write the poem. Just like that.'

He chuckled as if only to himself, as if sharing the joke with himself.

'What is funny, Joseph?'

His name sounded odd, coming from her. It sounded like a command, rather cold and forlorn.

'Well, you can't go writing a poem just like that,' he said.

'Why not?'

He laughed, rather nervously. 'Poems need inspiration. The Muse—'

'Perhaps I am your Muse,' she said.

He looked at her.

'Yes, you could be.'

'Well, you can pretend I am. Go away and write it.'

He shook his head. 'I don't want to write a poem about a blasted reaper-binder.'

He was uncomfortable, she was feeling her way towards his inner self. The poem business was a way in, that was all.

'I'll write you one soon and send it to you,' he said.

'Send it to me?'

'In Germany.'

'Oh, I might not go back to Germany. I might go to South America.'

'Really?'

'Or India. Somewhere I can devote myself to the poor. Perhaps the lepers.'

'Why the lepers?'

'They lose bits of themselves, don't they? I think Gabral, our *punkah-wallah*, lost his nose that way. I lost my son. When you lose your child – a bit falls away from you. A bit of your aura falls away. A big chunk, actually. It never heals, you know.'

Silence.

'I can imagine that,' he said.

Though strangely he could not, not deep inside himself.

She looked at him. He remembered her feeling his face on the salient.

'You've taken off your spectacles,' she said.

'Yes. Do I – did your son look anything like me?'

She frowned. 'Nay, as you say. No one looks like my son. He was *very* handsome—'

'Oh,' laughed Joseph, 'thanks very much!'

She broke into a smile. It was amazing, the way nothing remained sad and bitter for long, with this woman. And yet in one way she was all sadness, all lead weight.

'Working for the poor, the sick, the unloved,' he went on. 'That's good. Very good.'

'Is it?'

She was regarding him with a supercilious angle to her head.

'I think so,' he said.

'Why did you cut your hair very short? Like a soldier?'

He ran a hand over his scalp; it felt like the coarse plush on a cinema seat.

'I upset the barber.'

She laughed. 'It suits you. I like it.'

'Do my ears stick out?'

'Oh no! Not very much!'

The trees whispered as if musing on something dreadful that had just happened and was now over. Joseph felt himself careering, suddenly, into happiness. There was a great warmth in his mind and his thoughts were swift flowing; he only had to crouch to them to drink.

'I'll tell you what,' he said, after a moment, hugging his knees. 'I'll start my novel with the reaper-binder, and the clothes wrapped up in its blades. The whole novel will be about the owner of the clothes. That'll be the plot. It'll start off with clothes and a naked man.'

'That schoolmaster?'

'No, someone quite different. But he's suffering from shell shock, like Mr Jonson-Lois. Amnesia. He recovers, and then the heat starts his amnesia again.'

'Your hero?'

'No, my hero is handsome and young and is killed in action which means that he falls off a troop train outside Ypres, dead drunk.'

'Oh. Why?'

'Well, half the army were tipsy at any one time, it's just his bad luck. But the truth about him is hidden. Only the naked man knows.'

She nodded, wary of his excitement.

'I thought you had started your novel,' she said.

'I have. A hundred pages. Now I'm going to burn them.'

'Oh, really?'

'Yes. Wait here.'

He rushed inside and quite loped upstairs to his room and took the wad of pages out of his bag. He was more than a touch breathless, wheezing with it. There was the taste of chlorine in his mouth. This was terribly annoying, this lurking of the war within him. It really annoyed him, now, when otherwise he was seething with happiness, a great warm geyser in his soul, his mind pealing with bells from its highest towers.

He opened the window. The annoyance went with the cool air and its scent of hay and trees, along with a certain amount of his excitement. He felt very calm and clear, instead. He could have walked through a brick wall and emerged unharmed, the way he felt.

'Watch the chimney!' he called down to her. 'Marda! Watch the chimney!'

He leaned into the air and flapped the wad of pages about. Without his spectacles, he saw her as no more than an indistinct form on the grass, the pale oval of her face turned towards him.

'You just watch that chimney!' he shouted again.

He went down into the kitchen and opened the little square door of the range. Smoke curled up over the lip. He held, in both hands, the wad of paper crawled over by his writing and slowly made a tube of it. He half-hoped, half-dreaded that she would stop him. The fire glowed in its iron husk. But no one came to the door. She must be watching the chimney. He held the tube close to the heat. He was badly treating it, he thought. He saw the pages quite suddenly as something alive that he was badly treating. Not part of him at all. Something that might wriggle in pain and leap out of his hand, with a quivering, rabbity feel to it – only much cleverer than a rabbit, cleverer even than a hare! Something separate from him, at least. It might be rubbish, he said to himself, but I can't go killing it. It would scorch him inside. It was as if his past self was separate, as separate as a twin, or that blasted Hubert Rail – even yesterday's self, even the self on the morning train: that was separate, too. Only the present self, the self of this instant, was not separate from him. He glanced out at the garden through the open door. Through the leaf-shadows he was aware of her again as something heavy and indistinct. He was annoyed by the fact that she was letting him do this. The smoke was gathering rather thickly under the beams, tickling his throat. He closed the range door with a clang and dropped the paper onto the table.

Months of work, he thought, months of soul-stuff poured in.

The geyser had sunk inside him to a little spout. It struck him how unhappy he was, most of the time. Or maybe unhappiness is not to be measured by a word; maybe it is the very condition of life, broken by the odd beam of irrational sunlight – the blessing of joy, against which everything less light-filled is measured and found wanting. When, really, a wedge of scrawled-upon pages is the thing to be measured against. Much better to measure oneself against that.

Marda was standing in the doorway.

'I watched the chimney,' she said.

'I couldn't burn it. I'm feeble. Very feeble, very shabby. One of Bunyan's "feebler sort", that's what I am.'

'Ah, you are exhausted,' she said. 'We are all empty, you know. We are all empty, our wells are all quite dry.'

She sat down in one of the cheap wooden chairs and covered her eyes with a hand. Her hand trembled.

'I am not much of a Muse,' she said.

'Oh, you'll do. All the best Muses say that.'

He laughed – and she did smile then, looking at him. She looked almost prim, sitting there in that crude little bodger-chair.

'When – when is the next train due, to London?'

'Soon after five. In about half an hour,' he said, glancing at his watch.

There was a silence. The trees blew and whispered outside. She would not be staying the night. Much better, that way.

'You'll be off tonight, then?'

'Of course.'

'You can take some biscuits with you. And plums. Take as many as you can.'

'You are kind.'

Oh, so much better that way, he thought, I must not regret it. I *will* not regret it. She was looking distant and, of course, rather sad. He definitely wanted her to go, now. She was weighing on him terribly, with her grief. The lost chunk of her: he could almost see it, around the left shoulder. She was quite lost in her grief, drifting under its black sails over the abyss. Nothing he could do would ever relieve it. And he also knew that nothing he could write would ever match this grief. If he could roll this grief up into a little ball and send it to, say, Frank Pitts, it would kill the fellow, blow up in his face like a whizz-bang. Blow his face right off, with its firm-jawed certainties. Right off. Nothing left at all – except a pair of ice-cold eyes.

He must have this black powder of grief scattered right through the book. Dangerous, in its plain way.

And then it struck him that he might dedicate the book to Pitts, as the gunners would chalk *For Fritz* on their shells. Yes – he smiled at this idea: he could almost see it on the page. *For Mr Frank Pitts of Chertsey, objectively dedicated—*

'Why are you smiling like that – such a cruel smile?'

He dropped the smile. He looked at her, his face softening but very serious. 'I think it's for the best, really. We will get our own lives, then.'

She nodded, although he was not at all sure what he had meant.

38

The Wild Man

H E SAW HER off at the station, briskly and without fuss on either side – just a dry-lipped kiss and a brief embrace, rather chaste, and the solemn waving through the steam and smoke of the 5.22.

'You will take coffee with me one day,' she said. 'Fresh coffee in my cosy new home.'

'I hope so, one day. You will write and let me know where you are.' He nearly made a joke about her walking around this cosy home naked, but the joke stopped at his lips.

He was quite sure he would not see her again. She leaned from the carriage window and waved as the train puffed away, and he waved solemnly back. Then he walked briskly back to the cottage and took some fresh paper and filled his pen from the ink-pot.

It was so crisply done, the goodbye. Exactly as on the salient, by the Lille Gate. She was sad, yes, but she had kept her dignity. She might so easily have lost her dignity, staying after there was no hope. He felt just a touch of pride, that it had been dealt with so crisply; he did not feel too uncomfortable with this. And he bent to the paper with a small, satisfied sigh.

He wrote for about two hours, taking a break once for some Bass and a few biscuits. He did not feel hungry. The table shook, all right.

Then he walked in the evening gloam down to the manor grounds, sitting for some time in the gazebo. The light was very dim and only the white puffs of old man's beard could be distinguished clearly. He knew she had gone for good, now. He was amazed at the way he had written over the last two hours, and yet had no doubt about *why* he had written thus: he was being guided in the invisible. The words had come easily to him, as if he had indeed been writing a poem in an inspired state. The reaper-binder, the bundle of clothes, the labourers staring down: these came easily to him. He had no idea to whom the clothes belonged in the novel, no idea at all. He was launching the words as Noah launched the dove: in pure faith. It was for others to judge whether the words had found land, greenness and solid earth, a fresh life.

It was not his task, to touch land before launching the dove. And that spring moment a few months ago, on the heath in Middlesex with Baz, in that lost little village – that came back to him now, that revelation of his faith amidst the rough beer and the old mumbling men of Heathrow. He nodded to himself. It was as if he was meeting his own eyes, far from any mirror, and acknowledging what he saw as good. He would not be destroyed, after all.

He walked down to the inn, quite late. The breeze had dropped, it was quite warm again, warm and dampish. He had a need to plunge into people, and entered the tap room for the first time. Mrs Hamilton was in the snug as usual, but he did not go in there and neither did he go into the smoke room with its chairs and pictures of hunting dogs. No, it was the tap room tonight. Walter served him with tired eyes, bringing him a cool glass from the cellar. He even felt a love for Walter, through the din of the labouring types. There was a great thirst for love in that place, he could detect it under the din and burliness.

'Not eating, then?'

'No. If you can tell Mrs H., please. I'm not at all hungry, Walter. Make my excuses, if you would. And this is for her.'

He handed Walter the little leather-bound *Poems by Scott*. The big man stared at it.

'She likes pottery, y'know. I gave her some Lancashire pottery for her birthday. Cream jug and two dogs.'

'That's grand.'

'Is it? It's normal. It's playing fair, Mr Monrow. It's what life is, playing fair.'

Then he grunted and went off with the little fat book to the snug. Samuel was seated in the corner, quite tipsy, chaff in his hair. He waved Joseph over.

'We were jes missin' you, Mr Monrow. I were jes sayin' as how you be a true genneman, Mr Monrow.'

Joseph nodded and spread his hand in a manly way, although he did feel a faint disgust, too; he was no saint, that was the trouble. Could he have worked with lepers? He doubted it. The others were raising their mugs to him, cheerily. He sat down on the bench and placed his beer on the scrubbed table. The faces were swirled from him by the smoke of cigarettes and shag from the old boys' clay pipes. He set his feet squarely on the brick floor in front of the bench and nodded and laughed and drank in a kind of passionate stupor. It was warm and snug and he bought many rounds on the slate. Samuel would wink at him now and again, rather knowingly. There was a pact there. Joseph felt cheered by this. He began to feel part of the company, an indistinguishable sheaf in the field of labouring men.

Mrs Hamilton came through quite late and gave Joseph a kiss on the cheek, which brought forth a whoop from the assembled throng. She smelt of warm bread and he stood up and told her, in the raised voice of supreme confidence, that she was the finest woman in Christendom – only the word 'Christendom' was fiendishly difficult to get round. Then they all toasted her and she left, her eyes glazed with tears. An old man recited a ballad interminably and Joseph was rocked by it – stopped struggling against the interminable, wheezy voice and let himself be rocked in the warm fug.

On the way back to the cottage, he sang. The trees sang, too. The very earth sang as it rolled like the sea. He found himself on Tillie's bed – he still thought of it as Tillie's bed. He hugged the pillow and wrapped himself up in the sheets. It smelt of Marda now, but he did not mind. It was all tommy-rot, that he did not love Tillie; he called her name out loud, many times. Nobody else was saying it aloud as he was, nobody else in the world, not even Hubert bloody Rail. Oh, Tillie. The smell of Marda on the sheets and pillow was like an autumn church, all mothballed coats and violet drops, but he did not mind – he really did not mind at all. She would come to him. She would come home, would Tillie, in time. And if she did not, he would seek her out. He would go to the ends of the earth to seek her out. And win her.

He took the torn, stained shawl out of the drawer and laid it on the pillow, as a delicate gold chain is laid on a cushion. Then he buried his face in it for a while.

Too hot, the floor pitching somewhat, he staggered into his room and sat down and read what he had written that afternoon. It struck him as very wonderful, though the words kept sliding away out of the corner of his eye. Then he lay on his own bed with all the windows flung open. Cool puffs of sweet night air stroked his face. He floated deliciously in the coolness, feeling that death might be as delicious. He lay and let the wonder of the cool, moist, slightly autumnal breeze stroke his face like his mother had once stroked it when he was ill in childhood. If only he could be another person, he thought – then was cross with himself for thinking this. His book would be a splash of blood on the dead white stone of the Cenotaph. It would say everything he could say and would include the cool, moist stroking of this very air over the bottomless grief.

Like a cat, he would move, like a great cat – so cunning over the shadow, so light and cunning would his words be.

He went down in his nightshirt and relieved himself in the bucket closet. Above the clattering of his piss in the bucket he heard a sound, a sort of baby cry – it might have been that, yes. A baby's high cry.

He stood there quite still for some minutes, rather frightened, but there was nothing. He did not believe in ghosts. In the invisible, yes – but not something as crude as a ghost. He came out gingerly, though, and climbed the stairs with his spine aprickle. If only the stairs did not creak so! Lucifer matches – the infant had died sucking lucifer matches. He tried not to picture its agony. He tried to put the whole thing out of his head.

He went into Tillie's room – this was how he thought of it now – and lay again on the bed, summoning her. It helped him to get over his strange, childish fear. He held her silken shawl in his hand and stroked his face with it, took it into his mouth. It was his fetish, really. He would keep it forever beside him, like a knight's love-token. Then he lifted his nightshirt and rubbed the shawl over his groin, stiffening into it.

Another sound – perhaps the same night creature, only its baby cry had turned into a kind of whoop. A great cat, or a fox – no, more owl-like than a fox or a cat. From the garden, perhaps. He lay there blinking like an idiot, heart thumping, the shawl sinking

369

back over his groin. Then he stumbled to his feet and made his way – three, four steps – across the landing and into the study.

A shape in front of the window. A human shape, hooded. He went rigid with terror, absolutely rigid with terror at the sight of it, this dark shape before the window. The sheer surprise.

It was her.

She was dressed exactly as he had left her, as he had left her waving from the train, through the smoke and steam. He could not utter a word. She was beckoning to him, a rather excited little gesture.

'Come and see,' she said, very softly, as if not to disturb something. As if she had never even gone. 'Come and see, quick.'

And immediately – an unearthly cry from the garden, really unearthly. A kind of whoop, but not an animal's whoop. He walked up to the window in a kind of thought-trance and stood right beside her, looking out through the open window. They looked out together, quite calmly side by side. There was something flitting about, pale and thin, between the trees and shrubs. It flung its arms up and jumped and whooped. It was like a pale star, jumping on forked legs, flinging its arms out and leaping and then vanishing and then again reappearing somewhere close by on the lawn.

It was, Joseph saw, a naked man. Quite wild and naked. He found himself lifting his hand and waving, waving slowly at this naked, wild apparition as it swept about the garden. Then it vanished with a whoop into the darkness and never once came back, though they both waited by the window for a long time, very quietly and calmly staring into the darkness of the garden and the busy night woods.

'Well, I'll have a bit of supper with you, I think,' she said, eventually.

'All right.'

'What have you got?'

'Some eggs. Bread. Paste. Not a lot.'

'Enough,' she said, smiling. 'Enough for a honeymoon.'

'I see.'

He led the way downstairs with a candle, his footing uncertain, feeling the fool in his long white nightshirt. He had to prove to her that he was not recovering from a binge: his movements were very deliberate. Oh, he wasn't ready for this. Honeymoon! Oh, God.

Her eyes glittered across the table, the other side of the flame. Moths flapped about it, very lively.

'What's that around your neck?' she asked.

He looked.

'Oh, a shawl. My grandmother's.'

He gave a strange little chuckle. 'You'll—'

Then the laughter took hold of him, rose up from his stomach and could not be quelled. He could not stop laughing while she looked on in astonishment. And he simply went on with it, surge after wheezy surge, worrying the candle's bright flame while she watched him in readiness from the other side.

ACKNOWLEDGEMENTS

With grateful thanks to Peter Metcalfe for Ypres documents; the staff of the Imperial War Museum for their help; Robert Avery for painstaking research concerning boats and trains; my editor Robin Robertson for timely suggestions; and my wife Jo for encouraging me to continue when I wanted to stop.

Certain events and details owe much to the unpublished memoirs of Captain L. Gameson, medical officer at the Front, and to the reminiscences of Gilberte Rougeron.

THE VINTAGE WAR COLLECTION

www.vintage-books.co.uk